FLORA KIDD

the loving gamble

Harlequin Books

TORONTO • NEW YORK • LONDON
AMSTERDAM • PARIS • SYDNEY • HAMBURG
STOCKHOLM • ATHENS • TOKYO • MILAN

Harlequin Presents first edition March 1989
ISBN 0-373-11154-1

Original hardcover edition published in 1988
by Mills & Boon Limited

CHAPTER ONE

THE feeling that she was being watched by someone she couldn't see made Rachel's skin prickle all over. Slowly she turned her head and glanced over her shoulder.

He was still there, in the shade of two graceful silver birches. He was standing, as she was, slightly apart from the group of laughing, talking people who were clustering about her cousin Jenny Vanway who had just been married to Dr. Charles White. It wasn't easy to see what he looked like because he was dappled with the shadows of birch leaves, but she had the impression he was tall, his physique symmetrical, broad shoulders tapering down to lean hips. He was elegantly dressed in a silver-grey double-breasted suit.

She looked away from him and down the sloping lawn to the River Hudson, wide and shining in the mellow sunshine of late September. On the other side of the river, from the tops of reddish cedar-crowned cliffs the land rose up gradually in green curves to the summits of the Catskill Mountains. The slopes of the hills were ablaze with the colours of autumn, scarlet of maples, gold of elms and birches, threaded with the greens of cedars and pines.

Still aware of being stared at by the stranger and resenting what she considered to be his rudeness, she began to wander away in the direction of the path that wound down the steep bank to the narrow, stony beach that edged the river. Even though she

and her brother Giles had been made very welcome
when they had arrived in this part of the State of
New York, three days ago, having flown over from
Scotland to be at the wedding, she still felt like a
stranger in a strange land.

Everything was so much larger here than it was at
home in Scotland. The river was wider than any
other river she had ever seen, the trees grew taller
and there were more of them, and the land seemed
to go on and on for ever. Houses also were much
bigger than any she had known, and the Vanways'
sprawling split-level was more comfortable and
luxurious than any house she had ever stayed in
before. The people, too, were different: noisier,
livelier, more outgoing and, she had to admit,
friendlier than any people she had ever met before.
Even her Aunt Moira was thoroughly Americanised
now in her ways, and in her speech, too, so she also
was a stranger.

Reaching the beach, Rachel strolled along, enjoying the warmth of the sunshine and watching a big
tug pulling several loaded barges down-river. Some
sailing boats from the nearby marina were trying to
race in the almost windless air, their white sails
glinting against the dark cliffs. For a moment she
paused, trying to fix the scene in her mind, wishing
she had her camera with her.

The crunch of stones under someone's shoes made
her look back over her shoulder, and immediately
she felt resentment flare up in her again. The tall
man had followed her. His well brushed, fashionably trimmed hair shone with the reddish glow of
polished mahogany in the sunlight. That was all she
allowed herself to see before she walked on swiftly,
her head held high, as she hoped to convey to him

her dislike of being stalked by a complete stranger.

Beside her the historic river flowed, tranquil and unhurried. The tug and barges chugged by, the yachts lolled about aimlessly, sails empty and shaking. The beach ended, unfortunately, where an old wharf once used by transport barges jutted out into the water. The only way she could escape from the man, who was stalking her, was to climb either up the pilings of the wharf or up the steep bank to the top and to trespass into the garden of the house next door to the Vanways' house.

It was while she was eyeing the pilings, wondering where she could best get a foothold, that the stranger came up behind her and spoke. There was an undercurrent of amusement stirring beneath the pleasantly modulated tones of his voice.

'I wouldn't risk it if I were you,' he said. 'Not in those shoes or that pretty dress. You'll ruin them. Also the timbers aren't to be trusted. You could fall.'

She turned slowly to face him. He had taken off the jacket of his suit and was carrying it slung over one shoulder. The knot of his sleek silk blue and grey tie was loosened and the collar of his stark white shirt was undone. From between thick dark lashes his eyes, violet-coloured in the sunshine, surveyed her narrowly. While she stared at him in haughty silence, resenting her innate response to his physical attractions, he smiled at her, his lean, lightly tanned cheeks creasing, his well shaped teeth gleaming white.

'I could wait for ever to be introduced to you, so I've decided to introduce myself,' he continued smoothly, and she noticed there was hardly a trace of accent in the way he spoke English. He sounded neither British nor American.

'I'm Ross Fraser and I know you're Rachel Dow, Jenny's cousin, and you're from Edinburgh, Scotland. You and I have something in common. I was born in Edinburgh, though I've lived in the States since I was twelve and I'm a friend of Charlie White, Jenny's new husband. You were walking so fast I got the impression you were running away from me. Why?'

'I don't like being followed by someone I don't know,' she retorted, looking away from him at the river, her chin up, her eyelids drooping.

'Well, now you know who I am shall we walk back together?' he replied equably. 'Or are you really set on doing some mountaineering? Perhaps I should warn you that even if you did make it to the top of the bank the Perkins, who own the house and land up there, have two fierce Doberman dogs, trained to attack any intruders. I'm much less vicious.'

She glanced sideways at him from beneath her lashes. His pleasant mockery of himself did much to allay her resentment. Judging by the way he spoke and the expensive cut of his suit and shirt he was not only well educated but also wealthy. Suddenly intrigued by him, she decided to abandon her plan to evade him. Turning to face him, she smiled.

'Jenny did tell me she and Charles hoped you would be at the wedding,' she said. 'But she wasn't sure if you'd get to the church in time.'

'I just made it to hear them say their vows,' he replied, smiling back at her, and it seemed to her as if his smile was a ray of sunlight shining into her and warming the cold knot of caution and reserve inside her. 'I've not been to a wedding before,' he added as they began to walk side by side back the way they had come.

'Not even to your own?' she asked and he laughed.

'No, not even my own. How about you?'

'Oh, I've been to other weddings, at home, in Scotland, but none of them were as grand as Jenny's. In fact, until we arrived the other day my brother and I had no idea that Aunt Moira's husband was so well to do, nor that they lived in such a beautiful place.'

'I suppose, like many Brits, you had the impression that New York State is all industrial, with chimneys belching forth smoke everywhere and textile mills polluting rivers, like the Midlands and north of England, to say nothing of the Lowlands of Scotland,' he scoffed.

'Well, I had read that this river was badly polluted,' she retorted spiritedly. 'And it still doesn't look very clean.'

'It was even worse some years ago. But thanks to people like Pete Seeger, the folk-singer, it's been cleaned up, and although it's not completely free of pollutants yet, the fish in it aren't dying any more,' he replied. 'But you haven't answered my question. When I said how about you, I meant have *you* been to your own wedding? Are you married?'

'No.'

'Have you been?'

'No. I've never met anyone I've wanted to marry and I feel I never will.'

'Never will marry or never will meet anyone you'd like to marry?' he queried.

'Never will marry. I'm much too interested in trying to make a career for myself as an artist,' she answered lightly.

He stopped walking to turn to her. She paused

too, returning his gaze frankly.

'No time for a man in your life, then?' he asked.

'Not seriously. I don't mind having men friends, but so far I haven't felt any great desire to give up my freedom to marry one of them.'

'What a waste,' he murmured enigmatically, his glance drifting over her face and then her figure.

'What do you mean?'

'I mean that you'd be so nice for a guy to come home to every night of his life, but if you never marry that won't happen and all your female beauty and expertise will be wasted, never shared with a suitable mate, and never passed on to your children.'

'If I'd known the conversation was going to run along these lines I'd never have agreed to walk back with you,' she replied as coolly as she could. For a moment she had imagined what it might be like to have him come home to her every night of his life, and she had wished it could be.

Disturbed because he had, in a very few minutes, made a violent impact on her, she turned away and began to march quickly back along the beach, angry, not with him exactly, but more with herself for allowing him to get under her skin in such a short time. In her haste to get away from him she didn't look where she was going. Her left foot, in its neat low-heeled black pump that gave little or no support to her ankle, slipped on a stone, her ankle twisted, pain shot through it and she sat down abruptly, moaning a little and bowing her head in agony.

'Well, well, I guess the old adage is right after all. Pride does come before a fall,' he mocked her. 'Let me help you up.'

'No.' She got up quickly but as soon as her left

foot touched the ground she yelped, pulling it up sharply.

'What's up?' he asked.

'I think I've sprained my ankle,' she muttered weakly, and, without looking at him, she began to limp along, flinching at every step. Although not far away, the path that twisted down the bank from the Vanways' garden looked very distant at that moment.

'You'll never make it,' he said with aggravating male arrogance.

'Then what do you expect me to do?' she challenged, stopping to turn on him. He gave her another raking glance that did nothing to appease her. It seemed to her he was actually measuring and weighing her in his mind. With a swift movement he shrugged on his jacket.

'I'll carry you,' he said forcefully.

'No.'

She stepped back defensively, forgetting she was close to the edge of the beach, and found herself standing in the river. Moving quickly and decisively, giving her no chance to avoid him, he stepped forwards and scooped her up into his arms.

Like bars of iron they supported her. Her head was close to his shoulder and when she looked at his face she could see the darker skin where he had shaved, the quirk of amusement at the corner of his sensually carved broad lips, the bold straight line of his nose, and the determined jut of his cleft chin above the strong column of his throat, the heart-appealing length of his eyelashes, only a few shades darker than his reddish-brown hair.

'I'd give anything for this not to have happened,' she muttered, uneasily aware that she longed to give in, to lay her head against his broad shoulder and relax, to let him take the load and be responsible for her.

His eyes flashed briefly down to her face and then looked straight ahead again as he walked along the beach.

'Pride again?' he taunted. 'You want to watch it. Pride never did anyone any good.'

'I hate being dependent on a stranger,' she persisted.

'I sense a feminist,' he scoffed. 'Don't you really mean you hate being dependent on a man? Actually I'm not a stranger. Not any more,' he added as he started to climb up the pathway, apparently effortlessly. 'I feel as if I've known you all my life, even though we never met until today. I'm the guy who is going to marry you.'

'Oh, that does it! Put me down at once. Put me down.' She began to wriggle in his arms and he stopped walking.

'Be still or we'll both go backwards down the bank,' he rapped. He frowned down at her, his face hard and implacable, and she had her first taste of his steely determination to have his own way.

'Then put me down. I'll walk the rest of the way by myself,' she ordered.

'I'll put you down when we're on level ground and not before, you stubborn wench,' he growled, and forged on up the path.

'I could call you names too,' she said sniffing haughtily.

'So go ahead. There's nothing I enjoy more than a good slanging-match or argument, especially with a woman. Clears the air.'

She didn't say anything, guessing that he would win in any verbal sparring-match they might have

because, like many other Americans, he was
unreserved and he wouldn't care who overheard him
or what anyone else might think of him. He didn't
put her down when they reached the lawn but carried
her up the steps to the deck, where several of the older
guests were sitting and talking. Among the many
exclamations of concern, she heard her aunt's voice
with a feeling of relief.

'Rachel, what's happened?'

Dark-haired and immaculate in her blue mother-
of-the-bride dress, Moira appeared beside them.

'She's sprained her ankle,' said Ross Fraser.
'Where shall I take her?'

'Oh, right into her room,' said Moira. 'This way,
come through the kitchen.'

'It's all right. I can manage on my own,' said
Rachel, trying to assert herself, but no one took any
notice of her. Ross's arms tightened about her and he
heaved her a little higher as they passed through the
kitchen, in Moira's wake, and then went along a
passageway to one of the spare bedrooms of the big
sprawling house.

He laid her down on the pink quilted cover of the
single bed and stood up straight looking down at her,
a slight mocking smile curving his lips.

'You're a lot heavier than you look,' he gibed and
turned to Moira. 'I guess, having been a nurse, you
know what to do, and we don't have to ask Charles to
examine her ankle?'

'Charles has already left with Jenny to go to
Kennedy. We looked for you and Rachel all over to
come and say goodbye. They dared not wait any
longer,' Moira replied briskly, bending over the bed
and studying both of Rachel's ankles. 'You'll have to
take your pantyhose off, dear,' she continued. 'It's

the left one isn't it? Looks as if it's swelling nicely. I'll bring a bowl of water and you can soak it for a while, then I'll bind it up. I'm afraid you're going to have to rest it. No gadding off to Manhattan tomorrow to visit the art museums.'

'It's so disappointing,' Rachel complained, wincing when Moira touched the tender spot on her ankle. 'Giles and I were looking forward to visiting the city so much.'

'Giles?' queried Ross, who had been looking in the mirror of the dressing-table and fixing his tie. A wave of his hair had slid down over his forehead and now he combed long fingers through it to lift it back as he turned to look at her. Again she was smitten by his physical attractions; his muscular strength sheathed in a silk shirt and fine worsted wool; that glint of warm violet in the cool greyness of his eyes, like a flame encased in ice, sending strange delicious shivers tingling through her.

'He's my brother,' she murmured.

'Well, Giles will just have to go without you,' said Moira practically.

'If I had crutches . . .' Rachel started hopefully.

'Not even on crutches. You'd be worn out before you even got to the second floor of the Modern Art Museum.'

'Don't they allow wheelchairs?' asked Ross casually.

'Now I never thought of that,' exclaimed Moira in surprise, swinging round to look at him.

He was leaning his hips against the dressing-table, his long legs stretched before him, his hands in his trouser pockets, and he was staring at Rachel intently, eyes slightly narrowed, on the verge of smiling at her. Feeling warm blood creep into her cheeks she looked away from him.

'But then she would have to get to town,' added Moira thoughtfully. 'She and Giles were going on their own on the train.'

'If a wheelchair could be found in Riverpark, the folding type that would go into the boot of a car, I'd drive you into Manhattan, take you round the museums and bring you back here,' he said softly to Rachel. 'It's the least I can do, since I'm partly responsible for your having sprained your ankle.'

'That's really kind of you, Ross,' said Moria warmly before Rachel could answer.

'I guess Giles is around somewhere,' he said, pushing away from the dressing-table, 'I haven't met him yet.'

'He was playing tennis with Kathy Van Dorp last time I saw him,' said Moira, following him to the door. 'I'll just fetch the water and a bandage, Rachel. Be back in a jiffy.'

Moira went out, but before he left the room Ross slanted a glance at Rachel, and once again his lips curved in that slight knowledgeable smile that made her pulses leap unexpectedly.

'See you soon,' he said softly.

'Don't count on it,' she managed to retort tartly, but her retort only seemed to amuse him. His smile widening to a grin, he made no reply, and disappeared from her sight.

When Moira came back carrying a large bowl of water, towel draped over her arm, she said, 'I don't know what's come over Ross Fraser. He's not usually so helpful or forthcoming. I introduced him to Giles and he invited him and some of the youngsters over to Chestnuts for the rest of the evening. I'm sure I don't ever remember him doing anything like that before. Now just sit up on the edge of the bed and put your left foot in the bowl, dear.'

Rachel did as she was told and the hot water engulfed her foot and ankle soothingly.

'What is Chestnuts?' she asked.

'Morton Fraser's estate, further up the river. The house isn't as big or as ostentatious as the Vanderbilt mansion that is near here, but it is lovely, and it gets its name from the avenue of chestnut trees leading up to it. Ross usually stays there when he comes upstate.'

'He told me he was born in Edinburgh. Is that true?'

'As far as I know, it is,' replied Moira, sitting down on the bed beside Rachel and beginning to unwind an elastic bandage.

'And who is Morton Fraser?'

'He's the descendant of a star-spangled Scot who made a fortune when he emigrated here in the nineteenth century, something like Andrew Carnegie did. Now Morton is President of Fraser and Allanby, a Wall Street investment firm. He's also on the board of directors of several important companies. He's rolling in money. Ross is his adopted son.'

'Adopted?' Rachel exclaimed.

'Yes. Such a romantic tale really. Morton never married when he was a young man because he was disappointed in love. Apparently when he was overseas during World War Two he met and fell in love with a Scottish girl, but she was engaged to someone else and refused to marry him. Anyway some years ago he began to regret he hadn't married and hadn't had children of his own, so he decided to look up his old flame. He learned that she was living in Nova Scotia, so he went up there to see her. Seems she had married the Canadian soldier she had been engaged to and had returned to Canada with him. But her husband, Bill MacPherson, had been badly wounded during the war and had eventually died, a little after their son Ross was born. Unfortunately when Morton found her she was already suffering from cancer. Even so, he asked her to marry him. She agreed and he brought her and her son to live at Chestnuts. They had only five years together before she died. At least they were five happy years. Morton was devastated when she died but he had Ross, having legally adopted him as his son. Ross also works in the investment company. He went to school and university with Charlie and they have always been good friends which is why Ross came to the wedding today. Now, let me look at that ankle.'

When the ankle was firmly bound up Moira announced her intention of phoning around to find a wheelchair.

'No, please don't bother,' Rachel said urgently. 'I'd rather stay here with you and rest my ankle.'

'But I thought you were so keen to see all the works of art in the city museums,' exclaimed Moira looking puzzled.

'I was and I still am, but not in a wheelchair. I'll wait until my ankle is better.'

'Then you might never see them,' Moira pointed out. 'By the time you can walk on it without pain you'll be in Scotland. Remember you and Giles are booked to fly back next Thursday. Oh, I feel so disappointed for you, dear.' Moira's kindly face creased with distress. 'I'd planned so many outings for you.'

'You're very kind. And I'm sure within a couple of

days I'll be able to get about on crutches. I . . . I just don't want to go into town tomorrow with Ross Fraser.'

'You don't like him?' Moira seemed surprised.

'It isn't that,' Rachel muttered, having difficulty in expressing exactly how she did feel about Ross. He attracted her more than any man she had ever met, and yet his lack of reserve in pursuing her that afternoon along the beach and in describing himself as the guy who was going to marry her had offended her. She felt he had been far too presumptuous and her feminine instinct was warning her not to let him have any advantage over her because, once she submitted to his powerful will, she would never be able to call her life her own any more. Forcing herself to smile, she looked at Moira and added, 'You know me, Auntie. I hate to be under an obligation to anyone.'

'Just like your mother,' Moira said drily. 'And I've no patience with such an attitude. You might as well know that many of the women out there are just green with envy because you were carried into the house by the most eligible bachelor in the State of New York.'

'I don't care if they are. I didn't want him to carry me. I found him far too—too—oh, I don't know, too overbearing, I suppose, and I've no wish to see him again or be under any further obligation to him,' said Rachel coolly, even though she knew she was lying in her teeth.

'Well, that's plain enough,' said Moira with a laugh, and then suddenly hugged Rachel. 'Oh, how like dear Dottie you are, so independent and obstinate. She always had to have her own way and to be the boss.'

'Yes, I know, and perhaps it's a good thing she was

like that, since she married someone as easy-going and irresponsible as my father,' said Rachel with a sigh.

'But Hugh was such a nice man,' said Moira. 'So kind and generous. And you mustn't forget, Rachel, you inherited some of his characteristics, too. He was always very artistic, even if his attitude to life was a little happy-go-lucky.'

'Except that he was often unlucky in his financial dealings,' said Rachel drily. 'And Giles is more like him than I am. I'm so worried about Giles, Aunt Moira. I'm afraid he's inherited Dad's lack of thriftiness and also his gambling fever. Do you think you or Uncle Jack could have a word with him about it?'

'We'll try, dear. We'll try,' said Moira. 'But he is a grown man now, twenty-one years of age, and there's nothing much anyone can do after a person has turned eighteen. You shouldn't be mothering him, Rachel. You have your own life to live.'

'I know. But you see, when she married again and went to live in Australia three years ago, Mother asked me to keep an eye on Giles, and even though he's twenty-one I just can't help being concerned. I do hope he won't get into any trouble while he's here.'

'And if he does, let him get himself out of it without your help. He'll never learn to be responsible if he doesn't,' replied Moira sharply. 'Now suppose you let me help you walk back to the deck. There's no reason why you should miss the rest of the party.'

Rachel didn't see her brother that evening because she had gone to bed before he returned from Chestnuts. Nor was he at breakfast the next morning when she managed, with the help of the crutches that

Moira had hired from the local chemist, to make her way to the bright morning-room that overlooked the river.

'Giles has gone into town with Kathy and some of the others,' Moira told her. 'He said to tell you he's sorry about your ankle and he'll see you when he comes back on Wednesday.'

'But where is he going to stay until Wednesday?' exclaimed Rachel.

'At Ross Fraser's apartment in Manhattan. He'll be OK, Rachel, so for heaven's sake stop worrying about him. You're worse than a hen with her chick, yet you're only three years older than he is.'

'Did you tell Mr Fraser I wouldn't be going into town with him?' asked Rachel. In spite of her resolve to forget about her encounter with Ross Fraser, he had been at the forefront of all her thoughts, all last night before she had fallen asleep and this morning ever since she had woken up.

'Yes. I did that when he arrived to take Giles into town. Now let's talk about you. In view of what has happened to your ankle Jack and I wonder whether you would consider postponing your return to Edinburgh and would stay on with us for a couple of weeks? We'd both love to have you. I always wanted Dottie to come and visit, but she said she couldn't afford the fare, because your father had lost so much money betting on horses or had gone bankrupt for some reason or other. And now Jenny's gone away.' Moira sniffed and wiped away the tears that had welled up in her eyes at the thought of her only daughter having left home. 'Do you see what I'm getting at, dear? Jack and I would love to have your company for a little while longer.'

'But Giles has to be back at university. The term

begins next week,' Rachel demurred, looking out at the view, at the coloured hills and the smooth water, at the birds flitting about the bird-table, and wishing she could stay longer in that pleasant, comfortable house where time passed so serenely and nothing seemed to be a trouble.

'Then let him go back. It's time he learned to cope on his own,' retorted Moira, suddenly authoritative. She stood up and began to collect used dishes together. 'Anyway, think about it. You look so pale and thin, as if you need a holiday and some good home cooking. And it would be best if you rested that ankle really well before attempting to walk on it properly.'

Rachel thought about the suggestion all day as she lay out on the deck and sunned herself. In Edinburgh she worked in a department store, and to come to the wedding she had taken her annual holiday of three weeks. There was really no need for her to go back to Scotland yet. Possibly Moira was right, Giles should be allowed to cope on his own by now. By that evening she had come to a decision. She would stay on with the Vanways for the rest of the holidays.

Giles returned on Wednesday none the worse for his visit to New York City. He seemed not at all surprised by Rachel's decision to lengthen her stay, and was very enthusiastic about it.

'Be good for you, Rach,' he said to her as he packed in the bedroom he had used while staying there. 'And give you a chance to visit the museums and galleries.'

'Did you go to any of them.'

'Now you know I'm not into that sort of thing,' he parried.

'Then what did you do in New York?'

'Saw all the usual sights, Statue of Liberty, Empire State Building, Brooklyn Bridge, Central Park. But best of all, we went to a couple of nightclubs where the jazz playing was really super. We also took a run down to Atlantic City.'

'Oh, no,' groaned Rachel. 'I hope you didn't go to a casino.'

'Of course I did. Everybody did.' He avoided her eyes as he stuffed underwear into his case.

'But you had no money to gamble with.'

'Ross Fraser lent me some.'

'He was with you?'

'Sure he was. How else do you think I got there? I went in his car. You should see it, Rach. It has all the options you can think of.'

'Did you lose much money?' she demanded, refusing to be sidetracked by his enthusiasm for Ross Fraser's car.

'Won some, lost some.' His grin was, as usual, cheeky and cheerful, and his golden brown eyes, the same colour as her own, glinted with merriment. 'I had a whale of a time. But not to worry, Rach. All that's taken care of.'

'Meaning, I hope, you don't owe anything to Ross Fraser,' she said sharply.

'I've told you. It's all been taken care of. I'm a big boy now and can look after myself. I don't need you hovering around and watching everything I do, watching for me to make a mistake. Time you got off my back, Rach,' he replied testily and went over to the cupboard to take out the few shirts he had brought with him.

'Here, let me fold those for you,' she said taking them from him. Although hurt by his remarks, she acknowledged the truth of them in the light of Moira's advice. 'Where else did you go in New York?'

'Ross showed me round the offices of Fraser and Allanby, the investment company of which his adoptive father, Morton Fraser, is the president, and where Ross works too. It seems he's a whizz at knowing how to make money, buying and selling companies, stocks and shares and so on, and he's already a millionaire in his own right as well as being all set to inherit more millions when Morton Fraser kicks the bucket.' He gave her a curious glance. 'Just what happened between you and him when you met down on the beach, when you sprained your ankle on Saturday?'

'Nothing much. Why?'

'I just wondered. You see, he told me he'd like to marry you.'

Rachel stared at him, her mouth open. Then, snapping her teeth together, she said coldly; 'Well, I'm not going to marry him.'

'Why not?'

'Because . . . because. Oh, Giles, surely you know why? I hardly know the man, have only had a short conversation with him, and what I know of him I don't like.'

'I think he's a great guy,' said Giles, who seemed to be picking up Americanisms fast. 'I wish I could live the way he does. You should see his apartment. Has every luxury you can think of. And he goes skiing in the winter to all the best resorts and sails in the summer from Newport, of all places. He knows all the right people, too.'

'He's just a rich playboy, then, who makes his living gambling on the stock exchange with other people's money, and I don't like or admire people like that,' Rachel said haughtily. 'He behaves as if he owns the world and all that's in it and he's far too bossy and arrogant.'

'That's just female prejudice talking,' Giles jeered. 'You don't know what he's really like as a person. And it could be that he's just the match for you. You're awfully bossy yourself and you need a man who'll stand up to you. Anyway I gave him my permission, in our father's absence, to propose to you. I'm rather keen on getting a real live millionaire, who knows how to gamble and win, as a brother-in-law. I'm tired of us always being poor.'

Rachel flung down the shirt she was folding.

'Just for that you can fold your own shirts,' she retorted. 'I'm going to bed.'

Giles left for Britain as scheduled. Rachel's ankle slowly improved during the next few days and she was able to go out with Moira when her aunt went shopping in the small nearby town of Riverpark, hopping around with the help of the crutches.

She found she enjoyed being mothered by Moira, and realised for the first time how much she had missed her own mother ever since Dorothy had married again two years after the tragic death of Hugh Dow, her first husband and Rachel's father. And, though reluctant at first to admit it, she was enjoying not having Giles around. Overseeing her lively and mischievous brother had not been an easy task for her, and had forced her into growing up a little faster than she might have done otherwise.

The surprisingly warm autumnal weather combined with the picturesque beauty of the countryside had a tranquillising effect on her. It was hard to believe she was only seventy miles from the hectic traffic and bustling life of the city of New York. Moira's friends were also soothing. Mostly married middle-aged women, they seemed quite happy to drop in for an hour in the morning or afternoon to chat and drink coffee and discuss various subjects ranging from local politics to the latest birth of a baby. One of them was actually a well known artist, and she brought a pad of D'Arches' watercolour paper, paints and brushes so that Rachel could use her enforced idleness to practise her recently neglected art of painting.

One sunny afternoon, over a week after Giles had gone back to Scotland, Rachel was alone on the veranda trying to capture in paint the scene before her. Her ankle had recovered sufficiently for her to manage without crutches, provided she didn't overdo the walking, and she had one more week left of her holidays.

Absorbed in what she was doing, she wished that she could spend all her time either painting or printing when she returned to Britain instead of having to work at the department store. It had always been her ambition to earn her living from practising and selling her art, but so far it had been more important to be able to earn enough money to keep herself and to help support Giles until he had graduated as a lawyer.

Sitting back in her chair, brush in hand, waiting for the paint to dry a little before adding another detail, she was looking out at the now familiar Catskills when suddenly the view was blotted out as a pair of hands covered her eyes.

Surprised that Jack Vanway would play such a trick on her, Rachel grasped two sinewy male wrists and tried to pull the hands away from her eyes.

'Guess who?' whispered a voice behind her and, recognising it immediately, she stiffened and let go of the wrists.

'Mr Fraser,' she said coolly and the hands dropped

immediately from her eyes.

'Mister Fraser.' Scorn rasped in his voice. He stepped round to the other side of the table and hitched a hip up on the rail of the deck, blocking her view of the river. In a faded blue sweatshirt and jeans, his eyes covered by sunglasses and his tawny hair dishevelled, he looked younger and even more attractive than he had in his silver-grey suit at Jenny's wedding reception. 'Mister Fraser is Morton. I'm Ross. And don't you dare tell me you've forgotten me, because I know you haven't. How's the ankle?'

'Much better, thank you,' she said frigidly, nose in the air.

'Still on crutches?'

'No.'

'Can't have been such a bad sprain, then. Come and have dinner with me tonight?'

'No thank you.'

'Why not?'

It was one thing to tell Moira and Giles that she didn't like Ross Fraser but quite another to tell him to his face how she felt about him, that really she was afraid of liking him too much if she dared to be in his company for too long. 'I think Moira has made other arrangements for this evening,' she began evasively.

'You think. But I happen to know,' he interrupted. 'I know because I've just met Moira in Main Street and she said you're free this evening. I'll call for you at seven.'

'No. Oh, please don't. I don't want to have dinner with you.'

'But it isn't a question of what you want, darling, right now. It's what I want that matters,' he replied, smiling at her confidently, and she felt as if her bones were melting under the warmth of that smile. 'And

that narrowed his eyes. In a well tailored suit of charcoal grey and shirt of a lighter grey, his hair shining with the smooth reddish glow of chestnut skins, he was the epitome of the wealthy and sophisticated New York businessman.

'You look great, a real Highland princess,' he said in his open forthright way, the expression in his eyes leaving her in no doubt of his appreciation of her appearance.

'Thank you,' she murmured. 'What time shall I tell Moira I'll be back?'

'Do you have to tell her any time?' he asked raising his eyebrows.

'I'm her guest. It would be good manners to.'

'Are you always so considerate of others?'

'I try to be.'

For a moment his eyes were hidden by their lashes and his lips twisted as he thought. At last he said, 'Tell her . . . No, I'll tell her myself and then she'll know for sure.'

Turning on his heel, he strode out of the room and into the kitchen where Moira was dishing up dinner for Jack. Although she followed him, Rachel didn't catch what he said to her aunt, only heard Moira's answer.

'That's fine with me. Have a nice evening, both of you.'

Outside, the car gleamed opulently in the light shed from the standard lantern-shaped lamps that lined the driveway. He was everything she resented, she thought irritably, as she slid into the seat next to the driver's. He possessed more money than was good for him, spent it on luxuries like the car, led young men like Giles astray to places like Atlantic City and behaved in an arrogant way towards women. And to crown it all, he was an American, even if he had been born in Edinburgh and his real father had been a Canadian. If she was at all consistent in her opinion of people like him she shouldn't be there in his car or be going out to dinner with him.

But it was too late. The car was already moving smoothly and fast like the stealthy animal after which it was named. Headlights illuminating the high stalwart trunks of old elm trees, it swept along the riverside drive and turned right up the hill at a junction towards the town.

'What did you tell Aunt Moira?' she asked.

'To expect you when she sees you.'

'That was hardly specific.'

'I wasn't aiming to be specific. And having brought up one daughter and two sons she knows better than to demand to know the specific time of the return of someone like yourself after a night out. The way it is, she won't worry if you don't get back before morning and she doesn't see you until some time tomorrow. She knows you'll be with me,' he replied smoothly.

'But I'm not staying with you until tomorrow,' she said, even though a queer little tremor of anticipation about what might happen if she did stay with him all night tingled through her.

'Maybe you're not. But then maybe you are. Who knows? Relax and let the chips fall where they may,' he replied lightly.

The gambling term chilled her in a way no other words would have done, and for the rest of the drive through the town and on the fast highway she sat upright and tense, staring ahead, feeling as if she had been taken captive by some marauding pirate and that during the next few hours she was going to have to fight for her freedom.

CHAPTER TWO

THE full moon was rising, a yellow ball in a blue-black sky, as they drove along a two-lane road. On one side it was edged by thick woodland interrupted by dramatic spurs of rock where the way had been forced by blasting. On the other side a plantation of trees and grass divided the road from another road along which the lights of traffic going in the opposite direction lit up the foliage. Together the two roads were called a parkway, Ross told her, designed for motorists who wanted to avoid towns as well as the heavy commercial traffic they would find on the fast interstate highway.

After a few miles he took an exit road off to the right. The lights of a small town twinkled beckoningly. Soon they were driving along a main street of stone and brick houses. To Rachel they looked, with their rows of sash windows, wide panelled doorways and fanlights, as if they had been built in the eighteenth century.

Ross parked the car at the kerb in front of one of the biggest buildings outside which a sign hung from a wrought-iron bracket.

'It used to be a coaching inn,' Ross explained as he opened the car door for her. 'Now it's one of the most fashionable places to dine out in this neck of the woods.'

Big brass lanterns attached to walls on either side of a double front door set under a wide porch gave out a warm yellow light. An inner glass-panelled vestibule door opened into a wide hallway panelled in pine. The floor was made from shining strips of maple and was scattered with colourful rugs. Against the walls antique side tables and chairs were arranged and before a log fire in a wide stone hearth there were several wing chairs and wooden settles.

They were welcomed by the owner of the restaurant and his wife, who were both dressed in clothes that innkeepers might have worn in the late eighteenth century. The host wore homespun breeches, thick stockings and heavy shoes with buckles, and his coat and waistcoat were both of blue cloth, fastened by brass buttons. His shirt had a high collar around which was fastened a white cravat. The hostess's dress, of the same blue, had a long full skirt and a wide white collar edged the neckline. On her thick blonde hair she wore a white mob cap.

'Welcome to our home,' said the host, shaking hands with them. 'My wife will be pleased to take you to a table and to show you our bill of fare.'

'We like the diners to feel as if they are indeed guests in our house,' the hostess explained to Rachel in answer to her question about the host's greeting. 'If you had arrived earlier you would have been able to mix with our other guests in the reception-room and to have aperitifs with them. And when dinner is over everyone goes into the lounge for coffee and liqueurs. We give you a choice of only two main courses and the recipes are based on the sort of meals that might have been served in this place just after the War of Independence. Most of the food is fresh today. If we use anything that has been preserved it has come out of our own gardens and has been canned, frozen or preserved by ourselves or our staff.'

She led them into a room on the right where candles in brass candelabra glimmered on tables. The windows were draped in green velvet looped back with golden tassels. White linen, silver and glassware shone in the flickering flames. In the wide hearth, with its white Adam-style mantel, a log fire blazed.

There were already many people in the room. Bare shoulders of women shimmered, jewels glittered, teeth flashed as someone laughed, and several male voices called out greetings to Ross which he acknowledged with some pleasantry and a wave of a hand.

Their table was by one of the windows. The hostess introduced them to the blond young man who was to be their waiter. He was also dressed in period style, breeches made from homespun, thick stockings, a white collarless shirt and a green waistcoat.

They both chose to have the roast beef and drank a local Hudson Valley red wine which Rachel found surprisingly palatable.

'So what do you think of this place?' asked Ross.

'It's very elegant.'

'There's a lot of this sort of restoration going on, especially in the eastern states, where many of the places built in the seventeenth and eighteenth century are still standing. I guess you could say Americans have at last discovered that they have a heritage worth preserving.'

'I'm beginning to realise that,' she murmured politely.

'And you'd see much more if you visited Maryland, Virginia, the Carolinas and Georgia,' he said, putting his elbows on the table and resting his chin on his folded hands to look at her intently.

'I won't have time to go south. I'm going back to Edinburgh next week,' she replied, looking down at the table to avoid that intent stare of his. She had an odd feeling he was trying to mesmerise her.

'Why do you have to go back?'

'My three weeks' holiday will be over and I'll have to go back to work.'

'What sort of work?'

'I'm a display designer in a department store.'

'I thought you said you were an artist.'

'I went to art college and the work I do is artistic, but I'm not able to make my living by selling my own artistic creations yet.'

'You mean you'd like to paint pictures and sell them?'

'Mostly I like making silk-screen prints more than just painting. I do batik work also for scarves and dress materials as well as designing decorations on silk that can be framed and hung on walls. But it's difficult to get established as a free-lance artist and I have to eat.'

'No wealthy patrons around to support you?' he asked with an amused quirk of his lips. 'Give me half a chance and I'd be your patron for life.'

'No wealthy patrons,' she agreed lightly, although she felt blood warm her cheeks at his insinuation. 'What do you do for a living.'

'Don't you know? I thought your brother would have told you. Or Moira.' His lips twisted cynically as if he knew he must have been discussed since their last meeting.

'I've been told that you're with an investment company, but I don't really know what that involves in the way of work,' she replied. 'I can only guess that you buy and sell stocks and shares with other people's money.'

'And you don't approve,' he guessed accurately.

'No, I don't. It seems to me to be only another way of gambling.'

'You're right there. It is a chancy business to be in. Why don't you like gambling?'

'Because gambling ruined my father. He was always making unlucky investments and losing money. And he could never resist a bet or a wager on anything.'

'But I'm not like that,' he remarked. 'I don't suffer from gambling fever. When you're handling other people's money you have to keep a cool head and do a lot of research and analysis into the various businesses offering stocks and shares on the market to be able to predict their future behaviour. And I never make a bet on anything unless I'm sure I'm going to win. Also, I don't intend to do it for ever. One of these days, when I've made enough money to live on without having to work, I'll leave Wall Street, find something else to do.'

'What could you do?'

'Do I detect a note of scepticism?' he challenged with a grin. 'Don't judge a person by outside appearances or by how he earns his living.' She couldn't help flushing again. 'Basically I'm really an outdoors guy. My real father's father was a farmer in Canada, and so my father would have been too, if the war hadn't ruined his health. I'm only in Wall Street because Morton had me educated to follow in his footsteps and I didn't want to disappoint him by refusing. But I don't intend to be trapped in the city for ever, much as I enjoy all it has to offer in the way of bright lights and entertainment. Nor do I want to end up like Morton . . .' He broke off as if changing his mind about what he had been going to say about his adoptive father, and emptied his wine glass. 'I guess what I'd like to do most is buy some land and farm it, do something productive or creative.'

At that point the waiter came so Rachel made no comment. She had to admit to being surprised by what he had said. She had been sure he was really what he appeared to be, a clever and possibly unscrupulous materialist who cared only for money and whatever luxuries it could provide, a smooth and selfish sophisticate interested only in satisfying his own appetites. His confession that he would like to do something more creative or productive impressed her and subtly her attitude began to change even more. Not only was she fast falling in love with him because of his appeal to her senses, she was beginning to like and respect him.

When the waiter had gone with their order for dessert, and before she could say anything else, Ross took command of the conversation again and directed it away from himself by asking her opinion of a certain artist. From then on they talked mostly about art, and she found he was very knowledgeable about the subject, and she remarked upon it.

'That's thanks to Morton,' he replied. 'He prides himself on being a connoisseur of paintings. He owns many by famous artists, including a couple by Picasso, a Matisse and one by Marc Chagall, whom he once met personally, when the artist was over here some time ago. Originally he started collecting for investment purposes but now he buys only if he thinks the painting is good by his rather high standards. You could say Chestnuts rivals some of the museums in the city.'

It was a bait she couldn't resist.

'I'd love to see them,' she said, her enthusiasm for art completely overriding her prejudices.

'Then I'll come for you tomorrow and take you to see them,' he said autocratically. 'I'd like you to meet Morton. Or I should say it the other way round. I'd like Morton to meet you. He's very pro-Scots, his own grandfather having emigrated from Glasgow to New York. Morton wanted to marry my mother years ago, when he met her for the first time in Edinburgh.'

'Moira told me about that,' she admitted, and again his glance in her direction was knowledgeable and a little cynical.

'So you were interested enough to ask her about me. That gives me hope. I wouldn't mind having a Scots girl for a wife myself if she were like you,' he said softly.

In response to another intent look he gave her over the candle-flame she felt a strange flicker of nerves in the lower part of her body, a primitive physical reaction that disconcerted her. She was quite aware of what he was doing. By every look and almost every word he uttered he was wooing her, attacking her sensibilities with every weapon he possessed. And he possessed many, she admitted, glancing at his lean, aquiline features, still tanned by summer suns, at the humorous slant to his generous curving lips, at the sudden flaring of violet flames in the greyness of his eyes when he looked at her. Listening to the pleasant cadences of his voice as he told her an amusing anecdote about Morton Fraser and watching for the sudden charming flash of his smile, she wished suddenly that she could be with him for ever.

By the time they left the restaurant she was totally disarmed and caught in a spell of enchantment from which she was reluctant to break out and, after another long drive along the moonlit parkway, it was with a certain sense of disappointment that she found herself back at the Vanways' house half an hour before midnight.

'You see, I can also be considerate when I want to,' Ross said with a touch of mockery.

'Especially when you want to make an impression,' she said, feeling sufficiently at ease in his company to tease him gently.

'Especially then,' he concurred with laugh. 'I'll see you tomorrow about ten, and take you to Chestnuts to view the paintings and the garden.'

'Don't I get a chance to refuse your invitation?' she retorted lightly. 'Supposing I have another date?'

'You'll just have to call it off,' he replied turning to her.

'And if I don't?' she retorted, pretending to be irritated with his cool assumption that she was ready and willing to fall in with anything he suggested, but knowing that in reality his confident approach was fast destroying her few defences.

'I'd challenge whoever he is to a duel. Pistols at dawn in the woods behind Chestnuts,' he said with mock fierceness. 'So you'd better be ready at ten tomorrow if you don't want to be the central figure in a local scandal.'

She couldn't help laughing. 'Then I'll expect you at ten. I wouldn't like you to be sent to jail for disturbing the peace on my account. And thank you very much for taking me out to dinner tonight.'

'You were very welcome. Goodnight, Highland princess.'

His head tipped towards hers. Against her cheek his lips were warm. But such a chaste and considerate kiss from him was suddenly not enough for her, so she turned her head until her lips touched his, gently yet invitingly.

'Nice,' he whispered, and slid an arm around her shoulders.

Beneath the harder pressure of his lips she parted hers voluntarily, giving in to a delicious headiness and kissing him back with an almost innocent fervency. Not for a long time, not since the time she had imagined herself in love with one of the teachers at the art college she had attended, had she felt so strongly that she wanted to kiss someone of the opposite sex. Forgotten were all her prejudices against this man. Suddenly he seemed very close to her, a companion with whom she could share not only thoughts and opinions, but much more, and in that brief moment of communication she recognised him as a person with whom she could happily share the rest of her life.

Much of what she felt was expressed in the short embrace, and in his response to her kiss she sensed passion within him flowing deeply and strongly, all the more exciting and appealing because he kept it under control and withdrew from her, pushing her away from him gently, before it could burst through his restraint. In the light cast by the driveway lamps she caught the gleam of his eyes, the glint of his teeth as he laughed softly.

'That was good, but let's not be greedy. Let's save something for tomorrow and all the other days we're going to be seeing each other,' he murmured.

'We'll enjoy each other much more if we take our time.'

He let her out of the car, walked up the steps to the front door with her and saw her into the house. In a daze of romantic excitement she went straight to her room and for a long time lay thinking about him and all they had talked about. For a few hours he had been the perfect companion, attentive and not at all overbearing. That tomorrow couldn't come soon enough for her, was her last thought before sleeping, and she wasn't at all surprised or dismayed by the way her attitude to him had changed so quickly. Love had stepped into her life and, to borrow Ross's own phrase, she was going to gamble on it and let the chips fall where they might.

Next morning, casually dressed again in sweat-shirt and jeans, he seemed somehow bigger and tougher and, in the close confines of the front seats of the car, she was very aware of him on a physical level. She wanted to touch him, to feel the sinewi-ness of his arm, of his thigh so close to hers, taut under tough denim. The purely primitive physical desire shocked her a little because she had never experienced it so strongly before.

Apart from her brief association with the art teacher, her previous relationships with members of the opposite sex had always been on a cerebral level and she had felt no strong desire to be physically united with any of them. Even the art teacher hadn't aroused in her an ache like this. Ruefully surprised at herself, she realised she wanted to possess this man totally and on every level. She wanted him to be not only her lover but also her husband, to belong to her alone and to no one else.

After greeting each other they didn't talk. They

didn't have to. It seemed as if their minds met and were in tune immediately. He drove up to the town and then out along a road that wound past green fields and patches of forest with occasional glimpses of the sun-dazzled river. Shadows of tall trees slashed the sunlit paving. They reached stone gate-posts on the right and turned in between them to follow a straight avenue edged by sturdy chestnuts, their fingered leaves brown and withered, ready to fall.

The house sat among a clump of cedars and birches. It had two storeys and was built in classical New England colonial style, with two rows of long sash windows and a panelled door set under a portico supported by pillars. The views from the front steps of the river and Catskills beyond were panoramic.

Once they were inside he took her straight to the picture gallery, an addition at the back of the house where temperature and lighting were carefully controlled in the interest of preserving the paintings. And yet the outside world was not shut out. The graceful trees, crammed flowerbeds and shrubberies of a well tended landscaped garden were invited into the gallery through two wide windows.

The paintings held Rachel spellbound for more than an hour, during which time Ross left her twice, called to the phone by the housekeeper. When he returned the second time she was still sitting in front of one of the paintings, apparently oblivious of anything that was going on around her.

'Hey, I know I can't compete with a painting by Matisse, in your estimation, but I am the guy who brought you here. You could show a little appre-ciation,' he taunted, sitting down on the bench beside her and slipping an arm around her waist.

'Oh, I'm glad you brought me! They're marvellous. Thank you very much for letting me see them,' she said, turning to him her brown eyes alight with joy.

'Is that all?'

'What more should I say?'

'I'm not really interested right now in words,' he mocked softly, his glance going deliberately to her lips.

She knew what he meant, and didn't find it hard to comply with his suggestion. Leaning towards him, she kissed him on the mouth.

'Thank you once again for bringing me here,' she whispered.

'You'll stay to lunch and then we'll walk round the grounds,' he said, still holding her, both his hands at her waist.

'Only if you'll agree to come back for dinner at Moira's and Jack's house. It's the only way I can pay back your hospitality,' she said seriously.

'You just hate to be under an obligation to anyone, don't you?' he said. 'That darned pride of yours again. You don't have to be like that with me, you know.'

'I can't help it. And it's not just pride. It's the way I was brought up.'

'It's stubborn Scottish pride. I know because I have more than my fair share of it, too. But between friends it shouldn't exist. And I'm hoping we're already friends, Rachel. Aren't we?'

'We will be if you'll come to my aunt's for dinner tonight,' she persisted.

'OK, I'll come. And tomorrow we'll go to the city. We'll visit those museums you want to see and then go on to a concert at Avery Fisher Hall. You can't go back to Edinburgh without spending at least one day in the Big Apple.'

His reference to her imminent departure upset her for the rest of that day, although she tried hard to hide her distress at the thought of leaving. When she was alone that night in bed she took herself to task about it. What had happened to her? Where was her much vaunted independence of spirit now? What about that career she had mapped out for herself? Where had that immunity to romantic love gone which she had once believed she had possessed?

Here she was, head over heels in love with a man she had known only a few days, and already she was crying inside because in three days' time she would have to leave him and would probably never see him again. Nothing in her life to date had prepared her for this disturbance of her emotions. She longed to stay and be able to see him every day, to hear his voice, his laughter. And not only that, she wanted to do things for him, cook meals for him, please him in any way she could think of. Above all else she wanted to make love with him, be close to him in every way, go to bed with him at night and be with him in the morning when she woke up. It was incredible that this had happened to her, and she had no idea how to cope with the situation because she didn't really know what his real feelings were about her. For all she knew she could be just a passing fancy for him, a woman he could date conveniently while he was waiting for a yacht to be made ready.

The day in Manhattan passed all too quickly. There was too much to see in too short a time. As it turned out she saw only two of the art museums, the

Museum of Modern Art where again she stood in awe of the paintings and paper art of Matisse for far too long, and the Whitney gallery where she admired the paintings of twentieth-century American artists. Then on to the concert, where she sat enraptured by the playing of one of Bruch's violin concertos by Itzhak Perlman. All the way back to Riverpark, driving along in companionable silence with Ross, she was haunted by the romantic bittersweet melodies.

In the darkness of the car in front of the Vanways' house she kissed him fervently to show her appreciation, and as always, much to her disappointment, he was the first to withdraw.

'Tomorrow we'll go on the river in Morton's yacht. It's all shipshape now and ready for going south,' he said.

'It will be my next-to-last day here,' she murmured, wondering what she could do to break through the barrier of her own pride and caution to let him know how she felt about going away from him.

'I know,' he said, his voice low. 'That's why we have to make the most of it. See you at noon.'

She liked Morton Fraser's yacht as soon as she saw it. Its sleek, rakish lines appealed to her sense of design. Over forty feet long, it was what is known as a motor sailer, having two masts on which sail could be hoisted but also having twin diesel engines to power it for hours at a time when sailing wasn't possible. Down below it was fitted out with every comfort possible, with a saloon for eating and socialising in and two sleeping-cabins, one for'ard and one aft. The fittings were made from oak and the cushions on the settee berths were covered in a sea-green tweedy material.

For three hours that day they chugged up and down the river, up as far as Rip Van Winkle Bridge and down as far as the town of Poughkeepsie. He showed her how to steer and told her about days he had spent ice-sailing on the river when it had been frozen in the winter. While they were out the sky clouded over and the air grew heavy and humid. The threat of thunder in the atmosphere seemed to underline the heaviness of spirit Rachel was experiencing because this would be the last time she would be with Ross.

When they returned to the yacht club and tied up at the dock, Ross produced cans of beer and they sat in the centre cockpit, drinking. On edge because parting from him was so close, Rachel could bear the thunder-threatening silence no longer and said abruptly, 'When are you going south?'

'Soon. I'd like to be in Annapolis, Maryland before the end of the month. Would you like to see the route I'll take?'

'Yes, please.'

In the pilot-house surrounded by electronic navigation equipment they leaned side by side over the chart he spread out on the sloping chart-table.

'From here I'll go down river and across the entrance of New York Harbour to Sandy Hook on the New Jersey coast,' he said, pointing to the places on the chart. 'If I'm lucky with the weather, from there I'll take a long trek down the Jersey Coast, around Cape May and up Delaware Bay. Then through the canal to Chesapeake Bay. I should be able to make Annapolis in three or four days from here. I'll stay there for a while to look up some friends, do some sailing. You'd like Annapolis. It has many old houses, some built before the War of Independence and some just afterwards. They've been preserved and restored. After Annapolis I'll go into the Intercoastal Waterway at Norfolk, Virginia and wend my way south with other like-minded sailors taking their yachts to the sunshine for the winter. Many of them will be from the northern states and Canada. Snowbirds, they're called because they're escaping, before the severe winter weather comes and freezes the lakes and rivers, and so that they can continue to sail all winter.'

'What is the Intercoastal Waterway?'

'It's a series of canals and cuts joining natural waterways that lie behind the long islands and banks of sand that edge the eastern seaboard. It was engineered so that shipping between the north and south could avoid the areas of bad winter storms, such as Cape Hatteras, here.' He pointed to the chart. 'Many hundreds of ships have been lost off that particular cape in the past.'

'Will you take a crew with you?'

'Not this time.' He paused for a moment, then said slowly, 'Unless you would be my crew. Would you like to come with me?'

He turned to look at her. Leaning as they were, they were very close. If she turned to him, their cheeks would touch and possibly their lips. Already her head was spinning a little in reaction to the nearness of his warm temporarily unrestrained sensuality, so she kept her face averted from his gaze and stared down at the blue of the sea and the green of the land on the charts.

'Yes, I would like to go with you,' she admitted in a whisper.'

'Then come.' His voice was deep, seductive.

'I can't. You know I can't. I have to go back to Edinburgh tomorrow.'

'You don't have to do anything you don't want to do,' he said, taking one of her hands in one of his. 'Don't go back to Britain,' he urged. 'Stay and go south with me.'

'I have to go back. Giles . . .'

'Never mind Giles,' he interrupted her roughly, his eyes blazing with violet light. 'Think of yourself and of me instead. Think of what it would be like, Rachel, just you and I on the boat from sunrise to sunset, the long dark nights together and alone, away from everyone else.'

'I can't.' She tried to pull her hand free of his and somehow found herself within the circle of his arms as they stood facing each other. 'Oh, please try to understand. It isn't because I wouldn't like to be alone with you. I have to go back to earn my living. I can't afford to stay on and go with you.'

'You could if we were married first.'

It was the first time he had mentioned marriage to her since the day they had met.

'You're not serious,' she began.

'I was never more serious in my life. Remember the day we met when I told you I was the guy who was going to marry you? I meant it. I was serious then and I'm serious now. I want to be married to you.'

'But you hardly know me,' she demurred, even though excitement was boiling through her veins. 'Why choose me?'

'Let's just say I recognise a good investment when I see it,' he said, mocking himself and his money-making ability as he drew her closer. 'I liked the way you looked, and after I'd talked to you I liked you even more and was determined to see more of you. Luckily for me, Moira understood how I felt and agreed to invite you to stay on until your ankle was a little better.'

'You asked Moira to invite me to stay longer?' she gasped, staring at him in amazement.

'Yes,' he admitted, with that slight smile which she realised was not only mysterious and mocking but full of mischief too. 'Having researched your background and analysed it, I was able to predict a great future for you and me together, so I had to make sure you wouldn't slip away before I had time to make my bid. And now I'd like to persuade you to stay on for a few more days so that we can get married and take a cruise south on Morton's yacht by way of a honeymoon.'

'I . . . I don't know what to say,' she whispered, completely overwhelmed by his proposal. It was beyond her wildest dreams.

'It's quite easy,' he said, mocking her. 'Just say yes and leave the rest to me.'

'But Giles . . .'

'If he weren't your brother and if I didn't believe you'd take umbrage, I'd say to hell with Giles. This has nothing to do with him. Anyway, last time I saw him he gave me his blessing, for what it was worth. In the absense of your father, he gave me his permission to marry you. Not that it would have made any difference to me if he hadn't.'

'I know. He told me. But . . .'

'And if you're going to go all feminist on me and bring up the matter of your career as an artist and throw it down as another obstacle to marriage with me, just let me point out first that as my wife you would be able to free-lance at last. I would be your patron. You wouldn't have to work for a living. You'd be financially independent.'

'No, I wouldn't. I'd be dependent on you,' she retorted. 'Anyway I wouldn't, couldn't marry you or anyone else just for that reason.'

'Then for what reason would you marry me?' he asked tantalisingly.

'Only for love,' she whispered and hid her face against his chest.

'Are you trying to tell me you don't love me?' he asked.

'No, I'm not, but . . .'

'Then stop butting. As far as I can see there are no impediments to our marriage. I know you don't like the way I make my living, but we do have some things in common, and we should be able to make a success of marriage. So we'll take a chance on it and tie the knot as soon as we've both had the necessary medical examinations and can get a licence,' he asserted autocratically.

He didn't give her another opportunity to argue but kissed her with a domineering possessiveness he hadn't shown before and that she had secretly longed for him to show. At last she was able to give expression to the desire she had been struggling to suppress for days, the desire to touch and caress him, to stroke his face and the nape of his neck, to lift her fingers through his hair and to press herself invitingly against his hard muscular body. Eyes closed, lips clinging, hands moving caressingly, they swayed together, caught in a storm of passion and only vaguely aware that outside thunder was rumbling ominously.

Not until rain started to drum on the roof of the pilot-house did Ross let go of her and lift his lips from hers. He closed the hatches and turned back to her. No smile curved his slightly parted lips and his eyes flared with violet light as he reached for her hand.

'Sounds like the giants are playing ninepins amongst the Catskills. We're going to be stuck here for a while until the storm is over,' he said softly in her ear. 'I know of a place where we can spend the next hour very comfortably finding out much more about each other in the best possible way.'

He led her down the two steps into the wide after cabin and, lying close to each other on the double bunk, they entered a new world that belonged only to the two of them. They talked as they had never talked before, sweet lovers' talk that was interrupted often by sense-arousing kisses that grew longer and longer as their mutual desire to be even closer grew more and more intense.

'I can't help wondering why you haven't married before,' Rachel whispered, her lips moving against the strong pulsing column of his throat. 'Why has no other woman snapped you up?'

'I could ask you the same,' he murmured, his fingers sliding seductively within the open neck of her shirt and down to the first fastening just above the cleft between her breasts. 'Haven't you ever been in love before?'

'Not really. It was more like an adolescent crush,' she confessed, laughing a little at the memory of her brief liking for the art teacher. 'He just wasn't right for me. He was too old, had a roving eye and was a bit randy. He'd been divorced twice, both times for having become involved with other women. When I found that out I was put off him completely. Knowing he'd been guilty twice of infidelity, I guessed he would be unfaithful to me too. So I got out of that relationship as fast as I could, before I got too involved with him. I never slept with him.'

'I guessed something like that must have happened to make you so cautious and aloof, so anti-marriage, and, dare I say it, so anti-male. You were damned prickly and prejudiced when I first met you.' His smile robbed his words of any offence they might have given.

'I suppose you're right. That silly affair did put me on the defensive with regard to the opposite sex. And it's also why I have to know more about you. Although you're as handsome and fit as any twenty-five-year-old, I know you're older than that,' she said, daring to slide her hands beneath the edge of his sweat shirt. The skin of his waist was as smooth as silk. Encouraged by his lack of resistance she let her hand wander upwards, her palm tingling, to the rough hairs that criss-crossed his chest.

'I'm thirty-three, nearly thirty-four, according to my birth certificate,' he said nipping the lobe of her ear with sharp teeth. 'In my prime. You think I'm too old for you? Nine years too much of a difference? You don't see me as a father-figure, I hope.'

'No, far from it.'

'Good. I wouldn't want that. I feel we're equals. Do you?'

'I hope we are, but what I was going to say was, because you're the age you are, you must have been in love before.'

'That's true. But not like this. This is the forever stuff,' he said softly and, framing her face with his hands, kissed her slowly but with passion.

'So why didn't you marry her?' said Rachel, gasping a little when they both came up from the dark and drowning depths of passion to catch their breaths.

'Who?' His fingers were busy with the buttons of the shirt she was wearing, slipping undone each button slowly, almost tormentingly, while she watched his face, the slight mysterious smile slanting his lips and narrowing his eyes.

'The woman you were once in love with.'

'I guess because we weren't right for each other,' he replied, and stroking the shirt away from her breasts bent his head to kiss the smooth white skin he had exposed.

'Were you hurt when you and she broke up?' she asked, her eyes closing as delicious sensations tingled through her and her body grew taut, arching to his touch.

'Not for long,' he said, and sliding a leg between hers, trapped her for ever with another burning kiss on her lips, stifling any other questions she might have asked and obliterating them from her mind.

The thunder rolled away, the rain stopped, the sun came out but neither of them noticed or cared as they caressed each other and stroked away clothing. Feeling his life-force throbbing under her hands, she lost all control. Her brain awhirl in darkness, her body moving against his urgently, she kissed him wildly, longing for him to come into her and to possess her completely.

'There's no going back now,' he said softly, a shake of laughter in his voice. 'After this you'll have to marry me to make an honest man of me.'

'I love you, I want you,' she moaned and after that she was aware only of the taste, smell and feel of him tantalising her senses and a growing ache within herself that could only be assuaged in one way and by him.

'Then will you marry me?' he whispered in her ear. 'You haven't said you will yet.'

'Oh, yes, I will. I will. I'd love to marry you, please yes, please,' she cried out of the desperation of her need, her hands clutching him closer.

'Thank you,' he whispered, and kissed her with such a sweet reverence she felt her heart would burst with emotion.

From then on he dominated her totally and she enjoyed every touch of his long fingers, every burning pressure of his lips, every probe of his hard, hot tongue, her body rising and lifting to the thrust of his desire until at last they ceased to be two separate beings and were fused together by twin internal explosions. Shaken by her own complete submission to his demands, Rachel also felt oddly triumphant too because this man, who was considered so eligible by many other women, had chosen her to be his wife.

In a subdued yet happy mood, entwined with each other they dozed a little, both of them becoming suddenly wide awake when they heard voices close by.

'The storm is over, and so is our own particular storm of passion, until the next time,' said Ross, pushing up on one elbow to look down at her. With his hair tousled, his eyes heavy-lidded, his lips parting sensually, his bare skin golden in the shaft of light that came through a porthole, he was the lover she had always dreamed of but had not believed she would ever meet. 'And there will be many, many, next times,' he added, sliding a hand along her cheek and turning her lips to his. 'Shall we go and tell Moira and Jack now?' he asked when the kiss was over.

She agreed, and soon they were dressed and leaving the yacht. The two men whose voices they had heard were inspecting the boat tied up in the next berth, which seemed to have filled with rainwater and to be half sunk. They greeted Ross and then glanced curiously at Rachel, but he didn't introduce her to them.

Arms about each other's waists, they walked along the floating dock to the main concrete dock and then up, past the yacht-club building to the car park. Daylight was fading fast from the sky as they drove along the riverside road to the Vanways' house and electric light was glowing from the windows of the few houses they passed. On the way they discussed when and where they would be married, agreeing that they didn't want any fuss.

'Moira and Jack will be very surprised when we tell them,' said Rachel as they went up the steps to the front door.

'Why should they be?' Ross asked, pushing the doorbell.

'Because we only met about two weeks ago. We've not known each other very long.'

'Not in days, or weeks, or months, I agree, but we know all that matters; we know the essence of each other,' he argued. 'The rest we'll discover over the years. Wouldn't be much fun being married if you knew everything about your partner. Best to have some mystery in the relationship. And I don't think Moira will be surprised. Want to bet on it?'

'No. Of course not.' She was suddenly sharp. 'I don't make bets.'

'Now that's a pity, because I was going to bet a nice long kiss that Moira will say when she hears the news: "I'm not surprised. I could see it coming." But since you won't bet I'll just have to grab that kiss now.'

They were still kissing when the front door opened.

'I was beginning to wonder what had happened to you two,' said Moira. 'That was some storm that came through and I was anxious in case you were still on the river.'

'No. We'd just tied up when it broke,' said Ross as he followed Rachel into the hallway. 'We waited until the rain stopped before leaving the yacht. And now we have something to tell you.'

'Really?' Moira's eyes glinted knowledgeably. 'No, don't say anything. Let me guess. You've proposed to Rachel and she's accepted you.'

'Right first time,' said Ross.

'I'm not surprised at all. I could see it coming,' said Moira complacently.

'I thought you might have done,' mocked Ross and couldn't resist slanting an 'I-told-you-so' glance at Rachel. 'We plan to be married here as soon as possible and then we'll go south on Morton's boat.'

'Oh, how wonderful!' Moira suddenly lost her smugness and hugged Rachel. 'I'm so happy for you both. Let's go and tell Jack and get him to open a bottle of champagne. And then we must phone Dottie. What time do you think it will be in Brisbane right now? But if you marry in such a hurry she won't be able to come. Couldn't you wait a while, until Christmas? Then we could have a real family gathering. Giles could come, and Jenny and Charlie would be here. Perhaps you could even persuade Morton to come up for it, Ross.'

'He never comes back north until May,' he said coolly. 'Anyway, that's the sort of wedding both of us would like to avoid. We don't want a lot of people around. The quieter the better, the more

secrecy the better. This is just between Rachel and
me. We'll go off one morning to the town hall and
do it, just as soon as we can get the medical
certificates and go for the licence.'

And that was exactly how it happened. One
golden morning with a slight touch of frost, Ross
called for Rachel as if to take her out for the day and,
followed by Moira and Jack in their car, he drove
her to the town hall where the brief ceremony was
performed by a justice of the peace. Later the same
day, aboard Morton's yacht, they left the yacht club
and motored downstream, following the bends of the
great river until, soon after they had passed the
imposing fortress of West Point Military Academy,
they reached the deepest part of the river where it
narrowed between high cliffs on the eastern side and
the State Park of Bear Mountain on the western
side. As the sun set in a deep red glow behind the
spectacular mountain and long purple shadows
shook across the silvery water, they anchored in a
cove between an island called Iona and a wharf.

Long and dark was that night, their first together
as a married couple, and its silence was disturbed
only by the haunting wail of a train passing by.

CHAPTER THREE

IN Annapolis, capital of the State of Maryland, the last day of October was warm and windy. Pale sunlight slanted down into the street called Cornhill that connects the State Circle with the Market Square, an open area at the head of the inner harbour. It glinted on the white paintwork of houses and gave old bricks a warm glow.

Rachel, wearing jeans, sweatshirt and sailing shoes, her smooth dark brown hair tied back in a pony-tail, sauntered down the street, pausing now and again to admire one of the old restored houses. She knew by now that the street had been called after the busy mercantile street in London, and had originally been an artisans' street with a workingmen's tavern, the home of a silversmith and a coachmaker. The houses dated from the seventeenth to the nineteenth century and none of them was very big. It was her favourite street in the whole of the town, and she had to admit to coveting one of the tiny terraced houses, wishing she could have bought it and set up a studio in it.

She had just been to the post office to send a letter to her mother and a postcard to Giles and was on her way to meet Ross at the Market House. They had been almost two weeks in the historic town, and during that time had sailed many times on Chesapeake Bay as well as taking trips to the city of Washington, DC in a rented car. They had cruised over to the yachting-centre of St Michael's where they had watched an exciting sailing race between Skipjacks, the low and rakish over-canvassed workboats of the Chesapeake region. They had visited the Naval Academy where one of Ross's ex-schoolfriends was an officer on the teaching staff and had also called on other friends of his who owned houses or yachts in the area. And everywhere she had gone Rachel had been surprised by the warmth of the weather for the time of the year as well as by the warmth of the welcome extended to her by Ross's friends. But most of all she had been impressed and overwhelmed by Ross's warm affection and generosity to herself.

Anything she wanted, it seemed she could have. Never before had her wishes come first with someone else. It was a heady experience for her to feel wanted and appreciated, and as a result she completely lost her caution with regard to him, the caution she had learned the hard way from her experience with the art teacher. Naturally loving and generous herself, she was at last with someone with whom she could show her deepest emotions. Loving and living with him, learning with him about sailing, she blossomed, realising at last her feminine potential. Not once during those first two weeks did she have reason to regret having married in haste.

Reaching the end of Cornhill she crossed the road to Market House and entered. At once her nose was assailed by a variety of smells, the aroma of coffee percolating, the scents of fresh vegetables and fruit, of smoked meats and fresh fish. She found Ross as she had expected in a corner store that sold mostly cheese, American and imported, choice foreign preserves, such as Scotch marmalade, and wines from South America as well as from France, Italy and Germany.

As always when she saw him her heart did a little leap of pleasure. Dressed like herself casually in jeans and sweatshirt, he looked lean and tough and thoroughly competent. During the time he had spent steering the yacht his skin had darkened to a golden brown and the sunshine had bleached his hair a little so that now his whole head looked like that of a Roman statue cast in bronze. She wanted to shout aloud to the rest of the women in the Market House, 'Hey, look over here. Look who I've got for a husband,' and then revel in their envious glances.

Smiling at her own silly fantasy, she had just reached his side and was looking at the bottle of wine he was holding and examining and giving her opinion of it, when she heard a woman's voice call out to Ross, and turning she saw a short plump woman, dressed in beige cotton trousers, an open-necked navy blue shirt and the inevitable rubber-soled dockside shoes, approaching them. Her blonde-rinsed hair was cut very short and her teeth looked very white in her sun-tanned face.

'Ross, great to see you,' she gushed, shaking hands with him. 'Larry told us you were here on *Trillium*. Is it true, what he says? Are you married now and have your wife with you? Congratulations.'

The woman's bright hazel eyes slanted a glance from Ross to Rachel. About to offer her hand to Rachel, she opened her eyes wide in surprise. Her eyebrows shot up and the hand fell to her side.

'Oh, but you're not . . .' she started to say when Ross cut in.

'This is Rachel. Rachel Fraser now, I'm glad to say,' he said authoritatively, sliding an arm about Rachel's shoulders. 'Meet Carrie Duval, sweetheart,' he added.

'Well, this is a pleasant surprise,' said Carrie, recovering her poise and letting her smile widen. She and Rachel shook hands. 'I bet Morton is pleased with you.'

'He and Rachel haven't met yet, but they will in a couple of weeks' time,' said Ross easily. 'I guess you and Spence are on your way to the Abacos for the winter.'

'We sure are. Spence is in Middleton's Tavern right now having a few beers with a couple of sailing cronies, also Abacos-bound. Why not join us there for lunch?'

'We're leaving in half an hour. We've just been picking up a few last minute items,' said Ross easily. 'It's good to see you, Carrie. Say hello to Spence for me. Come on, darling.'

In the determined way to which she was fast becoming accustomed, Ross swept Rachel out of the market without buying the wine they had chosen. Across the traffic circle, past the small green park, where the city flag hung from a tall pole, and over to the pavement beside the long inlet of the inner harbour, spiky with the masts of fishing boats, they walked at speed, turning the corner into Compromise Street on their way to the marina where *Trillium* was berthed.

'Do we have to walk so fast?' Rachel complained lightly. 'And do you have to grip my arm as if you're afraid I might lag behind or not come with you?'

His grip above her right elbow relaxed at once and he laughed. 'Sorry.'

'Why don't you like her?'

'I don't dislike her,' he said with a lilt of surprise. 'What makes you think I do?'

'The way you spoke to her and your refusal to go to Middleton's for lunch with her and her husband. Your decision to leave today instead of tomorrow.'

'I can see I'll have to be careful when you're around,' he taunted. 'You're far too observant. But you drew the wrong conclusion from the observation you made just now.' He let go of her elbow, slid an arm around her waist and squeezed her gently. 'Don't forget we're on our honeymoon,' he whispered. 'We don't want to be hanging around with people like the Duvals. We don't need company. At least I don't. I need only you. I thought you felt the same.'

She did, of course, and so she said nothing more, but as they sailed down the wide, blue, sunlit, white-capped bay that afternoon, a brisk north-easterly wind behind them, she couldn't help wondering what Carrie Duval had been going to say before Ross had interrupted her.

'But you're not . . .' Carrie had started, and there had been no mistaking her expression of surprise. What name had she been going to say? Whom had she expected to see with Ross? To whom had she expected him to be married?

They crossed to the eastern shore of the bay that day and, entering the mouth of the river, put the anchor down in a secluded anchorage overhung by trees where a solitary heron stood looking for all the world like a piece of driftwood washed ashore. No other yacht followed them into the anchorage. They had it all to themselves. The autumn evening was warm, and after a meal they sat for a while in the cockpit listening to the water lapping the shore and the rustle of a breeze among the trees. Above the moon sailed in a clear sky.

'Is there no habitation near here?' Rachel asked.

'There's a fishing village further up river, that's all. This side of the bay is very rural and unspoilt and the people who live here want to keep it that way. They still cling to the old ways, and have little liking for the hustle and bustle of the commercial world. You'd find if you talked to some of them that they still speak English like people in the west of England, from where their forebears came long ago.'

'It's so quiet, too. Quite different from anything I ever expected to find in this country. It seems as remote as any island in the Hebrides.'

'You've been to the Hebrides?' he asked, turning to look at her.

'Often. My grandmother owns a cottage there, on the island of Mull. My mother used to take Giles and me for our holidays in the summer when we were children. Didn't you visit the islands when you were over in Scotland?'

'No. I only went to Edinburgh to visit my mother's relatives. I didn't have time to take in the islands. But I'd like to. I have friends who have sailed among them. They say it's one of the best cruising areas in the world.'

'Then maybe next summer we could go. The islands are so remote and romantic,' she said with a sigh of nostalgia. 'I always used to be sad whenever I had to leave Mull at the end of our holidays there and I've always had an ambition to live there.'

'Then we'll go,' he said, taking her in his arms. 'Romantic and remote is what I like, and don't you forget it. And from now on no more marinas for us. We'll anchor off-shore and avoid the madding crowd.'

'And people who know you and are surprised you're married to me?' she queried lightly, disguising her sensitive reaction to Carrie Duval's behaviour under a teasing note.

'What do you mean?' he demanded.

'That woman, Carrie Duval, was surprised when she looked at me. She was expecting to see someone else.'

He stiffened and his arms dropped away from her. Immediately she felt chilly and wished she had kept her mouth shut.

'You read too much into her reaction,' he replied smoothly, rising to his feet. 'She was probably surprised at my good taste in choosing someone like you to be married to.' He yawned and stretched his arms above his head. 'I don't know about you but I'm pretty tired. I'll just check the anchor-line before turning in.

That night there was no lovemaking and no talking either as they lay side by side in the wide bunk in the after cabin. Although Ross lay quietly on his side with his back to her she knew he was awake. Several times she tried to reach him, to break through the wall of reticence behind which he had hidden ever since she had mentioned the meeting with Carrie Duval, but whenever she snuggled up against him and slid her hand over his lean waist and upwards to fondle his bare chest he didn't respond. He had left their private world and she guessed, with a feeling of what was very close to rejection, that he was thinking of what might have been if he had married the woman Carrie Duval had expected to see with him in the Market House.

Next day he was up early, his withdrawn mood evaporating under the warmth of the sunshine.

Deciding that perhaps he had been right and she had read too much into Carrie Duval's reaction, Rachel abandoned suspicion and negativism in favour of hope and optimism. Ross had married her. The future was theirs, and not to be shared with the ghosts of old flames.

A brisk wind sent the yacht bounding down the bay over white-crested slate-grey waves, and they spent the next eight hours working together as a team to steer the yacht and trim the sails so that they could reach another secluded almost landlocked anchorage on the Virginia side where they spent another quiet night alone.

The following afternoon, after several hours of splendid sailing, they reached the busy shipping-lane approaching Norfolk, Virginia. Keeping to the right-hand side of the channel, they squeezed past huge container-freighters and oil-tankers, navy frigates and even surfaced submarines.

Ignoring the two marinas, the Waterside in Norfolk and the one under the towers of the Holiday Inn on the Portsmouth side, which sported the masts of many yachts, they entered the narrow canal or Intercoastal Waterway, that threaded past the hulks of abandoned or cocooned warships and aircraft carriers. Swing bridges swung and lift bridges lifted to let them go through and, after the lock at Great Bridge that lifted the yacht and several other boats into a higher reach of the canal, they motored on until sunset and anchored in another small cove, away from any habitation and other boats.

Next morning, after hearing a weather forecast predicting that a hurricane was coming up the coast and might hit the area where they were on the following day, Ross decided to push on to find shelter. Across two shallow sounds of water they crossed, keeping to channels marked by buoys, lurching on the short, choppy waves, the winds sweeping in from the Atlantic just beyond a line of low-lying islands to the east, and howling ominously in the rigging.

Shelter was found that night in the Alligator River of North Carolina, where again they anchored in a remote, deep pool, surrounded by cypresses that grew out of the water and where the only sound was the call of the night heron.

Only once during the next week did they berth at a marina and go ashore. After passing through the beach resorts of North Carolina they lingered for a while in the beautiful Waccamaw River, its calm waters winding between untouched forests of yellow pines and cypresses, draped with Spanish moss and crowding right into the water. After the Waccamaw they wandered along the twisting waterway through abundant life-giving marshes, golden in the sunshine where white herons and other birds waded in the mud, until they arrived in South Carolina. Giving in to Rachel's request to see Charleston, that most romantic city of the American south, Ross berthed the yacht at a marina.

In weather that seemed very hot to Rachel for that time of the year, they wandered hand in hand through the old city, the architecture of which was richly cosmopolitan and showing the influences of many different cultures: British, French, West Indian, German and Jewish. Huge houses with shutter-edged windows and wide verandas decorated with lacy ironwork fronted many of the streets. Others of an earlier period were glimpsed behind high walls or through wrought-iron gates hanging between stone gateposts. The pointed white steeples of elegant old churches soared against a vivid blue sky, and local black women sold baskets on the pavements. They dined at an expensive hotel and stayed the night in one of its bedrooms and the next day shopped for clothes for Rachel that would be suitable for the summer-type weather they would be experiencing for the rest of the trip.

From then on it seemed to Rachel they were never alone on the waterway as many yachts, both sail and power, caught up with them, all migrating south to warmer climates for the winter. In Georgia, once again Ross avoided marinas, seeking out anchorages in narrow creeks and river mouths. They visited the site of the old British Fort Frederica which had been established to defend the British American colonies from attacks by the Spanish and was destroyed by fire long after those attacks had ended. It was a pretty place, hidden in a backwater, among magnolia trees and live oaks, and all that was left of the settlement were a few walls of the fort and the cleared land still laid out in the lots where once the original settlers' houses had stood.

Across wide inlets of the sea where shrimp boats were silhouetted against a bright eastern sky and along winding rivers they motored until they eventually crossed into Florida. On a stormy day with thunder booming and lightning crackling they reached St Augustine, the oldest surviving settlement made by Europeans in the United States, and stayed a day there to visit the old Spanish fort which had been built to protect the Spanish colony from British and French assaults.

'Not far to go now,' said Ross when they left the anchorage and again entered the confines of the waterway. 'We'll be in Palm Beach in three days' time. And that will be the end of our honeymoon, I guess.' He made a wry grimace. 'Morton will be wanting all his friends and relatives to meet you and it will be one social occasion after another. We won't get much time alone together. Think you'll be able to stand it?'

'How long will we stay with him?'

'Until just after Christmas. I have to be back in the city before New Year's Day for various reasons to do with business.'

'I'll be able to stand anything as long as you're with me,' she whispered, leaning against him.

'Good. And I won't be going far without you,' he replied.

'Where will we live when we go back to New York?'

'In my apartment. It's near Central Park at the top of a renovated brownstone house. You'll be close to all your favourite museums and art galleries. OK with you.'

'OK with me,' she agreed, surprising herself, because a big city like New York was the last place she had ever imagined herself living in.

The rest of the journey down the waterway was not as interesting or exciting as the previous part, as they passed sprawling urban developments, condominium towers and tourist resorts. Only the Indian River, wide and island-dotted like an inland sea, caught Rachel's interest. Many of the islands were refuges for wild life and everywhere there were warnings to boat-owners to be careful not to collide with and damage the manatees, those mysterious sea-animals whom many believe to be the original mermaids.

The sun was setting when at last they motored down

the long stretch of Lake Worth on the last part of their journey. High-rise buildings, glittering with lights, made dark shapes against the crimson-flushed sky. They entered a marina, and soon after they had stepped ashore were whisked off in a limousine sent for them by Morton.

Rachel's first impression of the fabulous town was of the graceful shapes of tall palm trees lining the approach road. After a left turn along a main street they turned right to drive down a residential street until they reached the exclusive road beside the ocean, where wealthy people not only of the United States but also of other countries owned huge houses and the beach in front of them.

Screened from the road by high laurel hedges, Morton's oceanside house was as different from Chestnuts as the shrub is from the big deciduous fruit-bearing tree. Again, for that particular place it wasn't big.

'Only twelve rooms,' Ross replied with a grin in answer to Rachel's question as she stared in admiration at the stucco façade of the Spanish-styled house. 'Bedrooms, that is, and each one with its own bathroom.'

'You're joking,' she said as they entered the cool hallway with its black and white tiled floor. 'It must be like a hotel.'

'Don't ever let Morton hear you say that. It's his pride and joy, his status-symbol. Just being allowed to live on this particular street in this particular town means he is someone, not only in this country but in the international set. Here, every winter, his neighbours are not only the wealthy, they are out of the top drawer. Here he can rub elbows with European royalty and aristocracy as well as top-notch American New England families and the descendants of Southern aristocrats. It gives him a real kick.'

Rachel had made up her mind that she couldn't possibly like Morton, knowing that he derived pleasure from having made a lot of money and found entertainment in having aristocrats and celebrities as his neighbours. He was bound to be insufferably snobbish, she thought, and possibly vulgar as well.

Hearing from the housekeeper that Morton was waiting for them in the solarium, Ross led her through a long living-room furnished with heavy Spanish-style furniture, carved from oak and upholstered mostly in red and gold, into the room of glass where some of the blinds had been drawn earlier against the heat of the noon-day sun.

'Here we are, Morton, right on time,' Ross said cheerfully.

The man turned. Of medium height, he had silvered dark hair and bright blue eyes set in a lined sun-weathered face. He was dressed casually in well-cut trousers and a golfing shirt. In his right hand was a pair of secateurs with which he had been trimming one of the many tropical shrubs that flourished in the solarium. Carefully he put the secateurs down and held his hand out to Ross.

'Good to see you, boy,' he said in a husky voice, and gave Rachel a quick shy glance. 'I see you've brought a friend.'

'She's more than friend. Rachel and I got married end of last month in Riverpark.' There was a note of quiet triumph in Ross's voice.

'Well, well.' Morton' face creased into many lines as he put back his head and laughed outright. 'I should have guessed you wouldn't let any grass grow under your feet once you'd made up your mind to a course of action. Congratulations. You too, young lady.' Rachel's right hand was seized and shaken by two large hard hands. 'Rachel, eh? That's a fine old name.'

'Not only does she have a fine old name, she's from a fine old country,' said Ross, seeming intent on crowing about his conquest. 'Tell him where you were born, darling.'

'I'm from Edinburgh, Mr Fraser,' said Rachel, who couldn't help feeling a little self-conscious at all the fuss about her name and birthplace.

'Then you're doubly welcome,' said Morton, his face sobering, his eyes taking on a wistful expression. He glanced quickly at Ross. 'Am I allowed to kiss her before we get into the champagne?'

'Of course you are,' said Rachel quickly before Ross could say anything, all her prejudice suddenly pushed aside by a sudden rush of liking for this shy man and, leaning forwards she met his lips with her own.

The next few days passed in a blur as she came to terms with living in the luxury of that house where she had nothing to do but sleep and eat unless she was getting ready to go swimming, to play tennis or golf or to attend some social gathering at another even more luxurious house along the road.

The times she liked best, when she wasn't alone with Ross in their bedroom, were the moments they both spent with Morton either in the solarium or on *Trillium*, when they took the boat out through the narrow Palm Beach inlet to the ocean to spend an hour or two fishing with other yachts in the Gulf Stream.

But the curious dreamlike quality of living at the Laurels came to an abrupt end when Ross announced that he would have to leave her for a few days after all to fly back to New York to attend to some business for Morton.

Her first reaction was to cling, not to let him go without her, because she had a strange fear she might lose him, that he might never come back.

'Let me come with you,' she pleaded as she lay in his arms the night before he was due to leave.

'I would rather you didn't,' he murmured sleepily. 'It's only for three days and I'll be busy all that time. Better for you to stay here and help Morton greet his Christmas guests. The weather can be foul, wet and cold in New York at this time of the year.'

'I wouldn't mind as long as I was with you.'

'But you wouldn't see much of me. Please me and stay here, sweetheart,' he whispered, raising her face to his and raining light kisses over her cheeks. 'If I can I'll try to do what I have to do in two days instead of three and be back the day before Christmas Eve. And please believe I wish this hadn't happened right now, that it could have been avoided. But I guess we'll have to become accustomed to being apart, sometimes, much as I would like the honeymoon bit to go on for ever.'

After that she didn't press him because common sense dictated that he was right and they shouldn't expect the honeymoon to go on for ever. Also she had never wanted to be seen as or even to be the sort of woman who clings. He had accused her of being proud, so now she stiffened her backbone and brought out her pride. She could manage without him for three days, of course she could, and yet immediately after saying goodbye to him at the airport and seeing him walk away from her she felt depressed.

Morton did much to cheer her up that day, taking her with him to the élite country club to play golf, introducing her to some of the well known people who were there, and treating her to dinner.

'I'm not much for expressing my feelings,' he said as they lingered over coffee and liqueurs. 'I always hope a person will guess how I feel from the way I treat them. It's a mistake I've made too often in my life. I'm a little shy and not good with people on a personal level. Only on a business level. So I want to tell you, while Ross isn't around and I've got you to myself for a while and before my sister and my neice and two nephews arrive tomorrow, how glad I am that he met you and had the good sense to marry you before you had a chance to escape back to Scotland.'

'You're not shocked that we married in such a hurry, then?'

'Good God, no. I think you did the right thing. Wouldn't have done any good to hang around waiting just to please a few relatives. Also I've been afraid, you see, that Ross might never get married, that he might behave as I did when I was younger, and wouldn't marry because he had once been disappointed in love. And I didn't want that for Janet's son. I didn't want him to grow into a reclusive bachelor with only one thing to do in life, make money, as I was until I was able to find Janet again and marry her, too late for us to have children.'

'Was Ross disappointed in love at some time?' she asked, trying to sound offhand and casual while all the time her brain buzzed with conjecture.

'Well, now, he's never said as much to me. Very secretive about his private life, is Ross. Proud, too. Not liking much to admit to ever making a mistake or failing at anything he undertakes. He likes to win, always. But I've known that there was someone he wanted to marry and couldn't because of some impediment or other. Anyway, that's all in the past and he's married to you now and that's all that matters. Don't you agree?'

She agreed, and kept telling herself over and over again that her marriage to Ross was all that mattered, yet she could not help wondering about that disappointment in love he had suffered, especially when she recalled how withdrawn he had been the night she had told him she believed Carrie Duval had expected him to have been married to someone else. For the first time in her life she felt the stirrings of jealousy of the woman he had wanted to marry but hadn't.

Next day the serene quiet of the Laurels was invaded by Morton's surprisingly noisy sister Wendy Cox, her twin sons Gerry and Todd, and her daughter Meryl.

'Ross married to you?' Wendy shrieked when Morton introduced Rachel to her. 'Oh, my God.' Small and grey-haired and apparently a bundle of nervous energy, Wendy rounded on her daughter who was just behind her, a slim, slight woman of about thirty who was, for all her plainness and paleness, dressed very elegantly and in the height of the prevailing New York fashion. 'Well, what do you think of that, Mer? Seems you've missed the boat again.'

'I wish Rachel every happiness,' said Meryl, offering Rachel slim red-tipped fingers and showing small white teeth as she smiled.

'And so do I.' Wendy showed her teeth too in a wide, insincere smile at Rachel. 'Believe me, you're going to need all our best wishes, since you've been foolish enough to marry that cheating rogue and . . .' She broke off, as if realising she was being tactless, and swung to Morton, 'Well, which rooms have you put us in?'

'Marley will show you,' said Morton as his English-trained butler appeared quietly in the doorway. 'We'll see you all later at dinner, I guess.'

'Don't expect us for dinner, Uncle,' said one of the twins. Rachel couldn't be sure at that moment whether he was Gerry or Todd because although they weren't wearing similar clothes or colours they were identical in their looks. 'We've already got dinner dates.'

Wendy and the twins left the solarium as noisily as they had arrived to follow Marley to their rooms, but Meryl stayed behind, seating herself close to Morton.

'It's really good to see you again, Uncle. Thanks for inviting us. This Christmas would have been deadly at home, our first without Dad,' she said quietly.

'That's what I figured, Meryl,' said Morton with a sigh. 'My sister's husband passed away a few months ago after a long fight with heart problems,' he explained for Rachel's benefit. 'I guess Wendy is still cut up about it.' A slight smile softened his lips. 'You'll find her a bit noisy and outspoken, Rachel, but underneath it all she has a heart of gold and means well. Right, Meryl?'

'Right, Uncle,' said Meryl, and she looked across at Rachel. 'Did I detect a Scottish accent when you spoke just now?' she asked.

'You sure did,' said Morton, smiling and answering for Rachel. 'Why don't you two get better acquainted while I just go and have a word with Marley about the numbers for dinner tonight.'

'I didn't know Ross had been in Scotland recently,' said Meryl, her pale blue eyes taking in Rachel's appearance, noting the good fit of designer jeans and the elegant simplicity of a loose sleeveless silk top, the silky darkness of brown hair falling straight from a centre parting to the shoulders, the lightly tanned perfect oval of her face.

'We met at my aunt's home in Riverpark, New York,' replied Rachel. 'At my cousin Jenny's wedding.'

'When?'

'At the end of September.'

'So it was a rush job,' said Meryl with a lift of her marked-in eyebrows. 'I guessed as much.'

'I beg your pardon?'

'Yours and Ross's marriage. You didn't know one another long before taking the plunge.'

'I suppose we didn't,' said Rachel coolly, feeling resentment rising within her at Meryl's derisory tone.

'Mother is surprised, but I'm not,' said Meryl, getting to her feet and going over to look at the lawn at the back of the house that swept down to a thick area of tropical shrubs dividing the land from that of another house. 'Ross had to do something in a hurry to stop the tittle-tattle that was going on in Manhattan.' She turned to look at Rachel across the length of the room. 'I work in the city too. I'm a financial analyst and I write for a financial magazine. What do you do in the way of a career?'

'I'm an artist,' said Rachel.

'I guess you married him for his money, then?' said Meryl and gave a little trill of mocking laughter. 'So it happened after all. After spending years dodging gold-diggers, Ross was caught by a penniless artist.'

She advanced towards Rachel and looked down at her rather pityingly. 'I suppose he bribed you to marry him.'

Rachel rose then to her full height and knew a certain malicious triumph in towering over the provocative Meryl.

'No, he didn't. And I didn't marry him for his money. I married him because I love him,' she said.

'Oh, my,' said Meryl tauntingly. 'Listen to the romantic. And I suppose you believe he married you because he loves you. Then why isn't he here with you? Why is he back in New York?'

'He had to go to attend to some business for Morton,' Rachel retorted.

'You really fell for that old trick?' jeered Meryl. 'My God, I didn't think it was possible for a woman to be so naïve these days. I bet you wanted to go with him and he persuaded you to stay down here.'

Rachel had no answer for that. She could only frown and bite her lip, remembering how persuasive Ross had been the night before he had gone away.

'I bet too he hasn't told you about Inci,' said Meryl, smiling slyly.

'Inci?'

'The name is Turkish. Female. She's very beautiful and an accomplished musician who is just beginning to make her way as a concert pianist. Ross has known her for years. He wanted to marry her but she turned him down. Imagine any woman having the guts to turn down the heir to Morton Fraser's millions. Ross was really cut up about it. A real blow to his ego, it was. But he still sees her when he can. I wouldn't be surprised if he's seeing her right at this moment, telling her about his marriage to you, explaining why he had to do it, to create a smokescreen so no one will suspect her of still seeing him whenever she visits New York. He probably had it all planned in that cold, calculating way he has of doing things. All he had to do was find someone like you, who didn't know him too well and was ignorant of his affair with her, and manipulate you into marrying him.' Meryl's lips smiled but her eyes didn't. 'You wouldn't be the first to fall for the charm he can turn on and off at will, you know.'

Rachel resisted the temptation to turn on her heel and leave the room. Her pride up in arms, she even managed to smile.

'Does that mean you have been a victim of that charm? Have you been in love with him, too, and did you hope to marry him for his money?' she jeered, and had the satisfaction of seeing her barb go home as Meryl's eyes flickered. 'Well, I'm not surprised. Ross is something rather special. But you're wrong in supposing he's meeting another woman at this moment. He is, in fact, flying back right now and should be walking into the house within the next hour. You see, he phoned me just before you arrived to say he'd managed to do what he had to do more quickly than he had anticipated. And if you don't believe me, I suggest you ask your uncle. That's why he wanted to talk to Marley. He wanted to tell him that Ross would be here in time for dinner.' Rachel forced another smile. 'But I do appreciate your effort to try and put me in the picture regarding Inci. I'm sure you meant it kindly, and I hope you enjoy your stay over Christmas.'

It was Meryl's turn to have no ready answer. Her pale eyes glittering, her thin lips pinched together, she swung on her heel and marched from the room.

Much to Rachel's relief, Wendy and Meryl were

not the only guests for dinner at the Laurels that night. Morton had invited several neighbours mostly to meet her, so she was able to avoid any direct contact with his sister and niece. Ross arrived just as they were all about to sit down at the long table in the dining-room. She was so glad to see him that her emotions threatened to boil up and overflow and, as he took her in his arms and kissed her hard, ignoring the interested onlookers, she sensed that he too was having difficulty in controlling his passion.

'As soon as we can, without giving offence to Morton we'll leave this lot and go upstairs,' he whispered in her ear. 'I can hardly wait to be alone with you.'

'It's the same with me,' she replied, all the doubts and suspicions Meryl had managed to rouse in her wilting for the moment under the hot blaze of his desire for her, and they parted reluctantly to sit opposite each other on either side of Morton, who was of course at the head of the table.

'Well, Ross, you certainly get around,' remarked the guest who was sitting beside Rachel, a rather fat man who had a very loud voice that could be heard by everyone. The other guests stopped chattering to glance at him attentively. 'Saw you in town only yesterday,' he added.

Rachel had soon discovered that the only town that mattered to most of Morton's friends and associates was the city of New York.

'I didn't see you, Harry,' said Ross easily.

'No, you were too busy chatting up your dinner guest. Wasn't that Ihsan Kapadia's daughter with you? What's her name? Inci? The concert pianist?'

All the joy she had been feeling seeped out of Rachel. Not looking at anyone she waited to hear, as everyone else was waiting, Ross's answer. He didn't hesitate, nor did he look disturbed.

'As always, you're right. Harry. What great eyesight you must have. Why didn't you come over and say hello,' he said drily. 'If you had I'd have introduced you to Inci and her brother. He's with the Turkish consulate in New York. An interesting guy. He speaks six languages. Made me feel really uneducated, since I can speak only one.'

The moment passed. Everyone started talking again. But for Rachel the damage had been done, and for the rest of the meal she avoided looking at or speaking to Ross.

As it turned out, they weren't able to escape to their room as he had suggested until most of the guests had left. As soon as the door of the bedroom closed he took her in his arms and began to kiss her but she didn't respond. She couldn't until everything was out in the open, until she knew more about Inci.

'What's wrong?' he demanded, refusing to let her go when she would have escaped from his arms. 'What's happened while I've been away?'

'Nothing very much until today when your aunt and cousins arrived,' she said coolly.

'If you mean Meryl, Wendy and the twins, they are not blood relatives of mine, only of Morton's,' he replied tautly, his face set in hard lines. 'I know they've hated me ever since Morton adopted me as his son. They always hoped to inherit all his money, you see, and believe me to be his sole heir. I don't really care for any of them, either, and I'm sorry Morton invited them, but I guess he felt he had to since Wendy has just lost her husband. If you don't like them we don't have to stay on. We could leave, take a trip over to Nassau for a few days.'

'And disappoint Morton?' she said. 'You must know how pleased he is to have us both here. No, we'll have to stay at least until Christmas is over.'

'Then tell me what's upset you,' he persisted. 'I bet that creep Meryl has been telling tales out of school about me. What has she said to you about me?' He gave her a little shake and then pulled her closer to him as if he knew he could melt her resistance with his physical warmth.

Her face hidden in his shoulder Rachel felt his fingers in her hair and found the courage to speak outright.

'She said she supposed I'd married you for your money.'

Hands sliding to her shoulders, he pushed her gently away from him so that he could see her face. His face looked grim and his eyes were a very clear penetrating grey. He was looking at her as if he suspected her of hiding something from him.

'And didn't you?' he said softly.

'No.' Her denial rang out angrily. 'Oh, surely you know I wouldn't do anything like that.'

'I kind of hoped you wouldn't, but I could have been wrong in my hope, knowing what your brother is like,' he said with a wry curl of his lips.

Twisting free of his hold she turned away from him and went round to the other side of the bed. Facing him, her head high, her chin tilted, she said,

'Just what do you mean by that?'

'Giles wasn't above borrowing money from me when he was in New York. Didn't he tell you?'

'Yes. But he said it was all straight between you and him, taken care of, he said,' she said shakily. 'But . . . if you thought I might be like him over money, why did you ask me to marry you?'

'I wanted to be married too much to care about any ulterior motive you might have had in wanting to marry me,' he replied. For a moment he stared intently at her, then, with a shrug, began to loosen his tie.

'Then perhaps the rest of what Meryl said is true,' she said in a low, shaking voice. 'And you have married me to create a smokescreen.'

He tossed his tie down on the dresser and looked at her reflection in its mirror.

'Meryl said that?' he said, his eyebrows slanting satirically. 'My God, what a wonderful imagination that woman has. She should go in for writing mystery stories. Her talent is absolutely wasted as a financial journalist. May I ask why I would want to create a smokescreen?' He laughed suddenly, and her heart leapt at the sound. 'Makes me sound like a navy frigate or destroyer, belching out smoke to cover the activities of a battleship.'

His suit jacket off, his shirt unbuttoned to the waist, he came towards her, laughter flickering across his face and in his eyes.

'Can you see any smoke coming out of my head, sweetheart?' he whispered bending towards her.

'It isn't a joke,' she muttered, her glance going to the opening of his shirt. Its whiteness contrasted with the golden tan of his skin. Her fingers itched to slide within the opening and to caress his chest.

'It is to me, and I'd like to share it with you, just as I want to share everything with you, so tell me why I would need a smokescreen.'

His mockery of Meryl made Rachel see that perhaps the woman had been melodramatic, and she hesitated now about bringing up the matter of Inci. But if she didn't it would always be there at the back of her mind, poisoning her relationship with him, so without meeting his eyes, now aflame with passion, as he reached out to caress her cheek with gentle fingertips, she went on, 'She said you'd got married to create a smokescreen so that you could go on meeting someone called Inci, with whom you've been having an affair for years.'

The fingers stroking her cheek were suddenly still.

'The bitch,' he said, his voice hissing savagely. 'Do you believe her?'

'I don't know what to believe,' she cried, raising her head to look at him earnestly. 'I didn't want to believe her but then that man, Harry, who was sitting next to me at dinner, said he had seen you dining with Inci last night and so I couldn't help wondering if what Meryl said was true and that you went to New York, not for business purposes but to meet Inci.'

His hands fell away from her face and he paced away from her, hands in his trouser pockets. Feeling suddenly weak from stress, she sank down on the edge of the bed. He came back to her, went down on his knees suddenly so that his face was on a level with hers. His hands slid along the silky stuff of her dress where it was taut over her thighs, an intimate and possessive action that caused desire to throb suddenly within her.

'Look at me, Rachel,' he murmured. She raised her head and looked into his eyes. 'And then tell me, if you can, that I'm lying to you. I didn't go to New York to meet Inci. I met her quite by accident. She was in New York to give a concert. My affair with her is over. It came to an end when she told me she couldn't marry me. She and I won't be meeting behind any smokescreen.' He paused, frowning, and when he continued his voice was harsh with bitterness. 'I guessed it wasn't going to be easy once the honeymoon was over and we had to mingle with other people like Meryl and Wendy, who don't like me and who would do anything to undermine my relationship with Morton or anyone else. Unluckily we've come up against the first stumbling-block while our marriage is still very vulnerable, while we're still learning about each other. All I can do is say that I won't be planning any meetings with Inci in the future, although there is always the possibility of running into her when she's in New York.' He leaned forward, rested his brow against hers. His lips only an inch away from hers he said, 'Believe me?' and it was hard for her to tell whether it was a plea or a question.

'But you did love her, didn't you?' she whispered.

'Yes, I did. But now you're my lover, my mistress and my wife, so why would I want to meet any other woman behind a smokescreen, or anything else?' His sense of humour got the better of him again and laughter shook through his voice. 'Forget what Meryl said, and don't let it come between us now. I've been looking forward to this night ever since I left you on Monday morning.'

'Oh, and so have I,' said Rachel with all her heart, and, giving into the desire that was suddenly surging up in her, she flung her arms around him and they fell across the bed together.

Their brief separation, plus the recent confrontation about his motive for marrying her, added a certain spice to their lovemaking that night. As if determined to obliterate from her mind the damage done by Meryl, Ross used every loving technique he knew to arouse her, taking time over each caress, seeking and finding what gave her most pleasure, his lips burning against her skin as they moved from her hips down her throat to her breasts and even lower, until, her senses aflame, she pulled him down on top of her and into her and soared with him to a height of ecstasy she had never known before.

Yet, later, when she was curled up against him, listening to his even breathing as he slept, although Meryl's insinuations about him were forgotten for the time being, the woman Inci wasn't. She lingered, a vague ghost between them, the lover he had lost, and over whose loss he had been deeply disappointed.

CHAPTER FOUR

PROTECTED by Ross's attentive behaviour from any more attacks on their marriage by Meryl, Rachel was able to enjoy the next few days in Palm Beach. The weather was perfect blue skies, warm sunshine and a placid blue ocean, so that it came as something of a surprise to her on Christmas morning to receive and give presents around a decorated Christmas Tree, imported from Canada, and to attend a service with Morton, at the Episcopal church where all the usual carols were sung. She and Ross spent the afternoon swimming and sunbathing, and after a traditional dinner of roast turkey and plum pudding they escaped from the others to walk on the beach beside the whispering surf under the stars.

Yet, in spite of Morton's hospitality and the warm weather, she was glad to leave the luxury of the Laurels and the hostility that seemed to emanate from Meryl and Wendy all the time, and to fly back to New York with Ross. His apartment, as she had expected, was furnished in the latest contemporary style and had every modern convenience.

For the first few weeks of the new year she was quite content, spending her days visiting art museums and galleries and her evenings, nights and weekends walking, talking and planning for their future with Ross. One day they would find a place in the country, he promised, somewhere with fields to be farmed; a place with barns and horses, where they could bring up their children together. Meanwhile

they would live right in the city near to where he had
to work.

And where he could continue to meet Inci.

In spite of Rachel's efforts to root it out of her
mind, the ugly seed of suspicion sown there by Meryl
would keep sprouting up, and she would wonder
whether he had been sincere when he had said he
wouldn't be planning to meet Inci secretly although it
was possible he might run into her. Then he would do
something for her, bring flowers home for her or take
her out to see a new play that had opened on
Broadway or to some other form of interesting
entertainment, and she would forget Inci and try to
convince herself that although he had never said so,
he must love her at least as much as he had loved the
other woman, if not more.

Big, noisy and dirty as New York was, it possessed
a vitality that was infectious. Ross seemed
determined to help her become established in her
chosen career as an artist, and he introduced her to
people he knew who belonged to the artistic
community of the city, encouraging her to look for a
studio for herself where she would be able to paint
and also to practise the art of silk-screen printing in
which she had specialised at college. Sometimes she
went up on the train to Riverpark to visit Moira and
Jenny, who was expecting her first baby, and
sometimes they came to town for a shopping-spree in
which she joined. Always there were friends of Ross's
to entertain. It seemed there was never a moment to
spare for introspection or reflection and rarely time
for doubts or suspicions about Ross's motive in
rushing her into marriage with him.

March was in, and the shoots of spring flowers
were beginning to show in Central Park where she

loved to jog in the mornings with Ross and other fitness-conscious people, when Rachel received a surprising phone call from her mother, who was in Edinburgh on a visit from Australia.

'Granny Dow is very ill and in hospital,' said Dorothy. 'She isn't expected to live much longer but she wants to see you very much. Can you come?'

'Of course I can. As soon as I can get a seat on a plane,' Rachel answered without hesitation.

'I'll have to go to see her,' she told Ross later that day.

'I guess you will,' he said, 'I'd come with you, only right now I'm really busy doing Morton's work as well as my own.'

'Couldn't you take some time off and join me over there? Surely the investment company can get along without you for a while.'

'I'm sure it could,' he agreed equably, 'but it seems that Morton can't.' Seeing her make a face, he stepped over to her and put his arms around her. 'Would you like to fly over on Concorde?'

'Could I?' The suggestion distracted her for a few moments.

'Of course. Nothing but the best and the fastest is good enough for my woman,' he teased her. 'Tomorrow suit you?'

'Only if it suits you.'

'I guess I'll survive, as long as we're not apart too long,' he murmured, and stifled all her misgivings as usual with kisses.

Early next morning she was giving her appearance a few last touches before she left the flat with Ross to drive to Kennedy airport, when the telephone rang. Since Ross was still in the bathroom she answered it.

'Hello,' said a soft female voice with a slight

foreign accent. 'Is this the residence of Ross Fraser?'

'Yes. He isn't available right now. May I take a message?' said Rachel, searching for and finding a pen and pad.

'You are?' the voice queried.

'His wife, Rachel Fraser.'

'Then I don't think it would be suitable for me to leave a message with you,' said the woman with a laugh. 'I guess I'll catch him later.'

She hung up before Rachel could say anything else and, puzzled by the mocking lilt in the soft seductive voice when the woman had said she didn't think it suitable for her to leave a message with Ross's wife, Rachel returned the receiver to its rest.

'For me?' asked Ross from the living-room doorway where he stood fastening the double-breasted jacket of his grey suit. As always when dressed for the city with his hair well brushed he looked very handsome and businesslike yet somehow coolly remote from her. She always preferred him in more casual clothes with his hair windblown.

'Yes. Most odd. I asked her to leave a message and she said it wouldn't be suitable for her to leave it with me. She'll catch you later, she said.'

'Really.' He was amused. 'She'll find it impossible. I've already been hooked by the most beautiful woman in the world.' Hands at her waist he twisted her round to face him. 'I wish you didn't have to go away.'

'I wish I didn't have to leave you,' she murmured, arms around his neck. 'But I have to; you do understand, don't you? Granny has always been so good to me. You'd go if it were Morton who was ill and wanting to see you.'

'I understand. Or at least I keep telling myself to

be understanding, even while all of me is rebelling against you going away without me,' he said seriously.

'You sometimes go away without me,' she pointed out.

'I know. But not far. Only to Washington or Chicago and I come back fast.'

'Please fly over to join me there.' She tried again to force him into making a commitment. 'It's time you met my mother.'

'I suppose it is.' His glance lingered on her lips.

'And you'd meet Giles again.'

'I guess so,' he said indifferently, and kissed her so long and hard that she was breathless when he had finished. 'That's so you won't forget me when you're back on your native heath and this place and all that has happened here seems just like a dream to you.'

'I won't forget you,' she said urgently, suddenly anxious about leaving him, the image of Inci rising unbidden in her mind. 'And please don't ever think it's been a dream. I do exist. Hold me tight, feel me. Am I as insubstantial as a dream?'

'I guess you're not,' he said with a laugh, squeezing her. Then, with a quick change of mood, he let go of her suddenly and turned away to pick up her cases. 'Come on,' he added roughly, 'let's get parting from each other over before I lose my cool and behave like a caveman and carry you off to the wilderness where no one can come between us.'

On the swift flight across the Atlantic she found herself thinking of his last remark about someone coming between them, and entangled with the thoughts was a woman's soft voice asking for him and saying it was unsuitable to leave a message for him with his wife. A voice with just the slightest trace

of an accent. Who? Inci? Jealous suspicion
mushroomed in her mind again and this time
wouldn't be banished. She wanted more than
anything to turn right round and go back to New
York to find out for sure if it had been Inci who had
rung him that morning, thinking possibly that his
wife had left for Scotland already, calling him to make
a date to meet him somewhere.

She was so worried that she rang him at the flat in
New York as soon as she had checked in at the hotel
near Heathrow, where a room had been booked for
her for the night so that she would be near the airport
to catch a flight next morning to Turnberry, not far
from Edinburgh. Only when there was no answer did
she remember it would still be mid-afternoon in New
York, so she dialled the number of his office. Hearing
his secretary on the line quite clearly she made herself
known.

'This is Rachel Fraser, Sheila. I'm calling long-
distance from London, England. Is Ross there?'

'Sorry, Mrs Fraser. He went out to lunch with a
client and hasn't come back yet. Is there anything I
can do?'

'No, not really.' Was he having lunch with Inci,
Rachel wondered jealously? 'Just tell him I arrived
safely at Heathrow and I'm in the hotel now. Please
give him the phone number here and ask him to call
me later,' she said, feeling disappointment flood
through her. When the secretary agreed, she gave her
the hotel's number, her room number and then rang
off.

Ross hadn't called her at the hotel before she at last
gave in to fatigue and went to bed. Although the
small room was cold and the bed felt damp, she slept
as soon as she lay down. But her sleep wasn't restful

because she dreamed nearly all the time, knowing she was dreaming and yet unable to wake up enough to shake off the dream. It seemed to her she was walking along a pathway. On either side there were high hedges. She was going to meet Ross, but as she walked the hedges seemed to crowd in on her so that the path grew narrower and narrower until she was fighting her way through a thicket of briar roses and hawthorns, the sharp thorns snagging her clothing and scratching her hands and face. Yet the more she tried to break through the thicket to reach Ross the further away he went.

Troubled by the dream, she decided to leave calling him again until she was in Edinburgh. The flight north didn't take long and she felt excited anticipation rising in her at the thought of being back in her native city as she looked out at the neat fields of the Midlands and then at the golden brown moors of Yorkshire and Northumbria sliding by beneath the wing of the plane.

As she waited for her luggage at the small airport, hearing familiar accents all around her, she felt as if she had never been away and had lived for the last six months in the States. Ross had been right. Her marriage to him, their honeymoon, Christmas in Palm Beach, the two months in Manhattan were all becoming rather dreamlike.

But she mustn't let that happen, she admonished herself, yanking one suitcase off the conveyor belt. She must always be reminding herself Ross really existed and was her husband. She fingered the rings he had given her. At least she had them, the tokens of his love and respect for her, to remind her that all they had done together hadn't been a dream.

Giles, seeming somehow a little taller and more self-confident, was at the airport to meet her, and soon they were in a taxi being whisked into the city and along familiar streets, under the towering slab of grey rock on which the castle sat, and out to the suburb where he said their mother was staying in a house lent to her by a friend who was out of town for a while.

'You look wonderful,' Giles said with a surprising lack of reticence. He hadn't been given, as a rule, to paying her compliments. 'Looks like being married to a millionaire is going down well with you. Must be nice to have money to spend and plenty of free time to spend it. Just wait until Mum sees you. I think she'll agree with me, at last, that you did the right thing in marrying Ross Fraser. Pity he couldn't have come with you.'

'He's going to try and come,' said Rachel. 'Has Mother said something to you about my marriage to him? About it not being the right thing for me to do?'

'No. But I think she's a bit worried about you. You know how mothers are about their daughters.'

'Not having a daughter yet, how can I possibly know?' retorted Rachel. 'You're not looking so bad yourself. How's your term been so far? Are you going to pass all your exams?'

'So far it's been fine. No problems. Having a bit of extra cash . . .' Giles broke off suddenly as the taxi lurched to a stop, throwing him off balance. 'Ooops! Sorry about that. Here we are. I hope you changed some dollars for pounds and can pay the fare.'

The house was typical of the neighbourhood, in a terrace of identical houses all joined together, and it had bay windows draped with lace curtains. The front door opened before they reached it and Dorothy, tall and slim, her still dark hair smoothly coiled about her shapely head, appeared. Feeling her

mother's arms around her, smelling the familiar
scents of her, Rachel swallowed back tears. It
wouldn't do to show too much sentiment in front of
her proud and extremely reserved only surviving
parent.

'I hope you had a good flight, Rachel. When did
you leave New York?' asked Dorothy, leading the
way along a narrow hall to a big living-room-cum-
dining-room at the back of the house.

'Yesterday morning, and I arrived at Heathrow
yesterday evening,' Rachel said, taking off her rakish
broad-brimmed black hat and shaking her shoulder-
length hair free. 'It was exciting to travel so fast. I
came on Concorde.'

'But that was very extravagant of you,' exclaimed
Dorothy. 'The one-way fare is more than most people
can afford to fly here and back again.'

'Not to worry, Mother. Rach wasn't paying. Her
millionaire stockbroker husband paid. One thing
about Ross that I learned when I was with him. He
isn't mean like some people I could mention.'
Catching Rachel's attention, Giles, his eyes glinting
with malice, jerked his head in the direction of the
man who was just getting up from an armchair by the
fire. He was Alec Burgess, Dorothy's second husband.

'Hello, there, Rachel. Nice to see you again,' Alec
said, his brown moustache twitching as he smiled at
her. A big man dressed in tweeds, he had a rather
high-pitched voice and spoke with an Australian
twang that sounded very strange to her after living for
months with Ross and hearing his pleasantly modulated voice speaking English without any noticeable
accent.

'How are you?' she said. She had never been sure
how to address Alec. She couldn't possibly call him

Dad or Father, because she had too many fond memories of her own father to do that. Nor could she bring herself to call him Alec.

'Can't grumble,' he said. 'Although I wish the weather was a bit warmer. Too bad we had to leave Brisbane before summer there was over. Not much difference in the temperature between here and New York, I suppose.'

'No, not much difference.'

'I'll take you up to the room you'll be sleeping in while you're staying here,' Dorothy interposed. 'Giles has taken your cases up.' Her dark glance went over Rachel's elegant black suede, fur-trimmed coat. 'I don't think I've ever seen you look so nice, Rachel. Is that real suede?'

'Yes, it is. But tell me, how is Gran?' Rachel asked as she followed her mother up a narrow flight of stairs to the next floor.

'I believe she's only waiting to see you before she goes,' Dorothy murmured sadly, opening the door into a small narrow room with a single bed. 'It was kind of your husband to let you come,' she added, sitting down in the only chair in the room.

'Ross is kind and very generous,' replied Rachel spontaneously, sitting on the edge of the bed. 'I'm hoping he'll be able to come over and you'll meet him.'

'I'd like to meet him. I'd have come to see you married but you were in such a hurry. It upset me very much that I couldn't be present at my only daughter's wedding.'

'I'm sorry you couldn't be there too. Aunt Moira wanted us to wait until Christmas and have all the family present but neither Ross nor I wanted a fussy wedding. I thought you'd approve of the way we did it.

After all it was the way you and Dad got married. And you and Alec.'

'But I'd known both Hugh and Alec for quite a while before I could make up my mind whether I wanted to marry either of them,' Dorothy pointed out. 'There was nothing hasty about either of my marriages. I didn't rush into wedlock as you seem to have done. I'm quite surprised at you. I thought you'd be more deliberate about marriage, somehow. I hope you didn't marry him for his money.'

'Oh, why do people always think that I might have done that?' Rachel complained. 'Do I look and behave like one of those women who marry a man only for his money?'

'No, you don't. And I would hope you, being my daughter, would never do anything like that. But you have to admit you and he married in haste. Perhaps there was some other reason he had for rushing you,' said Dorothy with an inquisitive glance, and immediately Rachel thought again of Meryl implying that Ross had married her to create a smokescreen behind which he could hide his continuing affair with Inci. The thought kept her silent.

'Oh, well,' Dorothy went on, rising to her feet. 'I suppose you think it's none of my business, but I wouldn't like you to have made a mistake. So many young people seem to marry without thinking seriously about it beforehand these days. And then, before you can turn around, they're getting a divorce because they have discovered that their life-styles and their opinions on important decisions such as whether or not they want to have a family are incompatible.'

'Is there a phone in this house?' said Rachel, quickly, uneasily aware that her mother was still fishing for more information about her sudden decision to get married. 'I must phone Ross later, let him know I've got here all right.'

'There is a phone but a transatlantic call must cost the earth.'

'Don't worry about it, Mother. I'll pay for it. I'll phone him when we come back from the hospital. He should be back at the flat by then.' Then, seeing the worried frown creasing Dorothy's high, white forehead, she said earnestly, 'I do hope you won't hold it against me or Ross because we rushed into marriage. So far we've been very happy together.'

'Well, I'm relieved to hear it,' replied Dorothy. 'Yet it's strange to think of you, of all people, living in such a busy commercial city like New York.'

'I know. And I'm a little surprised myself, because I like living there. Of course, it wouldn't be the same if we were . . .' She had been going to say 'if we were poor' but that would have been another reference to Ross's wealth, so she broke off and, leaning forwards, she touched one of Dorothy's long hands which was resting on the other one. 'And I hope you're happy, too, Mum. You look tired, and a bit anxious about something.'

Dorothy's brown eyes were hidden swiftly by their lids and her lips tightened.

'I'm as happy as it's possible for a woman of my age to be, given the circumstances,' she said evasively. 'but I have to admit that since Alec and I came to Edinburgh last week I've been worried about Giles.'

'Oh, dear, what has he done now?' Rachel felt a familiar sinking feeling at the pit of her stomach which always happened when Giles got into a scrape

'I'm not sure. But it seems to me he has more money in his pockets than he usually has. I thought

Harlequin's

Best Ever "Get Acquainted" Offer

Look what we'd give to hear from you

GET ALL YOU ARE ENTITLED TO—AFFIX STICKER TO RETURN CARD—MAIL TODAY

Look what we've got for you:

Get 4 FREE full-length Harlequin Presents® novels.

Plus
this lovely lucite clock/calendar

Plus
a surprise free gift

▼ PLUS LOTS MORE! MAIL THIS CARD TODAY ▼

Harlequin's Best-Ever "Get Acquainted" Offer

Yes, I'll try the Harlequin Reader Service® under the terms outlined on the opposite page. Send me 4 free Harlequin Presents® novels, a free digital clock/calendar and a free mystery gift.

108 CIH CAN2

PLACE STICKER FOR 6 FREE GIFTS HERE

NAME _____

ADDRESS _____ APT. _____

CITY _____

STATE _____ ZIP CODE _____

PRINTED IN U.S.A.

Don't forget...

. . . Return this card today and receive 4 free books, free digital clock/calendar and free mystery gift.

. . . You will receive books before they're available in stores and at a discount off the cover prices.

. . . No obligation to buy. You can cancel at any time by writing "cancel" on your statement or returning a shipment to us at our cost.

If offer card is missing, write to: Harlequin Reader Service,
901 Fuhrmann Blvd., P.O. Box 1867, Buffalo, N.Y. 14269-1867

BUSINESS REPLY CARD

First Class   Permit No. 717   Buffalo, NY

Postage will be paid by addressee

Harlequin Reader Service®

901 Fuhrmann Blvd.
P.O. Box 1867
Buffalo, NY 14240-9952

No Postage
Necessary
If Mailed
In The
United States

perhaps he had earned it doing some job or other, but whenever I've tried to question him about it, he's either evaded the matter or made some joke about it. Rachel, I wish you could find out where he's getting the extra money from.'

'I'll do my best. I think he might have been going to tell me something in the taxi. He started to say that having extra cash had made a difference to him this year but the taxi stopped before he could explain. I suppose you think he's been gambling.'

'No. I don't. If he was gambling he'd be losing more than he'd be winning,' Dorothy said drily. 'It's as if he gets paid regularly by someone. You see when we came I asked him if he had enough to get him through the rest of the university terms and he said I was never to worry about that any more. I do hope he hasn't got involved in something criminal, that's all. People seem to do such terrible things to make money, like selling illegal drugs . . .'

'I'm sure Giles would never do anything like that, Mother.' Rachel was shocked that Dorothy would even think her own son might do such a thing.

'I hope you're right.' Dorothy looked up and smiled, her handsome long-jawed face with its high cheekbones lighting up and gaining a sudden beauty. 'But you'll be wanting to unpack your clothes and to hang them up. I'll call you when lunch is ready and then afterwards we can go and visit Gran. We're not far from the hospital here. So kind of Jessie Mackay to lend us this house. You remember Jessie? She and I went to school together. She's retired now and is away at the moment on a cruise.'

The visit to the hospital was a sad and trying experience. In the big white bed Ethel Dow looked tiny and shrunken, yet she attempted a smile when she saw

Rachel and reached out her two withered hands to her.

'So glad you've come, darling,' she whispered. 'You look lovely.' Her eyes, once a deep warm brown but faded now, looked past Rachel. 'Where's your husband, dear? He's a Fraser, Dot tells me, and born here in Edinburgh.'

'That's right, Gran. His mother was Scottish and she married a Canadian soldier, went out to Nova Scotia after the war. I'm sorry Ross couldn't come with me,' Rachel said, feeling tears start in her eyes and thinking how much more emotional she seemed to have become since she had been married. 'But he will come. Just you hang in there and you'll meet him.'

'Hang in there, eh.' A little laugh that changed quickly to a cough shook Ethel. 'You've become quite American since you've been away. Now listen, child.' Ethel's face grew serious and her thin fingers tightened a little on Rachel's. 'The cottage on Mull is yours and there's a little annuity to go with it. I fixed it all up with the lawyer years ago. I could have left it to Giles, but I remembered how you always said you'd like to live on the island some day, and not have to work for anyone else. It'll give you something to fall back on in time of need, just in case your husband ever lets you down. Men often have a way of doing that. Don't forget, now. It's all yours. I'm so glad you came, darling. I can rest in peace now.'

Ethel closed her eyes and her hand slipped away, and although Dorothy and Rachel sat by the bed for another half-hour, the old lady didn't open her eyes again while they were there.

As soon as Rachel returned to the house where they were staying she rang Ross. She let the telephone in the flat ring a long time before hanging up and then checked the time. He should be home by now. Living and working in downtown area, he didn't get held up in rush-hour traffic. Twice more she tried to reach him before she went to bed and even got up to creep down the stairs at three o'clock, hoping to get him when he went to bed, but there was no answer.

She didn't try again because she fell asleep at last and didn't waken until late morning, when Dorothy came in to the bedroom with a cup of tea to tell her that Ethel had died peacefully in her sleep soon after they had left the hospital.

Helping her mother arrange the funeral, visiting Ethel's lawyer and hearing the reading of her will, took up most of the rest of the day and she wasn't able to ring Ross until just before she went to bed. He answered after the second ring.

'Oh, I'm so glad you're home,' she said. 'I tried all yesterday evening but there was no answer.' He didn't say anything so she rushed on. 'Did Sheila give you my message?'

'Yes. I'd have phoned you but had no other number to call. Give me one where I can get in touch with you,' he replied, briskly businesslike.

'Ready?'

'Shoot.'

She gave him the number then said sadly, 'Gran died last night.'

'I'm sorry.' How far away and remote he sounded.

'She said she was sorry not to have met you.' Again he didn't comment so she added, 'The funeral is the day after tomorrow. Please, Ross, will you fly over for it?'

'I can't. Too tied up. But you'll be coming back right after, won't you?'

'Not immediately. I have to go to Mull.'

'Why?'

'Gran's left me her cottage.'

'How long will you be there?'

'Only a few days.'

'And when will you fly back to New York?'

'I'll stay here until Mother and Alec leave in two weeks' time. Mother would like to meet you.'

'Then she'll have to come this way with you when you come back, bring her husband, visit Moira and Jack, see the sights.'

It sounded all so easy when he suggested it, the right thing to do.

'They can't afford it.'

'I'll pay. You make the bookings for them over there and charge it all on your American Express card.'

'She wouldn't let me.'

'So that's where you get that pride from,' he taunted. 'I noticed Giles doesn't suffer from it,' he added drily.

'It would be much simpler if you flew over and joined me here.'

'I can't. Not right now. I'm up to my ears.'

She suddenly got the impression that he wasn't alone in the flat, something to do with the terse way in which he was speaking.

'Ross. Is someone with you?'

'Yes.'

'Anyone I know?'

'No. Just someone who has dropped in for some advice.'

'Rachel.' Dorothy spoke sharply behind her. 'You've been on that phone long enough. You must be spending a fortune.'

'I guess you're not alone either,' Ross laughed in her ear. 'Is that your Mum? Put her on to say hello.'

Rachel turned and held out the receiver to her mother.

'It's Ross. He wants to speak to you.'

Dorothy stared at the receiver as if it was some wicked invention.

'Whatever shall I say to him?' she whispered in near panic at the thought of speaking to a stranger on the phone.

'Just say hello, how are you and ask him to come over to meet you and Alec.'

Slowly Dorothy took hold of the instrument and put it to her ear.

'Hello, Mr Fraser,' she said primly. 'Dorothy Burgess here. How are you?'

Rachel couldn't hear what Ross was saying so she watched her mother's face instead. At first Dorothy frowned then, slowly and unbelievably her face softened and she nodded her head as if agreeing with something he was saying. Then quickly but pleasantly she cut in.

'Oh no, we couldn't possibly let you do that, Mr . . . er . . . I mean Ross. It's very kind of you but we couldn't accept your offer. My husband has to return to work. He can't spare any more time off. Couldn't you possibly fly over before we go back to Australia? No? Of course. I quite understand. You're in the same position as Alec, and work must come first. Well, it's been nice talking to you. Perhaps you'll bring Rachel to visit us in Australia, will you? Next winter? Oh, good. I'll look forward to that. Goodbye.'

Still smiling, her fine skin just a little flushed as if she had received an unexpected compliment, Dorothy handed the receiver to Rachel and went back into the living-room.

'Ross?' Rachel said quickly.

'She doesn't sound like a dragon at all,' he mocked. 'We're committed to a holiday in Australia. OK? I've always wanted to go there.'

'I still wish you'd try to come here.'

'Sorry. Talk to you again soon, sweetheart. Must go now.'

He hung up, and the click cutting her off from him made her feel momentarily desolate because he was so far away. She hung up too and went into the living-room.

'What did he say to you, Mother?'

'He thanked me for having such a lovely daughter and offered to pay Alec's and my fare to New York if we returned with you. He's wanting you to go back this week.'

'I know. But how can I when I have to go and see Gran's cottage? Oh, I do wish he'd come here and go to Mull with me.'

Ross called her the evening after Ethel's funeral and once again she asked him to fly over to join her on the trip to Mull.

'I want you to see the place and advise me what to do about it,' she pleaded.

'I'd like to be with you, but I can't come right now. I have to go out of town.'

'Where? Where are you going?'

'San Francisco. I leave in the morning.'

If he had said he had been going to the moon she couldn't have felt more deserted. In San Francisco he would be thousands of miles further away from her than he was now, on the shore of a different ocean.

'Where will you be staying? Please give me a phone number,' she asked urgently.

'I can't yet. I'll call you when I get there.'

'But I might not be here. I . . . I'm going north with Mum and Alec tomorrow.'

'Then call me at the apartment when you get back,' he said briskly. 'Gotta go now. Night, sweetheart.'

He rang off and she hung up. He sounded impatient and now she felt as if he had cut her off because he couldn't be bothered to discuss the possibility of him flying over to join her any more. He didn't want to come to Scotland to be with her. That was becoming very clear.

The feeling of having been cut off from him entirely worried her all that night. Not only did she feel separated from him by miles of ocean but also she felt as if someone had come between her and him, preventing them from communicating properly. The soft, seductive voice of the woman who had called him the morning she had left for Scotland whispered in her ear, causing chills to go up and down her spine.

If only Ross had agreed to come over and join her she wouldn't be suffering from all this doubt and suspicion. If he really loved her he would have come, wouldn't he? Since he had told her a little bit about his affair with Inci at Palm Beach, she had tried so hard to come to terms with the feeling that she was only his second-best love because she hadn't been his first love; that he didn't love her and would never love her with the total commitment of a young man's love, as he must have loved Inci, but she still resented the woman she had never met and would never know.

Might as well face it, she was downright jealous of Inci, and even now was suspecting that Ross had lied to her when he had said he would never plan to see Inci again. She had almost convinced herself that the woman who had phoned him the morning she had left New York and who was perhaps in the flat now with him was Inci.

She spent a miserable night, wanting him and wishing he were with her holding her in his arms, and she was glad when daylight came and she was able to get up and start packing for the trip to Mull.

The sun shone out of a misty blue sky, and as Alec drove Dorothy and her to the islands over the moors and through the glens it seemed to Rachel that the whole countryside sparkled, as it wakened from its winter sleep. High on mountain summits snow glittered. Streams swollen by melted snow rushed down craggy hillsides and babbled under old bridges. Pussy-willows shone silver-grey and the buds of birches glowed purplish pink.

They reached the port of Oban on the west coast in time to see a spectacular sunset, crimson and gold clouds streaking a sky of pale green against which the mountains of Mull made dark mysterious shapes, and they stayed in an old-established hotel facing the small island of Kerrera across the strait of water with the same name. Next morning they boarded the car ferry and sailed across to Mull. Standing on the deck in the crisp yet calm air, Rachel recalled with Dorothy the many times they had travelled that way years before, and named familiar landmarks for the benefit of Alec.

From a ferry wharf on the island they drove along a winding road over brown moors where pools of water glittered and green was beginning to show. In the tiny hamlet of Boskillen, a group of old crofting cottages on the shores of a western sea loch, they were welcomed by Margaret and Archie Maclaine who lived on the croft next to Ethel Dow's and had always kept an eye on it while she was away.

To Rachel the cottage looked the same as it always had. It faced west, looking down the long inlet to the

Atlantic ocean, and its whitewashed walls were pale primrose colour in the light of the spring sunshine. Snowdrops drooped in its front garden and crocuses were showing their green sheaths. The house was one storey high, built of blocks of granite, and its roof was thatched. Inside there were two large rooms, a kitchen-cum-living-room furnished with table and chairs, a sofa and a winged armchair and a bedroom divided from the other room by a narrow hallway with a bathroom at the end of it.

Standing in the kitchen for the moment Rachel couldn't help being struck by the stark simplicity of the place compared with the homes she had stayed in in the States. The furniture looked very shabby and the whole place smelt damp. She couldn't help wondering, either, what Ross would think of it. Accustomed to living in luxury with every convenience, wouldn't he look down at it, perhaps make derisive remarks about it and refuse to stay in it with her?

'Are you going to keep it?' asked Alec as, after having some tea and home-made scones with the Maclaines, they walked to the cottage for a last look at it.

'I'd like to, but I'm not sure if I'll ever have much chance to come and stay in it. I don't know what Ross will think of it. It's so far away from New York and everything he likes to do,' said Rachel dubiously, trying to imagine her sophisticated husband staying in the cottage, hobnobbing with the Maclaines, fishing in the loch, and failing. 'I think Gran should really have left it to you, Mother.'

'She was trying to do what she thought best for you,' Dorothy replied. 'She made her will before you were married, when you were talking about wanting to come here to work and not have to be dependent on a nine-to-five job to keep your body and soul together. Remember

what she said to you? While you own it you'll always
have somewhere to come to that belongs to you. She
was glad of the place after Hugh's father died. And you
can never tell what might happen. You might be glad to
come here one day and do your own thing.' Dorothy
turned to look at the twinkling water of the sea loch and
took in deep breaths. 'It's beautiful and peaceful here,'
she enthused. 'And the air is so clear and fresh.'

'It seems damned raw to me, especially now the sun
is beginning to go down,' grumbled Alec, shivering in
spite of his tweeds. 'Come on, let's drive into Tobermory to the hotel. I'm looking forward to a dram of
malt whisky in front of a blazing fire. We can decide
what Rachel wants to do with the place there, in
comfort.'

Tobermory, the largest town on the island, didn't
seem to have changed any more than Boskillin had,
thought Rachel. The famous bay was smooth and placid in the late afternoon light, reflecting the tall, high-
shouldered Highland buildings edging the shore-line.
On its cliff top the well-known hotel still looked like an
old Scottish manor house complete with turret, strong
and sturdy, as if to withstand not only the often
boisterous Atlantic weather but also armed invasions by
an alien people.

After seeing their rooms, Rachel and Dorothy left
Alec to have his malt whisky before a blazing fire in the
lounge and walked back down the hill into the town to
renew their acquaintance with it.

'Let's walk that way and see if Bessie Gowan still has
her tweed shop,' suggested Dorothy.

'Didn't she always close for the winter?' said Rachel
as they reached the bottom of the hill and walked along
a pavement in front of the few shops.

'I'm not expecting to find her open. I just want to

see if she's still in business. She said something about selling the place and retiring last time I was over here, five years ago. Here it is. Look, someone is inside building shelves.'

Light streamed out of the window of the shop into the slowly falling dusk. Peering inside, Rachel saw two men and a woman. One of the men had a beard and was standing on a plank of wood supported by two trestles and was painting the ceiling. The other man was sawing a plank of wood in half. The woman, who was slim and small dressed in denim overalls, had waist-long, honey-coloured hair. She was painting another plank of wood, which was presumably to be used in the building of shelves.

'That's Morag, Morag Gowan,' Rachel said excitedly. She left the window to try the latch of the shop door. The door was locked so she went back to the window and tapped on it. When the young woman looked in the direction of the window Rachel waved to her. After a hesitation the young woman waved back and started towards the door. Rachel was at the door when it opened.

'Morag. Remember me, Rachel Dow?'

'Of course I do,' said the small fair-haired woman, her thin triangular-shaped face lighting up with pleasure. 'Ach, it's grand to see you. You too, Mrs Dow.'

'Mrs Burgess, now,' said Dorothy smiling. 'I married again.'

'Won't you come in for a wee while,' said Morag, standing back and gesturing towards the interior of the shop. 'We're in a wee bit of a mess as you can see, making alterations. What are you both doing on the island at this time of the year?'

'My grandmother died recently,' Rachel explained as they stepped inside. 'And we came over to see her croft, make sure everything was in order. She left it to me in her will.'

'Then will you be coming to live in the island?' asked Morag who, although the same age as Rachel, looked not much more than twelve or fourteen with her flat-chested slim figure, her smooth pink and white complexion and her straight hair falling almost into her round grey eyes.

'Er . . . no, not really. I might come and stay for a while in the summer,' said Rachel. 'What about you? Last time I saw you you were off to study dress design somewhere.'

'Ach, that was ages ago,' laughed Morag. 'I'm married now, to Lachlan Beton. He's the one with the beard and he owns a sheep farm on the island. Since Mother decided to give up this place we've taken it over and we're opening in May, still selling local tweeds, hand-made knits and home-spun wool but also offering other locally made crafts. Pete Corrie over there is our partner. He's a potter. I do the weaving and we have several island women doing the knitting.'

Morag introduced the two young men who acknowledged Rachel and Dorothy then went back to work.

'I'm quite envious of you,' said Rachel.

'Why?' Morag's eyes opened wide in surprise.

'You're using you skills as craftspeople and artists and you're going to sell what you create.'

'Aren't you? I remember you used to say you would like to set up a studio here on the island and turn out paintings and silk-screen prints and sell them,' replied Morag. 'What have you been doing since you left art college?'

'I've been working in a department store doing display designs. Getting started on one's own is really difficult when you don't have any financial backing.

You're lucky your mother already had an established business here.'

'You're right. I am. And of course being married to Lachlan helps. Most of the wool I use in the tweeds comes from his sheep. I do the dyeing of it myself, too,' said Morag, gazing at Rachel thoughtfully.

'Did I hear you say something about silk-screen printing?' asked Pete, coming over to them. Ever since she had been introduced to him Rachel had been aware of him watching her curiously.

'Yes. Rachel is a whizz at it. Won prizes at the art college she attended,' said Morag enthusiastically, and then clapped a hand against her forehead. 'Good heavens, I've just realised she went to the college where you used to teach pottery.'

'I thought I'd seen you somewhere before,' said Pete, his dark blue eyes crinkling at the corners as he smiled at Rachel. 'I was in my first year of teaching there when you were in your first as a student.'

'Yes, I remember you now,' said Rachel. 'But you left before I graduated.'

'That's right. I got fed up with teaching. Went abroad for a while,' he said. 'This is really a stroke of luck you turning up here today. We've just been discussing the fact that we could really do with another partner. Is it possible you'd be interested in joining our little venture? We're looking round for someone who could contribute a different sort of craft or art form and also share the financial load with us.'

'Pete's just taken the words right out of my mouth,' said Morag excitedly. 'And with your shop-display experience you'd be a great asset.'

CHAPTER FIVE

RACHEL stared at Pete Corrie for a few moments, trying to assess the sincerity of his suggestion. He smiled back at her encouragingly and another memory of him stirred at the back of her mind. He had been very friendly with Ralph Bates, the teacher of painting with whom she had become involved. She remembered that Pete had also possessed a roving eye and a couple of times he had made a pass at her.

'We'd love to have you with us,' he said, his glance drifting over her appearance admiringly.

'Yes, we would,' said Morag enthusiastically. 'Oh, Rach, do say you'll join us.'

'I wish I could, but at the moment I'm not free to make such a commitment,' Rachel replied cautiously.

'I understand that. I mean, you've only just heard about it, haven't you?' said Morag. 'But I wish you'd think about it.'

'I'm sure Rachel is going to be thinking about it for the rest of the day,' put in Dorothy with a glint of amusement. 'I know it's something she has always said she would like to do.' She glanced at Rachel. 'And it does seem to fit in somehow with you inheriting Gran's croft, dear. You'd have somewhere to live while you worked here.'

'Pete's setting up his kiln and wheel in one of the big rooms at the back of the shop, but you could have the other room as a studio,' said Morag. 'I do all my weaving in the barn at the farm.'

'It's very enticing, but . . .' Rachel began and broke

110

off, for some reason not wanting to tell Morag that she had succumbed to the charms of a wealthy New York businessman and had married him. Artistic to her fingertips as well as having a strong antipathy to big cities and big business, Morag would never understand how it was possible to be courted and eventually taken over by someone as worldly as Ross was. 'I wouldn't be able to live here all the time,' she finished lamely.

'You wouldn't have to. Just for the summer season.' said Pete. Not very tall, he was compactly built and was not unattractive with his black curly hair and brilliant blue eyes. 'Being natives of the island and having the sheep farm to look after, Mo and Lachlan don't mind living here all year round, but I like to go off to warmer climates, to Greece, preferably, in the winter. You could do the same.' Was it her imagination or was he hinting she could accompany him when he went abroad? She looked appealingly at Dorothy, hoping her mother could help her out.

'We have to go back to the hotel now, or we'll miss dinner,' Dorothy said smoothly. 'And tomorrow we'll be leaving the island to go back to Edinburgh.'

'Oh, what a pity,' sighed Morag. 'I was hoping we'd have more time together, Rachel, so that I could persuade you to come in with us before you left.'

'Could she get in touch with you by phone?' asked Dorothy, the determined organiser of other people's lives.

'Of course.' Morag found a piece of paper and wrote something on it, then handed it to Rachel. 'That's the number at the farm. Phone in the evening because in the daytime we'll be here in the shop finishing the alterations and haven't got the phone connected yet.'

'Thanks. It's been good talking to you, Mo.' Rachel put the paper in her handbag. 'And I'm really very interested. It's just that I have to consult someone else before I can make a decision.'

She and Dorothy didn't talk as they returned to the hotel. This was because they needed all their breath to climb the hill, but as soon as they were in the entrance hall Rachel said, 'I'll have to talk to Ross about it. I can't do anything until I've talked to him. I wonder if I can phone him from here, this evening.'

'You must do as you wish, of course, dear but it will cost a lot of money,' said Dorothy. 'Why not wait until you see him? He might arrive in Edinburgh soon. Then you could discuss Morag's suggestion with him and even bring him up here to see the place.'

'Yes, I think I'll do that,' agreed Rachel, seeing that she might be able to use Morag's and Pete's invitation to join them as a partner to persuade Ross to fly over to Scotland. She wanted so much to show him the islands, to share the places she knew and liked with him as he had shared the places he knew and liked with her during their honeymoon.

All the next day as they went back to Oban by ferry and then started off across country to Edinburgh she was silent as she held imaginary conversations with Ross, wondering what would be the best way to approach him, and she couldn't help thinking that if the opportunity had presented itself at the same time last year, before she had met Ross, she would have had no hesitation in agreeing to join Morag's venture. In marrying Ross she had lost her freedom to do something she had always wanted to do.

Not until she was back in the house in Edinburgh two days later was she able to ring him at the flat in New York. At last the telephone there was picked up. To her surprise a soft female voice said, 'Hello.'

Thinking she had got the wrong number, Rachel

apologised and put down the receiver quickly. Aware
that the sound of the voice had given her an unpleasant
shock, causing her heart to thump with unnecessary
vigour, she tried again fifteen minutes later, noting that
her hand was shaking when she dialled for the operator.
Twice she heard the ringing tone before the telephone
was picked up and the same silky soft voice spoke in her
ear.

'Hello.' It was the same voice she had heard the
morning she had left New York.

'I'm trying to reach Ross Fraser,' she said sharply,
and gave the phone number of the flat.

'I'm sorry, he isn't here right now,' said the voice.

'Then who is this speaking?' she demanded.

'Just a friend of his,' said the voice and there was a
click and the line went dead.

Slowly Rachel climbed the stairs to her bedroom.
She was sure she had just been speaking to Inci. The
woman was in the flat, in the place Ross had asked her
to think of as her home until they were able to find the
right place to buy in the country. He had lied to her
when he said he wouldn't be seeing Inci again. He, to
whom she had given all of herself, all her love, her entire
body and soul, had deceived her after all in the way
Meryl had insinuated he had. She wanted to sit down
on the stairs, then and there, and howl out her anguish
for everyone to hear. But, of course, she didn't. Calling
on her pride, she kept quiet about it, and tried to
pretend she had got a wrong number again.

Yet she didn't try to ring him again at the flat because
she was too afraid of hearing the same soft voice
answering her. She would wait, she decided, until Ross
rang her when he returned from San Francisco; if he
had really gone to California. Perhaps that had been a
lie too, to prevent her from ringing him at the flat while

Inci was there. Oh, God, was there to be no end to his deception of her?

For the next few days she went out as much as she could, sometimes with Dorothy and Alec, sometimes to visit old friends, doing anything rather than be in the house waiting for Ross to ring. She even called in at the department store where she had once worked and was at last able to get Giles to herself for an hour, when she invited him to have lunch in the store's restaurant. Afterwards, the day being fine, they strolled about the park in Prince's Street and sat on a bench in the sunshine for a while.

She told him about the trip to Mull and the offer made to her by Morag and Pete.

'But you're not going to go in with them, I hope,' he remarked, frowning at her.

'Why shouldn't I?'

'Well, for one thing, you're married to Ross.'

'It's something I've always wanted to do,' she argued. 'And he said when he asked me to marry him that he would have no objection to my having a career as an artist. In fact he has been encouraging me to set up a studio in Manhattan, but I'd prefer to go in with Morag.'

'But Ross works and lives in Manhattan,' Giles pointed out. 'Surely you don't want to be separated from him so soon.'

'If I agreed to go in with Morag I'd only be in Mull for the summer, say from May to the end of September, the usual tourist season. It's just possible he might come and stay with me for that time,' she said slowly, then decided to change the subject. 'What are you going to do this coming summer?'

'I've been hoping a certain relative of mine would invite me over to New York to stay with her and her husband for a while,' he replied with his cheeky grin. 'Ross said I'd be welcome any time to visit him.'

'When did he say that?'

'Last year, when I was over there,' he replied, rather evasively, she thought.

'Won't you be trying to get a job, to make some money to pay your way through university next year?'

'I suppose I should. But I'd rather visit you and Ross in New York and maybe travel around the country a bit. You were in Palm Beach, weren't you, among the nobs? That must have been quite an experience. What's Morton Fraser like? I'd really like to meet him. Perhaps he'd give me some leads on how to get into business in New York.'

'He's a very kind person, but extremely shrewd. I wouldn't count on him giving you any help.'

'He helped Ross, adopted him.'

'Yes, but he had a personal reason for doing that,' she pointed out. 'Giles, would you mind telling me how you could afford to come to the States for the whole summer? Have you been earning money in your spare time?'

'What makes you ask that?' he parried quickly.

'Mother has noticed that you don't seem to be so short of money as you usually are and asked me to find out where you were getting the extra funds from,' she said bluntly, realising an oblique approach wasn't getting anywhere.

'Don't you know?' He opened his brown eyes wide, as if he was surprised at her ignorance.

'How could I know?'

'I thought Ross would have told you.'

'Giles, stop hedging,' she snapped irritably. 'What do you think Ross has told me?'

'Last year when I was with him in New York he

offered to help me out financially until I graduated. I was pleased to accept his offer.'

Feeling suddenly chilled, Rachel stared at him in astonishment. 'You . . . you mean Ross has been lending you money ever since then?' she croaked. 'Why didn't you tell me he was going to give you a loan before you left the States?'

'Because I knew you would start objecting and might even tell him not to lend me anything,' he said defiantly.

'You're quite right, I would have. Oh, Giles, how could you sink so low as to ask him for a loan?'

'Now don't start criticising me before you know all the facts. I've just told you he offered to help me.'

'But you must have said something to him. I suppose it was when he lent you money to gamble with in Atlantic City that you got the idea of borrowing more from him. I can just imagine you going on about how hard you were finding it to make ends meet while you're still studying, whining, begging, playing on his generosity.'

'I didn't whine or beg,' he flared angrily.

'Then tell me how he came to offer to give you a loan?' she demanded.

'Rach, if he hasn't told you himself, I don't think I should,' he grumbled.

'Why not?'

'You're not going to like it.'

'That isn't any reason at all why I shouldn't know,' she argued.

'Oh, all right. Have it your own way. Ross told me he wanted to marry you and asked me if I thought he had any chance with you. I said he might have if you could get to know him better, but for you to do that he'd have to come over to Scotland because we would be leaving the States in a few days' time. He said he couldn't come to Scotland then because of other commitments but he thought he could get Aunt Moira to persuade you to stay longer. Then he bet me you and he would be married before the end of October. I told him I had nothing to bet with and he asked me then how come I was always so short of money. I explained why and that was when he said that if he succeeded in persuading you to marry him before the end of October he would lend me money to help me finish at university. It would be the least he could do for his brother-in-law, he said.'

Again she stared at him in open-mouthed amazement.

'So if I hadn't agreed to marry him he wouldn't have arranged to give you the loan?' she whispered.

'Right.' His lips twitched into a grin again. 'Now you know why I was so keen for you to marry him.'

'And also why you didn't tell me before you left? You guessed, didn't you, that if I'd known the loan to you was conditional on my marrying him I would never have married him. Never,' she said vehemently. 'You had no right to agree to such an arrangement. No right at all. You should have told me.'

'I think you're making an awful lot of fuss about something that has nothing to do with you,' he retorted with a touch of hauteur. 'The arrangement between me and Ross has nothing to do with you, really.'

'But it does have something to do with me. If I hadn't agreed to marry him he would never have lent you the money,' she insisted fiercely.

'Well, you did marry him and he arranged the loan immediately,' he muttered sulkily. 'It was done and can't be undone now.'

'Oh, yes it can. You'll have to pay back what you've

already had from him and tell him to stop the rest of the loan,' she said.

'Why?'

'Because I can't have him thinking I married him just so he would lend you money.'

'But I can't pay it back yet,' protested Giles.

'Then I will,' she declared. Then holding her head between her hands she moaned, remembering Meryl's scornful insinuations. 'Oh, I feel as if I've been manipulated by the two of you. I've been bribed into marrying him, bribed by a loan to you . . .'

'Don't be so damned silly and melodramtic.' Giles had never spoken so harshly to her before. 'I'm sure Ross didn't have bribery in mind at all.'

'Then why did he make the loan to you conditional on my agreeing to marry him?' she challenged him.

'I dunno. Maybe he thought he could be sure of me paying him back if I was related to him through marriage first. You'll have to ask him.'

'I will, oh, I most certainly will, the first chance I get. And you're not to accept any more money from him until I've talked with him and worked out how to pay him back.'

'But Rach, if you do that, if you stop the payments he's been sending to me every month I won't be able to afford my share of the rent of the house I'm living in,' he complained. 'And I won't be able to stay on and finish my courses at law school.'

'You mean you're not living in the place we used to share?'

'That dump? I should say not,' said Giles, his lips curling in disgust. 'Two of the fellows in my year and I live in an old house in the city. We share the rent, but I couldn't have afforded to move in with them if Ross hadn't been so generous. I tell you, my life has been much more comfortable as a result of you marrying him, so I hope you're not going to do anything stupid to mess everything up. I know how foolishly proud you can be. Pride, the never failing vice of fools—didn't some English poet once say that? I think it was Alexander Pope. It describes you to a T.'

'Oh, you're impossible,' Rachel hissed. 'If I have too much pride you have none at all, always borrowing money. How you could accept a loan from Ross when you hardly knew him I shall never understand.'

'You married him and you hardly knew him,' he sniped back. 'How do I know you didn't marry him because you knew he was wealthy and could finance any crack-brained arty scheme you might think up? I wouldn't be at all surprised if you're not thinking of asking for a loan yourself so you can put money into that business in Mull.'

'I'm not. I'd never think of doing that.' She was nearly spluttering she was so angry with him. 'You should never have accepted his offer to help you. Mother will be furious when I tell her.'

'Do you have to tell her?'

'Yes, I do.'

'Then see if I care. She can't do anything,' he taunted, getting to his feet. 'I'm going now. I've got a lecture at two forty-five.'

He stalked off and with a sigh Rachel stood up and went to wait for a bus to take her back to the house, oblivious of the signs of spring all around her as she tried to cope with this new attack on her marriage to Ross.

She was telling Dorothy of Ross's loan to Giles that evening when she received a call from Ross at last.

'I called you as soon as I got back from 'Frisco on Wednesday but there was no answer,' he explained.

'I did call you once but the woman who answered
the phone said you weren't in,' she replied stiffly.

There was a short silence then he said,

'When did you call?'

'Tuesday evening. A woman answered the phone. I
think she was the same person who called you the
morning I left. You remember? She wouldn't leave a
message for you with me. She spoke with an accent.
Who was she, Ross?'

Another short silence. Was he wondering how to
answer her, whether to lie to her or not?

'That was Inci,' he said at last. She drew in her
breath sharply. The truth hurt even more than a lie
would have done, she thought miserably.

'What was she doing there? You told me you were
never going to see her again.' She heard her voice
rising rather shrilly.

'I said I would never *plan* to meet her again,' he said
crisply. 'And I haven't.' She heard him sigh. Then,
'Look, Rachel, this is too complicated to explain over
the phone. Leave it until we meet on Friday.'

'I'm not coming on Friday,' she heard herself say in
a cool little voice.

'Why not?' He was very sharp. 'What's happened?'

'As well as finding out that you've been deceiving
me about Inci, I've also found out that you've been
sending money to Giles, that you've given him a loan.'

'I thought you knew about that. I thought he'd have
told you before he went back to Edinburgh last fall.'

'Why did you do it?'

'To help the guy out. He signed a promissory note
to say he'd pay it back as soon as he was working. It's
nothing unusual over here for students to borrow
money to help pay their way through college or
university. I thought he'd told you about it. In fact I

him. If you really don't want him to keep on taking the loan from your husband tell him to drop out of university and go and do some really hard work to pay off what he's already had.'

'I think Alec is right,' murmured Dorothy, 'Although I doin't like the idea of Giles not graduating now that he's so far on in his studies, he is old enough to be responsible for his own debts.'

'But where will ge get a job that will play the sort of money from which he can save enough to pay back what he owes Ross?' sighed Rachel. 'He isn't skilled in anything. It will take him ages to amass over two thousand pounds.'

'If you're so keen for him to pay it back why don't you help him?' Alec suggested. 'You'll be getting that annuity from your grandmother's estate.'

'Don't be ridiculous, Alec,' said Dorothy sharply. 'Rachel will be getting only about three hundred pounds a month from that.'

'You know it's really none of our business. It's just between Ross and Giles, and if Giles wants to go on taking the loan there isn't anything you two can do about it. Seems to me you're both getting worked up about nothing,' said Alec, getting to his feet. 'I'm off to bed. Dot and I have to make an early start tomorrow.'

As soon as Alec was out of earshot Rachel said to Dorothy, 'I've told Ross I can't go back to New York and live with him while Giles owes him money.'

'Oh, dear,' sighed Dorothy. 'Why did you say that?'

'Because if I'd known he was going to lend money to Giles I'd never have married him. Giles guessed that, so he didn't tell me about it. He deceived me deliberately and now I know that Ross has deceived me too.'

'In what way?'

'He's been seeing another woman while I've been over here.' In spite of her effort to remain calm and cool Rachel's voice shook.

'So soon?' Dorothy looked shocked. 'But you've only been married about five months.'

'He knew her long before he ever met me. He wanted to marry her but she refused for some reason. It's been suggested to me that he married me to make a sort of smokescreen so that he and she could go on meeting in secret.'

'I guessed that no good would come of your getting married in haste,' said Dorothy, looking grim. 'You should have made him wait, then you'd have probably found out all about him and wouldn't be in this position now.'

'I suppose you're right,' whispered Rachel miserably.

'Are you in love with him?' asked Dorothy.

'I was when he asked me to marry him. He seemed so sincere, so protective and kind. Now I'm beginning to think it was all an act, to rush me into marriage with him. He even made a bet with Giles that he would be married to me before the end of last October and he persuaded Moira to invite me to stay on so he could date me. He must have planned it all in a cold, calculating way that I don't think I can forgive.'

'How did you find out about this other woman?'

'Morton Fraser's niece told me. But I didn't want to believe her and Ross even told me the affair was all over. But when I rang him the other night a woman answered the phone. Tonight I asked him who she was and he admitted that she was Inci.'

'Didn't he offer any explanation?'

'No. He wouldn't discuss it over the phone, said it was too complicated.'

'Well, I agree with him there. Much better for you to have it out face to face,' said Dorothy.

'I'm not going back,' said Rachel stubbornly. 'And I'm not changing my mind. If he wants to have it out face to face he'll have to come to find me. I'm staying here.'

'That is one way of dealing with the matter, although it will take a lot of willpower on your part,' Dorothy remarked. 'But then if he really loves you he'll come running and looking for you.'

'And if he doesn't?' Rachel asked miserably, imagining suddenly what her life would be like without Ross.

'There are plenty more fish in the sea,' said Dorothy airily and unconsolingly.

Before Dorothy left the next day she had a few words to say to Giles that left him in no doubt about her feelings concerning his borrowing from Ross, but although his face was red afterwards he told Rachel, as they left the station after seeing Dorothy and Alec off on the London train, that he had no intention of giving up the allowance Ross had been sending to him.

'You won't do it even for me?' she said.

'What do you mean?'

'I can't go back to him while you're still taking money from him, that's all,' she replied.

'Have you told Ross that?'

'Yes.'

'What did he say?'

'He said OK.'

'I don't believe it,' whispered Giles, shaking his head incredulously. 'I don't believe that you're so stupid as to break up your marriage to him just because he has lent me money without consulting you first. You're nuts.'

'There is another reason why I'm not going back to New York,' she replied with a touch of hauteur. 'But I wouldn't expect anyone as lacking in pride as you to understand.'

'Are you trying to tell me he's been two-timing you while you've been over here?' Giles guessed shrewdly. 'Now that makes more sense as a reason for you to separate from him. But what are you going to do? Go back to the department store?'

'I'm going to Mull as soon as I can buy a second-hand car and move my printing equipment up there. You have still got it, haven't you? You didn't throw it out or sell it when you moved into your house.'

'I've got it,' he said, looking worried. 'Rach, I'm really sorry about what's happened. I like Ross. I think he's one of the best and I really believed he'd got your measure and could handle you. Isn't there anything I can do to help?'

'Other than paying back the money you already owe Ross and cancelling the loan, you mean?' she queried tartly, a little hurt to realise that he sided with Ross and not with her. 'Yes, there is. You can let me stay in your house for a few days and find a good used car for me.'

'All right. You can stay with us and I'll find you a car,' he agreed with a sigh. 'Have you told Ross about the business in Mull?'

'No, I haven't.'

'Well, you'd better. He has a right to know where you are and what you're doing. And if you're not going to tell him I will,' he threatened.

'I'll write to him as soon as I've settled in,' she said quickly. 'You don't have to tell him anything. Can we go to your house now? I'd like to ring Morag and tell her that I've decided to go in with them.'

Three days later, on a windy but sunny morning, the small second-hand car she had bought piled high with luggage and printing equipment, Rachel took the familiar road to the isles. Although it was warmer than when she had driven north with Dorothy and Alec, there wasn't much change in the appearance of the landscape. Maybe the moors were taking on a more greenish hue and there wasn't so much snow on the high peaks, but as yet there were no leaves on the trees. They wouldn't come out until late in May.

Primroses were peeping from the corners of the little garden in front of the cottage and the water of the sea loch was a deep turquoise blue when she drove into Boskillin the next day. On the distant sea some islands made blue smudges against the placid violet-tinged horizon. The whole scene was so peaceful she ached suddenly to have Ross there to see it, to share the romantic remoteness with her.

She called at the Maclaines' to tell them she would be moving in and staying for a while. Both of them were delighted to learn that she would be their neighbour all summer and would be working in the shop in Tobermory. They invited her to share their midday meal of fresh haddock and chips, and afterwards Margaret went with Rachel to carry luggage into the cottage and to make up the double bed with the brass ends.

'And when will your husband be coming?' Margaret asked.

'I . . . he . . . I don't think he will be coming,' Rachel said distantly, hoping by her manner to put the older woman off asking any more questions. Dorothy had told the Maclaines she was married during the visit earlier in the month.

'Ach, and why not? Is he away somewhere?'

He . . . lives and works in New York.'

Really now.' Margaret looked at her across the bed. 'So why aren't you there with him?'

'We came to an agreement that I should come here for the summer and work with Morag,' said Rachel evasively.

Margaret made no comment while she finished tucking in the sheet at the end of the bed, but when she straightened up she gave Rachel a rather pitying look from her small grey eyes.

'One of those modern marriages is it you have? Ye both gang in different directions. Ach, I don't hold with them myself. Ye'd be better off not married at all than to be separated in this way.'

Later that afternoon Rachel drove into Tobermory to the shop. Great changes had taken place since the last time she had been there. All the shelves and display areas had been finished and the place smelt of new paint. Only Pete was there to help her carry the printing equipment into the room that was to be her studio, next to his.

'Morag and Lachlan have asked us both to go out to the farm for supper,' he said, 'but before we go, come upstairs and see where I'm living. I'm rather pleased with the way I've decorated the place.'

In the long living-room which had views over the harbour to the hills beyond he offered her a glass of wine and they made a toast to the success of the summer season and their partnership.

'I'm really glad you decided to come and join us. Three tends to be a crowd in a partnership, but four should work out just right. Did you have any problems getting out of your other commitment?' Pete said looking at her curiously. 'We all noticed your wedding ring when you came before and guessed the person you had to consult before was your husband. Did he make any objection to you joining us?'

'No, he didn't,' replied Rachel honestly. She didn't have to admit that she hadn't consulted Ross.

'So will he be joining you later on?'

'I'm not sure.' She searched her mind for another subject of conversation, looking around the room appreciatively. 'You've done a great job in decorating this room.'

'Thanks. How long have you been married?'

'Five months.' She sipped the wine in her glass. First Margaret Maclaine and now Pete Corrie. Why were they so interested in her marriage?

'Is he an artist too?'

'No. He's a stockbroker.'

'Really?' Pete raised his thick eyebrows. 'Isn't it working out, then? Is that why you're here? You never did strike me as the sort of woman who would marry for money and be happy.'

Ignoring his insinuations, Rachel set down her empty glass and turned towards the stairway that came straight up into the living-room.

'I'd like to go over to the farm now,' she said coolly.

'Morag said she was surprised you had married. Seems you used to say marriage was the last thing you ever wanted to do, that a career in art would always come first with you,' Pete persisted, following her down the stairs.

'I must have been all of nineteen when I said that,' she replied lightly, reaching the floor below and going into the shop.

'And had just given Ralph Bates the brush-off,' he reminded her.

'I wondered if you'd remember that,' she retorted. 'Do you have any means of transport?'

'Yes. I have a jeep,' he said as they went of the shop into the street. The sun was going down behind the purple-dark hills and the sky was crimson. 'But at the moment it's in the garage down the road being tuned up. I wouldn't mind a lift over to the farm. I can walk back after supper. It's only a couple of miles away.'

Much to Rachel's relief, he said nothing more about her married state or her brief affair with her one-time painting teacher, but chatted amiably about the island and how he had met Morag and Lachlan the previous summer when he had crewed on a friend's sailing boat in the annual Tobermory Race from the Clyde to Mull. He had been impressed by the beauty of the scenery and also by the number of artists and craftsmen who had already settled there and on a chance encounter with Morag at a local *ceilidh* had mentioned he would like to find a place to rent where he could set up a pottery. Morag had suggested he go into partnership with her and Lachlan.

By the time they reached the farm they were on good terms and Rachel had forgotten the slight strain that had shown itself when he had about asked her marriage.

The first few weeks on the island passed quickly as she settled down to reviving her skills in printing. Every day she was up early, leaving the cottage soon after eight to drive to the shop and returning soon after five. Sometimes she went home with Morag and Lachlan to their farm and sometimes she stayed in the town to go to the local pub for supper with Pete. By sheer force of will she managed not to think about Ross during the daytime, but at night she couldn't keep him out of her mind. Several times she tried to write to him to tell him where she was and what she was doing, as she had promised Giles she would, but every time she gave up after the first few words as her pride got in the way of her expressing how she really felt about being separated from him.

If he loved her he would come running, looking for her, Dorothy had told her, she thought, one afternoon as she was slipping some new prints of a black and white drawing she had done of the house along the harbour into her portfolio, intending to take them back to the cottage with her to sign. It was the middle of May, two months since she had left New York, and the start of the tourist season on the island, yet still Ross hadn't come, nor had she heard from him. And she didn't really expect him, she told herself. She had guessed all along that he didn't love her in the way she loved him. He had given all his love to Inci and there had been none left over for any other woman. Oh, he had wanted her, had found her suitable to be his wife, but he hadn't let her possess him as she had wanted to. Always he had kept himself a little aloof from her so that she had never been sure of how he really felt about her.

'What's with you?' Pete's voice behind her mocked her. 'You've been standing there staring into space for the past thirty seconds and not heard a word I've been saying.'

'Oh. Sorry.' She turned and looked at him. 'What did you say?'

'You're beginning to let it show,' he said, walking over to her and looking at her closely. 'It's beginning to get you down, isn't it?'

'I don't know what you're talking about,' she snapped and slung her cloak of green tweed around her shoulders.

'I'm talking about your separation from your husband, love,' he said jeeringly. 'Haven't heard from him, have you?'

'No, I haven't. But then I'm not expecting to.'

'Gone off with another woman, has he? Given you the brush-off, like you gave poor old Ralph. Now you know what it's like to be rejected. But don't let it get you down. I'm here and you and I hit it off pretty well. There's no better way to get over a lost love than to start a new love affair.'

She let him kiss her then, just to find out what it was like, but his kiss didn't go right to the core of her as Ross's kiss would have done, to melt the cold knot of caution that lay there like a lump of lead. She went out to supper with him rather than return too early to the cottage, but when he asked her to return to his room above the shop and stay the night with him she refused coolly, telling herself that if she couldn't have Ross she didn't want any other man.

The stars were pricking the sky and on the water in the sea loch moonlight had laid a path of silver when she drove up to the cottage. All around the hills were quiet and dark. She parked the car in its usual place on the grass at the side of the road and, opening the door of the cottage, stepped inside the small hallway. She snapped the switch and the ceiling light came on. Closing the door, she dropped the portfolio of paintings and prints she was carrying on top of the antique silver chest, the only item of furniture in the hall, unwound the long scarf from around her neck and pulled the knitted angora cap from her head, shaking free her hair. Slipping her green tweed cloak from her shoulders, she flung it across the portfolio.

After stretching her arms above her head she whirled around to go into the kitchen. She stopped short before going through the doorway, her neat, straight nose wrinkling as she detected an unusual scent, unusual in that house anyway. It was the scent of an expensive cigar, something she hadn't smelled since she had been in New York.

Suddenly every nerve in her body quivered in alarm. Someone was in the room, lurking in the darkness waiting for her to enter. Suppressing a panicky urge to turn and run out of the cottage, she squared her shoulders and walked through the doorway.

CHAPTER SIX

HER hand reached automatically for the switch on her right. Light flooded the room. Someone was sitting in the wing chair beside the old-fashioned granite fireplace. She could see the top of a head showing just above the back of the chair. In a few strides she was in front of the chair. Her heart leaping excitedly in her breast, she looked down at Ross. Rubbing his eyes, he sat up straight, raked fingers through his tousled hair.

'I must have fallen asleep,' he murmured.

'How did you know where to find me?' she demanded.

'Giles told me,' he drawled, and rose slowly to his feet. The top of his head just touched the low ceiling of the small room.

'Oh. I asked him not to. I told him I would be writing to you.' In an attempt to control an urge to fling her arms around him in welcome, she folded them across her chest and paced nervously about the room, her pleated skirt swirling above the shiny black leather boots she was wearing. Stopping in front of the small window above the sink, she saw the reflection of her own face, pale as a pearl in the dark pane, then his shape as he came up behind her, darkly threatening. 'Why have you come?' she whispered tensely.

'To see you, of course.

'What do you want?'

'My pound of flesh. Isn't that what Shylock asked for when someone couldn't pay off a debt?' She saw the glint of his teeth in a familiar self-mocking grin.

'What's that supposed to mean?' Her self-confidence surging back, she challenged him, turning to face him, her chin tilting.

'Last time we talked you said you couldn't live with me until Giles's debt to me was paid off. I've been to see him and I've asked what he's going to do about paying up. He said he couldn't see his way to paying me anything yet and referred me to you,' he said coolly. 'If you pay me what he's had already I'll cancel the allowance I've been making to him and we'll start all over again.'

She picked up the kettle and began to fill it at the sink. Placing it on the counter, she plugged it in, moving deliberately and slowly, playing for time while chaotic thoughts skittered through her mind in all directions. As always, his direct approach had disconcerted her. He had come looking for her as her mother had said he would, but he had taken his time about it, and he didn't sound at all loving.

'Tea or coffee?' she asked.

'You know I don't drink either. I've raided your drinks cupboard. I could only find sherry. I drank all there was left in the bottle and will replace it as soon as I can get to a liquor store in the morning.'

'We don't go in for liquor stores in this part of the world,' she retorted.

'I'd noticed it's a long way off the beaten track,' he said drily. 'When I flew over from New York the night before last I wasn't reckoning on having to drive miles over moors and through glens and then take a car ferry to find you. I'm feeling really bushed. Jet-lag, I guess, combined with a sleepless night on a lumpy and damp hotel bed in Oban.' He stifled a yawn with the back of one hand.

She swung round to look at him. With his reddish

brown hair, he was well named Ross. Under slanted eyebrows, his slate-grey eyes had taken on the violet shade she had always admired. He was wearing a bulky Aran sweater and well cut tweed trousers and she could see no signs of suffering in his handsome clean-shaven face. He didn't look at all pale, had no dark lines under his eyes as if he had been spending sleepless nights pining for her, and contrarily she was annoyed. Why would he pine for her when he had had Inci, his former love, staying with him?

'I didn't see a car when I came into the house,' she said.

'That's because I parked it somewhere else,' he replied with another glint of mocking humour. 'I didn't want you to know you had a visitor until you were in the house. Do you always leave the doors unlocked?'

'There aren't any locks, only bolts on the insides of the doors. Anyway locks aren't needed in a small place like this where everyone knows everyone else and we're all good neighbours. This isn't New York City. Or Florida, for that matter,' she jeered.

'That's obvious. Why did you come to live here? Was it just to hide from me?'

'I came to live here because I like it, because I feel I belong here. My grandmother was born here and she lived in this cottage until she became too ill to live alone. She left it to me with a small annuity. I'm independent now and can live where I choose and do what I always wanted to do. If I'd had the opportunity to come and live here before I went to Jenny's wedding I would have done.'

'Implying that you wouldn't have been so tempted to marry me, I suppose,' he gibed. 'So, if you have money why haven't you paid off Giles's debt as you

offered to do and come back to New York?' There was
no humour in his face now and his eyes had lost the
warm violet colour, had become an icy grey.

Conveniently, the kettle began to boil, so she turned
away to take a small sachet of camomile tea from a tea
caddy and to put it in a mug.

'I haven't saved up enough to pay it off yet,' she
said in a low voice. 'But I will. I've gone into a
business with two other artists here on the island and
we're doing quite well selling hand-made pottery,
prints, paintings of local scenes and hand-woven
tweeds.'

'Small stuff. You'll never make much money that
way.'

She swung round again.

'I should have guessed you'd sneer,' she retorted,
flinging back her head to glare up at him. 'Making
money is all you've ever cared about.'

'That isn't true and you know it. I care about many
things that have nothing to do with making money. I
care about you,' he said softly, advancing towards
her.

'No, you don't,' she flared defiantly. 'If you'd cared
about me you wouldn't have tricked me into marrying
you.'

'I didn't trick you. I courted you fairly and
squarely,' he replied sharply, his eyes hardening
again.

'You rushed me,' she faltered backing into the
counter beside the sink.

'There wasn't much time for dalliance, I admit. I
wanted to be married before I had to go south and you
were due to go back to Scotland, so I had to apply
pressure. But everything would have worked out fine if
that creep Meryl hadn't told you lies about me.'

'Were they lies? I don't think so. There's rarely smoke without fire. You were in love with Inci and wanted to marry her long before I came on the scene. Can you deny that?'

'No. And I never have.'

'I'd hardly left New York when you started seeing her again, letting her stay in your apartment, living with her . . . ' She broke off, unable to go on because all the hurt she had felt on hearing Inci's voice answer her when she had phoned him rose up like unpleasant phlegm in her throat, almost choking her.

'She was staying in the apartment only while I was in San Francisco,' he replied coolly. 'I said she could stay there until I came back.'

'Oh, really,' she said scornfully. 'Is that the best you can do in the way of an explanation? I don't believe a word of it.'

'Then that's your loss, because it's the truth,' he snapped, his lips thinning, his shoulders stiffening, his head lifting proudly as he resented her lack of belief and trust.

She turned to the boiling kettle, unplugged it and poured water into the mug. Steam rose in her face, moistening her skin. She put the kettle down. She must make an effort to keep her cool.

'Would you consider a year's separation while I try to raise the money to pay off Giles's debt?' she asked.

'No.'

She turned again to look at him. He looked back at her, his eyes as hard and cold as grey glass.

'Then what would you consider?' she asked.

'That depends on how we get on together during the next few months.'

'I don't understand.'

'Since you can't pay the debt, nor can Giles yet, I

suggest we forget it and resume our marriage,' he said.

'You mean . . .?'

'Exactly what I say.' His breath hissed as he drew it in. She could tell by the ridging of muscle along his jawline and the cold glare in his eyes that he was only just managing to restrain his temper, and wondered what she would do if he got hold of her and shook her. 'I married you and I intend to stay married to you. I realise now that I should never have let you come back to Scotland. If I'd played the domineering husband and stopped you from coming we wouldn't be here snarling at each other now.'

'I'm not going back to live with you in New York,' she said, chin up, eyelids drooping. 'I'm committed to staying here the whole summer. I promised Morag and Pete that I would.'

'Then I'll stay here with you and we'll go back to the States when September comes. I think that's fair,' he asserted coldly.

'But you can't stay here.'

'Why can't I? I'm your husband and I have every right to stay and live with you,' he argued.

'There's no room.'

'I admit the place is a bit small and it needs some renovations and additions, but I'm a pretty good carpenter and have experience in house-building. I learned that from Uncle Duncan, my father's brother, when I stayed with him for a couple of summers in the backwoods of Nova Scotia. Between us we did up an old maritime farmhouse he had bought on the island of Cape Breton.' He must have caught the expression of scepticism on her face, because he added bitterly, 'I know you won't believe me. You've got it into your head I'm incapable of doing anything but gamble on the stock exchange. That's why I want us to have some

time together. We don't really know each other.' He
stepped closer to her, his expression softening, his eyes
beginning to glow with violet light again. 'In a place as
small as this cottage we'll soon become intimate again,
as we were on our honeymoon. Remember the long
nights alone together?'

To her irritation her whole body tingled in response
to the suggestiveness expressed in his voice and his
eyes. Reminding herself acidly that he was an old hand
at making love and had often made love to her to stop
her from asking him questions he had no intention of
answering, she tossed back her head and looked him
straight in the eyes.

'But I don't want you to stay and live with me,' she
said clearly and firmly, raising her voice a little as if she
thought he hadn't heard the first time.

'Give me one good reason why I shouldn't,' he said,
mockery beginning to curl his lips. 'I know that logic
isn't your strong point, but I'm willing always to listen
to your arguments.'

'Knowing you've been with another woman, I just
can't bring myself to take you back,' she said shakily.
'You married me only because you couldn't have Inci.
Now I suspect you and she have split again, so you
think you can come running back to me. Well, it's just
not on. I've had enough of being your second-best
wife. I don't want you living here because it's possible
I might . . . I might want a divorce.'

'Why?' The abrupt question caught her off guard.
She had given no consideration to divorce and had
spoken of it only out of irritation with him, in an
attempt to disconcert him.

'Because . . . because Inci stayed with you while I
was over here,' she stammered.

'You'd never be able to prove that,' he gibed. 'And

you'd have to have a better reason than that to get me to agree to a divorce.'

'Maybe I've met someone else,' she said haughtily.

'Someone better at it than I am?' he asked with mock surprise. 'Who is he?'

'I don't have to tell you,' she evaded.

'One of the arty guys you're in business with?' he suggested.

'Maybe.'

Turning her back to him Rachel sipped tea and watched their reflections in the window again. It seemed to her he hovered behind her like a predator and once again she tingled all over at the thought of him taking hold of her and asserting his marital rights.

'You'd never get a divorce in this country, because we haven't been married to each other long enough,' he said coolly. 'If you want a quickie you'll have to return to the States with me.'

'Never,' she said in a low voice, feeling a little thrill of malicious triumph. Was it possible she had shaken his self-confidence for a brief moment?

He stepped forward and, reaching round, took the mug out of her hand and put it down. Hands on her shoulders, he spun her round deftly. She had a brief glimpse of his face, white with anger, his blazing eyes, then too late she put her hands up to his chest to push him away. Like steel pincers his arms seized her and crushed her against him. She kept her head down hiding her face against his chest until, with a sharp tug on her hair that made her gasp, he jerked her head back.

The touch of his lips, cool and hard against hers, was an unforgotten torment, awakening memories of the uncontrollable passion that had erupted between them when he had proposed to her. She stiffened, resisting the tantalising probe of his tongue against the tight line of her lips. Keeping her eyes wide open, she struggled to rule her body with her mind. But when she felt his fingers at her nape, stroking it seductively, she couldn't help gasping with pleasure, and in that instant he was quick to take advantage, his lips pressing harder, his tongue entering her mouth to caress the tip of her tongue. Involuntarily her eyes closed and her body softened as the heat of passion flooded through her and she longed avidly for a return of the ecstasy she had experienced with him during the few months they had lived together.

Suddenly his mouth moved away from hers, although he continued to hold her close to him.

'We have company,' he murmured in her ear.

She pushed away from him and turned to look at the doorway. Archie Maclaine was standing in the small hallway.

'What is it, Archie?' she asked, moving towards him.

'Ach, it's sorry I am to be disturbing you, Rachel, but the wife was a wee bit worried about ye. She says she saw someone snooping about the house just at twilight and she sent me over when she saw the lights come on to make sure ye were all right. She was afraid for ye.' Archie's watery blue eyes looked suspiciously at Ross who had come to stand beside her.

'Tell Margaret I appreciate her concern,' Rachel was beginning when Ross moved forward, stretching out his right hand to Archie and saying,

'I'm Ross Fraser, Rachel's husband. Pleased to meet you, Archie, and to know that you and your wife look out for her.'

The suspicion fled from Archie's innocent blue eyes. He smiled and shook Ross's hand.

'Well, now. It's a pleasure so it is to meet you, too,

Mr Fraser, and to have you come to stay in Boskillin,'
he said. 'We were thinking you wouldn't be coming.
Rachel said you were too busy with your own business
to come here this summer. Have you ever been in the
islands before?'

'No, I haven't.'

'Then it's a treat you've been missing. You'll be
coming fishing in the loch with me one of these days?'

'I'd like that.'

'I'll be away now to tell Margaret everything is all
right,' said Archie.

'Goodnight.' Rachel followed him to the front door.
'And say thank you again to Margaret.

'I will. I will.'

The door closed, Rachel turned back into the
kitchen. Ross was standing on the hearthrug, long legs
apart, hands in the pockets of his trousers. Colour had
returned to his face and his eyebrows tilted satirically.

'I'm surprised you've admitted to being married,'
he challenged her.

'Mother told them when I came up here with her
and Alec in April,' she said.

'And what about the guy you've met whom you
prefer to me?' he queried mockingly. 'Does he know?'
When she didn't answer he continued tormentingly, 'I
don't believe he exists. I think you've invented him on
the spur of the moment to back up your demand for a
divorce, another spur-of-the-moment invention.' He
stepped towards her and put his hands on her
shoulders again. 'Now, where were we before Archie
came in?' he murmured provocatively, drawing her
towards him.

This time she was ready for him. With a quick
twitch of her shoulders she slipped from under his
hands, whirled into the hallway and through the open

doorway of the bedroom. Quickly she slammed the
door shut, regretting that there was no lock on any
door in that house. Expecting Ross to come after her
and push the door open, she leaned against it with all
her weight,

Nothing happened. He didn't lift the latch and push
the door, nor did he call out to her. She must have
leant against the door fully five minutes before she
moved, realising how cold it was in the room.

She switched on the light. The big old-fashioned bed
with its brass ends that had a tendency to lean inwards
over the mattress was still as she had left it that
morning, unmade. Ears pricked for the slightest sound
of movement on Ross's part, she moved towards the
bed and made it quickly. Then she plugged in the
electric fire and switched it on high. The fan began to
turn with a clatter and immediately the electric light
went out, plunging the room into darkness.

'Oh, hell,' she muttered and lunged in the direction
of the bedside table, her fingers seeking the switch on
the lamp there. Groping in the dark her hand collided
with the small lamp and knocked it to the floor. She
heard the bulb shatter. Muttering and cursing to
herself, she went down on her knees to search the floor
beside the bed for the lamp, hearing the latch lift on the
door. Straightening up she looked across the bed in the
direction of the door, expecting to see light slanting
into the room from the hallway. Everything was dark.

'Rachel?'

'Yes?'

'All the lights went out.'

'Oh, damn. I put on the electric fire. It must have
been too much for the fuse-box.'

'Got a flashlight?'

'Somewhere. I . . . I think it's in my car.' She got to

her feet and began to walk round the bed, keeping her hand on the mattress for guidance and then on the foot rail. It was so dark she couldn't even see the outline of his figure in the doorway.

'I'll go and get it,' he said.

She waited where she was until she heard the front door close after him, then she went into action. Her eyes growing accustomed to the faint light from the moon that slanted in through the window, she ran out into the hallway. Finding the two bolts, she slid them into position. Then she started to drag the old silver chest towards the front door by one of its iron handles. To her annoyance the handle came away from the chest in her hand and she realised the screws attaching it to the side must have rusted through. Dropping it she went to the other side of the chest and began to shove, but it still wouldn't budge. She was sitting on it, puffing and panting, after her exertions, when the latch lifted and Ross tried to push open the door.

As she had expected when the door didn't open immediately he pushed harder, using all the weight of his hard muscular body against it. The bolts held but only just.

'Rachel. Open the door,' he yelled and she flinched. He seemed to care little that he might be heard by Archie and Margaret or what they might think of him standing outside at night, shouting at her.

'No,' she yelled back. 'Go away.'

'If you don't open up I'll kick the door down,' he threatened loudly

'No. I don't want you.'

'That's a lie if ever there was one,' he retorted scornfully. 'Stand away from the door because I'm going to break it down now.'

The door shook as he launched himself at it and

then kicked it. There was a splintering sound as a panel of the old wood split. Rachel slid off the chest and faced the door.

'Ross, if you don't stop it I'll take you to court for wilfully damaging my property,' she shouted.

'Then be sensible and open the door. I'm not going to spend the night out here sleeping in a car when I could be in there sleeping with you.'

'Oh, please stop shouting. The Maclaines will hear you and they'll think . . .'

'They'll think you're refusing me my marital rights,' he taunted, making no attempt to lower his voice. 'And they would be right. Come on, open up and I'll fix the fuse for you.'

'Oh, all right.' Then very quietly she slid the bolts back and tiptoeing into her bedroom she closed that door and began to push the chest of drawers across it.

'Rachel?' He called to her again. After a few moments when she didn't answer him she heard him open the front door and step inside. She sat on the edge of the bed, shivering a little.

'Where are you?' he said when he had closed the front door again.

'In the bedroom,' she replied.' Did you find the flashlight?'

For answer he lifted the latch of the bedroom door and pushed it open against the chest. She saw the beam of the flashlight.

'What the hell,' he started, then broke off to laugh. 'OK, I get the message. But will you just tell me where the fuse-box is so I can get some lights on.'

'It's in the hallway, high up on the wall by the bathroom door. There are new fuses on the shelf.'

'Then unplug the electric fire. We don't want everything fusing again as soon as it comes on.'

She did as he ordered, and going back to the bed, got under the blankets and covers so as to keep warm. She could hear him moving about, then there was a short silence. After a while the ceiling light came on.

He didn't come back to taunt her through the opening of the door and she thought she heard him go into the kitchen. For a while she sat where she was, listening warily for his approach to the bedroom, but he didn't come. Eventually, feeling stiff, she slid off the bed and tiptoed over to the chest of drawers to push it away from the door. She couldn't possibly go to bed without visting the bathroom first.

There was no light on in the hall and none shining out of the kitchen. By the light from the bedroom she was able to see her way to the bathroom. A few minutes later she left the bathroom and went back to the bedroom. She closed the door quickly and dragged the chest of drawers across it.

Turning into the room, she pulled her sweater up over her head. When it was off she tossed it on the nearest chair, slid off her skirt and then took off her underskirt. Her skin goose-pimpling with the cold, she went towards the bed to get her pyjamas from under the pillow. She pulled up short with a gasp of irritation. Ross, wearing black pyjamas piped with red, was sitting up in the bed, his legs covered by the bed covers, his grey eyes slitted with the sardonic amusement that also curled his lips.

'You've put on a little weight since I last saw you,' he drawled, his glance drifting observantly over her body which was bare save for the briefs and tights she was wearing. 'I like it.'

'Get out,' she said through gritted teeth, covering her breasts with her arms, hoping he wouldn't guess that she was pregnant. She had only known it a short while herself, and had hugged the knowledge to her, telling nobody.

'Ah, come on. Be reasonable. I tried the sofa and found it too short and uncomfortable. There's plenty of room in this bed for both of us,' he said.

'I'm not sleeping with you,' she shouted, and grabbing her sweater she pulled it on again and turned to the door. The chest of drawers blocked her way. Suppressing a desire to turn on him, to rant and rave at him, she began to push at the chest. For some reason, possibly because she was beginning to feel weak with the intense strain of trying to keep him at a distance, it seemed to be very heavy and wouldn't move. Straightening up she glared across at him.

'What have you done to this chest?' she demanded.

'Nothing. You dragged it across the doorway yourself.'

'Well, come and help me move it.'

'In the morning,' he replied smoothly and slid down under the covers. 'Right now I'm going to sleep. Don't forget to put the light out before you come to bed.'

Rachel wasn't sure what happened to her then. It seemed as if a red haze danced before her eyes. Irritated beyond bearing, she lunged across the room intending to pull the bedclothes off and somehow drag him from the bed. It was a mistake. As she launched herself forward she tripped over the edge of the woven mat beside the bed and fell across him. Her violent landing combined her weight suddenly with his and was too much for the ancient bed. The irons on which the mattresses were resting came out of their sockets and clattered to the floor. The mattress fell, too, and the precarious brass bed-ends leaned towards each other, trapping the two people on the bed in a sort of tent.

'I knew you'd see it my way, after a while, and would come to bed with me,' said Ross with aggravating calmness.

Beneath her she could feel him shaking with suppressed laughter. Then his hands were sliding over her shoulders as he tried to lift her. Afraid she might give in to the sudden aching demands of her body and seek comfort close to his warm vibrancy she began to squirm backwards from under the bed ends.

'I've not come to bed with you,' she said tautly, as she managed to slide off the bed and on to the floor, where she sat cross-legged wondering what to do next. 'And now the only bed in the house is broken,' she wailed and buried her face in her hands. 'It's all your fault. Oh, how I wish you hadn't come.'

There was a short tense silence. Then the mattress creaked as Ross moved. He swore softly as he banged his head against the brass rods that slanted above him. A few more creaking sounds and he slid from the bed to sit on the floor beside her.

'You don't mean that,' he said softly, taking hold of her wrists and pulling her hands away from her face.

'Yes, I do. I do,' she whispered shakily, keeping her head bowed refusing to look at him. 'I was getting on fine without you. Please go away.'

'OK. I will if that's the way you feel,' he said, his voice taking on a hard edge. 'But not yet. Not before morning.' Dropping her hands he stood up. 'Come on, give me a hand to move these bed-ends and to slide the irons out. The mattress will be all right on the floor.'

'I still won't sleep with you,' she said stubbornly as she got to her feet.

'OK, OK, ' he said irritably. 'But you can still help me move the ends.'

Too dismayed by his sudden agreement to her

request that he should go away, she helped him move the irons and the bed-ends. When the mattress was flat on the floor and the covers were straightened, he turned to her and said, 'Do you still fancy sleeping on that old sofa? Shall I help you move the chest of drawers?'

'Yes, please,' she said wearily.

When she was curled up at last in a blanket on the sofa it didn't take her long to find out why he had given up trying to sleep on it. There was a spring jutting up right in the middle that either got her in the back or, if she was lying on her side, dug into her waist. For more than half an hour she tossed and turned, trying to find a comfortable spot and often losing the blanket. Finally thoroughly chilled, she crept throught the darkness into the bedroom. Moving cautiously, she lifted the bed covers and slid under them.

Ross was lying right in the middle of the mattress on his side with his back to her. Judging by the quiet steadiness of his breathing he was asleep. There wasn't enough room for her to lie on her back so she turned on to her side with her back to him. Heat from his body radiated out to her. She lay still, hoping to relax in the warmth and eventually to fall asleep.

Ages later, so it seemed, she was still wide awake, lying taut on the edge of the bed as far away from Ross as possible. She turned restlessly, punching at her pillow to make it more comfortable.

'What's the matter?' Ross spoke quietly as he turned towards her.

'I can't sleep.'

'I'm not surprised.' At her waist, under the edge of her pyjama jacket, his hand was hot and heavy against her skin. Slowly his fingers spread upwards over her breast and she felt his lips scorching the vulnerable curve between her neck and shoulder. The heat of his

hard muscularity was all around her, warming her.
The scent of his skin and hair was filling her nostrils,
going to her brain and turning her dizzy with delight.

'No. I can't,' she whispered, even while her body
was betraying her and arching to his touch.

'Sure you can. It will relax both of us,' he
murmured.

'But it won't solve anything, and besides I don't
want you.'

'Tell that to the marines,' he jeered and, jerking her
roughly against him, smothered any other protest she
might have made with his mouth.

Inevitably it seemed, her lips parted to the fierce
invasion of his tongue and against her loins she felt the
hard pressure of his maleness arousing her with a swift
suddenness that made her cry out against the heat of
his lips. His usual tenderness when undressing her was
in abeyance and he didn't bother to slip undone her
pyjama buttons but dragged the jacket off her, and she
heard the material hiss as it tore.

A wide and primitive hunger leapt up within her in
response to his ravenous caresses, and she forgot all
her earlier resistance to him. He had come looking for
her, and that was all that mattered. In spite of Inci, he
still wanted to make love to her, and for the time being
she was willing to be made love to by him. But only by
him. Only he could penetrate her and melt the knot of
cold caution that lay at her core. Only he possessed the
magic to make her mind spin out of control and her
body to erupt like a volcano. Only he could bring to
her the sweet fluid easing of tension, the relaxation he
had promised lovemaking would bring to both of
them.

They both slipped into sleep without saying
anything more, as if their physical union had solved all

the problems that separated their minds. Rachel slept long and deeply, waking with a start to lie blinking bemusedly at bright sunlight. She sat up quickly, became aware that the mattress was on the floor and remembered how the bed had collapsed last night when she had flung herself at Ross.

Ross. Where was he? Beside her the bed was empty, the sheet smooth, the pillow straight. No sign of anyone ever having slept there.

Had she imagined that she had found him in the cottage when she had returned to it last night? Had she been longing for him to come so much that she had experienced some sort of hallucination? Was she going out of her mind?

From the bedside table she grabbed her watch and peered at it. Nine-thirty. She had overslept. Putting the watch down, she scrambled off the bed and ran across to the open door. Into the kitchen to put on the kettle, out again to the bathroom to wash quickly, splashing the clear, cold water on her face to wash away the last vestiges of sleep and to shake off the morning sickness which, she was beginning to accept, was due to the fact that she was pregnant with Ross's child, conceived two months ago in new York.

Ross wasn't in the cottage. Nor was there anything lying about to indicate that he had been there. No flung-off pyjamas, no other clothes in the kitchen, no suitcase or travelling-bag anywhere.

Yet the mattress was on the floor and the bed-ends were stacked against a wall, evidence that the bed had collapsed when she had thrown herself at him last night. That couldn't have happened if he hadn't been in the bed could it? Surely she hadn't imagined the rest, the way they had made love, avidly and fiercely.

So where was he now? Had he left to catch a ferry

back to the mainland? Had he gone because he didn't like the cottage and its lack of amenities? Or had he gone because she had rebuffed him and had talked of divorce? Oh, she hoped not.

She had time for only one cup of very weak tea before she left the cottage, slamming the door shut behind her. Outside it was a lovely morning, the sun slanting down out of a clear blue sky. The sea loch shone like a mirror and the green and gold moorland was dotted with sheep. Waving to Margaret Maclaine who was pegging washing to a line, Rachel felt a lift of her spirits in response to the change in the weather, until she remembered that Ross had been to see her at last, she had said and done all the wrong things, and so he had left.

White houses sparkled in Tobermory and the bay was smooth and silken, reflecting the blue of the sky. She parked her car behind the Betons' van at the side of the building where the shop was located and hurried around. The shop door was wide open for the first time that season and there were actually three customers inside, obviously tourists.

'What happened?' Pete asked her when she entered the big room at the back of the shop where he had his potter's wheel and kiln. 'Flat tyre? Or petrol pump gone on the blink again?'

Neither. I overslept.' As she slipped off her jacket she eyed him surreptitiously, comparing him with Ross, and finding him lacking. No other man could compare with Ross, in her estimation. No other man could take his place in her life, so why had she rebuffed him last night? To try to hurt him, of course. To try to find out if he could be hurt in the way that he had hurt her.

'Rachel, now that you're here you might come and

help,' hissed Morag from the doorway. 'We've actually got four people in the shop now. Did you bring those new prints of the houses along the harbourside? You took them home to sign last night.'

'Oh, I'm sorry. I forgot.' Rachel smoothed her hair behind her ears and dragged her thoughts away from Ross. 'Shall I go back for them?'

'No, not now. Come and serve in the shop now.' Morag looked at her curiously. 'What's happened? You look all het up.'

'I'll tell you later,' said Rachel, and forcing herself to smile went back into the shop to try to cajole a customer into buying a length of tweed.

Not until it was almost noon and there were no customers in the shop did she have time to tell Morag what had happened to make her late that morning, and then she didn't offer the explanation herself but waited until her friend asked her.

After glancing about to make sure Pete wasn't in earshot she whispered, 'The strangest thing happened. When I got back to the cottage last night Ross was there.'

'Your husband?' Soon after having become a partner in the business, Rachel had told Morag about her hasty marriage to Ross and how she felt he had deceived her.

'Yes. But this morning, when I woke up he had gone.'

'Did you quarrel with him last night?'

'Well, we didn't agree,' said Rachel evasively.

'What did you say to him? You must have said something to annoy him if he left without saying goodbye or without making any arrangement to see you again,' guessed Morag shrewdly. 'I bet you gave him the cold shoulder so he took the huff and left. Oh,

Rachel, you are a fool. He probably came to make it up with you and you got all haughty and proud, the way you often do. How could you do it after all these weeks of wishing he would come running after you to ask you to start your marriage all over again?'

'I haven't been wishing he would come,' Rachel retorted.

'Yes, you have, because you're in love with him. I know you are because of the way your voice changes whenever you mention his name and your eyes go soft and dreamy. Why don't you drop the barrier of your pride and admit it? You love him and you want to live with him and make love with him. Why won't you give him another chance?'

'Because he's done things I find it difficult to forgive him for,' said Rachel forlornly. She glanced around again to made sure Pete was still in the kiln-room and said, 'Ross isn't in love with me. He loves someone else and he's been seeing her again while I've been over here. Could you forgive that?'

'No, I couldn't,' said Morag truthfully. 'But do you have concrete evidence he's been seeing this other woman?'

'The evidence supplied by my own ears,' said Rachel tartly, and thought how like Dorothy she sounded. 'One day I phoned his flat and she answered the phone. What conclusion would you draw from that? Wouldn't you think he was seeing her again?'

'It does sound rather as if he's in the wrong, but didn't he explain to you why she was there when he was with you last night?'

'Yes. But I didn't believe his explanation. And I said I might want a divorce.'

'Oh, lord,' Morag groaned. 'No wonder he left. But you don't really want a divorce, do you?'

'No,' sighed Rachel. 'I don't really. I only said it to
. . . well, to try and find out how he really feels about
me.'

'And what did he say?'

'He made a joke out of it. Asked me if I'd found
someone who could do it better than he could.' Rachel
felt the blood rise to her cheeks.

'Who can make love to you better, I suppose he
meant,' said Morag with a chuckle. 'And have you?'

'No.'

'Did you tell him that?'

'No.'

'Rachel, you are just about the silliest woman I've
ever met,' Morag said scornfully. 'You deserve to lose
him.'

There was no more chance for talk about Ross for
the rest of the day because they were busy in the
afternoon with more tourists. By five o'clock, when
they were thinking of closing up, Morag was quite
excited because they had sold two lengths of her tweeds
and also wool for knitting, a couple of Pete's big vases
as well as some woven place-mats and coasters.

'Like to come home for supper with us?' she said to
Rachel. 'Better than you being alone and brooding
about what might have been if only you'd held your
tongue last night.'

'No, thanks,' said Rachel. 'I have some washing to
do.'

'Well, don't forget to bring in the prints tomorrow.'

'I won't,' said Rachel and knew she wouldn't
because there wouldn't be any annoying but lovable
Ross around to distract her attention and make her
absent-minded. Immediately she felt her heart sink
into her shoes because Ross had gone and nothing had
been resolved between them and it was her own fault

he had gone.

She half-hoped he might be at the cottage when she returned to it, but he wasn't, and she spent a difficult night trying to decide what to do next. In the morning she felt washed out and weak, and it was a great effort to drive into the town.

Less than a month ago she had come to the island full of hope, believing that at last she was going to do what she had always wanted to do, establish herself in a career as an artist, Now she would have given anything to back out of the partnership and go back to being Ross's wife. Even if he didn't love her as he had loved Inci, she wanted to be with him again and not just because she wanted a father for their child.

If only she could see him again and tell him she hadn't meant what she had said to him when she found him in the cottage, explain to him why she had been so much on the defensive, if her pride would let her, that was.

'You look awful,' Morag said to her.

'I feel awful. I'm expecting a baby.'

'Oh, God,' breathed Morag. 'Ross's, I hope.'

'Of course.' Rachel was indignant.

'All right, all right. Keep your hair on. Does he know?'

'I haven't told him. But I wouldn't have wanted him to stay with me just because of that.'

'I would have,' sighed Morag. 'I keep trying to get pregnant but nothing has happened in four years of marriage to Lachlan and I'm beginning to wonder what's wrong.'

'You should go to a clinic, have some tests,' said Rachel urgently, rebuking herself for thinking she was the only woman with problems. 'Things can be done to help you have a child. You and Lachlan should both go. That is if you really want a child.'

'I'm almost dying with longing for a baby,' said Morag. 'And if I had been you last night I'd have shouted the news out to Ross as soon as I saw him. But then I don't have your pride. Do you know where he was going when he left?'

'No. I expect he'd go back to Edinburgh.'

'To your brother's place?'

'I don't know. I might phone Giles later, if you wouldn't mind.'

'Why should I? You contribute to the paying of the phone-bill.'

Rachel was lucky to catch Giles just before he went out for the evening. As soon as he heard her voice he asked quickly, 'Ross find you?'

'Yes.'

'So what happened? Is all forgiven and forgotten?'

'He left the next day. Giles, if he calls in to see you, would you let me know, please?'

'But I thought, at least I got the impression from him that if you refused to go back to the States with him he was going to stay with you all summer.'

'Well, he isn't.'

'Messed everything up again, have you? You need a good spanking, that's what you need. Pity Dad was so soft with you.'

'What a very chauvinistic remark to make,' she retorted loftily. 'No man is ever going to spank me.'

'I wish Ross would. I doubt if he'll come to see me, but if he does do you want me to ask him to phone you at the shop?'

'Yes please.'

Somehow she got through the next few days. There was no call from either Ross or Giles and she could only assume that Ross hadn't called in to see her brother on his return to Ebinburgh.

He had probably gone back to New York, she though disconsolately, and she would never see him again, unless she made the next move, trampled on her pride and asked him to take her back, and told him she would turn a blind eye to his affair with Inci if only she could live with him.

No. Never could she do that. She would rather stay on the island without him than do that.

So she struggled with the pros and cons of the situation while longing every day for him to be at the cottage when she returned to it at night, to be there sitting in the kitchen, even if he mocked her pride, her lack of logic. She loved him, she wanted him . . .

'There's someone in the shop asking for you,' Morag said, looking into the studio, where Rachel was working on the design of batik prints for silk scarves one afternoon.

Her heart leaping hopefully, Rachel turned to look at her friend quickly.

'Sorry to disappoint you, but it isn't him,' continued Morag, reading the expression on her face accurately. 'Her clothes are American but she speaks English with a rather mixed-up accent. She lookes as if she's from Greece or somewhere in the Middle East.'

Rachel stared at Morag, hearing a soft voice speaking in her ear.

'Did she give her name?' she whispered.

'Yes, but I'm sorry I can't pronounce it,' apologised Morag, her eyes beginning to glint mischievously. 'And she's come with an escort, someone you know very well.'

'Who, for heaven's sake?' said Rachel becoming irritated by her friend's teasing manner.

'Come and see,' retorted Morag and left the room.

CHAPTER SEVEN

STILL feeling somewhat annoyed at having been interrupted while working on a print, Rachel followed Morag into the shop. Morag had been busy serving a customer who had just come in, showing off a length of tweed at the counter. Over by the display shelves two people, a man and a woman, were standing examining some of Pete's pottery. They both had their backs to Rachel. The woman was small and slim and had thick jet-black hair that stood out from her head in an ear-length bob. She was wearing a narrow dark blue skirt and a white blazer. The man, tall and brown-haired, was wearing jeans, and a fisherman's knit sweater over his shirt and was easily recognised by Rachel. He was her brother.

'Giles, what on earth are you doing here?' she exclaimed, moving towards him.

Hello, Rach,' he said easily, turning to her. 'Just thought I'd take a trip up to see you before exams start. I don't think you've ever met Inci, have you?'

Inci! The name, so sharp and icy, seemed to stab through to Rachel's heart. She was aware that the woman had turned and was looking at her curiously with big black eyes that seemed to fill the whole of the upper part of her thin classically featured olive-skinned face.

'No, we haven't met, but we have spoken to each other on the phone,' said Inci, and at the sound of that soft, seductive voice chills went up and down Rachel's spine. 'How are you, Rachel?'

'I'm quite well, thank you.' Rachel had stiffened and she was glad that the other woman hadn't held out a hand to be shaken. 'But I'm surprised to see you here with Giles. When and where did you two meet?'

'Inci was one of the crowd I met when I stayed with Ross at his flat in Manhattan, last September,' explained Giles. 'I told her then to look us up if she was in Edinburgh to give a recital. And she did. Sent me a couple of complimentary tickets for her concert.' Giles looked excessively pleased with himself. 'Afterwards I went backstage to see her.'

'And I was so glad you did,' added Inci, flashing him a warm grateful smile before she looked back at Rachel. 'I was able to ask Giles if he would be so kind as to drive me to this island,' she continued seriously. 'We left very early this morning. Is Ross staying here with you?'

'Er. No, he isn't,' said Rachel awkwardly. 'He was here but he left.' She became aware that Giles, who was standing behind Inci, was signalling to her, twitching his eyebrows and pressing a finger against his lips as if in warning, and she made an effort to recover her poise. 'It's a pity he couldn't stay longer.'

'But he will be back, won't he?' Giles suggested to her, nodding his head at her as if urging her to agree with him. 'Before we have to leave, I mean.'

'I'm not sure. How long are you intending to stay here?' she asked, wondering what mischief Giles was up to now.

'Tonight, tomorrow and tomorrow night. We'll drive back on Sunday,' he replied. 'I have a tutorial on Monday morning that I must attend.'

'And I have to be back to catch a plane to Paris on Monday,' explained Inci.

'Inci is going to stay at the hotel, but I was hoping I

could stay at Gran's cottage with you,' said Giles.

'You can stay with me as long as you don't mind sleeping on the sofa,' said Rachel, thinking of the mess the cottage was in. Recently she hadn't felt like doing much housework and the mattress was still on the bedroom floor.

'I suppose I won't have to,' grumbled Giles disgustedly.

'It would be much better if you came to stay at the farm,' said Morag, coming over to them, the customer having left. 'You too, Miss Kapadia. We have two spare bedrooms. You'd be most welcome. It isn't often we have a chance to meet a celebrity and have her stay with us.'

Another charming smile irradiated Inci's dark face and her black eyes seemed to glitter light. She is beautiful, as Meryl said, thought Rachel with a sinking heart, beautiful and disarmingly gentle; no wonder Ross is still in love with her.

'I'm not a celebrity yet,' said Inci with a little laugh. 'I'm only at the beginning of my career as a concert pianist, I still have a long way to go. But I'd like to stay with you if it won't be too much trouble. I do get tired of staying in hotels and of hardly ever getting a chance to meet the real people of any town or country where I happen to be performing. It sounds like fun to stay on a farm.'

'Good. That's settled then,' said Morag. 'You can take Inci over to the farm now, Giles, if you like. I'm sure you know the way. Lachlan will be there. Just tell him who you are and that Rachel and I will be there in about half an hour, as soon as we've shut up shop.'

Inci and Giles left the shop. As soon as the door had closed behind them Morag said, 'What a charming person. So modest too. A bit old for Giles, though, I would think. How old do you think she is?'

'About thirty-two or three,' said Rachel coolly.
'And there's nothing between her and Giles. He'd
have told me if there was.'

'I wouldn't be too sure of that,' scoffed Morag.
'Brothers, in my experience, have a way of being very
secretive about their love affairs.'

'It's not my brother whom she's interested in. It's
my husband,' retorted Rachel tartly. 'And I think
she's got a nerve coming all this way to see Ross,
knowing I'd be here, too,'

'You mean she's the woman who was at his flat when
you phoned him?' exclaimed Morag, her eyes round.

'Yes.'

'You'll be wishing I hadn't invited her to stay at the
farm then,' groaned Morag.

'No, I'm not wishing that. You did what you
wanted to do and I know you can't help being
hospitable.'

'I felt a bit sorry for her. She seemed so lonely and
sad. It can't be much fun having a career like hers,
wandering about the world and playing the piano in
foreign countries, without the company of your husband
or lover. Wouldn't be my bag at all. I like having my
nice hairy Lachlan to cuddle up to every night.'

'I just wish I knew what Giles was up to, bringing
her here,' said Rachel.

'Well, you'll be able to ask him when we get to the
farm. I'll invite Inci into the kitchen while I'm getting
supper. I bet she knows a few good recipes from
Turkey I could use.

Its whitewashed walls gleaming amongst the pine
trees and clustered around it, the Betons' house looked
solid and square on its green knoll, its windows
brimming with golden afternoon sunlight. Only Giles

was in the old-fashioned parlour. It was cluttered with huge mahogany glass-fronted cabinets full of old china and souvenirs from India and Africa and big overstuffed sofas and armchairs, their backs still protected from the greasy hair of sitters by antimacassars which had been crocheted by Lachlan's grandmother.

'Inci has gone off with Lachlan to look at the pigs,' Giles explained to Morag, as he stretched and yawned. 'I was just having a little shut-eye. I'm not used to getting up at first light and having to drive nearly two hundred miles. The only time we stopped was when we were on the ferry.'

'Well, you didn't have to come,' said Rachel sharply, sitting down on one of the sofas. Morag had gone, closing the door after her. 'Why didn't you let me know you were coming and bringing her with you?'

'Didn't get a chance to,' he replied, evasively she thought. 'She was a little surprised when I told her you weren't in Edinburgh, but insisted that she had to see you. She seemed so desperate and helpless that I offered to drive her up here if she would pay for the rental of a car. She jumped at the chance.' He leaned back, his hands behind his head. 'I think she's the most charming woman I've ever met,' he went on, as if he'd had a lot of experience with women. 'It's a pity she's already got a lover, or I wouldn't mind taking my chance with her. On the way here she told me she had a man friend with whom she lives when she's not on tour.'

'You and she must have got really chummy if she's been telling you about her private life,' snapped Rachel.

'And she seemed quite positive Ross would be here with you,' Giles continued blandly, looking up at the ceiling. 'Haven't you heard from him?'

'No. I was hoping you had seen him or had heard something of him,' she said, her shoulders sagging. 'Oh, Giles, I don't know what to do. I think he believed me when I said I want a divorce and that he's left me.'

'It would serve you right if he has, that's all I can say,' retorted Giles with brotherly frankness, and that was the end of their conversation because the parlour door opened and Inci came in followed by Lachlan.

For supper there was roast lamb, tiny new potatoes and green peas followed by marmalade pudding and custard. Conversation was kept light and general, Morag, Giles and Inci doing most of the talking. Rachel was feeling too miserable to join in much and Lachlan was always shy and taciturn when strangers were present. When the meal was over Inci made some excuse to go to the room where she was to sleep and Lachlan and Giles went into the parlour to watch television. Rachel stayed in the dining-room to clear the table and carry the used dishes into the kitchen to Morag who had started to wash up. She had almost finished when Inci came into the room offering to help.

'They are talking about the sport they call rugby and I do not understand it,' Inci said with a shrug. 'And since you are alone in here I think I had better take the opportunity to say what I have come all this way to say to you. The trouble is I do not know where to begin.' She sat down suddenly on one of the dining-chairs. 'It's so silly,' she whispered. 'Look at me. My hands are shaking because I'm afraid of you.' She held out square, muscular hands. Both of them were trembling slightly.

'You are afraid of me?' exclaimed Rachel, also sitting down and facing the other woman across the corner of the big oak table that was still covered with a white linen cloth. 'Why should you be afraid of me?'

'You're so calm and reserved, so proud, so self-contained, a little like Ross in some ways, and I've always been afraid of him. Both of you make me feel I am too mixed-up, over-emotional and excitable.' Inci laughed self-deprecatingly. 'What I am, of course. I am better at playing the piano than I am at dealing with people.'

'Everyone tells me I have too much pride,' admitted Rachel with a rueful smile, as she wondered uneasily what it could be the pianist had to say to her. Was she going to ask her to give up Ross? 'But please don't be afraid of me. I can be mixed-up and emotional too. What is it you have to say to me?'

Inci drew a deep breath, clasped her hands tightly together and plunged.

'I have to apologise for not telling you who I was and why I was staying in Ross's apartment when you phoned him last month. I wasn't there with him, Rachel. He was really in San Francisco. You see Ross and I . . .' Inci broke off, her hands pressed against her cheeks, and shook her head from side to side. 'Oh, I do not know how to explain to you about him and me,' she said.

'You and he have known one another for a long time, haven't you?' said Rachel gently, suddenly feeling sympathy for the beautiful and talented woman.

'Yes, we have.' Inci seemed to relax a little and her charming smile appeared. 'Over ten years and once, when we were young, we were very much in love with each other. It is so wonderful to be young, to have no worries or responsibility and to be in love, Rachel.'

'Yes, I suppose it is,' said Rachel, feeling envy uncoil within her because this woman had known Ross when he had been younger and had experienced with him something she herself had never known, the ecstasy of a young woman romantically in love with someone equally young.

'But then we were separated, rather cruelly, by my parents,' added Inci.

'Why?' exclaimed Rachel.

'It will be hard for you to understand, I know, but my parents did not approve of my going about with Ross. And they wanted very much for me to be a concert pianist. So after finishing my studies at the Juillard School of Music I was sent to Vienna to learn piano from a great teacher. Some years later, when I returned to New York, Ross and I started seeing each other again. It wasn't quite the same. We had both grown up and had changed. Some of the magic had gone. And then my parents were still against my having anything to do with him.'

'You let them influence you against him?'

'I guessed you would not understand because you have always been free to make your own decisions,' sighed Inci. 'You see, my parents suffer from what it known as the "ghetto" mentality. Even though they have lived for many years in the States they have never adapted to the American way of life. Their friends are all from Turkey and they want my brother and me to be like them, all the time. They are afraid they would lose us if they allowed us to grow up to be Americans. They want us to be Turkish always.'

'Then why didn't they stay in Turkey?' asked Rachel.

'A good question,' said Inci with a sad little smile. 'Why does anyone leave their own country to go and live in another? Often it is for political reasons but mostly it is for economic ones. Many people emigrate

to the States because they feel they will have a better
standard of living there. And if they work hard, it is
true, they do. But often it is difficult for the children of
immigrants to a new country. They are pulled in
different directions all the time. My brother and I
always wanted to be like the American kids we went to
school with, to adapt to their culture and be a part of it.
When we went home from school we found our
parents wanted us to follow their culture and even to
speak a different language. It made for great tensions
in our family. You understand?'

'I'm trying to,' said Rachel.

'But to get back to Ross and me. A year and a half
ago he asked me to marry him. It was time, he said, for
him to marry and to have a family. He wanted that
very much. I had to refuse.'

'Because of pressure from your parents?'

'Not entirely, although that did come into it. I had
decided that my career was more important to me than
marriage ever could be. I have a single-track mind,
can only do one thing at a time. I knew I couldn't be
the sort of wife he wanted or be the mother of his
children. It wasn't fair to either of us to get married to
each other, but it hurt me very much to refuse him.'
Inci's voice shook with barely controlled emotion and
she wiped tears from her eyes with the tips of her
fingers. 'Especially when he would have nothing more
to do with me and refused to be my lover,' she added
in a low voice.

'You expected him to want to be your lover after
you'd rejected his proposal of marriage?' exclaimed
Rachel, feeling sympathy with Ross, knowing how she
would have reacted to rejection out of her own pride
and self-esteem.

'Yes, I did. I couldn't see why we had to sever our

relationship just because I had refused to legalise it,' replied Inci. 'He didn't see it that way. He dropped me suddenly, as if I was something distasteful.' Inci's lips trembled and again she wiped tears away. 'I was very upset. It affected my playing,' she whispered.

'But you still tried to see him?'

'Of course I did. And why shouldn't I? I was still in love with him.' Inci managed to sound affronted, as if she had been the only one who had been hurt. 'But what does he do? He goes off in a huff and looks for someone else to marry, even though he still loves me. He found you and married you. I do not think I can forgive him for that.' Inci sniffed and blinked back tears.

Rachel stared at her. It looked as if Meryl had been right after all when she had suggested Ross had married only to create a smokescreen to hide his continuing affair with this woman.

'Is that why you have come?' she said stiffly. 'To tell me you and he are still lovers and to apologise for that?'

'I am here because Ross ordered me to come,' said Inci, and drew a long, sobbing breath. 'And when he gets angry and orders you to do something you do it. I was so pleased to see him, when he came to see me at my hotel in Edinburgh.'

'When? When did he see you in Edinburgh?' Rachel interrupted urgently.

'On Wednesday evening.'

'This past Wednesday?'

'Yes. And he said I must come to see you and explain what happened last month in New York.' Inci's voice trembled and she clasped her hands together nervously. 'He threatened me,' she added in a shocked whisper.

'How? Surely he didn't . . .' Rachel broke off, afraid that Ross had let his temper get the better of him.

'Threaten to hit me?' Inci's smile was twisted. 'No. Ross is much more subtle than that,' she said drily. 'He threatened to expose my secret affair with another man not only to my parents but also to my agent and the press. He said he would ruin my career if I didn't tell you the truth about why I was in his apartment when you phoned him. And I couldn't risk him doing that. I couldn't.'

'Why were you in the apartment?' Rachel forced the question out between dry lips.

'I was there because Ross had let me stay in the apartment while he was away in 'Frisco,' muttered Inci', who was obviously not enjoying making this confession. 'I was there with Julian,' she added in a whisper.

'Who is Julian?'

'He . . . we are lovers,' admitted Inci in a choked voice. 'He cannot marry me because he is already married to a woman who won't divorce him. He is an opera singer and we meet secretly wherever we can and whenever we can. He was appearing in New York last month so I asked Ross if he knew of a place we could rent for a few days, where we could be together without anyone knowing. He offered me his apartment. Ross wasn't there at all while we were there and we left before he returned.'

Rachel was silent, bereft of words by this story of romantic intrigue.

'I suppose I shouldn't have answered the phone,' Inci went on. 'But you know how it is when it goes on ringing. You always think it might be a matter of life and death, something important. I was scared when I heard your voice but I couldn't tell you who I was or why I was there. I couldn't betray my affair with Julian to a stranger.' She looked at Rachel. Once again her eyes were shining with tears. 'I didn't think of how you would feel about hearing me. It just never entered my head that you would think Ross and I were . . .' She broke off to sniff and made a gesture with one hand. 'I'm sorry, Rachel. Truly sorry. I hope you will accept my apology. I wouldn't want to be the cause of the break-up of your marriage to Ross.' Now she sounded as if she was repeating a lesson she had been taught.

'I think you've come too late,' said Rachel, coolly. She no longer found Inci charming but saw her now as a selfish, egotistical careerist, caring sincerely for no one but herself.

'Oh, no. Never say that.' Inci looked horrified and jumped to her feet. 'Please don't say that. Ross told me you had threatened to divorce him because of me. But you mustn't do that. You mustn't divorce him on account of his friendship for me. And that is all he is now, a friend. A most generous friend. But if you divorced him because of me it would really put a blight on my career, and it might come out that I have been having an affair with Julian.'

'It's all right,' Rachel said trying to sound reassuring, when it was she herself who needed reassurance most, she thought wryly. And comfort. The comfort of Ross's arms around her and his voice in her ear saying he forgave her lack of trust. 'I didn't really mean it when I told him I wanted a divorce. I'll try to find him and tell him you've been here and that you've explained why you were in the flat,' she added, rising to her feet. She felt she had had enough of this spoilt child of a woman.

'Oh, thank you, thank you.' Inci's smile was dazzling in its relief and for a moment she looked as if she might fling her arms around Rachel and kiss her. But something in Rachel's cool expression and possibly the proud, upright carriage of her head deterred her. She backed off and said lightly, 'Shall we go and help Morag? I think she is wonderful, this friend of yours, having a career and being a farmer's wife too. How does she do it? I think she must be a superwoman.'

Inci's explanation and apology, far from soothing Rachel, had stirred up her emotions. She left the farm as soon as she could, after saying she would see Giles and Inci the next day, and drove over the moors to Boskillin. If she couldn't be with Ross she had to be alone, tortured by remorse because she hadn't trusted him enough. Where was he? She longed to know so that she could rush to him and confess she had made a terrible mistake and that she was ready to resume their marriage, to live with him anywhere he wanted to live, to be with him always.

There was just one streak of light left in the sky when she reached the cottage and the loch glimmered with faint ghostly light. As usual all was quiet. She went into the cottage and as soon as she put on the light in the hallway she missed the silver chest. Puzzled, she turned into the kitchen and flicked on that light and stared in amazement. All the furniture had gone. The mats had been lifted from the flagged floor, and worst of all, the sink, draining boards and cupboards had been removed. Apart from the old-fashioned hearth and coal-fired oven beside it, the room was completely empty, cold, damp and unwelcoming.

Turning she dashed across the hallway to the bedroom. The mattress had gone from the floor and the bed-ends had been removed. Even the old wardrobe had gone. That room was completely empty too. The bathroom told the same story. The bath, the hand basin and the toilet had gone. There were only plugged drainage pipes jutting out of walls.

Someone had been in the cottage and had stolen everything out of it.

She ran from the cottage along the road to the Maclaines' house to bang on the front door with her fist. The door was soon opened by Archie, in his slippers. He was puffing at his pipe.

'Ach, so ye're home at last and himself only gone in the last half-hour to the town to look for ye,' he said in his sing-song voice.

'Who? Who has gone to the town to look for me?' she demanded breathlessly.

'Mr Fraser.'

'Ross? Ross has been here?' she squeaked and swayed against the jamb of the door.

'Come in and sit down for a wee while. You're all of a dither,' said Archie kindly, and she stepped past him into the narrow hall from which a stairway led up to the first floor of the house. She turned into the room on the right. Margaret was sitting at the table, knitting. She looked up and nodded at Rachel, her glasses flashing in the light.

'What pity ye didn't come home sooner,' she said. 'Ye've just missed him.'

'When did he come?' asked Rachel, sitting down on the chair that Archie pushed forwards for her and realising as soon as her hands touched the arms of it that it was the wing-chair from the cottage.

'Soon after ye left this morning,' said Archie, settling into his own chair by the hearth. 'Ach, a great day we've had of it moving all the stuff out of the house. Everything had to come out, he said. And he made sure it did. Ye'll see your chair is here. We're just minding it for ye. The rest of the furniture is in the barn at the back and will do there, he said, until the place is fixed up and you could decide what you wanted to keep. He took the bathroom furniture and the sink away with him on that fine truck he came in, said he'd get rid of it to a junk dealer or just take it to the dump.'

'I didn't know Ross was going to do this,' exclaimed Rachel. 'I got such a shock when I walked in just now and found the place empty.' She struggled to her feet, resisting a desire to give in, curl up in the chair and go to sleep. 'Did he tell you where he was going when he left?'

'He waited as long as he could for ye, and then said he supposed you'd stayed on at your studio to finish some work and he would go there to look for you, 'said Margaret. 'I think he said he had booked a room for both of ye at the hotel. Ye must have passed him on the road if ye came straight here.'

'No, I didn't. I've been at the Betons' and came back the other way,' Rachel replied, and hurried out into the hallway. Not finding her at the shop, Ross might go up to Pete's flat to ask where she was.

'Drive carefully now,' cautioned Archie as he saw her out of the house. 'There's a lot of mist about.'

The mist came and went, drifting suddenly in white gauzy scarves right across the road in front of her and often causing her to slow down and stop until it had cleared, but there was none in the town nor on the water which reflected the clear starlit sky

Feeling flutters of trepidation in her stomach at the thought that Pete might have said something about her to Ross, she parked the car in front of the shop and went around to the side door, from which the stairs led up to Pete's flat, and rang the bell. Soon she heard his feet clattering down the stairs. The light over the doorway went on, the door swung open and Pete stood there, looking dishevelled. He finished buttoning his shirt, raked back his hair and gave her a hostile glance.

'Sorry I'm not available tonight,' he sneered. 'I've found someone who isn't as strait-laced as you are.'

'I haven't come just to see you,' she retorted. 'I was told that Ross, my husband, has come here to look for me. Is he here?'

'No. But he was here. We had a few words and he left.' He rubbed the side of his jaw with his fingers and she saw it was slightly swollen.

'What happened?' she asked, but felt she knew. She was fast learning that, when Ross went into action, he acted forcefully and without compunction.

'You could say I collided with his left fist,' Pete said.

'Ross hit you? Why?'

'That is between him and me,' he retorted. 'He's not exactly what I expected. I thought you said he was a city gent. Seemed more like a lumberjack to me. He's gone to the hotel and he's expecting you. And the best of British luck to you. He's got one hell of a temper.'

She knew about Ross's temper, thought Rachel, as she coaxed her little car up to the hotel on the cliffs. He had never lost it with her, although she guessed he had come close to doing so. Usually he just smouldered and went about in a thunderous silence for a while. Then a couple of hours later he would be cool and calm, whatever had roused his rage apparently forgotten.

What had Pete said to him to make him lose it tonight? Something sneering about Americans? Or something of a more personal nature? Oh, she knew too well what a virulent tongue and filthy mind Pete possessed. He wasn't above saying something derogatory about her to Ross, just to get his revenge on her, for having turned down not only Ralph Bates but also him, the evening she had had supper with him and he had asked her to stay the night with him at his flat.

Noting that there was a red half-ton truck, loaded with the bathroom furniture from the cottage, in the car park of the hotel, she parked her car beside it and went into the entrance hall. It was quiet and rather dimly lit. At the reception desk she pinged the bell and waited. After a few moments the proprietor of the hotel came through a door behind the desk.

'Ah, Mrs Fraser. You've come just in time. It's almost midnight and I lock the doors then, for the night. As I was explaining to Mr Fraser, this isn't the United States and this isn't a motel or one of those big city hotels, where they have a night staff and guests can come and go at all hours. We're a private family-orientated hotel and we expect our guests to be in by midnight,' he said primly. 'Mr Fraser is in room five. That's on the first floor. Just turn to the right at the top of the stairs and go along the passage. You'll want breakfast in the morning?'

'I suppose so,' Rachel said, feeling suddenly exhausted. She hadn't realised it was so late and was glad that Ross with his usual foresight had booked a room for both of them and had told the proprietor to expect her.

Her legs ached as she went up the stairs and she had to rest at the top. It had been a long and rather traumatic evening, and the most difficult confrontation was yet to come. She had to force herself to walk along the passage to number five, all the way wishing that Ross had been given a room closer to the stairs.

Raising her hand to knock on the door of the room was a great effort but she made it, although she doubted if anyone inside could hear the weak tap. She tried turning the doorknob and pushing but, as she guessed, Ross, who was accustomed to staying in hotels and apartments in big cities where strict security rules applied and every room had to be double locked from the inside, had locked the door.

She knocked again harder and, drained of strength, leaned against the door and closed her eyes, not noticing the grate of a key in a lock. The door swung open and she went with it. She heard Ross exclaim 'Rachel. What the hell?' And then his arms were around her, supporting her and lifting her like a doll and she knew she was safe and could let go and let him take the responsibility for her. Her head drooped against his shoulder and darkness swooped down all around her.

When she came out of the faint she was lying on a single bed and a blanket was covering her. Hazily she looked around the room. Lit only by the bedside lamp on a table between the twin beds it was full of shadows and the glint of mirrors on the dressing-table and on the front of the wardrobe.

'Ross,' she said and was surprised to hear her voice creak like a rusty hinge on an old door. There was no answer so she lifted her head slightly from the pillow, laying it back quickly when everything swam before her eyes 'Ross? Where are you?' Her voice rose to a note of panic. Had he been here and gone again? Or had she knocked on the wrong door and been caught and lifted up by a stranger? 'Ross, I want you,' she said out loud, and for some reason felt better immediately and, closing her eyes, drifted into a doze.

The sound of the door closing awoke her and she opened her eyes. In pyjamas and dressing-gown Ross was coming towards the bed, a glass of water in one hand. He looked very tall, his shoulders seemed very wide and his hair was tousled. More like a lumberjack than a city gent. She remembered Pete's recent description and smiled a little.

'Why did you hit Pete?' she whispered.

He came to the bedside, sat down on the edge of the bed and stared at her.

'I guess I decided the time had come for him to realise he couldn't get away with the sort of filthy remarks he was making,' he said curtly. 'Why did you faint just now?'

'I don't know. I've never fainted in my life before.' She felt rather affronted that such a weakness had overtaken her, of all people. She had always prided herself on both her physical and her mental stamina. 'I think I'd just got over-tired, that's all. It was such a muddle of a day.'

She noted the sceptical glint in his eye and curl to his lip. She pushed herself up and took the glass of water from him. 'Thank you. There's nothing in it, is there? No drug or alcohol or anything like that?'

'I didn't put anything in it. Everyone in this place has gone to bed so there was no one to ask for brandy or anything else. I had to get that from the bathroom tap. Hope it's OK.' He watched her closely while she sipped some water. 'Is it?' he demanded.

'Yes. It tastes very good. But then the island water always does.' She put the glass down on the table. He was still staring at her, his expression dour and unrelenting. She guessed he was severely critical of her. She recalled Inci saying that Ross could be frightening and now knew what she had meant.

'Where did you go when the shop closed?' he asked abruptly.

'I . . . ' she began and stopped to give him another wary glance. Bone ridged white along his jaw, and his lips had thinned and there was a smoky flare in his eyes. She couldn't see his hands because they were thrust into the pockets of his dressing-gown, but she guessed they were clenched. Looking back at his face she said coolly, 'Why do you want to know?'

'Because I have a right to know.' He leaned towards her suddenly, his face so close to hers she could smell the soap he had used to wash with, and the strange sense-titillating musky scent of his hair. 'I'm your husband, remember.'

'Really?' she taunted, pressing back against the headboard, away from the sexy roughness of his unshaven cheeks and jaws. 'Since you left me over a week ago without a word I thought you had decided to give up the privilege of being my husband,'

His lips curved back over his teeth in a dangerous and tigerish grin but he didn't move away from her. In fact he inched closer and put an arm out across to support himself and effectively trap her, his hand resting on the blanket that covered her.

'A piece of advice, sweetheart: don't ever twitch the tiger's tail. He's likely to turn and savage you if you do. Now answer my question. Where did you go?'

'You wouldn't be jealous, would you?' she taunted, then gasped as he took over her shoulders and gave her a rough shake.

'You're damned right. I am,' he said through gritted teeth. 'That's why I hit your arty friend. When I asked him if he knew where you were he implied that you were probably visiting a boyfriend somewhere on the island, that you'd had a reputation for sleeping with all and sundry when he had known you at the art college, that you had even tried it on with him only a few nights ago. I saw red and hit him. If that's being jealous then I'm jealous. Where the hell have you been since the shop closed?'

'Oh, how mean of Pete!' raged Rachel, all weakness forgotten in her anger at Pete's lies. 'I've never slept around with anyone. Never. I'm not the promiscuous type. And it was he who tried it on with me a few nights ago and when I was at college. He and Ralph Bates, the teacher I once told you about, were nothing but lechers, making up to all the younger women students, both of them thinking they were God's gifts to the opposite sex.' She broke off, her breath hissing in outrage. Then seeing he was still looking at her sceptically, she said urgently, 'You do believe me, don't you?'

'Why should I?' he drawled nastily, his narrowed glance sweeping her face insolently. 'You didn't believe me when I told you I wasn't having an affair with Inci. Give me one reason why I should trust you when you've never trusted me. And answer my question. Where did you go when you left the shop?'

'I went home with Morag, to the farm, to have supper with her and Inci and Giles,' she replied steadily, warning herself that nothing would be gained by remonstrating with him about his arrogance.

'And?' he prompted her.

'And Inci told me everything, about you and her, about how you lent her and her lover the flat so that they could spend some time there.' She paused, not looking at him any more but very much aware, as always when he was close to her, of the fiery passion that swirled within him just below the cool surface. 'Inci still loves you,' she went on in a lower tone when he didn't speak. 'And now that I've met her I can understand why you still love her. It's a pity she felt she couldn't marry you because of the career. But I think if you were free and you asked her again she would marry you . . . '

She broke off to look up quickly because, with a muttered curse, he had stood up and had walked away from her into the shadows beyond the shaft of light from the bedside lamp.

'Ross?'

He came back and looked down at her, his eyes cold.

'You'd better get this clear. You've as much chance of getting me to agree to a divorce and freeing myself from marriage to you as a snowflake has of surviving in hell,' he said between taut lips. 'While you're carrying my child and there's a good possibility of it being born I'll not be divorcing you, and I won't allow you to separate from me or divorce me.'

'How did you find out I was pregnant? I didn't want you to know.'

'You mean you weren't going to tell me?' he rasped, his eyes beginning to blaze. 'You weren't thinking of terminating it, I hope?' Sitting down on the bed again, he glared at her threateningly and his voice was silky with menace. 'If you dare to . . . '

'No, no, of course I'm not,' she said quickly. 'I didn't want you to know because I didn't want you to think you had to stay married to me just because you'd made me pregnant. How did you find out? Who told you?'

'No one told me. And I didn't know for sure until just now,' he replied smoothly, the suspicion of a wicked grin flickering across his face before it hardened again. 'I'll just say again, there will be no divorce.'

'But now I know that you and Inci still love one another I'd rather not continue to be your second-best wife,' she complained.

'I do not love Inci,' he said, and every syllable dripped with ice. 'I lost interest in her when she refused to marry me because of her career. I think my feelings for her had changed while she had been away in Vienna but I hadn't realised it until she turned down my proposal. Your pride objects to your being a second-best wife, so you should be able to put yourself in my place. My pride won't let me play second fiddle to a woman's career, not even to yours. I warned you I had more than my fair share of pride, too, when we first met. Remember?'

He leaned towards her again and she felt desire begin to stir low down in her body.

'Yes, I do,' she whispered, not looking at him. She began to play with the tassel on the end of his dressing-gown belt which lay on the bed between them.

'You're my first and only wife, Rachel, and I'd very much like you to stay in that position. I've done my best to show you that I want you. I've taken you places, spent money on you. I let you come to Scotland when you wanted to and, when you refused to return to me in New York, I came over to join you, as soon as I could, to be with you. I'm even prepared to live with you on this island while you fulfil your commitment to Morag. But I can't see my way to living in that cottage the way it is.'

'But you've never said . . . ' she began.

'How many times do I have to tell you to stop butting,' he snarled suddenly, and got to his feet. 'It's late and I have to be up early to start work on renovating the cottage.'

'And that's another thing,' she interrupted quickly when he paused to draw breath. 'You had no right to take everything out of the cottage. No right at all.'

'Do you want me to live here with you for the summer?' he asked with another hint of silky menace in his tone.

'Yes, I do, but . . . '

'Then stop telling me what you think my rights are or aren't and get ready for bed. Your clothes are in your travelling-bags in the cupboard and the bathroom is along the passage.'

'You are . . .' she began again, and saw him step threateningly towards her. She slid off the bed at once, glad that she didn't feel dizzy any more. It seemed as if confrontation with Ross had revived her. Or perhaps it was his dynamic presence in the room plus the knowledge that he didn't love Inci any more that had perked her up. She soon found her clothes and, taking a nightgown and a dressing-robe from among them, she left the room to go to the bathroom.

When she returned Ross was sitting up in the other bed. Going over to the wardrobe, she took off her robe and hung it up.

'Seems to me you're over-dressed,' he drawled, watching her walk towards her bed.

'So are you,' she retorted, as she got into bed. 'But you once said that having to undress me makes making love more exciting.'

'That must have been when I was feeling less impatient than I do now.'

He waited until she had settled her head on the pillow and had arranged the sheet and blanket over her, then he switched off the bedside lamp. After a while she said tentatively, 'I thought you wanted me.'

'I do and it's hurting like hell,' he growled. 'But what about you? How many weeks pregnant are you?'

'I'm not exactly sure. About nine and a half.'

'You gave me a hell of a scare when you passed out. How do you feel now?'

'I feel fine. I think I must have hurried too much, or got too worked up when I saw what had happened at the cottage. And then Pete was so nasty. I think it happened the night before I left New York,' she added.

'What did?' His bed creaked as he turned on his side.

'The start of the baby. You were very loving.'

'That was because I wanted you to come back,' he replied in a low voice.

'You almost convinced me you loved me.'

'Only almost?' His voice was sharp and she guessed from the sounds that he had sat up. 'Why weren't you convinced?'

'You've never said it to me. You've never said you loved me.'

'You think that words are more important than deeds, then?' he rasped.

'Yes. I do.'

'Ha.' His laugh was short and mirthless. 'Then I've been wasting my time these past few months trying to show you by my treatment of you how I feel about you.' More movement and she guessed he had lain down again, his back to her. 'OK. We'll do it your way, since words are enough for you,' he taunted. 'I'll just say I love you, darling, goodnight, and you can answer in the same trite, empty way, and then we can both go to sleep.'

'Saying I love you isn't trite,' she argued.

'Sure it is. Too many people have said it to too many other people and haven't been sincere,' he retorted. 'It only means something when it's backed by deeds, by loving behaviour. You've told me you love me many times, but I've yet to see you back it up.'

'That isn't true. I have. I've . . . I've . . . ' She realised suddenly that apart from letting him make love to her and having cooked a few meals for him she hadn't done much at all for him, and she stuttered to a stop. She hadn't even trusted him.

The silence between them lengthened, became tense. Rachel acknowledged that there would be no sleep for her and probably none for him either, until one of them overcame the barrier of pride and made an approach to the other. Sliding out bed she went to him and lifting the covers, she got into bed beside him. There was hardly any room between him and the edge of the bed to lie comfortably. She had to cling on to him, her hand sliding over his waist and resting on the smooth skin of his solar plexus beneath the pyjama jacket. She heard him draw in his breath sharply.

'What do you want?' he said gruffly.

'To tell you I'm sorry I didn't trust you while I was away from you. I didn't mean it when I said I wanted a divorce.' She rubbed the tip of her cold nose against his back to warm it.

'Then why did you say it?'

'I wanted to see if I could hurt you. And I did try to show you I loved you and would be happy to resume our marriage, in spite of still suspecting you loved Inci more than me, that night we spent at the cottage. I couldn't have made love with you if I hadn't still been in love with you. Yet you went off in the morning without telling me where you were going, as if you didn't care any more about me.'

'I'd got the message that you still wanted me all right,' he said drily. 'But I had to make sure there really was no one else you preferred to me so I left you, while you were still sleeping, to go to the shop and have a chat with your friend Morag.'

'You went to see Morag? She didn't tell me.'

Indignation made her rear up to glare down at all she could see of him in the faint light that slanted in though the window, across which he hadn't bothered to pull the curtains.

'Because I asked her not to,' he said coolly. 'And you want to watch it. One more move like that and you're going to fall out of the bed.'

'What did Morag say to you?'

'Only that she was glad you had decided to help her out this summer and that she knew you had been hoping I would come to the island to stay with you for the summer. From her I got a clear indication that there was no other guy in your life, not even that randy type who makes pottery.'

'Then why didn't you stay? Why didn't you wait for me to arrive at the shop? Or you could have gone back to the cottage to see me and tell me what you were going to do next.'

'Sure I could have. But I was sore because you still believed I was carrying on an affair with Inci behind your back and you'd threatened to divorce me. I knew that Inci was due in Edinburgh to give a recital because she had told me, when I handed the keys of the apartment to her before I left for 'Frisco, so I went to Edinburgh to turn in the rented car and to buy a truck. I saw Inci, made her agree to come and explain to you what she'd been doing in the apartment. I didn't feel that it was my place to tell you about her having a lover. It was her secret, not mine. I also saw Giles and asked him to make sure she got here if he wanted me to continue the loan to him.'

'And he pretended he hadn't seen you at all, didn't know where you were. Oh, just wait until I see him again tomorrow.'

'I also phoned Morton,' continued Ross calmly, ignoring her outburst, 'and told him I was taking six months off to be here with you while you do your thing. He was very understanding and wished me luck, as I knew he would. Then I came back here.'

'You've been in this country all the time!' she exclaimed furiously. 'Why didn't you tell me what you

were going to do before you left me? And why didn't
you let me know you were coming back?'

'I guess I wanted to you to sweat a little, believing
I'd left you for good,' he replied with a lilt of mockery.
'Call it my revenge on you for not trusting me and for
threatening to divorce me,'

'Oh, you . . . you . . . ' she spluttered.

'Are you speechless at last, my darling? Aren't
words of use to you any longer?' he taunted, turning
slowly to face her. Then, his voice sharpening
warningly when, after snatching up the pillow, she
began to hit him with it, he said,' Hey, look out.
You're going to . . . '

She fell out of bed and lay on the floor, all the breath
knocked out of her.

'I hope you didn't hurt yourself,' Ross whispered as
he knelt down beside her. He lifted her and held her
close to him. She could hear his heart beating strongly
beneath her ear. 'You're not crying?' Under her chin
his fingers were gentle.

'No, I'm laughing. And I'm not hurt. Not a bit.'
She touched his face. Beard bristles rasped against the
tips of her fingers.

'I did ask for a room with a double bed but it seems
they don't go in for them. The tourists they get must
be a lot of celibates,' he said.

His lips found hers in the darkness with the hard,
dominating kiss that she had been longing for and,
while he had her at his mercy, he began to slip the
straps of her nightgown down until her breasts were
bared. As soon as his lips burned against her delicate
skin her body arched against him and she moaned in
an agony of pleasure, her fingers sliding into his hair
and slipping down to caress his nape.

'I've been longing for you to do that,' she groaned.

'Please do it again.'

'You know what will happen if I do.' His voice was thick with passion. 'Dare we risk doing it?'

'I think so.'

'But not here, on the floor. Nor in one of those narrow beds,' he said, standing up and helping her to her feet. 'We'll take the mattresses off the beds and put them together on the floor.'

Soon they were lying entwined. He was very gentle with her, so gentle that tears brimmed in her eyes as she realised how much he cared for her welfare and for that of the embryo in her womb and, although she could tell he was eager to possess her, he kept his passion in check until she was fully aroused and pleaded with him to come into her, so that together they could experience again the magic and mystery of physical union and fulfilment.

'I love . . .' she began when it was over and at once he stopped her mouth with kisses.

'You don't have to say it. You're beginning to learn to show that you do,' he mocked.

'You didn't have to go to all the trouble of renovating the cottage,' she whispered, her head resting on the satin smoothness of skin, stretched taut over the bone and muscle of his shoulder. 'I was going to tell you, that morning you left before I woke up, that I was sorry I hadn't trusted you over Inci and that I would go back with you to New York.'

And what about the little matter of my loan to Giles?' he asked with gentle mockery.

'I'd decided to forget about that because I wanted to live with you again so much,' she admitted in a low voice.

'Good. I'm glad that it's sometimes possible to get through that pride of yours.'

'But I hope you still don't think I married you so that you would give him the loan,' she said anxiously.

'You were so adamant about wanting to pay it back and about asking me to cancel it that I believed you when you said you knew nothing about it when I proposed to you. I guess I should never have told him I'd lend him the money once I had persuaded you to marry me. Then there wouldn't have been any misunderstanding on your part. And I had no intention of bribing you into marrrying me. I wanted you badly but only on the up and up. There were to be no underhand deals. I know it was a hasty marriage, but I was scared you'd get away before I could catch you. I took a gamble on love and hoped it would pay off. Do you believe me?'

'Yes.'

'And trust me?'

'Oh, yes. It's going to be so wonderful living with you again without having to worry about Inci or Giles,' she said with a happy sigh as she snuggled against him.

'I agree with you. I like living with me, too, especially when you're around.'

And for once Rachel didn't argue with him. Warm and safe in his arms she relaxed, not wanting to spoil the intimacy of the moment. Through her own pride and wilful behaviour she had almost destroyed their hasty marriage. Now she could only be glad that he was proud, too, and determined always to get his way, using whatever means came to hand. If he hadn't been like that . . .

It didn't bear thinking about, she decided hastily. He was here, they were together, and never, never would she let anyone or anything come between them again.

Harlequin Presents

Coming Next Month

Available in April wherever paperback books are sold, or through Harlequin Reader Service:

In the U.S.
901 Fuhrmann Blvd.
P.O. Box 1397
Buffalo, N.Y. 14240-1397

In Canada
P.O. Box 603
Fort Erie, Ontario
L2A 5X3

Have You Ever Wondered If You Could Write A Harlequin Novel?

Here's great news—Harlequin is offering a series of cassette tapes to help you do just that. Written by Harlequin editors, these tapes give practical advice on how to make your characters—and your story— come alive. There's a tape for each contemporary romance series Harlequin publishes.

Mail order only

All sales final

CRESSIDA WAS SURPRISED TO FEEL RUSHTON'S HAND JUST BEHIND HER ELBOW AS HE BEGAN WHISKING HER TOWARD HER CHARIOT

"You planned this, didn't you, vixen!" he murmured into her ear as he saw Lord Somersby reprehensibly flirting with Daphne.

"Mr. Rushton," Cressida whispered with a sincere smile. "I beg you will believe this much, Somersby is not part of any scheme of mine, but I must see Daphne settled. You are not wrong to suppose I have not come here without design, but I forewarn you to stay out of my way."

"I shall be only too happy to oblige you, madam." He returned her gaze squarely, his thoughts inscrutable. A rather slow, wicked smile overtook his features.

Cressy felt in his expression the most dangerous tug upon her heart. "What absurdity is this?" she murmured softly, her pulse alive and almost wild suddenly. How could a smile do so much to her heart? It seemed impossible that such a man could have affected her so strongly. Especially because she despised Rushton! He was everything she disliked in a man—proud, officious, overbearing.

Why then did she feel positively dizzy?

A Lady's Gambit

Valerie King

ZEBRA BOOKS
KENSINGTON PUBLISHING CORP.

Chapter One

The roads in England were gradually improving ever since a certain John Macadam discovered a very simple method of laying a uniformly shaped rock on the road. Travel had become easier and safer and to some degree slightly more comfortable.

But to Cressida Chalcot, whose whip was poised high in the air over the back of the most recalcitrant and useless piece of horse flesh behind which she had ever had the misfortune to sit, the fine road of crushed rock was of little benefit. The horse—if the ancient creature could be termed that—had stopped in the middle of the King's highway and refused to budge.

What was worse, the mulish gelding had chosen just such a curve in the road, lined with trees, as to make her position rife with danger.

"Mr. Percival!" she cried, pleaded, and cajoled. "Do take a step! Just one for me! I promise a carrot, or two, or a bushel of sweetmeats if you should so desire once we are returned to the manor, only do but move!"

She was reluctant to employ her whip again, having already stung him twice alongside his flanks and once at just the tip of his ear in an effort to persuade him out of the sullens. All he would do, however, was look back at her with a pitiful expression as though to say she was a brute of no mean order for having required the trek of

5

him in the first place.

Cressida knew the truth. He was simply stubborn and old and wished for his comfortable stall and a bucket of oats rather than the noxious task of transporting a lowly companion, employed at Wellow Priory, to the village of Mendip Combe. Not a companion, precisely. If Cressy were to describe her duties, she would place herself somewhere between a lady-in-waiting to Mrs. Cameley and that of a lower servant. She penned all of Mrs. Cameley's correspondence, organized her societal functions, served tea to her neighbors, and played sonatas, airs, and dances upon the pianoforte for the same guests, but at the same time was generally expected to discharge every insignificant errand the priory's mistress wished accomplished.

She was headed for Mendip Combe to pick up a parcel of fish, for instance! Cook had need of it for the evening's dinner.

Feeling somewhat ill-used as well as wondering for the hundredth time whether or not her future would ever show a glimmer of advancing toward her, Cressida tied the reins securely to the creaking cart and carefully descended the serviceable vehicle. She did not wish to catch her fine pelisse on the splintered wheels, or the chipping paint of the body of the cart. Her clothing was nearly all that was left to her, and to her sister, for that matter. She protected every delicate fiber of it with the greatest of care.

Her half-boots had just touched the rock, when to her dismay she heard the faint sounds of an approaching carriage. Taking a firm hold on the halter, she moved quickly to the head of the horse and began drawing the gelding forward one slow step at a time.

The sounds of the approaching vehicle, however, loomed ever nearer. She could hear that the carriage was moving briskly—too quickly in fact for the narrow, winding country road.

"Oh, Mr. Percival," she whispered, her heart beginning to pound in her chest, her head dizzy with sudden fear. "If you have even an ounce of sense left in your short, heavy bones, please come!" She gave a hard tug, and though the horse resisted her efforts at first, she felt him finally acquiesce as he took several plodding steps forward and to the side, the entire unhandsome equipage moving to the left of the lane.

Even so, as a natty curricle and pair rounded the bend at a speed Cressy could only think of as suicidal, she could see there would be but inches to spare.

"Hell and damnation!" a dark, masculine voice cried out. "Get that confounded cart off the road! Imbecile!"

Cressy continued to pull and tug, as the curricle bore down on her cart and horse. A collision was imminent. The carriages would collide and the air explode with the sounds of shattering wood and screaming horses. No one could pass safely in such a confined space.

Squeezing her eyes shut, yet determined to keep a firm hold on her horse, she prepared for the worst.

Within three seconds, the curricle whirled safely by the cart. Impossible!

Cressy's eyes flew open as she patted her horses's nose, all the while stunned by the gentleman's feat. She stared at his back, a cloud of dust from his quickly spinning wheels billowing up around her. She had been so certain a terrible accident would ensue she could scarcely order her thoughts. What manner of skill did such a man possess? He did not even graze Mrs. Cameley's poor cart!

She began coughing from the settling of the dust as she moved away from Mr. Percival and prepared to climb aboard her vehicle once again. She still could not credit a collision had been averted and wished she could express her gratitude to the man for his extraordinary negotiation of the lane, when she noticed that the gentleman had brought his curricle to a halt, secured the reins, and was now retracing on foot the quarter mile which separated them. She supposed he meant to see if she was in need of assistance and began to feel quite warmly toward the apparent nonpareil who combined such marvelous skill with the wonderful attributes of compassion and consideration.

How kind of him! she thought.

She touched her shallow-brimmed poke bonnet, pushing away straying strands of her light brown hair, wondering if perhaps her face had become dirtied since having left the manor. Taking in the stranger's appearance at a quick glance, somehow it became supremely important that she appear, if not entirely modish, then at least elegant and neat.

He possessed a striking countenance, she noted, as he strode toward her with his arms in a wide, purposeful swing. His coat of what appeared to be a blue superfine was positively molded to a pair of broad shoulders. How many *fish*, she wondered, did it require to gain such perfection of cut and fit! The lapels of his coat, slashed with a neat "W" were neither narrow nor wide, permitting his fine chest to fill the lines of the coat. No need of buckram wadding there! His shirt points were of a medium height, and his neckcloth was tied and folded in a series of interesting creases. His own creation? The coat met a narrow waist and fell away to tails of simple design. Fawn-colored breeches, probably of soft doeskin, revealed muscular yet lean legs. An athlete, unquestionably. Top boots, covered in dust from the roads, and a hat of brushed beaver completed the portrait of a gentleman of some means. She longed to ask him whether Stultz or Weston had made up his clothes. She had a great interest in both men and women's fashions, and in the skill required to fit a garment so well to the human form.

As she surveyed the stranger, she knew the master who had overseen the construction of his coat alone, had probably rejoiced in how well his workmanship became the gentleman's figure. He was a very well-proportioned man.

When Cressy had sufficiently scrutinized his clothing, a habit she had developed years earlier, only then did she notice the man's face. He wore a rather stern expression, his gaze fixed to the road as though deep in thought. He took his hat off his head and began thumping it over his clothes as though to rid himself of at least some of the perpetual, clinging traveling dirt, then resettled the hat over his black hair.

As he drew near, within twenty-five yards, she took in her breath sharply. He was quite one of the handsomest men she had ever seen! His eyes, as he looked up at her, however sharp in expression, were a startling blue. His brows were thick and arched, the lines of his face very definite, almost rugged. His chin was firm, his nose straight, and his nostrils flared slightly. This last observation brought her up short. Compassion did not rule him in this moment, not in the least. The gentleman was clearly angry.

But why? she wondered.

Chapter Two

Mr. Gregory Rushton could not abide two things—a lady who set her cap for a man, *any man*, and an incompetent upon the highway.

Before him was the latter, and he had spent the past three minutes, while accomplishing the distance between his curricle and the wretched-looking cart up the lane, in rehearsing the severe dressing-down he meant to deliver to the ridiculous young woman now standing beside her cart.

He swept his gaze over her, and his first impression was a confused one. For though she wore a dull straw bonnet, neither fashionably trimmed nor fashionably large, her pelisse was of a beautiful blue silk, embroidered with acanthus leaves in a gold floss. Glancing at her feet, he saw worn half-boots protruding from beneath the hem. A country hat, expensive silk, scuffed boots? He didn't know quite what to make of her.

He wondered if perhaps she had "borrowed" her mistress's pelisse, and toyed with the notion of turning her over to the local constable, in—what the devil was this outlandish place?—Mendip Combe! Well, it was no concern of his whether she was a thief or some sort of eccentric. He had only one duty to perform—to tell the wench in no uncertain terms that she ought to leave off driving and make further and better use of her worn boots by walking to whatever destination beckoned her.

When he shifted his gaze to meet hers, he was impressed with how directly she regarded him. She did not lower her eyes, as he had fully expected her to in shame for her disgraceful driving skills, but rather regarded him in what he perceived to be a challenging manner. He almost felt a stir of interest, if that were possible. He had been on the town for so long, and had been made the object of so many ambitious females, that he could number on one hand the occasions in which a lady had actually captured his fancy—but then for scarcely more than a sennight. Not that he fancied this female, precisely. It was merely that he admired her unreserved manner of meeting his stare. No coquetry, no fear.

She was pretty, too, though in an entirely country fashion. Her hair, being an uninteresting shade of brown, was her least attractive feature. The rest of her seemed competently beautiful. Her complexion was creamy and touchable, and her lips were, if not inviting, then well-shaped. Her cheekbones were delightfully pronounced and gave a poetically Grecian cast to her looks. Her nose was small, though not pert, just very, very lovely. And her eyes—the devil take it!—the nearer he drew, he came to realize they were an unusual, quite exquisite shade, which he could only term as violet.

His interest was again ruffled, like a breeze rippling the surface of a lake. A country miss! Seducible? He wondered. The stiff manner in which she was standing did not encourage his thinking in that direction. If anything, she appeared prudish, almost disapproving.

Forgetting his interest in the young woman, since he had a serious duty to discharge, he took a sharp breath through his nose and opened his mouth to speak. But before he could utter a syllable, *she* spoke!

"You were driving far too fast, you know," she said archly. "A great deal too fast for our poor country lanes! I'm sure you don't mind my giving you a hint, for you

11

seem just the sort of amiable person as to welcome reproof. In the future, I hope you will be better able to keep your horses in check!" She then smiled, tilted her head in what he could clearly see was a facetious manner, dropped a small curtsy, and proceeded to clamber up into the hapless cart.

He was dumbstruck, a firm silence holding his tongue steadfastly quiet. Never, in his entire existence, had he met with such impertinence! And never had a young woman dared to cross him, and how dare she criticize his driving!

"Oh, dear," she simpered, her gloved hand held to her cheek in mock dismay. "Have I offended you? I daresay I must have for you have the distinct appearance of a satyr in this moment. Your brows are drawn together with such ferocity, and are those horns sprouting from just beneath your hat? Dear me! I vow I shall faint at such an angry look! How, sir—pray tell me, do *tell me*—how have I wounded your sensibilities? Until I know, I shan't have a notion how to go about begging your pardon!"

She wasn't merely impertinent, she was outrageous. "Cut the theatrics!" he snapped. "I don't see why, having not even been introduced to you, you must take to immediately playing off these airs and criticizing my driving! Especially when you and this ridiculous hack were nearly the cause of—"

"Hush, hush!" she whispered, glancing in a meaningful way toward her horse. "Mr. Percival is quite the most sensitive creature I have known in all my existence. He couldn't bear hearing your biting remarks upon his worth. Oh dear, I apprehend you are of a similar delicate disposition, are you not, for you are still frowning and have a pained glint in your eye. Well, you are most fortunate, since I am of a generous inclination and most graciously recant every word I have addressed to you and most sincerely beg your pardon!"

"I am not of a delicate disposition!" he countered, aware that he had somehow lost complete command of the conversation before it had begun.

She clicked her tongue and began untying the reins. "And proud, too! My goodness gracious what a dreadful set of flaws you possess. I have never before seen so many brought together in one man—proud, officious, ill-tempered, ill-mannered, and entirely lacking in compassion." She slapped the reins of her horse against Mr. Percival's back, clicking to him at the same time. The cart slowly moved forward, a fact which seemed to surprise the young woman. "Good day, sir!" she finished over her shoulder.

"You will not go!" Rushton cried, taking several steps toward the cart and setting his feet in stride with the slow movements of the equipage. "I refuse to permit you to leave me standing here when I have not yet even—"

"It would appear you are not standing at all," she observed, glancing down at his boots which were marching quite forcefully in step with the turning of the cart wheels.

He somehow could not keep from laughing. "You are quite the most audacious female I have met. But you must stop! I say you must!" He quickly leaped up, hooking a foot onto the bed of the cart and grabbing the reins from her. With a brisk tug he brought Mr. Percival to a halt, which set the old horse to complaining with a series of huffs and grunts.

"Now you've done it!" she cried. "I shan't get him to move another inch. I have spent the past hour trying to persuade this horrid beast to take me to the village and now that he has suffered a little excitement and was actually prepared to walk again, what must you do, but bring him to a halt! I am inclined to switch conveyances with you in order that you might suffer his ill temper instead of me!"

"You shouldn't live out the hour were you to try!" he retorted, sitting down beside her upon the cramped seat. "I don't permit anyone to drive my grays!"

Cressy folded her hands tightly upon her lap. She was

very nervous and held her back straight out of the sheer discomfiture she felt at having brangled with the man, who was now actually sitting beside her. She had not meant to come the crab over him, but when he had approached her with just the look in his eye of an angry governess she used to have, she resorted to an aggressive attack which she had hoped would set him about his business.

She had misjudged him, however, dreadfully so. Not only had he not been sufficiently repulsed, but he was now sitting uncomfortably close beside her. She had few hopes of winning the war at this point and desired only that he not realize how nervous she had grown. "What are you about, sir!" she cried. "I beg you will get down immediately from my cart. I have an errand to discharge for my mistress, and she is expecting me to return, er, at least before the sun sets!"

"Then you are a governess."

"No, that office belongs to my sister. I am a—" she found it difficult to speak the words. As a girl growing up and cherishing every hopeful vision of a beautiful future she had never thought that one day she would be serving as the companion to a nervous creature who obliged her to fetch fish at the receiving office. "I am a companion to a prominent woman in the neighborhood."

She sensed that something she had said had disturbed him. She glanced up at him and saw that he was staring at her with narrowed eyes. A hint of steel flashed in the startling blue of his pupils, and she felt a terrible dread prickle all over her.

But the expression passed, and in its stead was a softer look, even appreciative as he leaned closer to her and said, "You were right, of course, I oughtn't to have been driving my horses quite so hard. I'm afraid I let my enjoyment of the sport get the better of my good sense."

Cressy frowned slightly as she searched his eyes, wondering what he was about. She wasn't certain she trusted him and after inclining her head graciously,

14

responded, "That's very handsome of you! And I in turn apologize for my ungracious remarks. But if you wouldn't mind, I do have fish to retrieve. Besides, your presence in my cart would hardly be considered proper conduct."

He gave her the reins, which she took with a swell of relief, only to have him catch her round the shoulders with one arm, and with his free hand take her chin, forcing her to look at him.

"You're an exquisite creature," he breathed.

She was thoroughly, completely outraged as he held her in a fierce embrace and pressed a painfully hard kiss on her mouth. She wanted to struggle against him, but the confinement of the small cart as well as the knowledge that she held the reins, and therefore the recalcitrant Mr. Percival in her charge, permitted her to do little more than utter protests in her throat. She tried to move her face away from his, but each time she did, his lips found hers again and again. She felt ridiculous and angry all at the same time. Still he would prevail, and it seemed she had little choice but to submit to his horrid assault.

When she grew quiet, resigned to her fate, she tried to direct her thoughts to anything else—to the state of the weather, to the recent copies of *La Belle Assemblee* she had received, to whether or not Daphne would be turned off without a reference for the fifth time in the space of two years—but to little avail. She was drawn into the terrible kiss by how much it had changed. The stranger's insistent manner had completely disappeared and in its stead was a remarkable softness, a gentleness, which—heaven forbid!—had begun working a charm on her. She experienced a most peculiar sensation that in him she had somehow met her ideal. She remembered how struck she had been by the beauty of his person, by his handsome countenance, by the brilliant blue of his eyes, by the confidence in his stride when first she had seen him approach her cart.

15

To her horror, therefore, she found herself actually enjoying his kiss. But how could she? Not only was she unacquainted with the man, but he was just the sort she had always despised—proud, overbearing, willful.

Why then did she feel she had been kissed by heaven? His touch seemed to reach some hidden part of her, burrowing up longings she had suppressed for years, wishes which had no part of her precarious future. For this one moment, her girlish dreams seemed to rise all about her, and she knew a sense of loss so dreadfully acute that it felt like a physical pain in her chest.

He drew away from her finally, only to stare at her with an expression of confusion furrowing the lines of his face. He appeared as though he wished to say something, but could not.

She lowered her gaze, not wanting to look into his eyes, nor to see the future she would never have somehow held captive in his visage. "I wish you would go now," she said quietly.

"It was never my intention—" he began.

"Never your intention?" she queried, a strange, sudden anger taking hold of her. "Never your intention to do what? To kiss me? I wouldn't give it a second's thought or worry, if I were you. Do you suppose you were the first? Hardly. I exonerate you entirely from your guilt. Now you may go without a single blight upon your conscience!"

His face seemed to harden, his jaw working strongly as he watched her. "I suppose I would not be the first, would I? I imagine a young woman in your station of life has many such opportunities."

Cressy ought to have been angry, but since she had never before been kissed, even though several importuning gentlemen had attempted to do so, she now saw the situation as having an amusing aspect. "Oh, indeed, yes," she responded with a laugh. "A score of opportunities, to be sure!"

He did not seem pleased with her reaction and with a

light, quick movement, leaped from the cart, flourished a mockingly low bow to her, then returned to his curricle on a brisk step.

In her current state of restless unhappiness, Cressy gave the reins a hard snap, and to both her surprise and relief Mr. Percival, at last recognizing a command he could understand, jolted forward and began a final plodding trek to the village.

Chapter Three

Cressida bent her head over the fish, alongside Cook, the latter of whom did not hesitate to give her opinion. "La, it smells like rotting cabbages! And it were guaranteed fresh! 'Tis probably that girl at the receiving office—held it up, no doubt. She's half a brain if she's got one a'tall!" They were standing in the dark, gloomy kitchen of Wellow Priory, situated in the heart of the rolling hills of Gloucestershire, inspecting the dubious package Cressy had finally secured.

"Mrs. Cameley won't be pleased," was all Cressy could think to say. She was relieved of giving further comment by the sudden interruption of Mrs. Booth, the housekeeper.

"Miss Chalcot!" she cried. "Oh, do come at once and be quick about it! We've a terrible storm brewing. The mistress wishes to see you and I fear she's taken a terrible pelter!"

Cressy felt the blood drain from her face. For nearly a fortnight she had been experiencing a familiar anxiety. Not anything tangible, precisely, just a queer feeling she had come to recognize boded ill for the future of her sister's employment. Maybe it was the way Daphne had taken to floating about the halls of the ancient manor house that had first sent a queasy sensation twisting through her stomach, or perhaps Daphne's forgetfulness, more pronounced than usual, was the cause of her mounting disquietude, or it might even have been due to the decided mooncalf expression which had dominated Lord Somersby's countenance since his arrival a fortnight earlier.

Whatever the case, any of these wretched symptoms could have brought about the slow churning of her stomach which had begun afflicting her almost hourly. She might not have been entirely cognizant of the signs, but her stomach certainly was, and had been warning her of impending doom for some time now.

As it was, she had little doubt as to the object of Mrs. Cameley's dissatisfaction. It could only be Daphne and her influence upon Mrs. Cameley's guest, Lord Somersby!

Of the five excellent homes from which Daphne Chalcot had been dismissed over the past several years, four of them were for reasons involving the adoring advances of one or the other of the family's eldest sons. Her expulsion was always for the same reason—however extraordinarily beautiful Daphne might be, she was not considered a suitable bride for any gentleman with even modest needs for either a fortune or for sensible conversation. Cressy remembered in particular the accurate words of one former employer, a very fine, perceptive woman, who said, "She hasn't a dowry, nor a particle of either sense or intelligence! She is a beautiful, indeed, at times a delightful widgeon. But you would do well, my dear, to take her to Bath and see her settled upon some old gentleman who can support her in comfort and generally not give a fig for such matters as rational thought, order in his household, or the flirtations which would undoubtedly ensue from every buck within twenty miles of her home! Go to Bath, Cressida, and dispose of her however you might, otherwise you will be saddled with her the remainder of your days!"

Cressy had nodded several times throughout the woman's speech. She had found nothing in her lecture with which she could, as an intelligent creature, disagree.

It had been a most lowering moment. The only flaw in the woman's scheme, however, had been the impossible idea of taking Daphne to Bath. They had not funds enough to spend a sennight there, nonetheless enough time to woo a husband for Daphne. Polite society, *tonnish* society, could be rather hard on one's purse.

Neither she nor Daphne were situated well. Both parents had perished some five years earlier—drowned in a yachting accident. Afterward, it was discovered that her beloved father had been improvident in the extreme and had left his daughters without a feather to fly with. Of the two sisters, Cressy had a slight advantage, having received a small competence upon the death of a distant cousin of her mother's but a year prior to the funerals of her parents.

At one time she had indeed considered making use of it in order to establish her sister—it might even have been possible to spend an entire summer in Bath, provided she could prove clever enough with the managing of every tuppence which dared to pass through her fingers. But to do so, to risk such an enterprise without being assured of a happy result, would mean to perhaps give up forever that small portion which fate had allotted to her as a shelter, meager though it was, against the adverse winds of life.

For five successive employments, therefore, Cressy had refused to alter her plans of seeing Daphne well employed. Perhaps she was being selfish, even cruel by insisting her dimwitted sister apply herself to the task of earning a wage. She had always intended, once Daphne was self-supporting, to open her own shop as a modiste in whatever town happened to be closest to her sister. She would have preferred to have kept Daphne with her. But it soon became apparent that in order for her scheme to succeed she could not take on the added expense of a shatterbrained female, who set but the crookedest of stitches and who possessed a propensity to cause scandal—however innocently contrived such scrapes might be—upon whatever path she placed her small, pretty feet.

If only she could have been guaranteed of finding a suitable gentleman, she would surely have taken up an expensive residence in Queen's Square, in the very center of Bath, without a moment's hesitation.

Now, facing the prospect of Daphne losing her sixth position of employment, Cressy stood outside the doors of the drawing room, her hands clutched to her bosom. She did not wish to open the door and learn in its entirety the source of her mistress's dissatisfaction. Perhaps she was mistaken. Perhaps Mrs. Cameley had merely misplaced her best gloves as she had three weeks ago and had subsequently fallen into a fit of hysterics.

She leaned her head against the cool oak of the door and listened intently for the mewing sound the mistress was used to making when she was particularly overset. None issued forth. Cressy took in a difficult breath and tried to still the hammerings of her heart. She could be mistaken. It was possible!

Beneath her breath she murmured, "Possible? Were I living on the moon, it might be possible. Courage, Cressida!"

Finally, she pushed the door open and took several bright, quick strides deep into the chamber.

The room, littered with tables and overstuffed sofas and chairs, seemed to be alive as it rolled in a series of shadowy waves beneath the light spilling from several windows along the south wall. Cressy was struck by the vision of Mrs. Cameley, swathed in the delicate folds of several silk shawls, reclining on a chaise longue. Her ethereal form was bathed in one of several lakes of sunlight. The heavy fragrance of attar of roses permeated the air and blended with the bouquet of several spiced bowls of the manor's homemade potpourris. The effect was blinding, both to Cressy's eyes and nose. She wondered if somehow Mrs. Cameley's ailments didn't emanate from a chamber so overpowering in its sensory

21

displays. She herself had succumbed to the headache upon more than one occasion when she was required to remain within the confines of the drawing room for extended periods. A brisk walk through the manor woods, however, had generally sufficed to relieve the pain.

"Mrs. Cameley," she began politely, "Mrs. Booth has given me to understand you wished to speak with me, that you had a concern of some urgency to lay before me."

"Yes," the mistress whispered faintly. "It is a most grievous duty I must perform. I am referring of course to Daphne. Though I am quite fond of her and she is certainly a vision upon which to rest one's eyes— Somersby can attest to that, I'm sure—I fear I cannot possibly do otherwise than to dismiss—"

"Please, Mrs. Cameley," Cressida interrupted, standing very still except for the loud knocking noise of her knees banging together. She experienced the most desperate sensation as one might when engaged in a battle for one's existence. "I know what you mean to say, only I do beg of you to reconsider. I'm sure once Daphne has become more accustomed to the children and to your home—"

"Accustomed to the children?" Mrs. Cameley exclaimed. "They adore her, which makes it all the more unfortunate! I have no complaints on that matter, though I must say, Cressida, I was a bit misled as to the scope of her abilities. I have begun to wonder if she has even learnt all her letters."

"Well, of course she has," Cressy returned easily, knowing she could not err in this. She had drilled Daphne on her letters only last summer, and she was certain her sister could recite the alphabet by heart. She realized, too, Mrs. Cameley was naturally referring to how well Daphne employed such a vastness of knowledge. "It may of course be true that she does not read as well as some—"

"Cassie tells me she has to correct her every other word. Even you must admit when a child of ten exhibits greater ability than her governess—"

"Cassie is exceptionally intelligent, which can account for any disparity."

"Which only argues my case further. Cressy, I'm sorry, you and your sister must go. If the truth be known, I only took you both on out of consideration for—for the memory of your dear mama. Indeed, you, Cressy, have been of the utmost use to me. You have been far more efficient than any of the servants I have ever employed, and as for the carriage dress of twilled sarsenet you made up for me! Well, even Lady Brockley begged me to tell her from which London establishment I had purchased so elegant a creation. Though I did think it quite unhandsome of her to exclaim that she felt blue an unbecoming shade for my complexion.

"But I have wandered from the point! I do not regret a single farthing I have disbursed for your employment as my companion. As you know, I was not seeking to hire a companion and only agreed to it because I felt it to be my Christian duty. By the way, did you get the fish?"

Cressy nodded, thinking if she paid her servants as poorly as she paid her *companion*, it was no wonder they did not slave for her. "Yes, ma'am. But as I was saying, I wish you would consider giving Daphne a sennight more, perhaps, to prove her worth to you and to your daughters."

Mrs. Cameley, who enjoyed a serious weakness of will and temperament, fumbled for her vinaigrette through a maze of vials and boxes scattered upon a small table at her elbow. "It is not the girls only, it is—it's everything! I'm sorry, Cressida, but my mind is made up." When she had found the small gold box housing a little sponge soaked in a restorative inhalant, she popped it open and breathed deeply, the noxious fumes bringing about a delicate series of coughs which erupted from her throat. "I have nothing more to say. Oh, how dreadfully ill I feel all of a sudden. You may stay on until the week's end, at which time one of the grooms may take you to the village. Now, please have some compassion for my poor nerves. You know I dislike brangling."

Cressida stood in stunned silence. Something must have occurred while she was at Mendip Combe to have brought about such a sudden change of heart. "What has happened?" she cried. "I don't understand you. Till week's end? But that is hardly more than three days." She took a step forward and biting her lip hard finally found enough strength to query, "Pray tell me, is it Somersby?"

Mrs. Cameley groaned, her eyelids fluttering as she draped a shawl over her face. The fabric puffed up with her next words. "You must tell her, Gregory. I find I cannot speak another word."

Only then did Cressida notice the dusty booted foot that could just barely be seen jutting out from a winged chair which faced away from her. The chair had been cloaked in the shadows of the draperies and had been obscured from easy view by the glaring light which still bathed Mrs. Cameley.

Was it Lord Somersby? Throughout the duration of the horrifying interview, he had been present yet had not made himself known to her? It seemed so unlike the kind young viscount who always greeted her with such enthusiastic affection. *Gregory*. She had been given to understand by Daphne that Somersby's Christian name was Evan. *Gregory*?

She turned toward the chair and watched in stupefaction as his lordship rose from his seat. Only it wasn't Somersby at all, but—but that man in the curricle!

How wickedly he smiled upon her, as a cat might who has caught a lovely little field mouse and is now holding it captive by a single claw.

"Miss Chalcot, I presume," he queried, his eyes drooping lazily, arrogantly. He made his bow, but it was very small, inconsequential and rude.

Cressy did not hesitate to take her pelisse lightly in hand at the sides, and drop a returning curtsy so infinitessimal as to be nonexistent. "Sir," she responded coldly, "I apprehend you are in some manner connected to my employer?"

He shook his head. "No, as it happens I am Somersby's guardian. I have come to take charge of him. Mrs. Cameley was so good as to inform me not a sennight ago that he was currently enjoying her hospitality and that—" here he paused, dramatically removing a silver snuffbox from the pocket of his coat, and taking a pinch before responding. "Well, though I should prefer to speak with greater delicacy—"

"I'm sure you would," Cressy agreed, her distaste for the fine gentleman increasing with each word he spoke.

"Yes," he said inclining his head slowly. "As it happens, Mrs. Cameley has every reason to believe he has become the object of your sister's pointed interest. I am here to whisk him away and have of course suggested that she remove from her house an influence, which otherwise, given the tender ages of her dear daughters, could very possibly sustain the very worst of consequences."

Cressida heard a faint mewing sound from beneath the thin silk shawl covering Mrs. Cameley's face. Of the moment, she did not know at which person to direct the bulk of her anger. She despised her employer suddenly for not having had enough pluck to address the issue at hand with her and for placing that responsibility instead upon the tongue of a man she disliked immensely. At the same time, the terrible aspersions which the elegant gentleman did not hesitate to cast upon a young woman he had never before met in all his life were too horrid to be endured. Daphne's "pointed interest" indeed!

Since she believed it would be wholly ineffectual to address the figure shrouded in silk, Cressy pinned her gaze squarely on the haughty stare of the stranger. "Daphne," she said, straightening her spine, "in all her sweetness and gentleness, could never be such a terrible influence as you infer. She may not have perfection of mind or of discernment, but her heart is good and generous, which Mrs. Cameley's children understand quite well. I suppose you mean to suggest she has designs upon Somersby. You are making an insinuation out of your ignorance, and that is a fault I will most happily add to the rest of the ones I named earlier. If you are Somersby's guardian, than I can only say I understand with perfect clarity why he has hid himself in the country, no doubt to escape your officious, unhandsome, and quite ruthless interference in his affairs."

At this speech, for some reason Mrs. Cameley felt bound to rise from her pillows, the silk falling away from her face like a droplet of rain off the feathers of a goose. "Do you know to whom you are speaking?" she queried in astonishment.

Cressida lifted her chin. "It would make no difference to me were he the Prince Regent himself! None whatsoever."

Mrs. Cameley found this response entirely unsatisfactory. "The Honorable Gregory Rushton!" she exclaimed.

Cressida felt as though she had just been struck across her cheek with a whip.

Rushton!

She knew of him, of his reputation, of course. Everyone did. They shared the same county, Somersetshire. Though her family's home had been in the south while his was in the north, she was well acquainted with the exhalted name of Rushton—one of the wealthiest, oldest and most distinguished families in England. As for Gregory Rushton, he had been accounted to her a nonpareil, a *Go Amongst the Goers,* a Corinthian of exceptional abilities, a darling of society, in short the most famous Matrimonial Prize of them all!

Keeping in form with her earlier devilry, however, she placed a hand upon her cheek and exclaimed dryly, "Oh dear, not *the* Mr. Rushton! Well, then I must say it does seem to be an enormous pity!"

"And what is that?" he queried blithely, appearing pleased with himself.

Cressida could see that he was expecting either an apology or some other form of flattery, so she took great delight in retorting, "That your education has been so completely wasted. For a more useless man, who must take pleasure in disrupting the lives of persons completely unknown to him, I have never found!"

Chapter Four

"Cressida!" Mrs. Cameley cried, greatly shocked. Her horror at her companion's insolence so affected her that she rose from her bed of suffering and ranged herself close to Mr. Rushton. "You forget yourself! While you are employed in my house, I certainly expect you to extend every gracious civility, of which I know you are perfectly capable, to dear Mr. Rushton. His impeccable lineage and breeding, his own excellent manners, his rightfully earned place in society must demand respect, particularly from those situated in your unhappy circumstances. You will make your apologies at once!"

Cressy meant to drop a facetious curtsy and to express her opinion that since she was no longer employed under Mrs. Cameley's generous auspices she felt little obligation to pander to the vanity of a proud, disagreeable man, but Mr. Rushton was before her.

He lifted an imperious hand toward Mrs. Cameley, a gesture which caused the good lady to take a frightened step backward. Cressy had expected his words to impale the air further; instead, a surprising gentleness had crept into his voice. "It is I who must ask for your forgiveness, Miss Chalcot. It is certainly possible I have erred, and I do beg your pardon. I am unacquainted with your sister, as you have so accurately pointed out. It is also possible I am not in possession of all the facts in this particular case. If I seem strident in my protection of Somersby it is merely because the combination of his title, wealth and extremely amiable disposition have made him the object of just the sort of pursuit of which anyone of sense and decency must have an extreme aversion. Would you do me the honor, therefore, of presenting Miss Daphne to me? Perhaps, then, any erroneous misgivings I hold might be dispelled."

Cressy did not know what to make either of him or of this odd outburst of polite behavior. It was so unlike him! She blinked several times, tilting her head with wonder and not a little suspicion.

And then he smiled, a teasing, challenging sort of smile which had the uncomfortable effect of causing Cressy's heart to beat a little faster. Had she misjudged him or was he merely being charming and civil for his own scurrilous reasons? She had certainly not expected him to yield on any point, much less the most significant one at hand.

In response, she dipped a slow curtsy and replied with dignity, "If it pleases you, Mr. Rushton. I would be most happy and grateful to introduce you to my sister."

Daphne Chalcot squeezed Lord Somersby's hands in return, locked as they were within his tight grasp. "But how silly!" she cried, her enormous blue eyes sparkling with happiness. "Of course you are worthy of me. How can you speak so when you are indeed the most kindhearted, warm, considerate man I have ever met." She looked away from his adoring face and wrinkled her nose. "That is, of course, there was the gardner's son, once. He was ever so nice! And so well behaved for one of his station. He was used to bring me a rose every day during the summer months, climbing the drain pipes and leaving it on my windowsill—when it wasn't raining that

29

is. Mama used to be so angry with him, though I don't know why, save that he did steal the roses from her garden! But as for you, Somer—that is, Evan—oh, but are you sure it is proper in me to address you so informally?"

"Oh, yes," breathed his lordship, who gazed lovingly down into Daphne's eyes. "I think I should perish if you did not call me *Evan*. I have longed to hear my name upon your lips for these past several weeks—"

"Not weeks!" Daphne corrected him with a trill of laughter. "I only met you but a fortnight ago, silly. *Days!* We have known each other but a few days!"

"It might as well be years," Somersby replied, terribly smitten.

Daphne leaned into him and sighed with great satisfaction. "Do you know, I was just thinking the very same thing. I feel I have known you all my life!"

"Daphne!" he exclaimed, drawing her close.

"Oh, Evan!"

Lord Somersby did not need further invitation to press either his suit or his lips upon Daphne. He released her hands, took her strongly in his arms and kissed her.

Daphne received his lips quite willingly, as she was in the habit of doing with gentlemen who were ever so kind to her. It had quite astonished her to learn how very many *kind* gentlemen there were in the world. Why, she must have been kissed no fewer than a dozen times in the past several months alone! Quite remarkable. She supposed she enjoyed it very much—indeed, yes, she did! Of course, Cressy would probably not approve, but as Evan held her more tightly still, she could not help but think that to receive such kindness from a man was one of the sweetest experiences in her life. She never felt quite so lonely when held within the loving embrace of a man, and besides, the twins had told her it was her duty to submit to their kisses! Richard—or was it Robert, she never could tell them apart—had informed her quite sternly that any creature embued with such exquisite beauty was required by Olympus to impart at least one kiss when requested to do so. She had been so enchanted by them both, by their gentleness with her, by their jokes which she adored, that she had given them each two as a reward for their delightful ways!

Of course, it was very unfortunate that their mother had actually witnessed the event. She wasn't sure, but she rather thought her ladyship's knowledge of her sons's attentions to her had caused her—and therefore Cressida's—dismissal. When she had laid the matter before her sister, suggesting that perhaps her ladyship had been upset by seeing Richard and Robert kissing her, Cressy had merely taken refuge behind an already damp kerchief and refused to give answer. Daphne had not meant to make her sister so unhappy, but for the life of her she couldn't understand why Cressida had shed so many tears. Surely she understood how very sweet Richard and Robert had been!

The following day, however, Cressy had revealed the source of her unhappiness and had lectured her for a full hour on the necessity of being more circumspect. Daphne had listened attentively and from that moment on had never kissed a gentlemen where his mother was sure to be watching!

That was why she was permitting *Evan* to importune her lips so tenderly now—they were closeted snugly in the library, away from Mrs. Cameley's watchful eye. She wasn't his mother, of course, but since she seemed like his mother, Daphne instinctively felt the relationship probably worked in the same manner. She prided herself in having finally become circumspect and thought with great pleasure that Cressy, were she to see her now, would be terribly pleased with her progress. She knew she wasn't clever like Cressida, but she was able to make sense of some things, if given enough time and repetition of dressing down. Why, she had even learnt her letters finally!

With Mrs. Cameley and Mr. Rushton in tow, Cressy lifted her skirts slightly and climbed the stairs. The butler, Banwell, had informed her he believed Miss Daphne to be in the library. He then cleared his throat, shifted his gaze to both Mrs. Cameley and Mr. Rushton in turn, opened his mouth to speak, then closed it again. After which his face took on a distinct stony appearance. Cressy turned away from him with a frown knitting her brow. What had Banwell wished to say, only to think the better of it, she wondered. Was it possible Lord Somersby was with Daphne? Even if he was, what harm could there be in it, particularly since the children would no doubt be clustered about Daphne's knees, reading or chatting harmlessly to one another. She glanced down at the large clock adorning the wall opposite the stairs and saw that the hour wanted five minutes to three. Daphne should be ensconced in the schoolroom teaching the use of the watercolors at this hour! But what difference did it make if she chose to take her wards to the library instead. Mrs. Cameley ought to be pleased that Daphne was making such excellent use of the quite impressive collection of books Mr. Cameley had been acquiring over the past fifteen years.

Her doubts somewhat assuaged, Cressy lifted her head and mounted the remainder of the stairs with a lightening of her brow. She felt hopeful of the moment. She knew she had but to convince Mr. Rushton that Daphne was not in any way a threat to Lord Somersby's heart or title, and she was certain Mrs. Cameley would relent and keep them both on. It was clear to her that in this particular situation her mistress would follow Rushton's lead.

But as they reached the top of the stairs, from the opposite direction of the library, three towheaded young ladies, aging from ten to fourteen, bounded from the direction of the schoolroom. Mrs. Cameley quickly brought them to heel, begging them to make their best curtsies to Mr. Rushton, and afterward learned from the eldest—who blushed in giving her responses—that Daphne had gone to the library alone some fifteen minutes earlier in order to procure books for their afternoon lessons.

Cressy saw the stricken look in Judith's eye as she offered her explanation to her mother; she noted with horror how Amelia chewed her lip and kept her gaze cast toward her feet, and saw with dismay that even young Cassie frowned with a look she could only conclude was guilt-ridden.

Panic took strong hold of Cressy's heart. With a jerk, she set her feet quickly in motion toward the library, only to have the urgent whispers of the girls behind her confirming her fears.

"I knew she should not have gone today!" Judith wailed.

"It is Lord Somersby's fault," Amelia added. "He insisted upon following her everywhere!"

Even Cassie said, "I thought he looked stupid, always staring at her as though he had a stomachache!"

Cressy reached the library door, and wanting only to know the complete truth, set her hand firmly on the doorknob, gave it a hard twist, and shoved the door wide.

There, as though bringing her worst nightmare to life, stood Daphne, held tightly within the amorous embrace of Somersby, the afternoon light sparkling on her blond hair. It would have been a touching, charming scene, had it not been a confirmation of Mr. Rushton's terrible opinion of Daphne's intentions.

Cressy turned away from the sight and glanced at Mrs. Cameley, Mr. Rushton and the awestruck faces of the young ladies, each in turn. She felt a knot of tears swelling her throat, and only after swallowing three times, was she able to address her mistress in a whisper, "I will remove my sister from your house immediately. I do beg your pardon. I do. I had no idea. I could only wish—" She could not finish such a hopeless thought.

She did not remain to see Mr. Rushton's look of triumph, but brushed past them all and hurried to her chamber on the second floor.

Chapter Five

"I wish you would stop crying, Daphne," Cressida said gently, her arm held tightly about her sister's shoulders. They were seated in Mrs. Cameley's creaking, poorly sprung barouche, the carriage listing from side to side with each turn of the wheels. "I suppose I simply haven't made clear to you why you must not kiss every gentleman who takes your fancy."

Daphne sniffed and lifted her head from Cressy's shoulder. "I don't kiss every gentleman who takes my fancy. I didn't fancy chubby Mr. Wrotham at all. Do you remember him? He had more spots than a—a fig has seeds!"

Cressy glanced down at the tear-streaked face and with a horrified laugh, asked, "Then why ever did you kiss him?"

"Because Richard said it was my duty."

"Richard?" Cressy asked. "You mean one of the twins."

"Precisely so. He said because Venus had touched my face and figure I was duty bound to share her blessings with him and with Robert and any other man who begged a kiss of me. Though I do think Robert was more fun to kiss than Richard. On the other hand, Richard could make me laugh ever so much! I miss them both, Cressy!

I do, I do!"

Cressida pushed her sister away, turned toward her, caught her by the shoulders and gave her a single hard shake. "Now listen to me, you wretched simpleton. Richard only said as much because he wanted to kiss you! Don't you understand?"

Daphne appeared to lend her every faculty to the intense cogitation of Cressy's meaning. "Are you saying I don't have to kiss anyone?" she queried, a brilliant luminescence entering her blue eyes.

Cressy shook her head. "No, my dear. In fact you should never kiss any man, only if he is to become your husband."

"Well, how would I know if a man is to become my husband?" Daphne asked, completely bewildered.

Cressy groaned. "Darling, if a man asks you to marry him, then it would follow he would become your husband, at which time it might be considered proper to permit him to kiss you once or twice before the wedding. If a man has not asked you to marry him, then you should not kiss him. It's really very simple."

"Have you ever been kissed?" Daphne queried.

The question, taking Cressy so thoroughly by surprise, conjured up an image she had by far wished left unseen by her mind's eye ever again. Her stomach seemed to take flight, as though powered by a battalion of butterflies. Had she ever been kissed? Very much so, she thought, remembering the way Mr. Rushton had forced himself upon her and had in the end caused her to feel such unconscionable things! Oh, but she did not wish to think of Mr. Rushton. Discovering Daphne in the telling embrace of Lord Somersby had caused her to feel such intense mortification that any remembrance of Rushton brought a fierce heat flooding her cheeks. Her only consolation, and that a pitiful one, was that she would never have to see either Somersby or Rushton again.

But, yes, she had most definitely been kissed!

36

She glanced at Daphne, wondering whether or not to tell her the truth. Poor Daphne! Whatever was she to do with her?

Daphne's mind was so loose and unteachable, yet never had the earth created a creature as exquisite. She was utterly faerylike in appearance, her blue eyes sparkling with vivacity, her blond hair dancing about her face like spun gold, her teeth so white, even, and perfect, her lips enchanting, her face heart-shaped! It was no wonder Richard had set about tricking her into kissing him! Her warmth of temperament and the beauty of her person simply begged for kissing. And no matter how sweet or how ornery the children she had taken into her charge, her tutorlings had loved her so! She had never been discharged because the children wished for it. All three of Mrs. Cameley's pretty girls had surrounded Daphne upon her departure, shedding tears, wailing, berating each other for not better protecting her against Lord Somersby's unhappy advances. They clung to her until even Mrs. Cameley was sniffling behind her kerchief and begging one of the maids to fetch her vinaigrette.

Whatever was she to do with such a hopelessly addled-brained, yet generously disposed being?

"No," she said at last in response to Daphne's original question, not hesitating to tell a whisker. "I have never been kissed." She was fully convinced she could neither explain to Daphne how the kiss had come about nor keep the kiss she had shared with Rushton from further confusing her dear, bird-witted sister.

"It can be wonderful," Daphne sighed dreamily. Her beautiful face then puckered into a serious frown as she continued, "I only wish I had known I didn't have to kiss Mr. Wrotham. He drooled, you see. I could hardly bear it!"

Cressy would have laughed at her sister's hapless admission had it not brought forcibly to mind the predicament Cressy faced. The weight of the world suddenly seemed to descend upon her shoulders, the hopelessness of Daphne's limitations sinking her spirits to a depth she had not experienced since the death of their parents. She was discouraged beyond belief and hadn't a single notion what next she ought to do, or where she ought to go, or what plans she should make for their joint future.

Mr. Rushton was worried. He sat opposite his ward, who was a mere thirteen years his junior—but might as well have been a hundred!—and could think of little to say. He had never quite seen so stubborn a set to Somersby's jaw before. The interview had gone badly, almost from the outset.

Somersby was in love with Miss Daphne—or so he claimed—and she with him. If he hadn't been interrupted in so brutish and untimely a fashion, he had meant to offer for the impoverished, addlepated governess! Why was Rushton always casting a rub in his way? Didn't he want to see him happily settled? Didn't he give a fig for the sensibilities of others? Didn't he think Daphne's gown was the same color as her eyes? Didn't he think she would look pretty in the grand drawing room at Somersby Hall? He wanted a miniature of her, too, and perhaps a set of ceramic buttons, painted with her likeness, for a new waistcoat he had in mind. Weston would be just the man for the job too, or would Rushton advise seeking out Stultz for such a project? What did he think?

Rushton felt like he was going mad!

He rose from the burnished copper-colored winged chair in which he had conducted the frustrating interview, and letting out a breath of air rife with exasperation, crossed the library to stare out the window at the pretty Gloucestershire countryside. It was June, early enough that London refugees, exhausted from the Season's trials, had not yet returned to Bath, and spring was already bursting into summer.

Mrs. Cameley's gardens, which the library overlooked, were well stocked with every shade of rose, with peonies, foxgloves, stocks, and columbine. The lawn, sloping down to a thick wood of beech trees, was scythed to a smoothness matching his own estate located some five miles south of Bath. Above the beech trees, shimmering in the late afternoon sun and shivering in a brisk wind, a clear blue sky reached into the heavens. Such a perfect day.

Such a ridiculous day! Such a strange day!

The meanderings of his thoughts brought to mind his initial encounter with Miss Chalcot. The beauty of the spring day seemed to reach through the paned windows and to grab at his heart in a funny way. He pressed a hand to his chest, his memory caught up with the feel of Miss Chalcot held tightly in his arms. Her lips, which had refused him at first, turned as sweet as any honeyed pastry he had ever tasted. He had wanted only to punish her for her rudeness, for her distasteful manners in actually having accused him of driving too fast. But after a moment, his thoughts were only of making this brazen young woman savor his embrace.

And savor it she had, or so he was convinced! Her slim young body had leaned so delightfully into his, the answering response of her lips was all that he could have wished for and the soft moaning sound issuing from her throat, barely audible, had aroused in him a surprising desire to know more of the intriguing "companion"! He regretted suddenly that Somersby had been discovered kissing Daphne, for then he would have persuaded Mrs. Cameley to keep on her delightful companion and her hopeless governess—at least for a few days more—if for no other reason than he would have enjoyed getting up a flirtation with Miss Chalcot.

But Somersby had kissed Daphne, and there was nothing to be done but drag him back to Bath where he would resume his constant vigil of keeping fortune- and title-hunting females away from the vulnerable peer.

Thoughts of Somersby caused Rushton to glance over his shoulder. His lordship, all of two and twenty years, sat fully upright in a matching copper-colored chair, his spine straight, his upper body nervously distanced from the comfortable cushions behind him. He had all the appearance of a schoolboy about to be rusticated for a terrible prank, his brown eyes cast toward the floor, his knees shaking as he chewed on the twisted corner of his kerchief.

"Come, Somersby," Rushton prodded quietly. "You must admit, however pretty Miss Chalcot is—indeed, however beautiful she might be—she is neither suited by her limited intelligence, nor by her station in life, nor by her lack of fortune, to become your wife."

"She was very kind to me," Somersby offered, jerking the cambric kerchief from between clenched teeth and twisting it around his fingers. "I don't think I know very many kind people. At least the ones who are, you always seem to chase away."

He sounded very bitter.

Rushton knew a profound desire to take the bronzed bust of Shakespeare sitting upon a cherrywood table at his elbow and throw it at Somersby's thick skull. He doubted that it would make even a small dent. If anything, he was certain Shakespeare would suffer instead from the exercise!

He was not used to be so out of patience with the young viscount, but of late—after having spent a month in London at the beginning of the Season putting an end to no fewer than three completely unsuitable *tendres,* the third of which had nearly ended in an elopement—he had grown fatigued with keeping a check on his ward's amorous adventures. He would have liked to have provided Somersby with a mistress, but he had a sincere dread that his clodpoll of a cousin would marry the wench out of hand! And that would never do!

Somersby had only been on the town for a little over a year. His friendships were severely limited by the size of his brain, and his interests had grown to encompass the pursuit of love almost exclusively.

With a despairing sigh, Rushton chose a different tack. "I hope you will meet up with a great deal more kindness in Bath, where I intend to take you next. Miss Pritchard informed me—"

"Olivia?" the viscount queried, his brows drawn together into a frightened wrinkled.

Rushton smiled thinly, locking his hands behind his back, as he tried to remain calm. "Yes, Olivia Pritchard—"

"I don't like her a bit. She called me a dolt. And even if I am a dolt, she'd no right to say as much in front of your mother and—and Mrs. Wanstrow. Miss Pritchard is mean-spirited, which is why I think you never offered for her!"

Rushton felt a strange coldness invade his mind. He didn't know Somersby had been informed of his past intentions toward Miss Pritchard, and though he marveled at the fact Somersby could actually form a conclusion of any kind—nonetheless a somewhat accurate one—he did not like being reminded of the fact he had been within seconds of begging for Miss Pritchard's hand in marriage. Although she was an elegant young woman, he had discovered at the eleventh hour that her motivations in encouraging his suit had been based solely upon her ambitions and were as far removed from the purity of her heart as anything could be. The worst of it was, he had fancied himself quite in love with her, and the experience had left him wondering if he understood very much about love after all. If he had any consolation in the broken affair it was that his subsequent coolness appeared to have had a profound affect upon Miss Pritchard. Her manners during the ensuing years had softened considerably, and toward him she now showed a gracious distinction, hitherto lacking. Was he being vain to think she was still hopeful after so many years? He was sorry for it if she was. He still counted her among his friends, but his affections, once betrayed, were lost to her forever.

Refusing to be drawn into a conversation about his former attachment to Miss Pritchard, he addressed Somersby's opinion of her instead. "I cannot imagine Miss Pritchard calling you a dolt! You must have misunderstood her. I have known her for any number of years and have never heard her utter a single like blandishment—"

"She wouldn't dare in your presence. She still hopes to become your wife. I wish you will not marry her, Rushton. She looks like a witch. She has a nose like a hawk and cold, green, staring eyes. She is cruel and selfish—and, and—"

"And you are greatly mistaken in her character—"

"And you see only what pleases you!"

Rushton was startled by the vehemence in his voice as well as by so succinct a criticism. He felt an uncomfortable prick of conscience. Had Somersby spoken a wretchedly profound truth?

"I see only what pleases me? Are you saying I am blind to the virtues and faults of others?"

"Yes! For if you were not, you would know that Daphne is all that is wonderful and kind and generous. While Miss Pritchard, for all her perfect curls and mincing and wafting her fan about as though she were a princess, is nothing but a platter-faced—"

"May we please stop discussing Olivia Pritchard!" Rushton cried, afterward dropping his head into his hands with a smack. He felt twisted up and thrown around as though he had been overturned in a careering

42

mail coach. How had their conversation come to such a pass as he must now be shouting at his ward! Between his earlier conversation with Miss Chalcot and his current one with Lord Somersby, Rushton could not remember a day when his temper had been more sorely chafed than today.

Taking a deep breath, he lifted his head from his hands and stared into the worried face of his cousin, who had begun chewing nervously upon his kerchief again.

Rushton apologized for his outburst. "I am sorry, Evan!" he said. "I can't imagine how I came to speak so harshly. There, there, don't hide your face." He crossed the room and dropped down beside his ward, sitting on his heels and giving Somersby's arm a friendly shake. "Let's forget all about Miss Pritchard. All I was trying to say initially was that there are many wonderful friends awaiting us in Bath for the summer. We will go to the Pump Room every day, to the Spring Gardens, to the New Assembly Rooms—I'm certain you remember from last year how delightful the assemblies are. I suggest we forget all about what has occurred here and set our eyes toward the future!"

"I'll never forget Daphne!" was all that Somersby could think to say as he sank back into his chair and let his kerchief droop out the side of his mouth. He averted his gaze to a window nearby and with a series of mooncalf sighs made the state of his heart clear to his guardian.

There was nothing Rushton could possibly say to persuade his cousin he had erred in encouraging the governess's affections.

Stilling the vexation which ruled his nerves, Rushton took several more deep breaths and finally cajoled Somersby by dangling a sweet in front of him. "Mama has made up your favorite brambleberry tarts."

At that Somersby shifted his gaze to meet Rushton's. "Crispy on top?" he queried, his expression and words those of an innocent child rather than a man who had attained his majority.

"Crispy on top," Rushton responded.

"If I must go then, I should like to go now," Somersby stated with finality, rising from his chair.

Rushton rose to his feet and patted his friend, his ward, his nemesis, kindly upon his shoulder. "That's the fellow," he said.

As he followed Somersby from the library, he made a mental note never to mention Olivia Pritchard again and to send a letter ahead to his mother to make certain Cook has made up a dozen brambleberry tarts before Somersby's arrival.

Chapter Six

"But we have never even met our Aunt Lydia," Daphne protested, biting her lip nervously. "She will not like having perfect strangers accost her upon her doorstep."

Cressy felt that every nerve in her body had been rubbed raw in the space of the three days which had transpired since Daphne's dismissal from Mrs. Cameley's household. After considering with great care and consternation the alternatives before her—trying to find another suitable place of employment for Daphne, or staking her small fortune on a summer in Bath—she had at last chosen the latter. Between Daphne's mental flaws and her irresistible beauty, there seemed nothing for it but to find her sister a husband, and quick! But the decision, once made, had left her feeling nervous and depleted of her usual buoyancy. The happy prospects for her own future had for such a long time been so nearly bound to her small competence, that to spend it—however well considered the scheme—upon the expenses of a summer's sojourn in one of England's most famous watering places, was a risk she disliked taking.

At the same time, Daphne had been unusually trying since their decision to seek refuge with Mrs. Wanstrow. She responded firmly to her sister's concern regarding their aunt, "We will not be engaging her in a bout of fisticuffs, Daphne. And as for intruding into her world, I am recently become convinced it is high time we made her acquaintance."

"She will not like it," Daphne responded gloomily. "She will probably turn us away from her door. She will think we are—are roasting mushrooms!"

Cressy, taking another jolt of the rough roads hard on her shoulder, turned toward her sister and stared at her in some confusion. "Roasting mushrooms?" she queried. "I don't quite understand you—oh! No, no, my dear! You mean, *encroaching mushrooms*. I daresay you are right. She will undoubtedly think unhandsomely of us, and not without some cause, since I mean for her to introduce us to Bath society this summer."

The post-chaise in which they were traveling moved along the highway at a brisk, steady pace. The postillion seemed a nerveless fellow whose only interest was in reaching his destination at a goodly hour. It was not surprising therefore when the Cotswolds of Gloucestershire gave way to a lovely valley surrounded by lazy hills, and the city of Bath came into view.

"She will not like it!" Daphne reiterated.

"Oh, do stubble it, Daph! Of course she will not like it. But we've no other choice and the more I think on it, the more I am absolutely certain we ought to have pursued her acquaintance the moment I was released from the schoolroom. The past five years have been entirely wasted, I fear."

Daphne's voice dropped at least two notches, and though Cressy was not looking at her sister, she could hear suspended tears constricting her throat. "I have been a sad disappointment to you, haven't I? But I did learn my letters, I promise you I did, you know I did!" She then began to recite, "A, B, C—"

"Oh, my darling girl!" Cressy exclaimed, pulling her sister close to her and giving her shoulders a squeeze. "I am not disappointed one whit! Of that you must be assured. You are not to blame for the failure of my

46

schemes! I should have known how it would be from the beginning. I shouldn't have tried to see you settled in the post of governess, since your beauty could only attract every amorous gentleman within five miles of whatever situation you undertook!"

"I don't understand, Cressy," Daphne said, chewing upon the inside of her cheek. "Why do the gentlemen make such cakes of themselves when I—well, I have only to smile and the strangest expressions are wont to overcome their faces."

"There is no comprehending how men think—or perhaps, *not think!* It is a mystery except that I believe, somehow, from the beginning of time, man has pursued beauty as a worthy object in and of itself. And whatever good and wonderful things you are, your beauty surpasses all your attributes. Your extreme comeliness is an advantage you possess over the rest of us mere mortals. An advantage not of your own making and therefore not a circumstance for which you can possibly be held accountable. It is unreasonable for anyone to blame you for every stripling who writes you a sonnet or steals a kiss from your lovely lips!"

Daphne fell silent, her brow puckered as though she were lending her every mental faculty to discerning the meaning of her sister's words. Cressy, on the other hand, left Daphne to her ruminations and looked out over the narrow valley which cradled the object of their journey. Hills rose on every side of the small, elegant town built almost entirely of local stone. The wheels of the post-chaise rolled across the hard stones of Pulteney Bridge, the crisp sounds echoing into the River Avon below. They had arrived in Bath at last.

Relief and trepidation vied for supremacy in her thoughts. Would their aunt receive them? Or would they be turned away as Daphne feared?

Lydia Wanstrow. She had never even laid eyes upon her mother's sister before. An ancient feud, presumably over a pair of earrings—or so her mother had told her—

had separated them ever since Cressy could remember.

Sisters. She glanced at Daphne and wondered if she and her featherbrained sibling would one day find it necessary to part company. It seemed unlikely. For all Daphne's faults and her quite serious cerebral deficiency, Cressy could not imagine life without Daphne's bright, simple companionship and the childlike way she took pleasure in everything around her.

Daphne's brow grew light with comprehension, and with a satisfied smile which lit her angelic features with a delightful, joyous glow, she said, "I can't be blamed then for being beautiful since I had nothing to do with it, can I?"

"Precisely so!"

Not even Rushton can blame her, Cressy thought. It seemed odd she would think of him in this moment. She realized it was likely she would be meeting him in Bath since she had learned from Mrs. Cameley just before they parted from her manor that he had an estate nearby.

It hardly mattered though. He could think what he wished, of either of them for that matter, so long as he remained respectful and did not interfere in her desperate schemes to see Daphne settled upon a worthy, wealthy, older gentleman—one who could enjoy her beauty, provide her with every comfort and not expect a sound word from her, one out of a thousand!

Daphne sighed. She had left so many places of employment in recent years that she had grown used to leaving behind her friends with only the mildest of regrets to mar her spirits. Though she did find herself wishing upon more than one occasion that she could pen a letter and keep up a correspondence with some of her former charges, seeing new places and meeting new people generally held enough charm to coax her out of the sullens of having been torn, yet again, from a comfortable home, bed and fire.

Something about this departure, however, was bothering her more than she could ever remember, and she couldn't understand why. She felt irritable, anxious and ill-tempered, grating sentiments which were ordinarily quite foreign to her. She shook her head in bewilderment. Of course she would miss the girls, Cassie especially, who had gotten into the habit in the past fortnight of sitting upon the foot of her bed late at night and reading her the most wonderful romantic novels when they were both supposed to be tucked up in bed, their candles long since put out. And as for Lord Somersby, well! Whenever she thought of him, she felt like weeping! Imagine that! She had never been particularly saddened by parting from one of her beaux before. Why now? All she could think was that she might be suffering from a fit of the ague, or possibly she was falling into a decline and would soon die!

She shuddered. What morbid thoughts. She wanted to ask Cressy what was wrong with her, but some instinct warned her against it. Cressy was bound to make more of it than would be at all conducive to her general sense of comfort. She only wished she had someone to talk with, someone like Somersby! He was ever so nice, and never stopped her midsentence begging to know what the devil she was talking about. The truth was, he seemed to like to hear her talk. He had even said her words were like a pretty melody in his ear and that she could say anything she wished to. Why even Cressy had grown irritable when she would prattle on about her charges or the foxgloves at the nearby rectory or the recipe Mrs. Cameley's cook had given her for preparing an oyster sauce.

Yet, when she had told Somersby about the sauce, he had begged to know every ingredient and did not chide her even once—not so much as a smirking lift of one of his brows—when she could not remember a single one of them!

She missed Somersby and Cassie and the way the geese

49

would steal into the flower beds and she and the children would have to chase them away.

A tear plopped onto the sleeve of her lavender silk pelisse, and she quickly averted her gaze to stare out the window at the passing dull stone buildings, wiping the telltale streak quickly from her cheek. Cressy mustn't know of her unhappiness.

As she gazed out the window, she could not help but think how dreary a place Bath was. Of course a light rain had begun to fall, hardly improving her first impression of the town which was supposed to hold her future, but still—wet stone was so *dampening!* She smiled to herself. She had made a joke! Somersby would have laughed and laughed!

If only he were nearby to cheer her up by flicking her chin with his finger as he was wont to do.

She sighed again, slipping her hands deep into her swansdown muff. If only Somersby resided in Bath!

Cressy's thoughts took an abrupt turn as the carriage passed by a delightful row of shops. One sold tea and the like, another was a charming millinery with lovely poke bonnets arranged enticingly in the window, and a third displayed a variety of brass cooking pots. She glanced quickly at the remaining number of shops, straining to see if a modiste made up one of the number of small stores, and then she saw a sight which caused her heart to positively leap within her breast—an empty establishment, sporting a bow window with a dozen charming paned windows and a sign propped on its sill which read TO LET! She sensed Fate had gently tapped her upon the shoulder, and she felt strange and dizzy with excitement. She knew that one day she would have a shop, right there, on Union Street, in that precise location, and that she would count among her patrons not only her aunt, but every lady of quality who resided in or visited Bath during the course of a twelve-month. For these ladies she would create the most fashionable gowns they had ever had the pleasure of wearing! Was it her teeming imagination or could it actually happen? Could she really set up a shop here, or was she merely spinning silly daydreams again?

The post-chaise began to slow, and she glanced through the front, rain-washed glass. A cart and horse—not unlike the quality of Mr. Percival and the equipage he was used to pull at Mendip Combe—had overturned and was blocking the street.

How providential, she thought, as she returned her gaze to the empty shop situated across from her coach! Another indication her path would one day include this delightful establishment. She again perused the outer facade, noting the false Doric half-columns which flanked the front door, and with each passing second she grew more and more enamored of it. She thought, too, the beauty of its appearance was enhanced dramatically by the presence of a flower cart to the left of the shop.

The flower seller pulled his hat lower about his ears and drew his coat more firmly about his bulging middle against the early summer rain. Cressy tilted her head and looked at him, caught by the contented smile on his face as he nodded to her. His little spot on earth might consist only of a cart and the daily hope that enough souls would pass by and purchase his humble flowers enabling him to live, but by God it was *his* cart and *his* flowers and *his* life! How very much she wanted the same, rather than having to be dependent upon the questionable beneficence of an unknown relation or the pitiful hope she would be able to see Daphne wed to a proper gentleman by summer's end.

Would her gambit succeed? She was wagering her inheritance upon Daphne's ability to secure a husband within the scant thirteen weeks before the autumn tumbled upon them. If Daphne was still unattached at that time, Cressy was convinced her lot would fall to becoming a governess herself—a future she detested only a little more than the alternative—that of becoming a companion to some dour, lifeless creature whose final years were confined to a Bath chair.

She leaned back against the squabs. The drizzle ceased as the post-chaise began a forward progression. The postboy, apparently longing for his supper, began moving his horses along at a brisk trot, and the empty shop moved further and further away from her.

Cressy closed her eyes and after a moment felt a slight prick of anxiety that the coach was moving as fast as it was. She heard her sister murmur, "Oh, dear. It looks as though that black carriage is going to run directly into our horses!"

Cressy's eyes flew open instantly. At the same moment, she saw the blur of an approaching vehicle coming toward them at a frightfully rapid pace. She could not quench the shrill cry which erupted from her throat as she quickly locked arms with Daphne, their mutual fright at the impending collison causing both young women to bury their heads in the other's willing shoulder.

Cressy squeezed her eyes shut and waited.

Chapter Seven

For the duration of what could only have been a mere five seconds but which seemed an eternity, the shouting of male voices, the screaming of horses, the splitting and wrenching of wood, as well as the groaning of the post-chaise as it twisted sideways, ripped through Cressy's hearing. She and Daphne were propelled from one side of the post-chaise to the other, then back again, their respective bonnets thrust askew, as the curricle and the traveling coach ground against one another.

Then all the sounds of mayhem stopped, almost as abruptly as they had started.

The horses ceased their unhappy squalls, the post-chaise, though sitting awkwardly on the street, landed upright and motionless onto its four wheels, and silence weighted the air. The sisters, as one, each let out an enormously relieved breath of air.

"I thought we were doomed," Daphne whispered, clutching her swansdown muff to her bosom.

"I, too," Cressy responded, taking in a deep lungful of air in an effort to still her racing heart and soothe her shattered nerves. Only then did she take notice of the hapless curricle which had engaged her post-chaise in a battle for right-of-way of the street.

If her nerves had hitherto been rubbed raw by the difficulties of her present circumstances, if they had just been rent asunder by the devastation of having been involved in an accident, they were positively flayed open by the sight of the driver of the curricle.

"Rushton!" she exclaimed. "I might have known! Who else would be setting his horses to with such ferocity in the middle of a crowded thoroughfare?"

Daphne glanced first at Cressy, then followed the line of her sister's gaze and gasped aloud. "Good heavens!" she cried in her girlish voice. Her next words, spoken joyously, sliced through another uncomfortable nerve in Cressy's overtaxed body. "Somersby must be with him. Oh, look! There he is!" She then turned a brilliant shade of red, hugged her muff to her flaming cheeks, and then turned abruptly away from the sight of the handsome peer.

Cressy looked at her sister and knew a feeling of disorientation which threatened to undo the remaining knotted threads of her composure. She did not know what to make of Daphne's rather strange and violent reaction to the mere sight of Somersby. She would have questioned her upon the meaning of the vermillion cast to her complexion had not the sight of a furious Mr. Rushton rapidly approaching her postboy with all the appearance of desiring to tear each limb from his body arrested the queries dancing upon her tongue.

Pushing Daphne's incomprehensible reaction to Somersby to the farthest reaches of her mind, she set her sights upon Rushton's imposing figure. Without giving the least heed to either Mr. Rushton's exhalted consequence or to the propriety of intervening on behalf of her postboy, Cressy popped open the door of her post-chaise, leapt lightly down onto the pavement without making use of the steps, and quickly placed herself in Mr. Rushton's path before he could make use of the clenched fists which he was at present holding menacingly at waist level.

Her sudden appearance so brought him up short that he actually started and took a step backward. "You!" he exclaimed, clearly horrified. "Do not tell me it is you to whom I am to offer my extreme thanksgiving that I have lost a wheel of my curricle, that my leader has suffered a strained fetlock and that my life was nearly damn well forfeit!"

"It is your own fault, Mr. Rushton," Cressida answered vehemently. "As you very well know! You forget that I have been witness to the care with which you are wont to tool your curricle about even upon the most dangerous of country lanes! But this folly is beyond words, beyond belief! The town is full to brimming with every manner of conveyance, not to mention persons on foot who could have been killed by your reckless and irresponsible driving! I will not permit you to speak one unkind word to my postillion, either, though I don't doubt you are just the sort of man who is perfectly willing to lay the blame for his every erroneous deed upon those in stations beneath his own! So, you may put away your weapons"—here she glanced purposefully at his fists, which resembled the knots found within the ancient trunks of hard oak trees—"and see to your horses, to your carriage and to the *precious cargo*, which you have born away from my sister's unfortunate influence."

His face was pale. Nay, beyond pale. Cressy thought it had the look of cold alabaster and that she could see clean through it to the dangerous thoughts which caused his jaw to work strongly. He was struggling mightily with his emotions and with his temper, his blue eyes sparking like hot flames on a log fire.

"If you were a man—" he murmured through pinched lips and a tight jaw.

"Oh, that I were," Cressy did not hesitate to respond. "I should be ever so happy to teach you the lessons you are so badly in need of. Since, however, fate has not so decreed any such mode of satisfying either your temper or my complete and utter indignation at your conduct, I shall have to take my leave of you instead with the hopes that you will attend better in the future to my admonition

55

that you alter your ways before it is too late." She turned on her heel at that and moved to the horses' heads where the postboy was standing and staring at her, his mouth agape, his gray hair sticking out at irregular angles from his head, his eyes bulging from their sockets.

The right Honorable Gregory Rushton stared at Miss Chalcot's back and felt as he had some few days earlier when confronting her about the deuced glue pot she had been driving to Mendip Combe—that he had been entirely knocked out of stride by this, this infuriating, self-assured, countrified, yet excruciatingly intriguing female! At the very same moment he felt such a sensation of rage that he scarcely knew how to politely vent his anger. He would have preferred to have picked up the young woman, tossed her over his knee, and struck her posterior a dozen times until she begged for forgiveness for her audacity and insults. But of course this was impossible!

And he had not been driving too fast! The fact that his curricle had severely grazed the wheel of the post-chaise was entirely the fault of her postboy, who had clearly been springing his horses and could not, at the eleventh hour, check them properly!

For that reason, he clenched and unclenched his fists rapidly several times, permitting his towering emotions to drain away through each finger as he did so, afterward approaching Miss Chalcot and her postboy. The latter appeared to be abjectly explaining his culpability to her.

By the time he cleared the several feet remaining between himself and Miss Chalcot, he could hear the astonishment in her voice as she responded to her man's explanations.

"What do you mean, you are to blame for the accident? You are being far too obsequious because of Mr. Rushton's station and far too harsh upon your own actions. Surely!"

The postboy, who had lost his hat during the course of the accident but who had retrieved the same wet, limp article from the pavement, was now turning it nervously between his fingers. With every few words he spoke, he made an entire circle of the black, dripping object. "'Twas that I were hungry, miss! I were thinkin' only of a tankard of ale and one of me wife's pasties. I oughtn't to have been drivin' like the devil were at me coattails. 'Twere me fault! I saw the curricle, but I thought I could reach Milsom Street afore he turned into the highway! I was wrong!"

Mr. Rushton took up a place beside Miss Chalcot and crossed his arms over his chest, a feeling of immense satisfaction warming his heart as he observed her blushing countenance. All his rage died in that moment like a fire that has been doused by a bucket of water. How delectable was the mere anticipation of the apologies she would no doubt offer for having castigated his character in public. Glancing about him, he noted with great pleasure that a considerable crowd had gathered around the vehicles. He positively savored the moment she would open her mouth to utter humble words and eat the pie of the same name! He would have chuckled aloud at the thought but instead, feeling he ought to take some pains not to add insult to injury, contented himself instead with smiling broadly.

Daphne glanced nervously forward, her gaze shifting several times from the back of her sister's burgundy pelisse to Mr. Rushton's oddly smiling visage. When she was satisfied she would not be the object of their scrutiny for several minutes, she pressed her forehead against the side glass window next to her and scratched upon the glass. Lord Somersby was not more than eight feet from her, but he was standing with his back to her, examining the leg of one of the gray horses harnessed to Mr. Rushton's curricle. She could not call out to him, else she was sure to be heard, but Somersby apparently couldn't hear the soft scratching sounds her gloved fingers were making.

Still, she continued doing so, every now and again adding a sharp rap to her efforts. But only after a full minute did his head finally perk up. He set the horse's leg down and turned around with a curiously questioning expression on his face which disappeared the moment he saw her.

How quickly the lines of confusion left his visage as he recognized her, a light of pure affection glowing from his warm, brown eyes. How handsome he was, how gloriously familiar and kind was the smile which overtook features she had come to cherish. Gone from her own heart was the desolate sense of loss which had been chasing her hard the entire way to Bath. He approached the window and mouthed her name. He placed his gloved hand upon the glass directly opposite her own. He regarded her with complete devotion.

Oh, how much she loved him! *She loved him!*

For the first time in her existence she knew what love was!

"Why do you not say anything to me, Miss Chalcot," Mr. Rushton said smugly. "You have heard your postboy admit his guilt, and yet you remain mute! Why is that, I wonder?"

Cressida stared blankly at Mr. Rushton for a long, awkward moment. She ought to apologize, but it seemed a rather silly thing to do, given the fine and well-deserved speech she had just delivered to him. She rapidly considered everything she could say to him in such a moment and quickly concluded there was only one thing to be said—two, actually.

"First, it seems perfectly clear to me," she began in a forthright, confident manner, "that after hearing my postillion admit that he had been encouraging his horses along at a pace which apparently contributed to the accident, I can only say that I believe you were *both* equally to blame and that therefore we ought to part company satisfied that no one party has been unjustifiably injured." She was completely delighted that another expression of astonishment again filled Rushton's eyes, replacing the smug look which had dominated his features from the moment he first approached her a few minutes earlier.

When she offered her hand to him in a friendly manner and smiled with an equally amiable expression, he extended his hand with pained slowness to receive her own as one who had been struck dumb. Full of deviltry suddenly, she continued, "Daphne and I will be residing with my aunt in Landsdown Crescent for the summer, Mr. Rushton. I hope you will have occasion to call upon her once we are settled there. And do bring Somersby with you. I am sure Daphne will wish to reacquaint herself with his lordship once she knows he is in Bath. Good day."

She then dropped an offensively slight curtsy, as she had done at Wellow Priory, directed the postillion to remount his horse and whirled about to return to the post-chaise.

Only then did she see that Lord Somersby was quite reprehensibly flirting with Daphne through the side window glass of the post chaise. "Oh, dear," she murmured into the damp air. She longed to turn around and steal a glance at Rushton in order to observe how he was affected by the sight of his ward pressing his lips to the glass of the post-chaise and feigning a salute upon Daphne's fingers.

The words which erupted from the sorely tried Mr. Rushton were sufficient, however, to bring a gleeful joy to Cressy's vengeful heart. "The devil take it!" he cried out in a barely muffled whisper.

She was surprised afterward, however, to feel Rushton's hand just behind her elbow as he began whisking her toward her chariot. "You planned this, didn't you, vixen!" he murmured angrily into her ear.

Cressy couldn't keep from chuckling beneath her breath. He was a rather hopeless man, she decided. "Oh, indeed I did," she responded facetiously as he swooped her up into the interior of the post-chaise. Settling herself upon the squabs and ignoring the frightened shrieks from her sister at having been caught flirting with Somersby, she continued, "I begged the postboy to crash into your curricle. Only he failed me dreadfully when he only but grazed your wheel! I had meant for the curricle to overturn and for at least both your legs to have been broken that I might not be required to meet you in company here!"

"You are being nonsensical," he retorted. He made as if to shut the door, but Cressy leaned forward and stopped him.

"Mr. Rushton," she whispered with a sincere smile, "I beg you will believe this much: Somersby is not part of any scheme of mine, but I must see Daphne settled. You are not wrong to suppose I have not come here without design, but I forewarn you to stay out of my way."

"I shall be only too happy to oblige you, madam."

"Thank you," she responded sweetly, permitting him at last to close the door, which he did with a hard snap. He remained standing opposite the post-chaise, and for some reason Cressy could not help but watch him as the postboy set the horses in motion. He returned her gaze squarely, his thoughts inscrutable. Just before the carriage moved away, a rather slow, wicked smile overtook his features. Whatever did he mean by it?

Cressy felt in his expression the most dangerous tug upon her heart. "What absurdity is this?" she murmured softly, her pulse alive and almost wild suddenly. How could a smile do so much to her heart? It seemed impossible that such a man could have affected her so strongly. Especially because she despised Rushton! He was everything she disliked in a man—proud, officious, overbearing. Why then did she feel positively dizzy?

To her surprise, Daphne seemed to think her question was directed toward her. "It wasn't anything, Cressida, really it wasn't! I don't know what possessed Lord Somersby to kiss the window glass. I told him to go away and not bother me anymore. I did! I promise you I did!"

Cressy turned to face her sister and taking one of her hands in the circle of her own, said simply, "You must not fill your head and your heart with hopes which can never be realized. Somersby is not for you and never can be! You must trust me in this. Even if Rushton approved of an alliance, I would not! You are in need of a kind, warm, generous man who has had much experience of the world—which Somersby has not!—one who will want to shower you with love and affection and—and as many comforts as you can bear to enjoy! The moment all is settled with Aunt Lydia, I mean to find just such a gentleman for you. Do you understand, Daphne?"

To Cressy's surprise, Daphne smiled brightly and replied, "Oh, indeed yes. Indeed, I do. I mean to be very good and to do just as you say." She then turned away from Cressy to gaze out the window and began commenting at random about the various persons she saw strolling about the streets.

Cressy felt happy for the first time in ages. She was in Bath, and Daphne was being wonderfully acquiescent. For the moment she could wish for nothing more. She was convinced that so long as Rushton did not interfere in her schemes, she was sure to succeed!

That is, so long as Aunt Lydia might somehow desire to take to her bosom the orphaned children of her cast-off sister, Amelia!

Chapter Eight

"But you were in Bath once before," Daphne cried. "How is it you cannot recall these hills?"

Cressy surveyed as much of the scenery as she could from being squashed between the driver of the gig and Daphne. "I think it would be due to the unremarkable fact I was only an infant at the time," Cressida responded wryly.

Bath was a bustling town situated beside the River Avon in a somewhat narrow valley that gradually opened out to the west. Her aunt's town house was located upon the side of Landsdown Hill, and the elegant crescent shape of the row of attached houses had been aptly named Landsdown Crescent. The journey from the posting inn to her aunt's dwelling was a rather steep one as the two heavy-boned horses strained to bear its load onward.

Daphne giggled at Cressy's response, a delightful, melodious sound which went a long way to easing the anxious tightness surrounding Cressy's heart. Every tuppence spent upon their venture in Bath was a decidedly uncomfortable experience, and the extra cost of hiring a vehicle to transport herself, Daphne and the sum of their baggage to Landsdown Crescent added to Cressida's increasing disquietude. Uppermost in her mind, however, was the terrifying fear that Aunt Lydia would turn her nieces away from her door without a single glance backward.

When she and Daphne were ushered into an elegant chamber decorated *en suite* with red silk damask covering the furniture, walls and windows, Cressy felt a surprising mist of relief overcome her, a sensation she could ill-define or explain. Something in the elegance of the chamber, the arrangement of chairs and sofa near the fireplace, the portrait of an amiable young woman above the mantel—presumably her aunt—a gleaming harp and glossy, rosewood pianoforte presiding over the corner opposite the windows, the fine quality of the textiles, all contributed to an instant comprehension of her aunt as a woman of excellent taste.

How had it come about, then, that Lydia and Amelia would have quarreled so ferociously that silence had dominated their relationship, even to Amelia's early grave?

Both young ladies stood before the cold fireplace staring up into the countenance of their aunt.

"She's very pretty, isn't she, Cressy?" Daphne queried softly.

"Why, thank you," a rich feminine voice called from the doorway of the receiving room.

Cressida turned her head in the direction of the speaker and was a little shocked to discover that Aunt Lydia bore only the smallest resemblance to the reflection of the young lady who had once posed so elegantly for the brush and oils of Sir Thomas Lawrence. Aunt Lydia, it would seem, had grown quite stout in the fifteen years which had transpired since she had sat for her portrait, and though her countenance was lit with intelligence and her blue eyes sparkled with an irrepressible sharpness and will, the beauty of her youth had been to a great degree lost in the folds of her chin.

"Aunt Lydia?" Cressida queried in a whisper. Suddenly the audacity of her schemes in presenting herself boldly upon her aunt's doorstep swept over her in a feeling of humiliation so strong that she took several steps forward and began rattling off the first words which occurred to her, "We should not have come! It was a fool's errand! I am sorry! We were wrong to have disturbed you when we have no rightful claim upon you, upon your generosity. We've no right to expect the smallest—"

Lydia Wanstrow lifted an elegant hand and silenced her niece. She moved forward into the room on a decorous tread, her demitrain of amber silk swishing like a soft breeze against the patterned Aubusson carpet as she passed by Cressy and took up a place on the sofa by the fireplace. "Sit down, my dears. It would seem we have much to discuss. Now, tell me what brings you to Bath, and perhaps more significantly, to my home?"

Cressida sat opposite her aunt, as did Daphne, and presented her requests haltingly at first. But Mrs. Wanstrow, as she preferred to be addressed by her nieces, gently encouraged her to lay a complete history of her difficulties before her. She gained confidence in her recital, dwelling in particular upon their lack of fortune as the real source of their hardship, ending with, "So we are here, very simply, to find Daphne a husband. I have enough funds to provide our wardrobe for the summer, to present a supremely fashionable appearance, which I believe is the most important requirement in such a condition as ours, but nothing more I fear. I know it is the greatest piece of impertinence to beg for your assistance, but could you possibly present us to Bath society this summer and—?" She found it nearly impossible to complete her request.

"Yes?"

"Take us into your home, as well?" Cressy felt her heart sink to the very pit of her stomach, her hopes dashed by the expression on her aunt's face.

Mrs. Wanstrow frowned slightly and dropped her gaze to the white smoothness of her hands. She gently touched each of three heavily jeweled rings on her left hand and adjusted them in turn. For a long moment she did not speak, and Cressida realized she was having some difficulty in discerning her aunt's character. She had come to know several mature women in the course of the past few years, partly due to the quantity of posts she and Daphne had held during that time, but never had she met such a woman as her aunt. She comprehended that *Mrs. Wanstrow*—how difficult it was to think of her in such a removed manner—was a creature of taste, elegance and refinement. She also appeared to enjoy a certain degree of wealth. Her intelligence seemed in no way lacking, but there was a degree of calculation in the piercing way she had looked each of the sisters over when Cressy had presented her history which imparted a sense that Mrs. Wanstrow did nothing unless it somehow served her interests.

Having intuited as much, she was not surprised when her aunt responded, "For my sister's sake, who was taken from you at a critical time in your lives, I will be happy to permit you to stay for two, possibly three days, but," here she paused and again adjusted her multijeweled rings, rocking an amethyst ring the longest, "I am afraid I haven't the resources to properly offer you shelter. For all the appearances of my furnishings and establishment, I am a woman of meager fortune and am able to sustain my house only by use of the strictest economies." And with the thinnest of smiles, she concluded the interview. "Now that we have matters settled, may I offer you some tea and then I should like to hear about all your adventures of recent years."

Chapter Nine

"Yes, Daphne, I am certain that our aunt—that is Mrs. Wanstrow—stated that eight o'clock was the appointed hour for taking the waters at the Pump Room." She mimicked her aunt's full, authoritative voice, "And not a single minute late! I have a custom of appearing precisely upon the hour, so that the Tompion clock near Beau Nash's statue marks my arrival. I move in a very strict, select circle and desire above all else to observe the established mode. You would do well to follow my lead. Sleep well, my dears."

"Oh, and as for sleeping," Daphne cried, rubbing her arms and grimacing, "Cressy, my bed was nearly intolerable. In all the years we have moved from one post to the next—including having slept in the garrets of that horrid manor in Oxfordshire—I have never known such a lumpy mattress as Mrs. Wanstrow's."

"Hush! Here is our aunt now! You will not wish to appear ungrateful."

"But I am!" she continued in a hushed whisper. "I don't like to mention it, Cressy, but the undermaid was telling me Mrs. Wanstrow keeps three carriages and at least six horses!"

Cressy turned her head sharply to stare at her sister. "You cannot be serious!" she responded rapidly beneath her breath. "After all her incessant complaints at dinner regarding the poverty she endures, and that throughout the duration of a meal I could only consider princely—well! Daphne, methinks there is something rotten in Denmark!"

"Denmark?" Daphne queried. "But we are not in Denmark, we are in Bath."

Cressy would have attempted to explain, but Mrs. Wanstrow was bearing down on them with her sharp blue eyes narrowed to slits as she examined every inch of their respective costumes.

After circling each of them three times and checking to see if their gloves and slippers showed signs of wear, Mrs. Wanstrow finally approved of them. "Well done," she said at last, standing before Cressy. "And it is you, I suppose, who has seen to your respective wardrobes so assiduously, only tell me, how much did this silk spencer cost you? I saw one exactly like it in *La Belle Assemblee*, down to the gold braid, not two months ago. Only a London dressmaker could have recreated such a design, but you said you have been in Gloucestershire for these six months and more. Tell me, did you by chance take a holiday in London? I don't see how you managed it."

Cressy, who had been giving a great deal of thought to her aunt's temperament and character, chose not so much to prevaricate as to avoid a complete revelation of her activities. "No, I did not go to London."

"Did you stitch this garment together yourself?" she asked, fingering the fine, blue silk fabric.

"Yes."

"I am mystified. The workmanship is remarkable. Where did you get the silk?"

"A shop in Mendip Combe."

"I would imagine you made it up very cheaply, then. Really, it is quite extraordinary!"

Cressy, who found the nature of her aunt's penetrating

questions both impertinent and ill-mannered, refused to respond to her observation.

"You needn't lift your chin to me, child! Though I can comprehend your pride perfectly well." She harrumphed a sigh. "For whatever it might be worth to you, I commend your taste and will be pleased to present you at the Pump Room to any of my friends who wish to make your acquaintance."

Cressida had not known precisely what to expect upon entering the Pump Room, but because of her aunt's great concern with modish conduct, she had rather supposed the establishment would be full of tonnish enthusiasts. Instead, much to her surprise, and to some degree her delight, a mixture of every manner of person was represented, from the unfortunate rheumatic individual restricted to a Bath chair, to common laborers in seek of some relief from their sufferings, to a general showing of the middle classes and, finally, to the quite obvious select circle in which Mrs. Wanstrow proudly peacocked.

Only when the clock marked the hour, however, did her aunt step across the threshold, her head held high, the single ostrich feather of her elegant bonnet swaying gently with each turn and nod of her head as she greeted her various acquaintances.

As the crowd, whose obsequious deference Mrs. Wanstrow sought, turned and lifted a kerchief here, bowed politely there, and responded appropriately to her entrance, Cressida realized her aunt thought of herself as a queen amongst the Bath dwellers. Here she presided, if not with grace, then with no small degree of dignity. A path parted instantly for her, allowing her immediate access to the pretty young lady who served glasses of the medicinal Bath water to all who required it of her.

Without making her request, certainly not needing to

do so, three glasses were immediately filled—three being the generally prescribed quantity to repair or maintain one's health—and presented to her.

Three more were pressed upon Cressida and the same number upon Daphne who, after taking a sip, exclaimed, "I vow it tastes of warm flat irons!" A polite tittering broke out from the various people nearby who overheard her.

Cressida smiled, but wisely refrained from adding her own sad opinion of the flavor of the water since Mrs. Wanstrow was frowning severely upon Daphne.

After the waters had been not so much enjoyed as tolerated, only then did Mrs. Wanstrow permit herself the pleasure of greeting her friends.

"My dear Mrs. Pritchard," she cooed gently with a curve to her lips which Cressy thought was decidedly false in affection. "How *do* you go on? You were suffering so from the headache the last time we met that I vow I was greatly moved to pity for you. I trust you are recovered?"

Mrs. Pritchard, a tall, thin, elegant woman with striking green eyes and black hair, responded with a polite, disinterested smile. "You know very well I was in perfect health the last time I exchanged words with you." She was accompanied by a handsome young woman, presumably her daughter since the younger female enjoyed the same elegant frame and general physical characteristics.

"Perhaps, then," Mrs. Wanstrow suggested, "it was some other malady which afflicted you. I vow the entire evening you wore the most pained expression on your face."

"I have often remarked," Mrs. Pritchard countered readily, "one frequently observes the world through the faults one possesses. If you saw pain and affliction, perhaps that is all you are able to see in those around you. Though I would not presume to suggest you are in any manner flawed, my *dearest* Mrs. Wanstrow, still, you might do well to examine your own heart. Now, pray introduce me to these charming young women, who, I am not in the least reluctant to tell you, have aroused in everyone's breast no small degree of curiosity. We cannot conceive of the nature of their relation to you, and I found it particularly odd that no resounding of four-and-twenty bells announced their arrival. It is the greatest mystery. And such handsome girls!"

Mrs. Pritchard's scrutiny—so similar to Mrs. Wanstrow's—poured over Cressida as well as Daphne. Her gaze took in every detail of their costumes, from the ruched silk of their bonnets, to the gold embroidery upon Daphne's emerald green pelisse, to the blue French knots and ribbons which traveled down the front of Cressy's round gown of soft white cambric. To Cressida's pleasure, a flicker of approval and jealousy sharpened the envious color of Mrs. Pritchard's eye as she completed her perusal of their clothing.

While Mrs. Wanstrow presented her nieces to Mrs. Pritchard and her daughter, Olivia, only then did Cressy meet the young woman's gaze. What she saw there caused her to rapidly conclude that whatever else Miss Pritchard was or might be, she was most certainly her mother's daughter. She was far prettier than her parent, yet she shared the same exacting eyes and penetrating manner of examining a new acquaintance.

Cressy, feeling equal to the task of making polite conversation with someone she sensed she could not like, commented upon the variety of persons to be found at the Pump Room.

Miss Pritchard's response was precisely what she expected. "It is unfortunate, isn't it, that we are forced to endure the presence of even the most degrading of creatures. I am only too happy to say that the assembly rooms are on a subscription basis and those who wish to attend must first be approved by the Master of

Ceremonies. I have suggested to Mama that a board of patronesses, such as rule Almack's in London, would be of even greater advantage than a single Master of Ceremonies, but nothing has come of it." With a condescending smile she added, "I do hope we shall be meeting you at the assemblies—when you have been approved, of course, or do you not intend to remain in Bath for an extended time?"

"My sister and I shall be residing here for the summer," she responded, regardless of the fact she did not know where or by what means yet.

"How very charming," Miss Pritchard added perfunctorily, and seeing an acquaintance entering the room, she excused herself by explaining, "For my dearest Miss Rushton, you know, would be seriously aggrieved and offended were I not to pay her the compliment of attending her immediately. We have been friends forever!"

Hearing the name of Rushton sent a strange sequence of thoughts coursing through Cressy's mind. First, was the surprise of learning there was a Miss Rushton, and therefore, no doubt, a mother. It was hard to imagine Mr. Rushton as having any female as part of his existence whom he addressed as *Mama!*

Secondly, was the unsettling notion that she might have to meet Mr. Rushton so soon after their exchange only the day before. Would he be civil? she wondered. Or would he ignore her entirely. On the other hand, she doubted he would have any interest in dancing attendance upon his parent and sibling and would therefore not be among their party, so she needn't worry.

Lastly, was a strong desire to see both sister and mother, whose identities her aunt corroborated. After directing her attention to the doors where the Rushton party was entering the premises, she was startled to find a handsome woman of medium height cross the threshold and extend her hand to Mrs. Pritchard. The latter had deserted Mrs. Wanstrow with an alacrity almost equal to that with which Miss Pritchard had abandoned Cressy's side.

The attentions of the two Pritchard women upon the Rushton ladies Cressy could describe as nothing short of obsequious. She found herself disgusted and would have directed her attention elsewhere had not the figures of Mr. Rushton and Lord Somersby darkened the doorway but a moment later.

Here, Cressida suffered a shock. She had not supposed Mr. Rushton the sort of man who would rise at such an inconvenient hour merely to attend his mother and sister to the Pump Room. She was therefore surprised and for some unaccountable reason, quite pleased. She found herself regarding Mr. Rushton steadfastly, and she experienced, as she had during their initial encounter on the country lane near Mendip Combe, the most profound admiration for him. He was taller than most and bore himself nobly, his head held erect, a demeanor which set his broad shoulders off to considerable advantage. He was dressed elegantly in a bottle-green coat, buff waistcoat and breeches, and glossy Hessians. His black hair had been groomed with fastidious care, and his neckcloth was tied in an elegant series of folds. He was without question an extremely handsome man, an unhappy fact which caused her heart to quicken and her senses to reel slightly as though a gust of wind had buffeted her off balance. If she had not hitherto been exposed to the diverse, untidy flaws of his character, she realized her heart might be in serious jeopardy.

But even as this latter, hopeless thought flittered through her brain, Rushton chanced to catch her gaze. She would have looked away immediately, but a teasing, most provoking smile overcame his lips, and she was instantly caught. Whatever did he mean by it? she wondered. And how much the smile gave his countenance an agreeable, appealing quality!

On impulse, she nodded to him, her own gaze fixed to his, and afterward felt a blush begin warming her cheeks. She was then betrayed into an answering smile which completely maddened her, since she wished to keep a firm distance between herself and the infuriating man. Fortunately the irritation she felt at having been coaxed into a smile empowered her to look away from him, which she did immediately.

The next object of her gaze was unlucky however. She discovered Olivia Pritchard staring hard at her, neat little daggers springing from her green eyes. She knew a silly instinct to duck her head, so tangible was the dislike in Miss Pritchard's gaze, and she realized she had just acquired at least one enemy for all her morning's effort.

She had not been in Bath above the length of a complete turning of the sun, and already her world was rife with envy, jealousy, and other complications at present too difficult to fully comprehend.

Daphne slipped her hand into the pocket of her pelisse. There she fingered the traitorous billet she had spent an hour composing only the night before. No one knew of the missive or of her intense hope that Lord Somersby would be present at the Pump Room this morning. But the moment Mrs. Wanstrow had stated her intention of taking the waters at eight o'clock Daphne had determined to somehow communicate with his lordship.

Now that Somersby had arrived, she could concern herself with finding a way to see that he received her impassioned letter. If only he would be able to detach himself from Rushton's side long enough to take her missive, she would be happy. Well, almost.

Her biggest concern, larger than finding a moment in which to slip the billet into Somersby's hand, was whether or not once he had possession of the letter he would be able to decipher her words. She wasn't at all convinced she had spelled out her message to him correctly—Cressy was used to checking all her correspondence. Naturally, she did not show the letter to Cressida! She knew all too well her sister's opinion of Lord Somersby! Why even last night she had described him as a charming half-wit, and even though she had apologized afterward it was clear she would not be happy to see her sister married to the viscount.

If only Cressy could understand her feelings—even a trifle!

But how could she possibly explain to Cressida—who had never been in love!—that when Somersby had first appeared in the doorway she had felt nigh to fainting, so fast beat her heart. He was even more handsome than she remembered from the day before!

Yet she was ever so careful not to betray her feelings to Cressida and for that reason had not even tried to capture Somersby's gaze, especially since Mr. Rushton was beside him and also disapproved of Somersby's interest in her.

She therefore stood staring blankly at the floor, uncertain where to look, wondering if she had spelled enough of the words in her letter correctly in order to convey her meaning to Evan, hoping Cressy did not divine her love for him, and chewing nervously all the while upon the inside of her cheek.

"I should have warned you how it would be!" Mrs. Wanstrow whispered angrily to her nieces. "I should have told you of Mrs. Pritchard and her bosom beau, Mrs. Rushton. Hoity-toity, the pair of them, acting as though they are above their company! Do stop chewing on your tongue or whatever it is you are doing, Daphne! And Cressida, do smile, you appear positively glumfaced! Goodness gracious! Your cheeks are as red as fire! I wonder what has caused you to blush so!" She returned her gaze to the interesting group by the door and startled Cressy by gasping, and then groaning behind a quickly unfurled fan. "Oh, my dears, do you see the gown Mrs. Rushton is wearing!" She gasped again. "It is beyond enduring! I had no notion she had been to the dressmakers! My sources are usually more efficient! I'll have to speak with that new maid I hired! She was supposed to learn everything that transpires at the Rushton house! Oh, my, my, my! Have you seen anything quite so—so elegant!" She clutched her own half-cape of gold silk and held it together at the bosom, heaving a sigh of despair. "I am ruined! Oh, for a cup of chocolate to calm my nerves!"

Cressy had been stunned by the exceeding distress she heard in her aunt's voice at apparently having been outdone by Mrs. Rushton. She had watched her during the course of her diatribe, and when Mrs. Wanstrow finally fell silent, Cressy said simply, "There is an unhappy pucker upon the bodice of the gown which the taking in of a 'little fish' would certainly have eradicated. And as for the choice of fabric, I should not have selected a twill, not with so much embroidery upon the sleeves."

When Mrs. Wanstrow glared at Cressy, she in turn inclined her head slightly. A certain intriguing notion had entered her head, and she hoped that her comment upon the workmanship of Mrs. Rushton's half-robe would give her aunt cause to consider what value Cressida could be to her. She then audaciously left her side to cross the room and view the statue of Beau Nash, which was situated in an alcove high above the heads of the assembled company for all to admire.

She had heard of the statue's existence in presiding over the Pump Room, just as Mr. Nash had reigned over Bath society for so many years before his death in 1761. She had always wanted to see the figure and was surprised to find that Mr. Nash, apparently, had been as stout as Mrs. Wanstrow. No one that she could remember had ever described Mr. Nash's physique thusly to her. And she had never conceived that anyone, having been known by such a charming appellation as "Beau Nash," would be so florid in expression and so high in the flesh.

Her ruminations upon the statue were abruptly brought to an end when Mr. Rushton addressed her. "Good morning, Miss Chalcot."

Cressida felt her heart take a small, dancing leap as she glanced to her left and returned Mr. Rushton's friendly greeting. "Hello," she responded politely. And because he was so near and smiling with just that look of easy arrogance which characterized him best, she queried, "Was the drive here more prosperous than the one of yesterday?" She batted her lashes provokingly.

"What?" he smiled more broadly still. "Do you expect me to rise so readily to the fly? You will need more enticing bait I fear. As it happens, my mother's house is not far distant. She and my sister were borne along in rather unfashionable sedan chairs while Somersby and I strolled in their wake. Quite unexceptionable, and to reassure you on at least one score, we arrived here without incident."

"I profess to being amazed," Cressy responded facetiously, which brought an answering glimmer of amusement sparkling in his clear blue eyes. She felt what was fast becoming a familiar tug upon her heart and returned her gaze to the statue. It was far easier to remember Mr. Rushton's faults when looking at the round face of Beau Nash than it was when she was dazzled by his strong good looks or mesmerized by his direct manner of speaking with her.

He shifted slightly to better view her face, an angle which Cressy noted also permitted him to glance about the room if he so desired. In an easy, polished manner he proceeded to engage her in conversation, desiring to know how long she meant to remain in Bath, how she was enjoying her first perusal of the city, and whether or not she meant to attend the Lower Assembly Rooms. "For if you do," he added, "I wish to request your hand for the cotillion or a country dance."

Cressy was not merely surprised by his forwardness, but shocked. Heretofore their interactions had been so charged with vehement disapproval or anger that she could not imagine from what motive he would so accost her. "You wish to dance with me?" Cressida queried, stunned.

He had been gazing at some distant object with a slight furrow between his brows, so that when he shifted his gaze to give her answer, he blinked first before speaking. "You sound alarmed," he said.

"I will admit to such a sentiment. And though I have little doubt as to your eagerness to escort me down the ballroom floor, for you seem genuinely desirous of doing so, I still cannot account for it. Pardon my frankness, Mr. Rushton, but it would seem more logical were you to give me the cut direct than to beg a dance of me."

"But love is not logical," he returned easily, leaning toward her in what she supposed he meant to be an intriguing fashion.

"Oh!" she cried, her brows lifted in mock surprise. "I understand at last. You are flirting with me!"

"No," he responded flatly. "I am *trying* to do so, but apparently failing miserably."

"Oh, not miserably. I will confess to being well entertained!"

He grimaced in acknowledgement of her hit and appeared as though he would have enjoyed continuing their tête-à-tête had something or other not suddenly enslaved his attention. His blue eyes grew sharp with awareness, a frown returning to his brow, his gaze fixed across the crowded chamber.

Cressy could not keep from directing her attention to the object of his concern and watched in horror as

Daphne tried to slip something into Lord Somersby's pocket, but failed. A small, white square dropped to the floor and instead of smoothly retrieving it, Daphne gave a little gasp, placed her hand upon her cheek, and remained frozen in the same ridiculous guilty posture.

Mr. Rushton, to Cressy's dismay, wasted no time in crossing the chamber quickly, retrieving what proved to be a piece of paper folded several times into a hard square and returned it to Daphne with a polite bow.

Cressida, who had remained fixed where she was below the statue of Beau Nash and almost as immobile as Daphne, watched as Mr. Rushton turned to shake his head disapprovingly at her, took Lord Somersby firmly in hand, and guided him away from her hopeless sister.

Mrs. Wanstrow had observed the various proceedings regarding both her nieces with utter amazement, particularly appertaining to the interest of the two most eligible gentlemen in Bath. She was of course astonished that Daphne would try to secrete a billet to Lord Somersby, and in such a clumsy manner, but what intrigued her more was that Mr. Rushton, known to be fastidious in his choice of females to the point of absurdity, had actually conferred upon Cressida a full quarter of an hour of his exhalted conversation. Really it was unheard of! What did he mean by it, and how had her niece come to know him in the first place?

She had much to ponder. She almost was prepared to invite the girls to remain with her for a fortnight or more, but the cost of candles alone would be more than her miserly heart could bear with even the smallest degree of equanimity. She would by far rather cut off her nose!

Still, what greater vengeance could she inflict upon Mrs. Pritchard than to see her niece wed to Olivia's heart's desire—oh, what nonsense was she thinking! A young lady without a portion! Ridiculous.

With that she settled in her mind to get rid of the young women as originally intended. It followed, therefore, that the mere thought of having averted the spending of a single groat more than was absolutely necessary to maintain her comfort so increased her appetite that she decided to treat the girls to an excursion to her favorite coffee house.

Chapter Ten

Later that afternoon Cressida stood at the counter of the linen-drapers on Milsom Street. She demanded of the clerk to unroll several feet of the amaranthine-colored silk. She held it draped over the backs of both arms, her mind enjoying a dramatic vision of the gown she thought would not only best complement her aunt, but would also set every envious tongue to wagging at the New Assembly Rooms.

She had chosen the delicate shade of purple which carried a tinge of rose in its hue, because she was convinced the color would set off to excellent advantage the lovely slope and milky white complexion of her aunt's shoulders.

Ever since she had become aware of her aunt's jealousy of Mrs. Rushton and Mrs. Pritchard, as well as the competitive manner in which she was constantly comparing herself to both women, Cressy had been formulating a bold scheme. Having become convinced her salvation rested with Mrs. Wanstrow's intense desire to retain her status as a ruling force in Bath society, she had realized there was one way in which she could assist her aunt in doing so. To be fashionably clothed was the first priority of any woman wishing to be known as a reigning deity, and Cressy knew fabrics, style, and cut as though she had been born with a pair of peacock scissors stuck upon her thumb and middle finger. From the time she could remember, the business of needlecraft and stitchery had been her hobby and her delight. She fully intended, once Daphne was well settled, to open her own shop as a modiste, hopefully in the charming little establishment on Union Street. But now, facing the bleak prospect of having to leave her aunt's house in only two days, she turned her efforts to proving her usefulness to Mrs. Wanstrow by creating an elegant, flattering gown and matching turban, designed to take the wind out of Mrs. Pritchard's eye.

"You will not find a better fabric in Bath," the male clerk informed her, speaking down the length of his long nose.

Cressida looked up at him and said simply, "It is flawed. See there, how the weft has snagged here along the warp." The clerk struggled to find the object of her dissatisfaction. When he did, his cheeks turned a faint shade of pink.

"It is quite infinitessimal," he said guardedly.

"Indeed?" Cressy asked. "You may consider the flaw neglible, but as for myself I don't see how my needlewomen can possibly work around such an ill-placed snag. Still, with a little judicious cutting and use of gold braid—" she paused, pursed her lips together, lifted her brow as though carefully making the measurements even as she spoke, then finally said, "I shall take eight yards if you will consider a reduction in the price."

"Oh, but I can't. It is not our policy—"

"Very well! Good day." Cressy carefully set aside the fabric, gathered up her reticule, tying it snugly over her gloved arm, and turned away from the counter.

"One moment," the clerk said anxiously.

Before she turned around, Cressy smiled. By the time she had completed her business, she had purchased a dozen feet of tasseled gold braid, eight yards of silk, three spools of thread, and a white ostrich feather for the original price of the fabric alone.

She was so well satisfied with her purchases that she was smiling when she opened the door to quit the shop.

"My sister had a cat once who looked just like that when he got at my mother's love birds!"

Cressy was startled into an indelicate "Oh!" upon nearly colliding with Mr. Rushton and his mother as she stepped upon the flagway. She quickly recovered herself, and though she knew a blush was stinging her cheeks, she nodded to Rushton and responded with a polite, "How do you do?" He returned easily that he was the happiest man on earth since he had had the delight of seeing her so pleased with her shopping. He then introduced her to his mother.

Mrs. Rushton extended her hand to Cressy, which she took readily. She was surprised at the warm manner in which the dowager smiled and said, "You must forgive Gregory, Miss Chalcot. He is forever teasing me about my penchant for purchasing all manner of frippery. I have tried to correct this incorrigible habit, but he is quite the most stubborn of my children. You would do well to ignore him, as I do."

"Yes, ma'am, indeed I believe you are right," Cressy responded with a sly glance toward Mr. Rushton. She had expected him to be affronted or to some degree embarrassed, instead he held her gaze with a warm smile which softened his blue eyes and again caused her own heart to set forward on a brisk Scottish reel. She found herself wondering how such a beastly man could possess such warm eyes and after a moment realized with a start that Mrs. Rushton had asked a question which she did not hear.

Tearing her gaze from Rushton's with surprising difficulty, she looked at the dowager with blinking eyes and begged her pardon. "I am sorry, what did you ask of me?"

Mrs. Rushton wore a somewhat astonished expression for only the particle of a second, then asked, "I have been given to understand that Mrs. Wanstrow is your aunt.

Will you be staying with her long?"

"Yes—that is, I don't know for certain. My sister and I wish to remain in Bath, but whether we are to stay with my aunt is as yet unknown. She is not used to guests, and I am afraid our visit would be a trying imposition."

Mrs. Rushton searched Cressy's eyes carefully and nodded politely. "I used to be acquainted with your mother, Miss Chalcot. We were schoolgirls together at a select seminary. I was sorry when she no longer came to Bath or to London during the Season. She was a very vivacious creature and sought after by every gentleman of my acquaintance. Your sister is very much like her, I think."

"Yes. Were they of an age I believe they would have passed for twins."

"You of course are in the mold of your dear father. I was so sorry to hear of both your parents untimely deaths some few years ago. I had expected Mrs. Wanstrow to take charge of you and was surprised when she did not."

Cressy felt her cheeks again begin to burn. At first she did not know what to say, then spoke the truth as she understood it, willing, for what reason she knew not, to confide in this gentlewoman. "I know not the cause, but a bitter quarrel separated my mother and my aunt from the time I was but a babe. I consider Mrs. Wanstrow's hospitality at this juncture in our lives a gesture of compassion for which I am very grateful."

"Then you are far more forbearing than I, my dear," she said with a concerned expression. "But on that score I shall say nothing more else I shall speak words which can only wound you and will do nothing to help your cause. If you are ever in need of a listening ear, I hope you will come to me. But do, at least, beg your aunt to call upon me when it is convenient. I have not met your sister and would very much like both of you to become acquainted with my daughter." She then bid Cressy good day.

Cressida was about to say her farewells to Mr. Rushton

when his mother, who had stepped toward the door of the linen-drapers turned and commanded her son, "Gregory, do see Miss Chalcot to her carriage, I shan't need your assistance for several minutes, and I'm sure she would be grateful if you were so kind as to lend her your hand." She then disappeared within, but not until her eye had gleamed with a decided twinkle of conspiracy.

Cressy was greatly shocked, and for the third time during the course of the exchange she felt a warmth upon her cheeks.

"How very curious," Mr. Rushton began.

"And what is that," Cressy responded quickly, summoning her courage and presence of mind in order to adequately counter whatever provoking comment he was about to make.

"Mama seems enchanted with you. She isn't with everyone, you know. You ought to be flattered."

Cressida moved toward her aunt's carriage and watched absently as the coachman let down the steps for her. "I am deeply appreciative of her attentions. She is a very good woman, isn't she?"

Rushton, who had taken Cressy's hand and was about to hand her up into Mrs. Wanstrow's smart and exceedingly expensive landau, held it for a moment and responded, "Yes, she is. A very good woman."

Cressy could not resist taunting him. "You should have learned better at her knee, then!"

"Vixen!" he cried. Aiding her to ascend, he released her hand as she stepped onto the carriage floor.

Rushton closed the door with a snap and nodded for the coachman to mount the lead horse. Resting his gloved hands lightly on the side of the landau, he drew his brow into a serious pucker and said, "I have been hoping for a moment to speak with you privately—about your sister, that is."

Cressy felt her heart sink. She had hoped he would spare her the mortification of referring to the matter of Daphne's grievous crime in attempting to place a missive in the viscount's pocket at the Pump Room. But apparently he felt compelled to bring forth a subject she had wished left unattended the remainder of her years.

"And what do you wish to tell me," she offered in a low voice by way of giving him permision to continue.

He nodded and taking a deep breath, stated, "I need not express to you, I'm sure, how shocked I was to witness your sister's *indiscretion.* I can only trust that you instructed her upon the impropriety of flirting with my ward?"

Deciding the best course to follow was to tease Rushton a little, she responded brightly, "No, I most certainly did not."

Mr. Rushton seemed both surprised and displeased. "But you assured me you had no wish to see Somersby attached to your sister."

"Indeed, that much is true."

"Yet you said nothing to her of how improper it was to conduct a secret correspondence with Lord Somersby? I think you were very wrong not to do so. For though I have been given to understand you are the younger sibling, your general sense of responsibility as well as your superior mental facility lend themselves to acting the place of a parent."

"Even so, I am convinced it would be useless to discuss the propriety or, as it were, the *impropriety* of her actions with her." Cressida was enjoying herself hugely. He was an easy man to plague.

"Why ever not?"

Cressy could not keep the smile from her face, and giving the coachman the office to start, spoke only when the wheels began to roll. "She would not understand what I meant by the word *impropriety.*"

"Surely—" Mr. Rushton began, but already the carriage was pulling away from the flags. Even so, he followed the progress of the vehicle for a moment, walking beside it, his expression replete with frustration.

"Rest easy," Cressy said at last. "Daphne has promised not to take up her pen again."

He let out a breath of air, brought his booted feet to a halt, and shook his head reprovingly at her. Cressy watched him mouthe the word "infuriating" and doff his hat. She then had the delight of seeing him smile and because of it could not resist waving to him. The last she saw, he had lifted his hand to her in a single salute.

Heaven help her, she liked him!

She liked him very much!

Chapter Eleven

Soon after dinner Cressida complained of the headache. Mrs. Wanstrow was first shocked and concerned, requesting to know if Cressy was succumbing to the ague. When she assured her aunt that she was perfectly well but frequently suffered from annoying headaches, her aunt settled back into her sofa—a sweetmeat clinging to her pudgy fingers as she continued to flip unconcernedly through the pages of Ackermann's *Repository*—and waved her away. She did recall she ought to express some concern for Cressida's discomfort, and just before her niece crossed the threshold recommended she purchase lavender water the next time she had occasion to visit the shops along Milsom Street.

"I have always found," Mrs. Wanstrow said, "that a kerchief drenched with lavender water and placed upon the forehead performs a considerable service in removing the affliction. I would offer you the use of mine, but my own supply is sadly depleted. And since my constitution is quite delicate, I must always take the greatest care not to jeopardize the various health remedies I keep perpetually nearby. For you must know the moment one is unwisely generous, disaster is sure to follow!"

Cressida murmured her appreciation for her aunt's kind intentions. Because she could not keep a slight measure of sarcasm from tinging her speech, Mrs.

87

Wanstrow glanced sharply at her, blushed faintly, then resumed her perusal of her favorite magazine. Cressy had little doubt her aunt's supply of lavender water was sufficient for an army.

It had not taken Cressida very many hours in her aunt's company to divine the exact nature of Mrs. Wanstrow's character. She could remember once her papa having said that Mrs. Wanstrow was a penny-pinching old fidget, hoarding every groat, who ought to be shot and stuffed, and her fortune given to charity. Her cupboards were stocked to the rafters, yet her servants were starved and the sole business of her life was her self-consequence. Yet in all the morass of her aunt's unhappy qualities, Cressida still found it impossible to dislike Mrs. Wanstrow entirely. For all her faults, she was an amiable, albeit selfish, companion and was both charming and amusing whenever it pleased her to be so—which was most of the time!

Cressy retired quickly to her bedchamber for the night. She had much to accomplish and was exhilarated at the prospect of setting her scissors and needle to the pretty violet fabric. In the process of determining how best to proceed with her scheme, she had admitted only the undermaid, Angelina, into her confidence. She was a tall, pretty young woman who was waiting upon both herself and Daphne while they remained under Mrs. Wanstrow's roof. Cressy had intended to keep her activities secret from all other members of her aunt's staff, but her request for a dozen working candles struck such a look of fright into the maid's round, dark eyes that Cressy found it necessary to inform the housekeeper of her mission as well.

Mrs. Pylle was a nervous creature with large hazel eyes and mousy hair. She had obviously been in Mrs. Wanstrow's employ for a long time, since her first comment was that the Missus was not likely to take kindly to having more than two or three candles disappear so sudden like. "For she is wont to take stock of all the foodstuffs and articles what has anything to do with her household, if not every day, then the days betwixt."

"Should she rebuke you, Mrs. Pylle, you must tell her I insisted upon the candles because I am frightened of sleeping in the dark, but by no means reveal what I am about."

Mrs. Pylle caught sight of the fabric laid out upon Cressy's bed and cooed softly. "Ah, 'tis lovely and will look pretty on you, miss!"

"Oh, it's not for me. I am making up a gown for my aunt, a surprise as it were. But if I am to have it ready by tomorrow night, I must work until the small hours of the morning."

Mrs. Pylle shook her head. "You won't have it ready, miss! 'Tis quite a lot of Mrs. Wanstrow that your stitches and fabric will be covering. I had best help you."

Cressy would have protested, but for all of Mrs. Pylle's fidgety fingers and blinking, nervous eyes, she possessed a firmness of will which closed the subject for Cressy and sent the young Angelina scuttling away at the command of the housekeeper in search of the latter's workbox.

By two o'clock in the morning, the garment had been carefully cut according to Cressy's experienced eye and well-thought out patterns. She had designed the garment taking as her model, pictures found in the *Repository*.

Since she knew the household would be alive by five o'clock in order to see Mrs. Wanstrow off to the Pump Room at the proper hour, Cressy sent a rather blear-eyed Mrs. Pylle to her bed and after snuffing carefully a guttering candle, crawled between the sheets.

In the morning she excused herself from a visit to the Pump Room, again with complaints of a severe headache. She was sorry to learn she was forfeiting as well a visit to Mrs. Pritchard's home afterward where several ladies were used to gathering every Tuesday after taking the waters. Daphne was more than willing to attend Mrs. Wanstrow, although her extremely happy and conscious looks disturbed Cressida.

The day prior, contrary to her teasing remarks to Mr. Rushton, Cressy had taken Daphne severely to task for having attempted to place a billet in Lord Somersby's pocket. She had dwelt particularly not only upon the scandalous nature of such an attempt, but upon the need for Daphne not to give Lord Somersby false hopes. "For you must know, Lord Somersby is so amiable a gentleman, he might misinterpret such a form of dalliance. He might believe you serious in your intentions. You would not wish to mislead him, would you?"

Daphne had instantly assured Cressy she would never want to mislead his lordship and promised earnestly never again to attempt to secret a billet to him.

Cressy had been satisfied with her sister's assurances until she saw how ecstatic Daphne was at the prospect of returning to the Pump Room. Since she would be taking the waters under the watchful eye of Mrs. Wanstrow—who had been carefully informed of Daphne's past indiscretion at Mrs. Cameley's house—Daphne would have little opportunity for getting into mischief. Still, as she set her stitches, along with two skilled maids and Mrs. Pylle, she felt a prickle of concern that all was not well with Daphne. Yet why she should feel the least anxiety, she did not know. After all, it was not as though Daphne was in love with Somersby, of that she was convinced. Her sister had conducted so many scandalous flirtations over the course of her career, however innocent, that Cressida was certain Daphne had as yet to know an affection that was true and everlasting. If only she could discover the right man for her sister, all would be settled, including the blossoming of love in Daphne's tender heart.

By noon, once the narrow gold braid had been properly affixed in a double row down the entire front of the gown, and the white ostrich feather had been attached to the matching turban in a gentle drape which would flow in a circle about her aunt's head, Cressy stretched herself out upon her bed and fell into a profound sleep.

She was awakened several hours later by her aunt, who touched her shoulder very gently, called her name several times, and bid her niece sit up.

Cressy rubbed her eyes and blinked several times. "Goodness!" she cried. "What is the hour? The room is quite dark! Have I slept so long?"

"No, no my dear! Mrs. Pylle merely pulled the blinds closed for you. But I must know!" she cried ecstatically. "Was it you, truly, who created this—this exquisite gown for me?"

Cressida felt the last vestiges of sleep desert her instantly as she watched her aunt pirouette several times, joy suffusing her plump face. The violet gown, enhanced by a charming necklace of diamonds and pearls, elegant long, white gloves, and delicate white satin slippers, fit her aunt nearly to perfection and had couched within its design the ability to smooth out the lumps of Mrs. Wanstrow's plump frame.

Cressy slid from the bed and crossed the chamber abruptly, causing her aunt to stumble in a final pirouette as she watched her niece's quick movements.

Cressy tugged on the bellpull summoning Mrs. Pylle. When that lady appeared, both women went quickly to work making several miniscule adjustments to complete the final fitting of her aunt's gown.

Mrs. Wanstrow was clearly shocked by the proceedings, unable to credit her niece's accomplishments. "How very clever you are, Cressida! But where did you learn such skill? Such an eye for line and detail?" She fingered the small gold tassels which accented each angled path of the gold braid.

"I have always drawn sketches of every manner of apparel, including bonnets, gowns, capes, even reticules, making use especially of my watercolors, playing with the use of color and texture. How do you like the feather?"

Mrs. Wanstrow rolled her eyes upward and catching a

glimpse of the feather, nodded gently, her arms outslung as Cressy pinned the seam beneath her arm.

"There!" Cressy cried at last. "You have but to remove the gown, and in about half an hour Mrs. Pylle will return it to you. But are you certain Daphne and I are to attend the assemblies this evening? I still cannot believe the Master of Ceremonies approved us so readily."

"I refuse to be offended by such an ill-considered remark, Cressida!" Mrs. Wanstrow's eyes twinkled as she spoke, the harsh nature of her words belied by the happiness in her blue eyes. "Of what use is it, I say, to work diligently to maintain one's standing in society, if one cannot persuade a mere Master of Ceremonies to approve one's nieces!"

Later that evening Cressy stood behind Mrs. Wanstrow—with Daphne behind her—and could not help but think that if the ostrich feather atop her aunt's violet turban had been an array of peacock feathers, the entire turban would have unfurled with pride. Though she felt there yet remained one or two flaws in the overall assemblage of Mrs. Wanstrow's gown, in general she could not remember her aunt appearing to greater advantage.

Cressy was not the only personage to note her aunt's charming ensemble. Within fifteen minutes Mrs. Wanstrow had received a dozen sincere and sometimes shocked compliments on the beauty and elegance of her gown—the most agitated one erupting from a seriously aggrieved Mrs. Pritchard.

"Why, how charming you look, my dear Mrs. Wanstrow. I—I had no notion you were having a new gown made up. And so utterly exceptional. I should like to see my Olivia in such a creation! I daresay she would appear to unequalled beauty, especially since even your defects of form are adequately compensated for by the extraordinary fit of the bodice and skirt!"

Mrs. Wanstrow, inured to such paltry attempts to overset her, replied, "But then Olivia is so frail-looking in her beauty, one might fear she would disappear entirely were she to don a gown meant for a more queenly figure. Now that I think on it, I feel I ought to give you a hint. Just a little one. On no account attempt to attire your daughter thusly, Mrs. Pritchard, for I fear you risk losing Rushton's attentions forever. Of course, it has come to my notice that Olivia's beau has experienced a decided shift in his interest." Here she cast a pointed glance toward Cressida. "Even Mrs. Rushton remarked on it not a moment earlier. Oh! I see my good friend Sir Leighton-Jones has returned from London. I must speak with him at once! Good-bye!"

Cressy and Daphne moved in her wake, each curtsying in turn to the stormy countenance of Mrs. Pritchard as they passed by. Cressy could not help but admire her aunt prodigiously with regard to her fencing abilities. As sharp as Mrs. Pritchard's sword was, Mrs. Wanstrow had no difficulty fending off each attack with as graceful a movement as the most skilled swordsman in England might parry the thrusts of his opponent.

Mr. Rushton's town chariot drew to a halt on Alfred Street at the carriage entrance of the New Assembly Rooms. In a curious way he was looking forward to the assemblies, which for several months now he had thought to have grown rather tedious and dull. When he was willing to admit as much to himself, he was particularly intrigued by the thought that Miss Chalcot would be present. Ever since learning of her arrival in Bath, then exchanging a delightfully sharp banter with her both at the Pump Room and later outside his mother's favorite linen-drapers, he had come to anticipate just what either outrageous or incisive remark she would make to him.

He was in no way in danger of losing his heart to her. Of that he was certain. She displayed scarcely a single quality he intended his future wife to possess in abundance. He wanted a woman with a gentle, yielding disposition, a mind devoted to study and improvement, and of sufficient fortune to match his own.

Cressida Chalcot could not meet any of these requirements. Not even the most generous of observers could qualify her as a meek, delicately nurtured female, and as for her mind, the object of her life was clearly not the development of her capacities, but of purchasing fabric and trying to leg-shackle her sister to the wealthiest simpleton she could find! As for her dowry, it was generally known that both young ladies were left destitute upon the unhappy deaths of both parents. For these reasons he felt perfectly safe in pursuing a flirtation with her and in general thought it would be most challenging to see whether or not he could breach the walls of her heart. Instinctively he knew she had never been touched by Cupid's arrow, and he wondered how a healthy infection of love might serve to put a glow in her pretty violet eyes. Indeed, it had, in the past several hours, become an obsession with him, to see her face awash with the light of *amour*.

However much he was enjoying himself one glance at his ward sufficed to inform him Lord Somersby was not. The hapless viscount, apparently unaware that the coach had stopped and that a footman had opened the doors and let down the steps, remained seated, staring out the window and chewing, as always of late, upon the corner of his cambric kerchief. The tortured viscount sighed and sighed again.

Rushton felt a pique of annoyance as he looked at his friend, wishing for the hundredth time that the heavens had seen fit upon his birth to place a little more sense within the vacuous space of his mind. Repressing his strong sense of irritation, he leaned toward Somersby. "We are arrived, Evan," he said quietly.

94

Lord Somersby jumped in his seat, startling Rushton.

"Good God, man!" Rushton cried. "Whatever is the matter? Are you not feeling well?"

Somersby stared at Rushton for a long moment, his mind appearing to work in fits and starts as he opened and closed his mouth a half-dozen times. Finally he nodded. "I'm perfectly well, thank you. Just a trifle blue-deviled. I—that is—oh, I suppose it is nothing of consequence." He shifted his gaze to again look sadly out the window.

Rushton considered his friend carefully. He knew the viscount had taken a hard tumble where Daphne was concerned, yet he knew not how to console him. All his attempts heretofore had only aroused his friend to a stubborn silence, a state which had taken Rushton completely by surprise. It was so unlike him. And no matter how strenuously he represented to the viscount the inequality of a union with Daphne as well as the unhappiness likely to ensue at the matching of two persons so *alike* in abilities—or rather the lack of them— Somersby would only stiffen his jaw, divert his attention away from Rushton, and set vigorously to chewing upon his kerchief!

Rushton had come to hate the sight of Somersby's damn handkerchiefs and knew a sudden desire to quickly wrest the one currently drooping from between his clenched teeth.

He restrained himself however and after patting Somersby on the shoulder could only offer the mildest words of condolence. "In time you will find someone better-suited to your station in society and to your temperament. Until then, I do not object if you go down one set with Miss Chalcot, but no more than one else you might raise unfortunate expectations in her heart. Even I am not ignorant of her decided *tendre* for you. But you must be strong and resist the desire to succumb to her exceptional beauty. If not for your sake, then for hers!"

Somersby was so surprised that his mouth fell agape, the kerchief dropping limply to his lap. "You will let me dance with her?"

Rushton was surprised and smiling faintly, said, "I am not such a beast as you must think. Of course you may dance with her. It would be impolite to do otherwise, especially since my mother means to pursue an acquaintance with both young women. She was a friend of their mother's at one time."

Somersby's expression was one of intense relief and joy. Without further ado he followed Rushton from the town chariot, nearly toppling him over in his excitement and rush to be near Daphne.

Chapter Twelve

Cressida sat in a chair next to Sir Leighton-Jones and tried to still the furious beating of her heart. He was a gentleman full of possibilities, and her mind was moving so swiftly that she was experiencing some difficulty in hearing what he was saying to her. She did think he was explaining in more detail than was necessary for her purposes precisely how it had come about he was using a cane. All that mattered was that Sir Leighton-Jones was talking, and she was more than willing to lend her ear for the remainder of the set.

Mrs. Wanstrow was dancing with the Master of Ceremonies, and Daphne had been claimed by a handsome man in regimentals, Major Heath, who had been introduced to her as a nephew of Mrs. Pritchard. Sir Leighton-Jones, who had had the great misfortune to fall from his horse in Hyde Park some three weeks earlier, was still relying upon his walking stick to move about and so could not dance.

Cressida thought it was a stroke of good fortune his injury must confine him to conversation instead of the intricate figures of the quadrille, else she most certainly would not have learned half of what she now knew of the handsome baronet.

He was the gentlest of men, possessing a temperament

above all others Cressida had envisioned for Daphne. His voice was well tenored and soft when he spoke. His brown eyes were direct, kind, and attentive when he listened. His expression was warm and generous when he smiled. He was tall, quite lean, and to some degree athletic in appearance. His coat of black superfine, the well-starched moderate shirt points, and the well-tied white neckcloth all presented an elegant appearance in the Brummell mode of which she heartily approved. And just before Mrs. Wanstrow had performed the introductions she had whispered to Cressida information of the most valuable—Sir Leighton-Jones was worth a very tidy four thousand a year!

He wanted only one, small, insignificant article with which Cressida could abundantly supply him—a wife! And Cressida meant, before the summer was over, to see him wed to Daphne!

"Then you and your sister will be living with your aunt through the end of the summer?" he queried politely, turning toward her and leaning his arm upon the back of the chair so as better to see her.

Cressida blinked at him, her ears struggling to catch up with his words. "My aunt?" she asked, knowing he had mentioned her within the body of his recent question.

"Yes, Mrs. Wanstrow. You will be residing with her?"

Finally Cressy heard him. "As to that," she responded brightly, unfurling her fan and wafting it gently across her warm cheeks. "We are not certain whether we wish to remain with her or to seek a chaperone and an establishment of our own. These matters must be handled with great delicacy."

Sir Leighton-Jones fixed a knowing eye upon Cressy and nodded wisely. "Yes, indeed! And I'm certain that if you choose to hire a house for the summer, Mrs. Wanstrow will help you pack your bandboxes!"

Cressida gasped, bit her lip, and tried desperately not

to smile. It was useless, however. He was a charming man and had said something most improper but highly amusing. His comprehension of her aunt's character was obviously astute.

He leaned close to her and whispered, "You may laugh if you wish, though I find your blushes and the smiles you are so ineffectively hiding to be quite enchanting."

Cressy cast her eyes down and looked at the tips of her shoes. "You mustn't try my sense of honor and decorum so mightily, Sir Leighton-Jones. My aunt has been all that is kind to have sheltered us for these several days. If I smile, I blame only you."

"Blame me all you wish. Just keep smiling and I am content."

At that, Cressy turned to look at him. She narrowed her eyes slightly as she met his teasing gaze. "You are flirting with me!" she exclaimed, laughing.

He nodded in a mockingly serious manner and responded, "Yes, I am."

Cressy laughed and felt very giddy and happy. It had been some time since she had let herself simply enjoy the company of a gentleman. The business of her existence had been so occupied in the tedium of survival that she had many times wondered if she could remember how to laugh, and skip about a ballroom, and smile, and say silly things. She knew now she could.

For several minutes more he teased her or regaled her with a favorite anecdote from the recent London Season. Cressy permitted him to lead her down whichever path he chose, but finally guided his thoughts and attention to Daphne. "Do you not think my sister a great beauty?" she asked, her own gaze watching Daphne smile at the officer now bowing over her hand as the set drew to a close.

"Indeed, who could not think as much!" Sir Leighton-Jones responded heartily. He, too, let his gaze dwell upon Daphne, an appreciative, masculine eye taking in every feature of her face, every blond, angelic curl of her hair, every detail of her embroidered blue gauze gown which traveled in a clinging drape to her well-turned ankles. "She is a vision from Olympus, there can be no two opinions on that subject. Tell me why she has not graced London with her extraordinary countenance. She would enjoy every manner of attention and courtship, with offerings of love clustered high about her feet. She would be worshipped."

Cressy explained in very simple and direct terms the origin of their misfortunes. She wanted the baronet to know at the outset how she and Daphne were situated.

Sir Leighton-Jones listened with concerned interest. "I can only guess at your sufferings," he suggested compassionately. "But I think you were wise to settle in Bath. You are sure to repair your fortunes here, with your aunt's patronage of course. I, too, shall do what I can to ease your path amongst the shoals of this sometimes unforgiving watering place."

"You are very kind," Cressy returned, feeling immensely pleased with the progress she had made.

She was about to invite him to pay a call upon her aunt tomorrow when Mr. Rushton's voice intruded.

"Miss Chalcot," he said politely, smiling down at her with a familiar gleam in his eye. He then bowed to her and to Leighton-Jones before continuing. "I am here to claim a dance you promised to me at the Pump Room. Or have you forgotten?"

Cressy stared up into Rushton's extraordinary blue eyes and felt her heart again set to leaping and jumping. Why did she feel this way, like a ridiculous schoolgirl, whenever she but looked at the man! Really, it was absurd! "No, I have not forgotten," she responded.

She then glanced toward Sir Leighton-Jones and knew a pique of annoyance that she must leave his side just when she was progressing so nicely with him.

There was nothing for it, however, but to smile and beg

him to excuse her. She had promised a dance to Rushton and did not wish in any way to give Sir Leighton-Jones a disgust of her by appearing disobliging to her promised partner.

As Cressida took Rushton's arm and moved to take her place among those preparing for the next set, she noticed for the first time the beauty of the chamber. The New Assembly Rooms consisted of a ballroom, a tearoom and a concert room or card room arranged around a central antechamber. The ballroom itself was over a hundred feet long, oblong in shape with tall Corinthian columns and pilasters ensconced in the upper half of the walls. Five chandeliers hung from the high, coved ceiling, and the orchestra was recessed above the floor in a charming semicircle overlooking the dancers. Elegance commanded the chamber, and when full of the finest of Bath society, adorned with jewels, feathers, starched shirt points, and tails, Cressida could not imagine a prettier or more festive gathering.

Mr. Rushton, much to her subsequent pleasure, had chosen to claim her hand for the waltz, a dance upon which Daphne had most wisely instructed her some two years earlier. At the time Cressida had thought it unnecessary to practice her steps when it seemed an impossibility to her that she would ever make use of such a skill. But now, as Mr. Rushton slipped his arm about her waist, and took her hand lightly within his own, she experienced a rush of gratitude for her sister's efforts. Still, she was not confident in her abilities.

As he gently turned her into the delicate sweeping rhythm of the music, Cressy grew very quiet and spent the first several minutes of the set responding in single utterances to his various civil questions and comments. She was concentrating assiduously upon the figure of the dance.

After several minutes she heard her partner call her by name, and afterward query, "Am I boring you?"

Cressy was startled and glanced up at him, aware for the first time how her responses to his attempts at conversation must have seemed. She was prompted to laugh and say, "To be quite frank with you, Mr. Rushton, I don't know whether you are boring me or not! I have been minding my steps. You see, I am quite unused to dancing in public, and most particularly, the waltz, though I will confess your own skill has made it quite easy for me to execute what little knowledge I possess of the dance."

Mr. Rushton looked into her smiling violet eyes and felt his ability to reason drift strangely away, along with his earlier intention of getting up a flirtation with her. There was something in the way she answered his slightly offended query with such candor and lack of affection which made the pursuit of dalliance with her something of an absurdity. That she actually confessed her incompetence as a dancer quite literally bowled him over. Of course, that would adequately describe his entire experience with her heretofore.

"I would not have known you were in any way lacking as a partner, Miss Chalcot. You dance with an ease and a lightness of step I find both remarkable and enjoyable!"

Cressy swallowed very hard. Rushton was looking at her with an unsettling light in his eye. And his words, however polite and kindly meant, were spoken with an intensity which went beyond mere consideration. Around he turned her, around again. Her heart was a butterfly, flitting wildly about, stirring up dangerous thoughts within her breast. She felt dizzy, but not dizzy. Light-headed, certainly. She felt caught in a powerful emotion she could not define. What was it about Rushton that slowed her mind down so that she couldn't think, yet sped up her heart so that she couldn't breathe? She wanted to speak, but words would scarcely shape themselves in her mind, much less make the long, impossible journey to the tip of her tongue. Why was such confusion holding reign over her faculties? Why was he so handsome? Why did he look at her so fiercely?

"Why did you come here?" he asked, but appeared not to desire an answer. Finally, he tore his gaze from her, a cloud of disquiet marring his features.

Cressida slowly began to hear again, as though all sounds had previously disappeared. The strains of the orchestra floated gently to her ears, the usual chuckles and giggles associated with a ballroom eventually returned to dominate the air, and even the whispering of her slippers across the polished wood floor rose to assail her hearing.

Only then did she realize that she was no longer concentrating upon her steps. Her feet seemed perfectly attuned to Mr. Rushton's mode of dancing and followed easily wherever he led. She wished she understood why Rushton affected her as he did, perhaps then she could counter the terrifying way in which she was beginning to take pleasure in his company.

In an effort to shift her thoughts away from the odd murmurings of her heart, she asked Rushton whether or not he was acquainted with Sir Leighton-Jones.

Rushton seemed relieved by her question and responded, "We have been acquainted for any number of years. He is a gentleman of honor, a notable shot, and is known to care for his lands with energy. I could not help but notice he had engaged you in conversation for some few minutes!"

"Almost the entire set. I found him quite agreeable. Just the sort of man—" she broke off, blushing with the realization she had meant to say he would make Daphne an admirable husband, "that is, just the sort of man to properly entertain a lady in a ballroom even when he is not able to stand up with her."

Mr. Rushton narrowed his eyes slightly. "That is not what you were about to say, was it?"

Cressida wished he were not such a perceptive creature and with a shake of her head, responded, "No, it was not! But I beg you will refrain from pressing me to reveal the truly dreadful thing I was about to say."

"May I guess the sum of your thoughts?"

Cressida, who was growing more and more embarrassed as each beat of the music swept them about the long chamber, glanced up at him and with a contrite note in her voice again beseeched him. "I wish you will not!"

"I think I should," he retorted. "You have already made your object in coming to Bath known to me. But I think you are very wrong to set about trying to fix your interest, or your sister's, however vicariously executed, with any man. It is most unbecoming conduct."

Cressida liked neither the content of his speech, which she felt a true gentlemen would not have spoken in the first place, nor the way he had fixed his stare upon her as though he meant to intimidate her. "I take it very unkind in you that you must give me a dressing down for seeing to my own or to my sister's affairs."

"Do you deny your motives?"

"Why should I? They are not, after all, so very different from most of the ladies present—not to mention a few of the gentlemen who lack fortunes and seek to align themselves with women of means."

"But must *you* follow suit?"

Cressida felt deeply frustrated by the subject at hand. "Do you think I take pleasure in the course I feel I must pursue? Had I a sufficient fortune, not only would we not be sharing this dance, but I daresay I would never have even laid eyes on you, and I most certainly would not have chosen to spend a summer in Bath! I should be fixed permanently in London, enjoying a leisured existence such as you enjoy!"

"Such as I enjoy?" he queried with a cold laugh. "Am I to now feel badly that my forebears had the sense and judgment to protect their property? I think not."

Cressy found herself offended by Rushton's reference to the manner in which her father had lost his fortune. Upon his death she had come to understand that his indiscretions at a variety of gaming hells were common knowledge. "How easily you condemn me," she returned quietly, her heart stung by his words and manners. "But this I will say, I have never met a more impertinent, unkind man in my entire existence. May I suggest you save your opinions and recriminations for one whose circumstances are slightly less desperate than my own. Until then, I confess I am grateful this waltz is drawing to a close."

Rushton appeared as though she had struck his face. "I didn't mean—oh, the devil take it, Cressida! I never meant to—I only wanted you to know that I dislike machinations of any sort."

"Well, you've certainly made your opinions known to me, haven't you?" she whispered.

Because the set was indeed ending, Cressy withdrew from the circle of his arms and dropped a slow, proper curtsy. Afterward, she moved away from him on a stately tread, hoping that their argument had not been obvious to the various spectators seated about the edge of the ballroom floor. She took up her place beside her aunt, drew in a deep breath, and composed her features. As she glanced about the long chamber she could see that she had become the object of some speculation, and though she tried to keep her embarrassment from affecting her, she could feel her cheeks grow decidedly warm.

Mrs. Wanstrow observed her heightened color. "Upon my word, Cressida!" she exclaimed in a hoarse whisper. "You have two rather ugly red spots burning upon each of your cheeks. What mischief have you been brewing, and whatever were you saying to our good Mr. Rushton to cause his countenance to become so stiff and unhappy? I trust you weren't giving offense, for you must know he is considered by most to be our Leader of

Fashion here in Bath. He certainly is invited everywhere, and it simply wouldn't do, you know, if your object is to see Daphne well settled, to go about setting up his back. You ought to apologize to him at the very first opportunity!"

Cressida, suddenly angry that her object must be to seek Rushton's good will, responded with a lift of her chin, "I should by far rather dye my hair a pretty shade of purple!"

Much to Cressy's surprise, Mrs. Wanstrow responded with a laugh. "Well!" she cried. "You are certainly full of pluck! I'll give you that much!"

Rushton quit the ballroom to take some air just at the entrance of the assembly rooms. An assorted melee of ladies and gentlemen made a constant progress in and out of the antechamber, some leaving, some just arriving, and some enjoying a respite from the exertions of dancing.

He stood watching the late arrivals, greeting some who he knew quite well, acknowledging those with whom he was but slightly acquainted, and ignoring the rest. His temper had been seriously ruffled by his unhappy conversation with Cressida. He didn't know what to make of her, or, more precisely, his incomprehensible feelings toward her.

The truth was, she disturbed him in a manner he had never experienced before. Why, there had even been a moment during the waltz he had shared with Cressida, when he had lost all ability to think, to give shape to his thoughts, to reason! Especially when she looked up at him with her enchanting eyes fairly boring into his soul. It was her candor which affected him most deeply, he realized. Never in his existance had he known a female to admit her faults or her ambitions so freely as Cressida was wont to do.

And he liked it! Heaven help him, he liked it very much.

Why then had he rounded on her so fiercely about her schemes where Daphne was concerned? He knew he had hurt her, and for that he was sorry. But he would be damned before he would approve in any form of her ambitions.

Chapter Thirteen

"But are you certain Mr. Rushton will not object to our dance and whisk you away?" Daphne queried of her most handsome, most wondrous love. She had placed her arm upon Somersby's and was permitting him to guide her onto the ballroom floor, her hand trembling as her fingers touched the sleeve of his coat.

Lord Somersby smiled and patted her arm, a movement he ceased abruptly, fearing he might be observed. He leaned his head toward hers slightly and responded in a whisper to her expressed concerns. "No!" he exclaimed. "It was he who suggested I go down at least one set with you, Daphne. Yes, you may stare! He felt it would be considered rude not to do so. I am ever so grateful for his sense of propriety! Never did I think civility would bring you close to me!"

"Oh, Evan!" Daphne whispered in return. "I am so glad we are to share this dance together, but pray tell me, who is *Civility?* Have I met her, though I must say I have never heard such a charming name before. Is it French?"

Lord Somersby emitted a crack of laughter. "You know her very well," he responded, taking up a place on the ballroom floor as far from Rushton as he could manage. "She is a cousin of Propriety and of Decorum!"

"Oh, *civility!* How stupid of me! But I do like how you tease me. But oh, my darling, whatever are we to do?

108

Cressy opposes our love! You can have no idea!"

"Oh yes I can!" he responded, bowing to her in preparation for the set. "Rushton won't hear of it either! He believes we are ill-suited, you and I! Can you imagine anything more absurd?"

"Oh, Evan! What are we to do?"

"Don't worry! We shall come about!"

It was not possible to exchange more than a few words during the course of the country dance, but what the thwarted lovers could not say, each made up for in the expressive smiles and looks they were able to generously bestow upon one another.

Cressida, having been accosted by Miss Pritchard at the beginning of the set, was alternating her attention between Olivia and the sight of Daphne comporting herself with some dignity and not a little absurdity, upon the ballroom floor.

Through all the ebb and flow of flirtatious, mooncalf glances the couple exchanged, Cressida was relieved to see nothing in either Somersby's or Daphne's demeanor to cause her any other sentiment than a strong desire to box both pairs of ears. Miss Pritchard was less confident the affair was as harmless as Cressida believed it to be.

"It would seem his lordship has tumbled violently in love," that elegant lady commented. "I have known Somersby these ages and more, and until tonight, I vow I have never seen him so blissfully attendant upon a partner as he is upon your sister."

Cressida, who believed Miss Pritchard said nothing unless it somehow served her interest, returned simply, "He is but barely shed of his salad days. I understand he enjoyed his first Season in London not many weeks past. I daresay he has many more to endure before he forms a serious attachment."

When Miss Pritchard did not respond immediately, Cressida glanced at her and discovered her features animated by the liveliest astonishment. "What is it?" she queried, surprised.

"I have never known anyone like you, Miss Chalcot. Your dispassionate comments upon what every other acquaintance of mine has already described as a singularly hopeful affair, has shocked me, particularly knowing how your sister is fixed. I should think you would be *aux anges* at the sight of Lord Somersby flirting with her. For myself, given his decided preference for her company, I should have already suggested she order her bride's clothes!"

"You are presuming I would wish for the match!"

"Would you not? I cannot credit it! What a strange creature you are, not to wish your sister married to a fortune and a title. I do not pretend to possess such disinterest in worldly concerns. Were I to have a sibling who showed herself ready to love such a man—and to be loved by him—I would be the first to encourage her heart to follow his lead, particularly since he appears to have already taken her in hand."

Since, at that moment, the movements of the country dance brought Daphne and Somersby together, and the exchange of smiles which followed was warm enough to light a dozen candles, Cressida could not immediately refute Miss Pritchard's opinions. She was struck forcibly by the manner in which Daphne's expression was replete with affection. Had she mistaken her sister's heart? Were Miss Pritchard's observations more accurate than her own? She could not believe it was possible, or perhaps refused to. Yet what if it was true?

She did not wish to dwell upon it. She had set her course and Daphne's, a path which did not include Lord Somersby as an appropriate spouse for her hen-witted sibling. Disaster could only ensue from such a union, of that she was convinced.

"There!" Miss Pritchard pressed her. "You must admit Cupid has spent at least three of his arrows on each of them. I have never known a couple to smell more of April and May than these two. Confess you have erred and I will be satisfied."

By now Cressida found her conversation with Miss Pritchard to be trying in the extreme. She could not resist, therefore, answering facetiously, a mode of response which she had begun to suspect was a particular failing of hers, "You are right, of course! Their's must be a marriage made in heaven. They look so uncommonly pretty together, how could I have thought otherwise!" With a conspiratorial smile, she added, "I have already seen to Daphne's bride's clothes—just as you suggested. I hope, nay, *intend,* to see her wed to Somersby before summer's end. I was only trying for a measure of discretion in the expression of my opinions earlier. But, tell me, since you are so interested in Daphne's welfare, what think you of the ceremony being conducted in a garden so full of flowers as to cause even the bees to sneeze? Hm?"

Miss Pritchard appeared well pleased with Cressida's answer, her expression taking on the look of a sly fox. "How quaintly you phrase your speech, Miss Cressy. The bees to sneeze, indeed! Are you a poetess as well as a matchmaker? But how charming. Oh! I see Miss Rushton is waving to me, and I simply must compliment her on her gown. She is one of the few women I know who can wear white to advantage. Perhaps we will converse again before the night is done—or the summer!"

She gracefully swept past Cressida, who was left with the strong sensation she had just exposed herself to someone who would serve her a bad turn the moment she could. She also could not keep from glancing down at the white sprig muslin of her own gown and tried very hard not to let Miss Pritchard's biting tongue, so reminiscent of her mother's, affect her judgment. She then recalled with pleasure how Sir Leighton-Jones had complimented her most specifically on the elegance of her balldress, in particular how the white proved a beautiful contrast to her light brown hair.

Thoughts of Sir Leighton-Jones was a happy occurrence since it turned her mind away from the unacceptable opinions of Miss Pritchard to the delightful prospects of the baronet falling in love with Daphne. She was able then to accept with equanimity the introduction of several of Mrs. Wanstrow's vast acquaintance. From this number, at least four were gentlemen who expressed a desire to stand up with her. She happily obliged them all.

The assembly drew to a close promptly at eleven o'clock, a tradition well over half a century old. For herself, Cressy was grateful to be returning to Landsdown Crescent. The ball was a mixture of both successful and tiresome encounters as had served to render the evening worrisome. She felt both Mr. Rushton and Miss Pritchard were disinclined to aid her in her cause to see Daphne settled with a proper husband, and that each, given the chance, might take pleasure in injuring her efforts were they so disposed.

Still, she was content to see Daphne both subdued and peaceful, seated as she was next to her, her gloved hands folded on her lap, and a soft smile lighting her face. No complaints passed her lips, not even an expression of sorrow that Somersby had not approached her again that evening. How unlike her, Cressida thought. On the other hand, when Sir Leighton-Jones had been introduced to Daphne, she had conversed with him in a serene ladylike manner, also unlike her, but which Cressy could see pleased the baronet. Her conclusion therefore was simply that Daphne had begun to mature.

Mrs. Wanstrow, on the other hand, was far from a state of peaceful contentment. She sat across from Cressy, her white feather bouncing as the carriage lumbered up the hill to the Crescent, her eyes glittering with triumph, her thoughts transparent in the excited expression on her face.

Her aunt had not spoken since settling herself against the squabs and beginning the journey home. It seemed, however, her enjoyment of the evening could no longer be held within.

"I have never known," Mrs. Wanstrow began enthusiastically, "such envy to flash in Mrs. Pritchard's eye as it did tonight! Oh, that I could experience such a victory every time we met! I shouldn't ask for more. My dear niece! You've no idea the success your workmanship has achieved this evening, and that with not one person the wiser. Do you know, I was not asked even once *who made up my gown,* but rather, *did I have it sent from one of the London shops,* for no one could believe a local woman to have accomplished such a masterful creation! Ah! I am overcome. If I were of nervous disposition I should begin complaining of the vapors and palpitations. I am delirious with joy!"

Cressida, aware that Fate had provided the opportunity for which she had been waiting to address her aunt regarding her and Daphne's need to remain under the shelter of her roof, suggested quietly, "I have just remembered, Mrs. Wanstrow. In my trunk is a sketchbook I have been keeping over the past year and in it are some two dozen paintings of balldresses which I have designed. I wonder if you would care to glance through it some time. I should be more than happy to create as many gowns as you like, and not only gowns, but I am quite adept at every manner of apparel—fichus, capes, redingotes, pelisses—oh, I have just had the most lowering thought!"

Mrs. Wanstrow leaned forward. She had clearly been hanging upon every word Cressy spoke. These last ones appeared to have seriously distressed her. "What? What is it, child? Speak!"

Cressy sighed. "I don't know if I mentioned it to you or not, my dear Mrs. Wanstrow, but Daphne and I will be departing tomorrow for Brighton. We have an acquaintance there who has promised to employ me as a seamstress in her quite fashionable shop, and given our dire circumstances, I have decided I must avail myself of her extreme kindness. I am sorry! It would have been so much fun, wouldn't it! I mean to have seen to the creation of walking dresses, carriage dresses, the most exquisite gowns you could ever imagine, bonnets—oh, and I nearly forgot! I have wanted forever to design a pelisse, of three-quarter lengths, made in fawn and lavender and trimmed with sable—or do you think fox fur might be more the thing! Oh, dear! I am running on! You must forgive me! I do become quite animated on the subject of fashionable clothing! Forget all that I have said and wish us well on our journey since we will be leaving at dawn's light. I have this moment realized we will in most likelihood not see you again. How very sad I feel!" She took a kerchief from her beaded reticule and pressed it to each eye in turn, drying nonexistent tears.

Cressy dared not look directly at her sister. She could see from her side vision that poor Daphne was nearly apoplectic with shock, and given her sister's limited mental facility, she was certain Daphne would not divine why she was fobbing off such a tale upon her aunt about going to Brighton, or even that she had fabricated the story in the first place!

At the same time, the expression on Mrs. Wanstrow's face was all that she had hoped it would be! Her aunt was clearly overset at the thought of having to relinquish so many potentially beautiful costumes as Cressy had just described. Her mouth was agape, her eyes bulged from her head, and her complexion had paled considerably. "You are leaving?" she whispered. "I mean, of course you are!" A frown ridged her brow, her eyes shifted to stare out the window, and a serious pout misshaped her lips.

Cressy waited, her chest tight with anticipation. She continued, for effect, to dab at her eyes and sniff while her aunt considered all she had said.

Daphne, apparently unable to bear the suspense, placed her hand on Cressy's arm and gave it a hearty squeeze. Cressy turned to look at her, but merely gave a warning shake of her head in response to the painful expression in her sister's questioning, beseeching eyes.

Daphne then burst into tears. "I don't want to leave!" she wailed. "I don't want to go to Brighton! I hate Brighton!"

Cressy, startled by her sister's sudden outpouring of emotion, thrust her kerchief into her hands. "But you have never been to Brighton. I am sure once we are become acquainted with such a charming town—"

She would have continued her charade, but Mrs. Wanstrow interrupted her, the firmness in her voice bringing Daphne's wails and tears to a halt. "You are not leaving! You both shall remain with me, in my house, until the end of summer! Why, I would be the unkindest creature on earth were I to permit you to take up such a post as you have described. You had by far better remain with me. Let it not be said that Lydia Wanstrow lacks compassion."

Cressida, a devilish impulse snagging her tongue, queried, "Do you wish to see my sketchbook before you retire this evening."

Mrs. Wanstrow cast a swift, harsh glance in her direction and after lifting a dampening brow, replied, "I don't know what you mean, Cressida, by that bit of impertinence in your voice. I will give you hint, though, that such a defect may cause you some future misery if you do not take care! And as for your sketchbook, tomorrow, after luncheon shall suffice."

Chapter Fourteen

Cressy could not remember a happier time in more recent years, than now. She moved quickly about the morning room at the back of Aunt Liddy's town house, from table to chair to fireplace where she had displayed at least two dozen of her sketches. She literally bounced from one to the other, making notes, sketching in changes, considering different fabrics, deciding on threads, embroideries, and other accents, and generally enjoying herself hugely.

She and her aunt, who had subsequently insisted the young ladies leave off such a formal appellation as *Mrs. Wanstrow,* and call her Aunt Liddy, had already decided on three of the many fabrics they would employ. One length of six yards was a lavender sarsenet, another, draped across a settee near the fireplace was a lemon-colored, lightweight jaconet, and spreading volumi-nously upon a wing chair was a length of billowing sea green silk.

She had been so delighted with the prospect of completing this stage of her quite massive project, she had done nothing more in prepartion for the day than to slip on a worn muslin round gown, ruffled across the bosom, and to tie her brushed hair in a knot atop her head. Her aunt and Daphne had gone to the Pump Room,

116

leaving her to her own devices, after she had reassured Aunt Liddy repeatedly that was she in perfect health and therefore did not require the waters. She also made it clear to her aunt that she was beyond contentment in spending her morning hours knee deep in ink, watercolors, sketching paper, fabrics, needles, and lace!

Humming to herself, she barely heard the door open.

She gave a little jump as the butler, his expression harrassed and disapproving, announced Mr. Rushton.

"Good heavens!" she cried, instantly pushing back several strands of hair which had become loose from her inelegant coiffure. "There must be some mistake! I—"

"I can see that I have inconvenienced you, Miss Chalcot," Mr. Rushton began. "But when I spoke with your aunt yesterday, begging to know when I might call upon you, she insisted eleven was a perfect hour." He let his astonished gaze drift about the wreckage of the room as he took in the nature of her industry.

"How very strange," Cressy responded, feeling awkward. Perhaps her aunt meant to have returned from the Pump Room by now, and she ought therefore see to Mr. Rushton's entertainment.

Absently smoothing out her gown, she said, "If you will be so kind as to await me in the drawing room, I shall attend you there in only a few minutes. Aunt Liddy must be detained for some unknown cause or other."

"If you please, I should prefer to remain here," Mr. Rushton said, a curiously intent expression on his face.

"You're not serious?" she queried, the question spoken before she considered how rude it sounded.

He smiled faintly and responded that indeed yes, he was very serious, explaining that in earlier years, when his mother was not afflicted with a rheumatic complaint which had more recently hindered the use of her fingers, Mrs. Rushton had enjoyed making up gowns and employing her needle with vigor. As a child, he had crafted several castles from the discarded spools she had

117

bestowed upon him. "I have a very fond memory of playing at her knee. The smell of these freshly dyed fabrics has put me in mind of happier days."

"Then of course you may remain here, if you are of a mind."

"Thank you," he said with a smile and a nod.

And with that, Cressy begged the shocked butler to have some tea brought round to the morning room.

Cressy was mortified, more than Mr. Rushton would ever know, by having been caught in a state of careless grooming. He may have adequately explained his desire to remain in the morning room, but she was convinced he must disapprove thoroughly of her appearance. He was clearly a man of fastidious tastes and was, if nothing else, extremely attentive to every detail of his apparel. He was dressed impeccably in a coat of blue superfine, a white waistcoat, yellow smalls, and gleaming top boots. To her surprise, however, he seemed oblivious to the state of her dress or her hair and merely settled himself in an undraped chair by the fireplace.

She stood on the other side of the room, the dining table between them. She scarcely knew what to say to him. It had been nearly a sennight since they had last spoken to one another at the New Assembly Rooms. Twice, in company since then, he had bowed politely to her, and she had returned this civility with an inclination of her head, but nothing more.

And now he was here, looking at her with a faint smile on his face, yet saying nothing.

She cast about in her mind for some bit of news or an anecdote with which to regale him, but nothing came to mind. After a moment, when he remained steadfastly silent, increasing the awkwardness of her feelings, she decided she would not even try to converse with him. If he wished to be uncivil, then she would oblige him by doing the same.

Therefore, she took a chair at the table, picked up her

pen, and began to sketch a variation on a cape she had seen in *La Belle Assemblee*. He seemed to comprehend the purpose of her silence and stated, "It was you I wished to speak with."

"I am honored," Cressy said flatly, not looking up from her drawing. She dipped the pen back into the inkpot and set to scratching on the fine paper of her sketchbook.

At her disinterested response he rose from his chair. "I can see that you are," he said facetiously, moving to stand directly across from her. Cressy stole a glance at him and saw that he was examining some of her sketches. "Are all these yours?" he asked, a tinge of astonishment in his voice.

"Yes," she again responded without expression. "You seem stunned."

"I suppose I am, a little." He then cleared his voice and moved to stand adjacent to her, at the head of the table. "You must wonder why I wished to speak with you."

Cressy looked up at him and said, "I would imagine you have some complaint you mean to address. You have as yet had no other reason to approach me. So, if it pleases you, have your say, and be gone. I have a great deal of work to attend to!"

She settled her silver-handled pen in the tray in front of her and rose from her seat. She was overset by his untimely arrival and by his curtness. She began gathering up some of the sketches on the table, and placing them in a single stack.

"You are right, of course," he began. "I do have a complaint. It has come to my attention that far from wishing your sister to marry elsewhere, you have made it generally known you wish to see her wed to Somersby."

Cressy placed another sketch atop the growing pile, her hand resting lightly on the last one. She could not credit her ears! "Are you deaf, Mr. Rushton," she said, sorely agitated. "How many times must I say to you that

119

nothing is further from my mind than seeing Daphne wed to your ward! We are in agreement upon this one matter at least, yet you repeatedly refuse to believe me! I don't hesitate to tell you I am offended by your disbelief!"

"And had I not been approached by three different persons, each saying you had boasted of seeing your sister wed to Somersby before the end of the summer, I should have ignored the first and even second report. But it seems to be a general consensus of opinion, both that Somersby will marry Miss Chalcot and that you intend to orchestrate it!"

Cressida stared at Rushton, truly shocked. She shook her head, "No. What I have said to you is the truth of my intentions! I cannot imagine how or why—" She broke off, remembering suddenly the manner in which she had responded to Olivia Pritchard's provoking remarks. "Oh," she said at last, realizing Miss Pritchard would certainly have recounted their conversation in the worst light possible.

"What is it?" he queried.

"It is my fault," she said, her gaze dropping to the sketch in front of her. She fingered the rippled, dry watercolor paper and continued. "I said something to Miss Pritchard which it would seem has been grossly misinterpreted. In fact, I fear I spoke precisely the words you repeated to me. But I was only speaking ironically. Surely Miss Pritchard did not willfully choose to believe such a silly speech?"

"Then you said, 'by summer's end'?"

"Yes, I'm 'fraid so. I know it was wrong of me, but Miss Pritchard had just such a look in her eye and a particular tone to her voice, as though she resided on a mountain and only attended to us mere mortals because she was required to—that I simply lost my temper."

"You are wont do so, you know."

"Well!" she exclaimed, mildly affronted. "I think it very unkind in you to say as much. And why is it I am perpetually admitting my faults and errors to you, and begging your forgiveness and explaining myself! I have never had to do so before, and I must say I don't like it one whit!"

"How very odd," he said, lowering his head slightly and staring at her with a warm glint in his eye. "I was just thinking the same thing! Now don't fly into the boughs, I beseech you! I was referring to myself, not to you."

Cressy watched him, the earlier coldness of his expression melting to an enticing charm. She felt her heart begin to soften. He could be utterly agreeable when his blue eyes twinkled in amusement.

She sighed. "I suppose we do rub one another, don't we?"

"Yes," he responded.

He remained looking at her thoughtfully, a smile lighting his eyes. What he was thinking, she could not guess. He simply held her gaze firmly, his thoughts inscrutable. She again tried to conjure up something interesting to say, especially since the air seemed fraught with tensions she was loath to comprehend. The anger had entirely disappeared from his features, but in its stead was another sentiment.

A familiar, gnawing weakness began overtaking her limbs. She thought with a start that she felt just as she had while waltzing with him, light-headed and strange. She wished he would take his leave, fearing the inexplicable state of her mind, yet dreaded the moment he did.

He turned to face the door abruptly for a moment, and she wondered if he desired to depart Mrs. Wanstrow's town house. Yet for some reason she was convinced he had no such intention. To all appearances, he seemed to be listening for something, or perhaps for *someone*. When he seemed satisfied with what he heard, he again faced her, only this time his expression was almost frightening in its intensity.

He began to close the small distance between them, rounding the table as he said, "I posed a question to you while we were dancing at the New Assembly Rooms. You didn't give me an answer."

Cressida felt her chest grow tight with an acute sensation of alarm. His approach she could only construe as containing the worst—or possibly, the best—of motives! In hopes of fending off what she now perceived to be an attack upon her sensibilities, she turned to face him, her quick movements causing one of her sketches to float to the floor at her feet.

"And what question was that?" she queried, trying to swallow and finding it impossible. She did not dare lift her gaze to meet his own.

"Why have you come here?" he queried. "No, don't turn away! Look at me!" He caught her chin with his cupped hand.

She quailed where she stood, her heart hammering out a loud cadence in her breast. She lifted her gaze to meet his and found herself trapped suddenly in his arms. She whispered, "I have to find Daphne a husband, I have told you as much. Can't you understand how important it is that I do so? You've met her, you've spoken with her! Surely by now you comprehend my predicament?"

"Must you be forever discussing Daphne?" he whispered, letting his gaze drift over her face, as though memorizing her eyes, her cheeks, her nose, her lips. "What of you? Are you seeking a husband for yourself?"

She shook her head. "No. I am convinced I would not *a good wife make*. I am not in the least biddable you know, and as for my temper, I need not expound upon that theme." He was far too close for comfort. She touched her tongue to her lips, hoping to relieve some of the dryness which afflicted her. "I don't look to marry. As it happens, I—I have another course laid out for my future."

"I don't concern myself with the future," he

122

whispered in response. And with that, he pressed his lips upon hers and kissed her very hard and very thoroughly.

The earlier sensations of weakness and dizziness increased to such a degree that Cressy found herself leaning helplessly into Mr. Rushton as though her body insisted upon betraying her. His arms encircled her waist more tightly still, as his lips made a thorough search of her own.

She was wrong to permit him to kiss her. It was a grievous folly to encourage him, yet she felt so tantalized by his presence. He held some power over her, some ability to rob her of her will. How was it possible? Why did she let him hold her, and why couldn't she have refused his advances?

The realization she could so ineffectively govern herself caused her at last to push him away, a rush of panic dampening the pleasures of his embrace. He frightened her.

"Sir!" she cried. "I beg you will stop importuning me. Your flirtations are ungentlemanly in the extreme!"

"Cressida," he began quietly. "I hadn't intended upon kissing you. In coming here, I meant only to ask you about the rumors which have run rife since last we met regarding your sister and Somersby. I am satisfied on that score. As for the rest, you're so deuced pretty, I seem to lose my head when I'm near you! As for the quarrel I instigated at the New Assembly Rooms, I do apologize. I have no right to sit in judgment on you, or anyone. And why is it, when I'm around you, I behave like the worst simpleton, I cannot imagine!"

"That is no compliment," Cressy returned in a whisper. She felt confused and overset by his nearness and by his apologies. She did not know what to make of him.

He stepped away from her and bowed. "You were right, Cressida. I have importuned you, and I beg you will forgive my roguish lips. I find myself drawn to your beauty in a way I can't explain. And I do not hesitate to say that something in your outrageous manners seems to cull my most wicked conduct."

"Worse and worse!" she exclaimed with mock dislike. "And how very much like you to blame me for your misbehavior! If I inspire you to misdeeds, then I heartily recommend you take yourself off. Your presence here compliments neither of us. Besides, should my aunt arrive and discover we have been closeted in a scandalous tête-à-tête, she will most likely eject you from her house!" This much Cressida admitted to herself was far from the truth. She had come to understand in particular that her aunt would have plucked out her eyebrows had she thought it would bring either Mr. Rushton or Lord Somersby calling at her front door! Mr. Rushton, however, did not need to know as much.

"You are right, of course! I should go."

He was a strange man who turned abruptly away from her and with several long strides of his athletic, booted, fashionable legs, crossed the portals of the morning room.

When he had gone, Cressida dropped into the chair behind her and bent down to retrieve the sketch which had earlier fallen to the floor. Her fingers were cold and trembling. She placed the watercolor upon the table and afterward gently touched her lips with her icy hands.

Why had she permitted him such gross liberties! Never in her existence had she known a man to turn her tidy world upside down as Mr. Rushton was wont to do. And what did he mean by kissing her and then admitting he was wrong to do so? Perhaps he wished to break her heart.

Fifteen minutes passed before Cressida felt her emotions had been brought to order. During that time, she lectured herself sternly upon the necessity of placing as much distance as possible between herself and the incomprehensible Mr. Rushton. Perhaps it was because she had not been in company with gentlemen a great deal and so was unused to conducting a flirtation in a proper manner, or perhaps it was because for the first time in her life she was actually enjoying herself, but whatever the cause, her heart was in an exceedingly vulnerable state. If she did not take great care, she thought it likely she would soon find herself in the basket!

From this moment on, therefore, she would try to ignore Rushton. Nothing good could possibly come from conversing with a man whose experience of life and of women was considerable, and whose object in making himself agreeable to her would not lead to her future happiness.

Chapter Fifteen

Gregory Rushton set off on a brisk step, the heels of his boots striking the hard Bath stone of the flagways with a resounding thud. The distance from Landsdown Crescent to his lodgings at the White Hart Inn near the Baths, seemed insignificant given his bewildered state of mind.

What the devil had he been about?

He had never intended to accost Cressida as he had! Never. In calling upon her he had only meant to get at the truth regarding the rumors of her intention of seeing her sister and Somersby wed.

The moment she had satisfied his concern, he should have quit her presence. And, if he wished to acknowledge the whole truth to himself, the moment he learned her aunt was not at home, he should have left his card and retreated instead of insisting upon seeing Cressy. What manner of sapscull had he become to so inflict his presence upon her?

He clacked his walking stick hard upon the stone in front of him, a frustrated shout raging about in his chest and longing for expression. He was, however, too much surrounded by Bath inhabitants to do more than grunt once or twice and mutter beneath his breath what a dreadful scourge woman, particularly a beautiful and unaffected one, could be upon a man's common sense and intellect.

Damn!

Well, he would not succumb to Cressida, however intriguing she had proved to be. He shook his head at thoughts of her, bemused by his interest in a young woman who embodied considerably less than his ideal. Why, she had even appeared as though she had thrown on the least attractive gown she could muster. And he would have been greatly surprised to have learned she had done more than run a hasty comb through her hair! And still, all he could think about the moment she confessed the ill-judged remarks she had spoken during a conversation with Olivia, was how pretty her violet eyes appeared in the morning light and how very much he wanted to kiss her again, as he had several days ago, whilst holding her captive in Mrs. Cameley's ridiculous cart.

Again he rapped his cane upon the flags!

Deuce take it all! Why the devil couldn't he have restrained such an impulse even a trifle. It was almost as though his sole purpose in calling upon Cressida had been to take her in his arms and discover whether or not the first kiss they had shared had been a mere accident, or whether she had indeed responded with warm vitality to his embrace.

Was this then a consolation—that he could now vouch for his initial impression of her, that she was a fiery, living, breathing creature who stirred up within his depths desires he had carefully set aside for years?

Fine consolation! To want a woman he was determined never to have!

Mrs. Wanstrow was infinitely relieved that one of her carriage horses had actually thrown a shoe just after having pulled away from the Pump Room. She had therefore no necessity of taxing her brain with the difficult job of concocting a reason why she must return to her town house beyond the hour of eleven and miss her appointed "at home" with Mr. Rushton. Thoughts of certain possibilities where Cressida and Rushton were concerned caused her heart to skip about erratically. He certainly appeared to have an interest in her niece—however much he pretended otherwise. And if she could encourage so glorious a match for her dear Cressida, then she would certainly avail herself of every opportunity which happened along.

Though her postillion was surprised when she insisted upon hiring slow sedan chairs to transport Daphne and herself up the tiresome hill to Landsdown Crescent, he did little more than bow and promise he would see the horse properly shod before returning the barouche to the mews. He repaired to the nearest smithy while she and Daphne were settled within the boxlike confines of two sedan chairs.

She was not happy, however, to hear her own chairmen groan and curse as they picked up their respective poles, but she was quite content to be separated from Daphne for the next hour or so. Her eldest niece had given her a great deal to ponder, as well, and she wished to do so in private. Narrowing her eyes, she settled in for a hard think.

Lord Somersby, quite red-faced and heartstruck, had approached Daphne within three minutes of his arrival at the Pump Room, a ritual he had repeated every morning for the past sennight—unless of course Rushton was present. On these days, of which most fortuitously there had been only two, Somersby would ignore Daphne entirely. If his perpetual mooncalf expression whenever he did approach her niece had not immediately indicated that he was terribly smitten with her, then the fact that he had hitherto drunk the waters but once or twice in his life—to her recollection—beat a loud drum upon her awareness.

128

Even a simpleton could see Somersby was very much in love with Daphne!

But what gentlemen wasn't!

The moment it became known that she, Mrs. Wanstrow, had taken both young women under her wing and had proclaimed that her darling relations would—at least for the summer—enjoy every advantage her vast patronage in Bath could offer them, both Cressida and Daphne had become thronged with instant admirers. Especially Daphne, whose delicate, alabaster beauty had brought several hopeful poets reclining at her feet in order to worship and to drink in gallons of inspiration at the mere sight of her exquisite face.

Even Sir Leighton-Jones made himself useful, hovering more than once at her elbow, begging to know if he might be of service to her in seeing to her niece's amusements. Very curious, that! She had never known Sir Leighton-Jones to dangle after any female, and particularly not one so bird-witted as Daphne! But there he was, appearing at every turn, almost as frequently as Lord Somersby, in evident pursuit of the fair Daphne's lovely, albeit impoverished, hand in marriage.

Curious and more curious!

As she set to nibbling upon the inside of her cheek, Mrs. Wanstrow reflected on the pleasure her nieces' visit was affording her. Though it went sorely against the grain to be obliged to part with one groat more than was necessary to keep her investments in the Exchange flourishing and growing, she could not help but think that she stood in very good stead to win an enormous victory over That Pritchard Female this summer!

Her mouth began to water with promised delights! Wouldn't it just take the wind out of Mrs. Pritchard's eye to see her darling Mr. Rushton wed to Cressida and the doltish Lord Somersby leg-shackled to Daphne? She leaned her head back against the seat and pressed a hand to her bosom. Sighing with deep satisfaction, she imagined the acute pleasure she would receive at being able to say to Mrs. Pritchard, "Did you see the advertisement in the *Bath Herald?* Yes, it is true! They are both to be wed during the same ceremony. And to think Cressida and Daphne actually conquered the hearts of our favorite bachelors! Who would have thought it possible!"

Mrs. Pritchard was like to spit guineas!

Mrs. Wanstrow laughed aloud and then chortled as she heard one of the chairmen curse her girth under his breath.

Life could hold such surprises and pleasures when one least expected it!

But what was she to do about Daphne's poor dilemma, she wondered. She had come to understand through several of her niece's sniveling sobs, that Cressida had forbidden her to even consider Somersby's suit and that Mr. Rushton was equally loath to countenance his ward's desire to wed the beautiful simpleton.

She huffed a pleased sigh. She was not a famous Bath personage for nothing! She knew well how to gently encourage every manner of intrigue, sliver of gossip, and clandestine assignation. She had been in the habit of doing so times out of mind. Why, she had even forced Olivia Pritchard, several years ago, to unwittingly expose her true motives to Gregory Rushton the very day he was to offer for her hand in marriage. What a stupid girl Olivia was!

Mrs. Pritchard had never forgiven her for that one! Yet it was Olivia's fault, after all, and as for herself, she simply could not bear the thought of Mr. Rushton wedding such a false female, however much his general air of arrogance and conceit rather demanded a justly punitive marriage.

She smiled to herself and fingered the amethyst necklace looped several times about her throat. How lovely to think she was to gain so much in having years earlier prevented Olivia's hoped-for alliance with the famous Rushtons of Somersetshire! If all went as she hoped it would over the course of the next few weeks, she would herself be connected with the august family when Cressida brought Mr. Rushton up to scratch.

She narrowed her eyes again. Cressida was a complicated young woman, one she did not as yet comprehend. She was certainly clever, and the more she thought on how it was Cressida had come about making up that exquisite gown for her, the more she had begun to suspect her niece's motives! She had since deduced Cressy had actually *hoped* she would persuade her to extend their visit through the use of the elegant creation. If that had truly been her aim, she had certainly succeeded in her object, a fact which engendered a surprising sensation of respect in Mrs. Wanstrow's breast for her quick-witted niece! She would therefore have to give careful consideration to the precise manner in which she would go about orchestrating Cressida's future.

Cressida and Rushton! Think of it!

Mrs. Pritchard would undoubtedly fall into a decline! What joy! What bliss!

When the sedan chairs finally completed the terrible ascent to Landsdown Crescent, leaving Mrs. Wanstrow's chairmen crimson-faced with effort, and puffing air in and out of exhausted lungs, Mrs. Wanstrow turned to Daphne, as the latter emerged from her sedan chair, and said, "I think tomorrow afternoon you and I shall attend the Spring Gardens by way of a water scow. You will enjoy the gardens, I think, and if I were on intimate terms with Lord Somersby I should ask him to attend us. Wouldn't it be odd if we were to accidentally meet him there? But then I suppose stranger things have occurred upon occasion." As she begged Daphne to take her arm and support her to the door, she added in a harmless way, "I think Somersby has become quite attached to me,

131

don't you Daphne?"

When Daphne appeared rather shocked, Mrs. Wanstrow only barely suppressed her irritation at the child's idiocy and continued chattily, "It has often been so with me, and with most women of a motherly appearance I think, that young men are wont to hang upon my sleeve a trifle. I am not at all surprised, for instance, that Lord Somersby paid me the compliment of addressing me this morning at the Pump Room. He is a most kindhearted young man, and I am a greatly desirous of becoming further acquainted with him. You must tell him so the very next time you have occasion to speak with his lordship, though I don't need to tell you that we shan't say a word to Cressida about it, knowing how she opposes your attachment to Somersby. I trust you to relay my sentiments to him, Daphne. You will, won't you?"

"Y-yes, ma'am. Of course, if you wish for it!"

"Oh, I wish for it very much, my dear. Perhaps he will come to the Pump Room tomorrow morning—I told him, of course, that you and I would be in attendance on the morrow. And if at that time you should happen to mention our excursion to the Spring Gardens, I shall pretend I heard not a word of it!"

Only after she had completed her speech did Mrs. Wanstrow turn to look at Daphne. What she found there took her by surprise, for Daphne's sparkling blue eyes were brimful of tears and her lips trembled as she spoke, "My dearest, most wonderful Aunt!"

Mrs. Wanstrow then had the most astonishing experience of finding herself nearly thrown backward as Daphne cast herself into her arms and hugged her very hard, birdlike sobs breaking from her throat.

"Why, Daphne!" Mrs. Wanstrow cried, finding that the exuberant expression of her niece's joy had brought unexpected tears to her own eyes. "My child, you mustn't cry! For heaven's sake, you are crushing me! Do stop!"

But Daphne did not cease hugging her, at least not right away, and there was nothing for it but for Mrs. Wanstrow to endure her niece's affections with an equanimity she soon found surprisingly easy to maintain.

If the butler, Mr. Brockley, appeared nearly apoplectic at the sight of his purse-pinching, groat-hording, singularly unaffectionate, self-centered mistress hugging her pretty niece, he somehow retained his faculties and merely bowed the sniffling duo into the house.

Chapter Sixteen

"But it is ridiculous!" Mrs. Wanstrow cried, pushing aside the length of thin tulle which Cressida had tossed in a gentle wave over her aunt's shoulder. "I have never been able to wear such a gossamer fabric, and I shan't do so now! It is quite absurd. Why I should have every Tom and Jerry laughing at me, besides making a complete cake of myself in front of Mrs. Pritchard, not to mention Mrs. Rushton!"

"You take their opinions far too seriously, Aunt Liddy!" Cressida argued. "But beyond that you must let me finish. I intend to give the fabric a lining of muslin, two layers if necessary—"

"And do you think a sheer length of muslin, or even two, will have the least affect? Why you are grown as shatterbrained as your sister! You have been three weeks now in Bath, and nearly the entire time you have kept yourself locked up in the morning room, and that so late in the evening that besides using up all my working candles and costing me more largess than I can afford, I think you are probably going blind! That must account for it! Can't you see how improper such a gown would be for one of my years, not to mention my—my matronly figure?" Cressy again draped the delicate tulle over her aunt's shoulder, and again Mrs. Wanstrow pushed it away. "I shan't wear it, I tell you! You've not only gone blind, you've gone mad, as well!"

"Do but consider!" Cressida returned firmly. "The ladies at l'Empereur's court wear a silk undergarment which covers their bodies entirely." She did not mention they wore the garments exclusively during the winter in order to keep the chill from their bones. "Were you to sport such a garment—do but consider!—beneath a lined tulle, I am convinced you would find the effect most dramatic as well as pleasing."

Mrs. Wanstrow stared at her niece. "Did Josephine wear as much?"

"Indeed, yes."

Mrs. Wanstrow was silent and pondering. She seemed very nervous as her eyes flitted over the tumbled objects scattered about the morning room.

"And the others at court as well?" she added after a moment.

Cressida nodded. "All of them, the ladies in waiting, the lot!"

"If you are sure—absolutely sure!"

"You will undoubtedly startle your friends at the next assembly, but not by what you fear to be the exposure of your limbs, but by the elegance of your gown. Oh, by the way. I failed to mention that the ensemble includes a trimmed half-robe of purple silk decorated with a Greek key in gold floss."

She held up the fabric, already embroidered with the traditional Grecian motif, and saw a light of amazement appear in her aunt's eye. "Oh, dear," Mrs. Wanstrow breathed in trembling accents. "I shudder to think how I shall astonish my acquaintance—and my enemies!" She touched worshipful fingers over the silk fabric which joined the tulle Cressy had for the third time draped over her shoulder. "You are a genius, Cressida. Positively, you are!"

"Then we are agreed?"

"Yes, but how much did the silk cost! No! Don't tell me! I fear a spasm should I know the truth. Cressida, you shall be the ruination of me! Of that I am convinced."

Cressida only smiled and carefully refolded the silk afterward stretching the tulle out on the table. Within a few minutes, immersed in the joyful process of bringing one of her creations to life, she had forgotten about her aunt entirely.

So it was that she did not at first realize either that her aunt had remained within the chamber, or that she was speaking.

"Cressida!" she finally heard her aunt cry out. "You are not answering me."

Cressy looked up from the fabric she was carefully smoothing out and blinked in surprise at her aunt. "I am sorry! I thought you had gone. What is it you wish of me?"

"What a strange creature you are," Mrs. Wanstrow returned quietly with a frown between her brows. She appeared to give herself a mental shake, then queried. "I asked, is there nothing you want for yourself?"

Cressida felt confused. "I don't know what you mean?"

Mrs. Wanstrow's frown deepened. "Most young women, particularly of your age—and certainly if they are endowed with your beauty and charm—are more nearly interested in attracting as many beaux as possible, than in making up gowns for their aunt. I remember between your mama and I, there existed a sort of competition—friendly, of course—to see how many hearts we could break. But you scarcely seem interested in attaching any man to your side, much less a score or two. I find it very singular. Why are you not engaged in a like pursuit?"

"Beaux," Cressida stated indifferently, picking up a pair of scissors and letting the smooth silver rings glide down her fingers and back again. "I suppose I haven't given it a great deal of thought. For so long my concern has been for my sister's welfare, and if you remember at the very moment when Daphne should have had her come-out ball, my parents—"

"Oh, don't speak of it!" Mrs. Wanstrow interrupted her, suddenly agitated. "I don't know how it is, but I keep forgetting—! I only wish—! Well, never mind. Keep on with your stitches! I can see you are happy when you have either a pen or a brush or a pair of scissors in your hands."

Cressida could see that she and her aunt had wandered down an unfortunate and painful path. "Indeed I am happy when I am thus employed," she returned brightly. "You must never doubt as much, nor that our joint project has brought me more pleasure than you can ever imagine." She wanted to tell her aunt of her intention of opening a fashionable modiste once Daphne was well settled, but the words seemed incapable of finding a route to her tongue, and so she remained silent.

Her aunt pulled a delicately embroidered kerchief from the long, ruched sleeve of her gown. Twisting and fidgiting with the lace confection, she responded, "Yes, of course it does, I can see that it does. Well, I promised Daphne we would take a trip down the canal, and today is the day. My goodness, how your sister enjoys getting about. You ought to join us one of these afternoons!"

"You know I am far too busy. Does Sir Leighton-Jones make up one of your party today?"

"Indeed he does."

"Oh, I am glad," she said, feeling greatly relieved. She had been so much engrossed in fashioning day dresses and evening gowns for her aunt that she had not been able to attend to her sister's plight so nearly as she would have wished for. "I hope you are encouraging his pursuit of Daphne. I believe he would make her an excellent husband."

"He always seeks out her company."

"Then you must believe me when I say I am very, very happy, indeed!"

"Yes, well! How delightful," her aunt returned enigmatically, then queried, "Will you be attending the

137

concert tomorrow night? The orchestra is performing Handel's *Music for the Royal Fireworks.*"

Cressida barely heard the question. She was envisioning a double row of lace about the hem of the skirt, then cast this idea aside for a silver embroidery motif of acanthus leaves. She murmured her acknowledgement that she would indeed be attending the concert, and with a sigh of relief heard her aunt cross the portals and the door snap shut. She had a great deal of work to attend to!

Half an hour later two seamstresses arrived, indigent ladies of gentle birth who had fallen on penurious times and whom Cressida had hired to do the actual stitching of her aunt's garments. Bath seemed to attract the needy and ill-fortuned of one sort or another. The beggars of Bath alone, who resided in the seamy, impoverished conditions of the Avon district to the east of the town, were world-renowned.

After several more hours of labor, Cressida, having been bent over the table for an unaccountably long time, felt several muscles in her back twist and bite until she was forced to set aside the task of marking a length of the tulle for embroidery placement. She reached her hands to the ceiling and arched her back, bidding her seamstresses to do the same if they were so inclined. Afterward, she promised to go in search of a pot of tea and some tarts or biscuits. The ladies smiled careworn smiles upon Cressy's declaration of intent and, setting aside their needles and thimbles, leaned gratefully back into their respective chairs.

Cressida glanced at them both just before she quit the morning room. She noticed the tracks of worry etched into each face and how no matter whether in work or in repose, the lines of their daily despair never receded nor did the pinched expressions relax. As she made her way to the kitchens and startled Cook by appearing so suddenly in her domain, she could not help but be grateful, for the moment, that she was well sheltered and fed beneath her aunt's roof.

"Miss!" Cook cried. "I would've brought you some tea! You 'ad only to give a tug on the bellpull!"

"I know as much," Cressy answered. "I suppose I was in search of a little diversion. And, to own the truth, I wished to see someone at a task other than stitchery."

"You've been workin' too 'ard, miss!" the kind lady clucked. "Go rest yourself in the library. I'll 'ave some tea taken to the ladies and some to yourself, with a bit of something sweet to lighten your spirits."

Cressy brightened at the notion of a measure of solitude with her tea. She thanked Cook for her thoughtfulness and repaired to the library.

The chamber was small in size but large in furnishings where several chairs and a sofa, all covered in the finest silk damask of royal blue, resided together in compact, familial comfort. She settled herself into a chair by the window, propped her feet up on a handsomely embroidered footstool, and gazed out over the prospect.

The library overlooked not only a handsome green, but much of the city of Bath, as well as an extraordinary view of the tree-shrouded hills on the other side of the valley. It was hard to imagine the valley empty of buildings and a legendary Prince Bladud, suffering from a leprous complaint, driving his herd of swine through the steamy swamps. According to the oft-told tale, the pigs were also afflicted with a like disease and cured themselves by wallowing in the vaporous muddy pools. Bladud followed suit, enjoyed a miraculous cure, and was restored to Court. Eventually he returned as King to establish his royal seat at Bath, afterward turning the swamp into a spa.

Cressy smiled at the notion of a prince and pigs wallowing together, since Bath in many ways existed very much akin to its unlikely beginnings—Bath society, from the lowest-born beggar to the wealthiest families of the aristocracy could bathe together in the hot bath and take waters, elbow to elbow, at the Pump Room.

Letting her gaze drift to the sky above the hills to the

east, she noted that intermittent clouds only slightly marred a beautiful July morning, a perfect day for an excursion such as a meandering trip down the canal. Cressida's thoughts turned quite naturally to Daphne. She remembered that Sir Leighton-Jones would be among the party, and she smiled. Upon the two occasions when she had joined her sister and her aunt in attending the ball at the Lower Rooms and a performance of MacBeth at the theater, she had conversed again at length with the gentle baronet and had had her first kind opinion of him reaffirmed. He was all that Daphne could need in a husband. The fact that he was in attendance upon her sister this afternoon enlivened her hope that Daphne's future was well on its way to being settled.

The room darkened in response to a cloud having floated in the path of the sun's rays, and in like response, Cressida's spirits seemed to lower in progressive stages. She was not even certain what thoughts had caused her heart to feel leaden, but as she retraced the weblike threads of her ruminations, she realized that the moment she recalled having spoken with Sir Leighton-Jones at the theater the image of another man also accosted her.

The face and tall, regal figure of Rushton came readily to mind, and the source of her subtle discomfiture suddenly became clear.

Nearly ten days had passed since Rushton had last kissed her in the morning room. During that time his demeanor toward her had been distant. Not that she would have expected anything different from him, particularly since she was certain he held her circumstances in disdain. But she had hoped to effect an apology and perhaps thereby ease what had proved to be a proper formality between them. As it was, the coldness which accompanied their discourse had become a source of malaise to her, fraying the edges of her peace and contentment. She did not like living at odds with anyone.

The sun peeked through the clouds and laid a gentle ray upon the sleeve of her white cambric gown. The sunbeam felt warm on her skin, and with the sensation came the memory of having been kissed by Rushton. Her heart glowed very hot for the briefest moment, and her whole body became as heated as the spot of sun on her arm. She didn't understand why it was so. His kiss had meant nothing to her save the enjoyment of simply being held very close.

A comfort.

Cressida scowled severely, her face feeling as though she had knotted it up into a ball. Comfort? Rushton's embrace was hardly what she would have described as *comfortable*. Yet it had been exceedingly pleasant. All right then, if not comfortable then at least *pleasant*.

Was it as uncomplicated as that? Did she feel nothing more? Why then had his embrace haunted her dreams and caused her upon each remembrance of the event the wickedest thoughts and hopes that one day he might assault her again?

There, she had admitted the truth to herself at last. She wanted to feel his arms about her again, only to what purpose? He could never have an honorable intention toward her since theirs was a disparity of station which could not be overcome easily, and certainly not in the face of his considerable pride. But beyond that, he was so dreadfully flawed!

Really, Sir Leighton-Jones was very much more the sort of man who would please her. Yet as the image of his kind, friendly face rose within her mind, she realized that for some odd reason she hadn't the least interest in ever knowing whether a hug from him would cause her knees to weaken as other, more delicious hugs were wont to do!

The clouds again victoriously shut out the sunlight, and with it her heart plummeted even lower still.

Rushton had all but ignored her both at the Lower Assembly Rooms and at the theater. At first she had been glad of it since she had already decided she must treat him with a cool civility in order not to encourage his advances again. But when he had spoken to her with a frosty look

141

in his eye and a stiffness of countenance which would have put to shame the most careful soldier on review before his commanding officer, she knew a sensation foreign to her—a sensation of loss.

Why was it all so complicated?

Still, she ought to be grateful for his indifference. He was being wise, and she would be wise, too. She would return civility with civility and nothing more, not a smile, not a bow, only the smallest inclination of her head to whatever polite comment upon the size of the room or the number of guests he might choose to make when next they met.

Chapter Seventeen

As Cressida followed her aunt into the concert hall of the New Assembly Rooms, she knew two sensations at once. First she felt confident and pleased that she was begowned becomingly and secondly, her stomach was fuzzy with anticipation. She had been secreted away in her morning room far too long than was at all desirable in order to maintain her ease in society—her aunt had been correct in mentioning as much to her.

Now, as she let her gaze glide over the countenances of her many new acquaintances, the fuzziness in her stomach began whirling into a dance of pure excitement. She was happy to be away from her pins and needles and sketches, to converse with her friends, to feel pretty and dressed to perfection, to forget her cares if only for an hour or two.

She was gowned in an evening dress of white muslin covered with blue-and-green appliquéd acanthus leaves, a low back, short puffed sleeves, and a long train. She wore her brown hair caught up in a careless knot of curls atop her head adorned by a tiara of silver leaves.

Daphne, though by far eclipsing every other female present with regard to her beauty, was begowned in a simple round gown of white muslin, embroidered with seed pearls across the bodice, and sporting white satin slippers tied at the ankles. Cressida could not help but notice that with every step her sister took down the aisle in seeking her aunt's favorite concert seats, heads invariably turned to look upon her exquisitely angelic face. It seemed to Cressy that her sister had never been in better looks. Her expresion was one of pure happiness, her complexion cast with a pearlescent glow which clearly originated from the depths of her heart.

When Sir Leighton-Jones stopped their progress, first bowing low to Mrs. Wanstrow and afterward clasping Daphne's hand warmly and affectionately, Cressida comprehended well the source of her sister's contentment. Daphne's smile never looked brighter as she returned the pressure of the baronet's hand, and she quite dazzled him with her prettiest curtsy. She then gestured to Cressida and said, "You have not seen my sister in some time, Sir Leighton-Jones. I wonder if you even remember her."

There was something teasing in Daphne's smile which caught Cressida by surprise, but she did not have time to consider the source of the twinkle in her sister's eye because the baronet descended upon her with a welcoming hand and his friendliest greeting.

"Well met, Miss Chalcot!" he cried. "And how charming you look this evening." He paused for a dramatic moment, then continued with some urgency, "I had meant to speak only the softest words of courtesy to you tonight, but I find instead I must press you with what I hope you will receive as but the gentlest of reproaches from my tongue. You distress your friends mightily by remaining locked away upon Landsdown Crescent—almost like a fairy princess—and I do not hesitate to say that your absence has been sorely felt by all this past fortnight and more. And not least, by me! I hope you do not mean to continue absenting yourself from the daily sojourns which your aunt and sister seem to enjoy most prodigiously! I am come to fear you harm yourself by staying within when all of nature beckons you to partake of her joys, without. Do I cross the bounds of propriety

144

by urging you to leave behind whatever homey tasks keep you bound to your aunt's lodgings, and in turn enter society with greater frequency?"

Cressida was a trifle shocked by the baronet's fine speech, but found it easy to respond with a prompt, "Of course you do not, though I must beg off for the present! Ordinarily, I should be most happy to oblige such a polite *urging*, but I am engaged in various employments, on behalf of my aunt—out of immense gratitude for her beneficence I might add—which must by their nature limit my daily pleasures."

Making only minimal use of his walking stick, he dropped into stride beside her as Mrs. Wanstrow—with Daphne elegantly in tow—began making a leisurely progress toward her seats. Her aunt's entrance was decidedly queenly as she marched down the central aisle wearing the half-robe of purple silk and the undergown of sheer tulle lined with muslin. The effect was all that Cressy hoped it would be as a general humming of whispers and gasps exuded from all who caught sight of, and marveled at, her elegant costume. Several acquaintance stopped her in her progress and exclaimed over the beauty of her gown.

Mrs. Wanstrow was positively pink with joy at her success and acknowledged her societal subjects with a regal wave of her hand.

The baronet lowered his voice and again addressed the subject of Cressida's tasks. "You refer, I presume, to the succession of quite charming day dresses and evening frocks which your aunt has been parading before us with such delight." Here he nodded toward Mrs. Wanstrow, who was still nodding and beaming.

Cressy cast him a startled glance and whispered in return, "Sir Leighton-Jones, I don't know what you mean, or to what you are referring. I—"

"You need say no more," he assured her. "As it happens, Daphne told me in some detail of your activities as well as the selflessness of your kind and generous

145

disposition. I shan't however, cause a blush of mortification to further suffuse your cheeks by dwelling upon your good deeds, though I do wish to say that I honor you for your industry and efforts on your sibling's behalf."

"You are talking utter nonsense," Cressida rejoined with an attempt at gaiety, hoping to stop what she felt to be an effusive compliment. She did not in the least like having her virtues held up to her. She knew she had her own, quite selfish, reasons for making use of her aunt's vanity. The establishing of a modiste for which she intended her aunt to be her best advertisement, was hardly the act of a selfless paragon. "And if we are to be friends, I hope you will never mention the subject again. Daphne, as you must know, does not always represent matters as they are."

He spoke intensely in response. "You may demur as much as you like, but I know your fine character for what it is. And if I choose upon occasion to offer you praise, you will be required—for the sake of our friendship—to endure my admiration with equanimity."

Cressy felt very uncomfortable as she glanced at Sir Leighton-Jones and tried to determine from what motives he spoke. The hint of a thought darted into her mind that she rather preferred Mr. Rushton's unflagging honesty to what she believed to be the baronet's desire to cloak her with qualities she did not possess. Seeing that a certain mulish expression had taken hold of his chin, however, she decided not to try to argue her point, but instead let the subject drop.

In true gentlemanly fashion, he took her lead and mentioned the size of the room and how delightfully comfortable the weather had been of late, ending with a polite, "I hope you do not take umbrage at my sitting with your aunt during the concert."

"Oh, no, how could I," Cressy responded candidly, "when you have shown yourself to be a true friend to my sister and to my aunt!" She then begged to know how he had enjoyed the journey down the canal. "For I promise you I found myself quite out of spirits yesterday when I was closeted within my aunt's town house and pondered upon the happy prospects which you must have enjoyed on your journey along the Kennet-Avon waters."

He responded gallantly, "I will say nothing then about the beauties I encountered on our trip, but rather will assure you that had you attended us, the sun would have shone brighter, the leaves of the trees would have danced more joyfully in the afternoon breeze, and I would have been the happiest of men."

"How kind you are to say as much!" Cressida responded with a warm smile, thinking again that except for the fulsomeness of his compliments he was precisely the sort of man to make Daphne happy. When several of the servants began extinguishing candles in the wall sconces, she cried, "Oh, dear! Are we come so late that the musicians are already picking up their instruments?"

In a conspiratorial fashion, he leaned his head near to hers as each of the party slipped into their respective chairs, and whispered, "Mrs. Wanstrow is renowned for taking her seat only a fraction of a second before the overture is struck!"

Cressida giggled then laid her fan hard upon her lips as her aunt turned to frown her down.

She was very content and found only one aspect of the concert displeasing as the musicians began Handel's *Music for the Royal Fireworks*—that Daphne was not seated beside Sir Leighton-Jones.

Chapter Eighteen

Gregory Rushton sat back three rows from Cressida, and far enough to the right of her that he was finding it difficult to fully enjoy the concert. His gaze seemed drawn to just that part of the audience where she resided with her careful posture and her head held elegantly erect. She was a horrendous distraction, he decided, and he wished he had sat a dozen rows directly behind her so that he might never be presented with the sight of her beautiful profile enhanced with what he conceded was a deuced pretty smile. A distraction, indeed!

The concerts had early on proved to be one of the more enjoyable aspects of the various rounds of Bath society for Rushton because, for over a quarter of a century, Handel had been properly revered and subsequently performed on a regular basis. As a child he had heard the unequalled Miss Elizabeth Linley sing a variety of solo parts from Handel's oratorios, and from that moment Rushton had been caught up in the composer's musical strength and brilliance.

But how was he to fully partake of the pleasures of the *Music for the Royal Fireworks* with Cressida's graceful neck, her smile, and the memory of her kisses shouting at him?

She was currently, in the intermission between pieces, laughing at something Sir Leighton-Jones had just said to her. From where he sat, he could see that her eyes were sparkling in the manner he knew they could when she was vastly amused—clear, twinkling, violet gems into which he had gazed more than once, and, more than once, had lost his way.

He had already determined he would not lose his way tonight, not again, never again. He looked away from her, scanning the assemblage, ignoring how Somersby sat on his right and chewed his kerchief, acknowledging Olivia's smile for the fifth time with a brief nod of his head, wishing the musicians would resume their instruments that he might be safe.

No matter how hard he tried, however, each time he heard Cressida's musical voice trill a delicious response to the congenial, but rather dull, baronet, he found his gaze drawn magnetically back to the curls of her brown hair wreathed with shimmering silver leaves. This time he noted how well her gown became her. Of course, the more he considered her costume, the more he realized she was always elegantly dressed, and something more. Something in her gowns, as well as Daphne's, bore a certain striking quality which easily distinguished the sisters from most of the ladies present.

Of course there was one occasion when he had not seen her begowned to perfection. When he had spoken with her *tête-à-tête* in her aunt's town house, she had sported a worn, serviceable gown, and her hair had been quite blowsy. Not that her unkempt appearance had stopped him from taking advantage of her!

Oh, the devil take it! he thought, knowing full well that remembering what she wore on that last fateful day was certain to cause unwelcome memories to overtake him. And before he could do more than wish it otherwise, he was caught up—as he had been a hundred times in the past fortnight—with the remembrance of having held her in his arms, and of having violated her lips again and again.

He folded his arms over his chest and stared at her,

willing himself to forget how delicious she had felt in his arms, but finding it impossible. He wished again, for the wildest moment, she weren't gently bred so that he might take her for his mistress. The more his thoughts traveled in this unfortunate direction, however, the more a sense of ill usage began to assail him. After all, she was the one who should have repulsed him at the outset, instead of leaning brazenly into him as she had done. What manner of female was she anyway, to give herself in an embrace so readily to any man who would demand it of her? He could not esteem her for such behavior. Would Olivia Pritchard ever have permitted him to violate her lips as he had Cressida's? Of course she would not!

He smiled mischievously at the thought. Olivia would probably have struck him hard across his cheek and called him a rakehell. He glanced at Miss Pritchard and wondered if perhaps he had not been, after all, a very fortunate man to have been warned away from an alliance with her. He might not approve of Cressida's enthusiasm, but by God, he had by far rather have a wife who enjoyed a little cuddling than a cold fish who approached the marriage bed as though it were merely another wretched duty among those many a wife must perform for her spouse.

Worse and worse! One moment he blamed Cressida for having a passionate nature, and the next, he blamed Olivia for not! What manner of confusion had stolen over him since first meeting Cressida Chalcot?

At last the musicians returned to their chairs, tuned each respective instrument, and again entered briskly into their various parts. A certain majestic quality characterized the several movements of the work. During one of the more lyrical segments Rushton could not keep, yet again, from glancing in Cressida's direction.

His mind suddenly envisioned fireworks dancing all about Cressida's head in response to the music. For a long moment he surrendered to his incomprehensible obsession with her and knew a longing which shocked him. He simply could not understand what was happening to him or why his thoughts turned incessantly toward her.

Cressy was enjoying the music immensely, as much for itself as for the fact that the concert had torn her away from her daily vigorous employments. However much she took delight in creating gowns for her aunt, she was coming to value her need for restorative entertainments.

The orchestra had just commenced a quieter more lyrical portion of the body of music when she felt a rather peculiar prickling sensation on the back of her neck that sent a river of gooseflesh rushing down her side. She had the profound prescience that someone was ogling her.

Chancing to glance over her shoulder she saw that Rushton, with Somersby beside him, sat but a few seats from her and was regarding her with an expression which caused a second wave of gooseflesh, like a lightning rush of tiny needles, to torture her side yet again. What was worse, she could not seem to tear herself away from the mesmerizing affect of his gaze as he held her own in a powerful grip.

Somewhere in the fuzzy recesses of her head she noted that the music had again become quite regal and marked in presentation as she continued to look at Rushton. She wondered what he was thinking. She felt as she frequently did in his company—light-headed and strangely vulnerable. What power was this that he exerted over her?

The music seemed to grow very loud in her ears, and everyone else present disappeared save Rushton. Somehow, through the dramatic beating of the timpani, she heard fireworks exploding and imagined that the concert room was suddenly filled with white, blue, and red bursts of light. What was happening to her?

Rushton did not realize how hard he was staring at

Cressy until Somersby queried, "What is wrong with Miss Chalcot? Her complexion is grown uncommonly pale? Why do you look at her as though she will disappear if you do not? Has she grown a wart on her chin?"

Only with the strongest effort did Rushton tear himself from Cressy's gaze, afterward experiencing a sensation very much like having been struck down by a mail coach traveling at a shocking ten miles an hour!

"Wart?" he queried in return. "Don't be absurd. She couldn't grow a wart if her life depended on it! She's too damned pretty!"

Somersby looked at him with his eyes bulging neatly from his head. "Damme, but if you ain't tumbled in love with her! Who'd have thought!"

"Don't be a sapscull, Somersby," he whispered irritably. Since he had not devoted himself to paying strict attention to the progress of the music, it was with no small degree of shock did he speak the following words in the electric space following the playing of the very last note of the movement. "*I'm not in love with Cressida Chalcot!*"

Rushton had not the smallest doubt that the entire audience, including every offended musician before him, had heard his ill-judged, ill-timed, and excessively rude remark. He could do ought else, therefore, but stand and make his apologies.

Facing Cressy, he spoke with as much dignity as he could summon under such a painfully humiliating circumstance and said, "I most humbly beg your pardon, Miss Chalcot. I can offer no excuse for such an unhappy incivility. Pray forgive me."

When Cressy inclined her head, he bowed low to her, then quit the chamber in good order.

Chapter Nineteen

Cressida sat stiffly, her gloved hands folded tightly upon her lap. The sound of Rushton's retreating footsteps echoed dully to the top of the plastered ceiling and smote her ears. She stared painfully ahead, her gaze fixed to the folds of a poorly arranged neckcloth belonging to an unknown gentlemen in front of her. Silence packed the concert hall, even the musicians seemed frozen in place. Intense mortification filled every pocket of her mind. She had exposed herself by looking at Rushton, and he had tidily made her an easy object of derision to those who lived for nothing more than to amuse themselves at the expense of others.

A smattering of feminine titters began first, behind hastily unfurled fans, of course. Then a growing buzz of conjectures filled the air as to who Miss Cressida Chalcot was and as to why the famous Mr. Rushton had been provoked into speaking about her as he had. When the lower tenors and basses of the gentlemen's voices were added to the throng, several deep-seated chuckles erupted, the gossip grew louder, and the ladies' titters evolved into trills of accusing laughter.

If Cressida could have snapped her fingers and vanished from the august chamber, she would have done so, but she could not. Turning to Sir Leighton-Jones, she politely asked him to request an encore from the musicians, if he would be so kind.

Earning her gratitude, the baronet rose and begged of the director of music for the assembly rooms, to have the orchestra play another opus of Handel's. The request was accepted and the audience immediately set aside their titterings, began to settle themselves back in their chairs, and grew quiet in successive waves.

If Cressy was still made the object of faint laughter and murmurings, the commencement of the music silenced these remaining incivilities. Sir Leighton-Jones leaned close and whispered, "Courage, my dear! A storm in a teacup, nothing more!"

Cressy knew he was right, of course. But what he didn't know was that Rushton's declaration had been not only an intense mortification, but had been, as well, a knife to a quiet place in her heart, hitherto unknown to herself. She glanced down at her embroidered, white muslin gown, and almost expected to see blood pouring out over the thin, finely woven fabric. She felt as though she were bleeding inside, that the rapierlike effect of his words had somehow sliced her soul apart.

Yet, she could make no sense of the enormous pain which had nearly robbed her of her breath.

I am not in love with Cressida Chalcot.

Well, of course he was not! She knew he was not. She did not seek his love, she did not want his love! Truly, she did not! Why then, did she feel this way? Was her mind keeping a careful veil over secret, unsuspected, unrecognized longings of her heart?

Impossible. Cressy had always known her mind and her heart. She knew herself. She knew her duties, she knew how to solve difficult problems. She had laid out a path for herself, one which did not include such fripperies as love and the companionship of a husband. She had long since reconciled herself to the fact that she was destined to support herself as best she was able, and to see to Daphne's care as well. She did not regret such duties, indeed she was deeply content that so far she had succeeded in always seeing to the sheltering and essential needs of both herself and her sister.

None of these concerns included the presence of a man.

If the truth be known, she had never permitted herself the luxury of thinking in such terms. Not once, since having sat in her father's library and having learned the extent of her papa's gaming debts from the pinched, disapproving lips of her parents' solicitor, had she allowed the impractical visions of home and hearth to affect her judgment or her actions.

Her survival had depended upon keeping a strict governance upon any fanciful or unrealistic hope which might, in their raising from the dead her schoolgirl wishes, make her path harder to bear or to execute, instead of tolerable.

Now, as she sat between her aunt and Sir Leighton-Jones, listening dumbly to the orchestra, strange tears clogged her throat, stung her eyes, all the while increasing the pain which still sliced through her.

She willed her heart to silence. She willed her tears to retreat. She willed the muscles of her throat to relax. She began to feel like a hot air balloon when the fire is removed. The balloon collapses and finally lies quietly on the ground next to its gondola. Something inside her felt as though it were collapsing and would soon lie inert within her heart.

So much the better. She had much work to do. And the first was to see that Sir Leighton-Jones married Daphne.

When the music had ended, when a proper acknowledgement of the achievements of the orchestra had been proferred through a burst of applause, when the audience began to rise in unequal stages preparing to leave, Cressy turned to the baronet and asked him to please join them on Sunday evening. "We are very quiet at that hour and day of the week, but I think you might enjoy being part of our little family circle."

She glanced at Mrs. Wanstrow, who immediately

added, "Yes do come! Daphne does so enjoy your company, and I would like you to reacquaint Cressida with the science of cribbage. She is far too reflective, bookish, or busy with her needle than can at all be good for her general health. You will be welcome indeed, if you can overturn what I know is a steady refusal on her part of any amusement broaching a state of pleasure."

Sir Leighton-Jones rose and offered his arm to Cressida, saying, "I intend to make such amends as are necessary to restore what I know must have been at one time a profound bloom to Miss Cressida's cheeks."

Mrs. Wanstrow smiled and nodded. Cressy suddenly felt uncomfortable. She was not certain what the baronet meant since, when she regarded herself in the looking glass she was not aware of any lack in her complexion. At the same time, she was vaguely disturbed by the warm, protective manner in which he wrapped her arm about his own, patted her hand firmly, and smiled tenderly into her face. She glanced back at Daphne, wishing she could find a way of trading places with her, knowing that such kindness would go a long way to winning her sister's heart. At the same time, she felt it would be rude to reject the baronet's considerate attentions toward her since he was clearly responding to Rushton's earlier mishap which had so effectually cut up her peace.

Rushton watched Lord Somersby's chest jerk in repressed laughter. How many times during the journey back to the White Hart, where he and Somersby were residing for the summer, did his ward begin to laugh aloud, check himself with a fit of coughing, and resume the spasmodic silent chuckles rolling around his ribs.

Irritated, Rushton finally said, "You might as well have your laugh or I fear you will go off in a fit of apoplexy!"

The dam broke and a roar of merriment filled the hackney. Rushton had never seen Somersby so amused in his entire existence. The young viscount laughed until tears streamed down his cheeks, he gasped for air, wiped his face with his kerchief, cast a single glance at Rushton, and was off again. He roared, chortled and chuckled, then roared again until he was clutching his sides in blissful agony. He rolled onto the seat next to him as the coach spun its wheels over the stone-paved streets, and roared again.

At first Rushton was angry, knowing that the merriment rioting about on the seat next to him was being enjoyed entirely at his own expense. But in the face of Somersby's hysterical mirth, anger was soon replaced by profound annoyance, which eventually gave way to a quietly mortified amusement which he began to accept as his due for having made a fool of himself at the New Assembly Rooms.

"I—I'm sorry," Somersby gasped, holding his stomach and trying to breathe. "B-but if you'd seen your face after—oh, Lord, I'm off again!" And with that, he again collapsed onto the seat, bumping into Rushton, laughing and choking in turns.

"It was your fault," Rushton said with mock seriousness. "You provoked me sorely, what with all your impertinent questions about Miss Cressida."

Somersby straightened himself up and chortled between rasping breaths until he finally said, "I happily take the blame for it was worth it to see your dumbfounded expression! Lord, what a cake you made of yourself! In all these years that I have known you as my guardian and as my friend, I've never seen you so gapped as you were tonight! And I'd give a monkey to see it all over again, damned if I wouldn't!"

"You make it sound as though it was the first time I'd ever committed a solecism in public. It's certainly not the first time, and I doubt it will be the last!"

"Yes, but you are so rigidly proper and take such care to appear in command of your sense and sensibilities."

"Heaven's man, I don't know which is worse! That you

laugh at me or that you make me out to be such a devilishly dull dog!"

Somersby stared at him in astonishment. "But that is what you are! I mean no offense, but even Sir Leighton-Jones said you could be a deuced bore on occasion, always smug and doing the pretty with the ladies, dressed as neat as a pin! I daresay you've never even worn a Belcher kerchief! I expect that's why you're blue-deviled so much of the time!"

"Why, because I don't choose to sport a ridiculous figure by tying a spotted handkerchief about my neck? And why do you say I am *blue-deviled!* I most certainly am not?"

"Must be! A man who doesn't kick up a lark now and again must suffer regularly from a fit of the megrims. Stands to reason! Besides, you don't smile very much, you know, or laugh, except lately, when Miss Chalcot is about. Funny thing, that, when you dislike her as much as you do!"

Rushton felt as though a clap of thunder had just exploded over his head. He glanced out at the night sky, sprinkled with stars, and knew the weather could not explain the loud rumbling in his head. He retorted, "I don't dislike her."

"I see what it is—she's beneath your company."

Lightning usually preceded thunder. This time it came afterward, a bolt piercing Rushton's head. Reeling from the shock, he found no words with which to respond to his friend, except to query in a stunned voice, "Beneath my company?"

"Yes," Somersby said, "In the same way, as you've said times out of mind, that Daphne is beneath mine."

"No," Rushton responded with a frown sitting heavily upon his brow. "I never said as much. Surely!"

"Not in so many words, I suppose," Somersby responded.

Rushton wanted to explain the difference between being above one's company and disliking the alliance of disparate fortunes, but he was oddly bereft of words. He had begun to wonder if there was a difference at all.

He turned his gaze toward the window, where the buildings along Broad Street passed by in hypnotic progression. His thoughts became full of Cressida and the manner in which she had unflinchingly returned his gaze during the concert. His heart seemed to swell within him at the remembrance of her lovely face and exquisite eyes turned toward him. How much she had entrapped him within her lavender eyes for those few seconds—or was it minutes?—that they had regarded one another. What had she been thinking,   wondered? What his thoughts had been, he could not recall, only that he wanted to look at her forever.

When the hackney turned onto Green Street, Rushton realized that his friend had fallen into a brown study. He sat quietly staring out the window, chewing upon one of the corners of the mauled square of soft cambric and sighing repeatedly.

Rushton could not help but notice the change in his ward's demeanor and in a concerned voice asked, "What is troubling you, Evan? I hope you know you can always rely on me, if you need an ear? Though I don't hesitate to point out that of late, I believe you have ruined more handkerchiefs than I have owned in the course of my lifetime."

Lord Somersby seemed a little startled as he held his kerchief up in front of him. He looked at it guiltily and after carefully folding it, returned it to the pocket of his coat. "My last one," he murmured absently.

When it appeared he intended to remain silent, Rushton prodded him gently. "You can trust me, Evan," he said.

"What?" Somersby queried, shifting his preoccupied gaze to look at him. "Yes, of course I know I can. The truth is I'm in the devil of a fix, but I mean to see my way clear by myself. So you needn't worry. I'll be all right and tight. Just have to see what I can figure out, that's all."

159

Rushton wanted to help his friend, but having been politely rebuffed, did not feel he ought to persist in his entreaties. Instead, he bent his mind to a more difficult task: how to become more comfortable with Cressida Chalcot's disturbing presence in Bath. He felt himself in imminent danger, but of what? Somehow, thoughts of Cressida brought Somersby's harsh opinions forcibly to mind.

A dull dog.

Cressida beneath my company.

These were not epithets he had ever expected to hear applied to his own person. As for Sir Leighton-Jones, he rather thought the shoe was on the other foot, for never was a duller dog born than the aging bachelor. The man must be forty, if he was a day, and what was he doing sitting next to Cressida and whispering in her ear? And was Cressy aware that Sir Leighton-Jones had broken his share of hearts over the course of his career?

Someone ought to warn her. Of course she had indicated her interest in seeing the baronet wed to Daphne, but what if the baronet tumbled in love with the wrong sister? Would Cressida marry him to secure her own future? He did not wish to consider such an eventuality and put the whole matter behind him. After all, what was Miss Chalcot to him? A mere acquaintance, as she always would be, and nothing more.

Later that night Daphne opened the wide doors of her gleaming dark mahogany wardrobe and from the upper top shelf retrieved a bandbox. She clutched it tightly to her bosom, took in several deep breaths, sighed reverently, and murmured a prayer, before she finally clambered between the sheets and settled down to open the box.

Untying the ribbons of the sacred container, she looked lovingly at the several letters lying scattered in the box. Each of them bore Somersby's seal.

MORE PASSION AND ADVENTURE AWAIT... YOUR TRIP TO A BIG ADVENTUROUS WORLD BEGINS WHEN YOU ACCEPT YOUR FIRST 4 NOVELS ABSOLUTELY *FREE* (AN $18.00 VALUE)

Accept your Free gift and start to experience more of the passion and adventure you like in a historical romance novel. Each Zebra novel is filled with proud men, spirited women and tempestuous love that you'll remember long after you turn the last page.

Zebra Historical Romances are the finest novels of their kind. They are written by authors who really know how to weave tales of romance and adventure in the historical settings you love. You'll feel like you've actually gone back in time with the thrilling stories that each Zebra novel offers.

GET YOUR FREE GIFT WITH THE START OF YOUR HOME SUBSCRIPTION

Our readers tell us that these books sell out very fast in book stores and often they miss the newest titles. So Zebra has made arrangements for you to receive the four newest novels published each month.

You'll be guaranteed that you'll never miss a title, and home delivery is so convenient. And to show you just how easy it is to get Zebra Historical Romances, we'll send you your first 4 books absolutely FREE! Our gift to you just for trying our home subscription service.

BIG SAVINGS AND FREE HOME DELIVERY

Each month, you'll receive the four newest titles as soon as they are published. You'll probably receive them even before the bookstores do. What's more, you may preview these exciting novels free for 10 days. If you like them as much as we think you will, just pay the low preferred subscriber's price of just $3.75 each. *You'll save $3.00 each month off the publisher's price.* AND, your savings are even greater because there are never any shipping, handling or other hidden charges—FREE Home Delivery. Of course you can return any shipment within 10 days for full credit, no questions asked. There is no minimum number of books you must buy.

4 FREE BOOKS

TO GET YOUR 4 FREE BOOKS WORTH $18.00 —MAIL IN THE FREE BOOK CERTIFICATE T O D A Y

Fill in the Free Book Certificate below, and we'll send your FREE BOOKS to you as soon as we receive it.

If the certificate is missing below, write to: Zebra Home Subscription Service, Inc., P.O. Box 5214, 120 Brighton Road, Clifton, New Jersey 07015-5214.

FREE BOOK CERTIFICATE

4 FREE BOOKS

ZEBRA HOME SUBSCRIPTION SERVICE, INC.

YES! Please start my subscription to Zebra Historical Romances and send me my first 4 books absolutely FREE. I understand that each month I may preview four new Zebra Historical Romances free for 10 days. If I'm not satisfied with them, I may return the four books within 10 days and owe nothing. Otherwise, I will pay the low preferred subscriber's price of just $3.75 each; a total of $15.00, *a savings off the publisher's price of $3.00.* I may return any shipment and I may cancel this subscription at any time. There is no obligation to buy any shipment and there are no shipping, handling or other hidden charges. Regardless of what I decide, the four free books are mine to keep.

NAME

ADDRESS _____ APT _____

CITY _____ STATE _____ ZIP _____

( )
TELEPHONE

SIGNATURE _____ (if under 18, parent or guardian must sign)

Terms, offer and prices subject to change without notice. Subscription subject to acceptance by Zebra Books. Zebra Books reserves the right to reject any order or cancel any subscription.

On the table beside her bed rested her beaded reticule, which she had taken to the New Assembly Rooms. With her heart beating happily in her breast, she withdrew from her reticule the most recent of his lordship's correspondence. Her aunt had received it from Lord Somersby after the concert and secretively passed it to her when Cressida had walked out of the rooms on the arm of Sir Leighton-Jones.

With her heart jumping in little bursts, she broke the seal and unfolded the sheet, drinking in each word.

My precious faerie queene,

A minute does not go by that I do not consider our difficulties. I am convinced Rushton, for all his affection for me, would not hesitate to stop our nuptials, even though we have both attained our majorities. He holds my purse-strings, which is the source of greatest distress. If only you would relent to my original scheme. I beg you will consider again that suggestion which I know you find Repugnant in the extreme—though I honor you in your Repugnance since your dislike of the scheme is a reflection of the beauty of your mind and heart. Or is it that you become dreadfully sick when you travel in a coach? If that is the case, I wish to assure you that we can stop as frequently as you might have need.

Whatever the case, though Gretna Green is a frightful distance from Bath, won't you relent that we might become husband and wife?

Yours, faithfully,
Evan

Postscript

We could carry a pot in the coach if you like. My mother used to do so when I was very young and we traveled from London to our country house in Oxfordshire. I was used to cast up my accounts every five miles. What do you think of that?

Daphne pressed the letter to her lips and swallowed hard. All Somersby's words of traveling sickness seemed to have affected her, somehow. After a moment, when she felt better, she held the missive close to her heart, closed her eyes, and smiled. She loved Evan ever so much, more than she dreamed possible. He was all that she could ever want in a man since he never said complicated things to her and always looked to her comfort.

She did not want to elope, however, and after pushing the bedcovers aside and retrieving her lap desk from beneath the bed, she set about penning a missive to her beloved, that she might tell him yet again she could not bring herself to be married over the anvil. When she was done, she sealed her letter and hid it in her reticule until tomorrow when she would give it to her aunt to deliver to Somersby.

Aunt Liddy had proved to be the very best of aunts. Through her kindness she had been able to exchange no fewer than a dozen letters with Evan and had spent hours upon hours in his company in the most delightful of settings all about the city—the Spring Gardens several times, the canal three times, the Pump Room every morning. She and Evan, under her aunt's tutelage, had also begun to learn the delicate art of discretion and so had been able to enjoy dancing together at the New Assembly Rooms and at the Lower Rooms several times when Cressida was not present—and once when she was!—without giving rise to the least speculation or gossip. She had even made one of a whist party with Evan, and that with Aunt Liddy and upon her insistence, Mrs. Rushton making up the fourth. It had even become a game with them to see how much they could keep from gazing longingly at one another.

Afterward Aunt Liddy said she was quite proud of her, and that to her own careful eye she was convinced no one could possibly be the wiser because they had both played their parts so well. Though she wasn't certain, she did not think she had yet grasped the whole of the card game. Still, it took her quite by surprise when both her aunt and Mrs. Rushton exclaimed they would never play whist with the pair of them again! For herself, she had enjoyed playing very much, but the best part of the event occurred when, upon rising from play, she had the delight of feeling Evan's fingers touch her own ever so lightly in acknowledgement of his love for her.

Oh, how much she loved him, only what were they to do?

Chapter Twenty

At the Pump Room on the day following the concert, it was with a small measure of relief that Cressida learned that Rushton had removed to his country home, Rushton House—otherwise known as The Hall—evidently to attend to some urgent business. He was not expected to return, according to Olivia Pritchard, for a full fortnight.

"He is quite assiduous in his attendance to every matter regarding his estates," Miss Pritchard pronounced. "I'm sure no finer property is better managed in all of England than The Hall."

Cressida wondered how it was a woman could be so obsessed with a man, as Olivia was with Rushton. She was always ready with a word of praise on his behalf, yet as for Rushton's leaving, Cressy could not help but think that the unfortunate incident at the end of Handel's *Music for the Royal Fireworks* had more to do with his sudden disappearance than any supposed *urgent business* might have.

She did not say as much to Miss Pritchard.

She did not have to. Miss Pritchard addressed the subject herself. "I imagine you are thinking he left because of the really odd thing he said last night at a moment when the whole concert room could hear his words, but I assure you, Rushton would not leave on so silly a pretext. You may trust me he had good reason for quitting Bath as he did."

Cressida sipped the water which her aunt was used to drinking every day and wondered yet again how anyone endured the vile taste. Afterward, she said, "I'm sure it's no concern of mine whether he left at all, nonetheless why."

Olivia smiled, and to Cressy's eye she seemed pleased. "You are right to speak thusly. I fear it is grown a habit among many of my Bath acquaintances to be far too concerned with the comings and goings of our mutual friends. Of course, Rushton's presence is always sorely missed. One does not meet with such an extraordinary blend of good breeding, manners, and impeccable taste, as in Rushton." She then switched subjects abruptly, her smiles increasing and a challenging glint overtaking her green eyes. "But tell me, are you still convinced your sister will be wed to Somersby by summer's end? Really, he pays but the smallest attention to her. I have been watching them, you see, in order to chart Daphne's progress. I only wish I could give you a better report."

Cressida found herself happily indifferent to the caustic nature of the young woman before her. As to her original question, she could not keep from glancing toward her sister—who was deep in conversation with Mr. Rushton's sister, Evangeline—and noticing that though Somersby was across the room, Daphne scarcely seemed to notice his existence.

Swallowing the remainder of her glass of the Bath mineral waters, she responded with mock sweetness, "Well, if in the end she does wed Somersby, perhaps Miss Rushton will help her choose her brideclothes." She then walked away from Miss Pritchard, knowing that this last remark was sure to sting, since Evangeline and Daphne had become fast friends in the past sennight or more. Olivia had been fairly surplanted.

As the days progressed, Cressy hired two more seamstresses and spent more of her time accompanying Daphne and her aunt upon their various excursions. The circle in which Mrs. Wanstrow traveled was quite large and energetic. Frequently a dozen or more would attend them to the Spring Gardens or to a promenade along the walk called the Orange Grove where an obelisk had been erected, in honor of William, Prince of Orange, who visited the city of Bath in 1734.

Large private balls and fetes were discouraged by the Master of Ceremonies, a tradition which hailed from early in the eighteenth century when Beau Nash reigned supreme. Still, morning calls were welcomed and the occasional alfresco luncheon, if not encouraged, was at least tolerated.

One aspect of Bath society pleased Cressida immensely—Daphne was positively blooming beneath the leisurely atmosphere and the congenial friendships she was enjoying. In particular, Sir Leighton-Jones was constantly at her elbow, begging to know how he could be of service to her or to Cressida. When Daphne remarked on it one day, she queried tentatively, "And how do you find the baronet? Is he a good man do you think?"

Daphne, plying her needle and setting a very crooked series of embroidery stitches on a lace handkerchief, responded with a warm smile. "He is one of the most agreeable men I have ever met with in all my life. He is forever friendly and says the kindest things to everyone! I like him prodigiously."

Cressida was very happy and after patting Daphne's hand, said, "Do not be afraid to encourage him if you wish for it, Daphne."

"Encourage him?" she queried, her brow knit. "Why? Has he been blue-deviled of late? I hadn't noticed it. But the next time I chance to see him I shall compliment him on his coat. That should lift his spirits. He always wears the prettiest coats. Have you noticed as much? Did you perchance see the one he sported yesterday? It was the color of claret!"

Cressy blinked her eyes and realized that somewhere within Daphne's response was the fact that she had missed Cressy's point entirely. As for Sir Leighton-Jones's apparel, she had thought more than once that he had a tendency to dandify his costumes, and a burgundy velvet coat, accented by a yellow waistcoat, had only confirmed her suspicion that he bordered on being a Pink of the Ton.

She said nothing more to Daphne on the subject of the baronet, or his clothing, trusting to Fate to see a happy conclusion in a few weeks' time. Though July was now well upon them, she felt confident that, with her aunt's help, Daphne would soon be properly wed.

Chapter Twenty-One

The linen-drapers on Milsom Street had quickly become a favorite haunt of Cressida's. She found everything she needed within the busy, well-stocked shop in order to supply her aunt with a steady stream of fashionable garments, and visited the premises at least every other day.

Once Mrs. Wanstrow's purse strings had been loosened, Cressida was pleased to find that her aunt spared no expense upon either the quality of fabric, or upon the smallest detail of trim. If nothing else, Aunt Liddy was a woman of exceptional taste, making it possible for Cressy to indulge her every artistic whim without regard to expense.

The young men who waited upon Cressida at the linen-drapers quickly became well acquainted with her and soon divined her purposes without once having the effrontery to rudely query, as Mrs. Pritchard had the other day, "And so you are determined to rig your aunt out in style, eh?" Mrs. Pritchard she could ignore and did so. The clerks won her appreciation by showing her more courtesy and respect in a day than Mrs. Pritchard was wont to show her friends and acquaintances over the course of a month.

When Cressy had established her patronage, she struck a bargain with the owner of the shop and subsequently received everything she purchased at a reduced price. When Mrs. Wanstrow learned of her savings, she fairly beamed with pride. "You are my niece, aren't you?" she exclaimed, giving Cressida a hug and placing a kiss upon each of her cheeks in turn.

At the counter, Mr. Perkins unfurled a roll of fine, Indian calico, an exceptional fabric printed with long rows of cherries and leaves and separated by narrow gold stripes running the length of the material. She was enchanted with the design and placed it next to a silk tulle which had also caught her fancy. Somehow, she thought, the fabrics belonged together, but she wasn't certain in what way or for which costume.

Heretofore she had been quite daring in her designs for her aunt, whose plump figure was not easy to fashionably circumvent. With skill, and the use of a small bolster of goose feathers secreted at the small of Mrs. Wanstrow's back to offset the disadvantages of an overly rotund derriere, Cressida had been able to employ every fabric which caught her eye. The cherries and stripes running vertically were a slenderizing aspect of the design which also made it possible for her to use the calico.

Oblivious to the presence of others in the shop, her gaze fixed to the delicate, sheer silk tulle, and trying to imagine how she could combine the fabrics, she was startled by the sound of a young woman addressing her.

"Cressida Chalcot?" a frail voice drifted through her concentration, finally breaking through to her hearing.

In a haze of imagined pattern cards, ruffles, darts, pleats, edgings, and linings, Cressida slowly turned her head to stare into the sunken eyes of a woman she did not recognize.

"Yes," she responded, trying to shake off the lethargy engendered by her intense involvement with the calico, and straining to identify a young lady who knew her by name. "I am Cressida Chalcot."

A smile, suddenly familiar, overspread the wan face of the woman in front of her. "Cressy," she said in almost a

169

whisper, tears burning brightly in her dove gray eyes. "I should have known you anywhere. You are quite as beautiful as I remember from school days. Have you forgotten me entirely, though I expect my appearance is something of a shock to you."

Cressy blinked once. Twice. She knew the voice at last. "Winifred Singleton. "Winnie!" she cried, stunned. The friend she had greatly enjoyed during her years at the seminary, stood before her in unrecognizable form. Only the color of her eyes, the perfect rows of teeth which had adorned her smile, and the musical quality of her voice, remained to lead a path to former days of health and beauty.

When Winnie coughed, Cressida knew there was no doubt but that her friend was ill with consumption. "How do you go on?" she queried politely, unable to broach immediately the subject of her health. "I remember you were to marry the squire's son, and after our final term together so much happened I fear I found it impossible to keep up with my correspondence."

"Oh, I did marry Charles," she responded, trying for enthusiasm. "And this is our son, Charlie."

For the first time, Cressy realized that a silent child stood at Winifred's side, clinging to her skirts. "He has your eyes," Cressy remarked.

"Indeed, yes. And his father's hair and nose and chin," she continued softly. She petted her son's head and squeezed his shoulders, her expression full of love as she watched him for a moment.

Cressida saw Winnie's affection for her son and watched with a sense of helplessness as a sadness overtook her friend's eyes. Afterward, she began coughing and pressed a kerchief to her pale lips.

Cressy gazed at the forlorn sight of mother and child and felt a rush of emotion overwhelm her heart. Pity was in the forefront of the assault on her sensibilities, intense, monstrous pity which twisted her sympathies and forced her into a state of profound gratitude that whatever she and Daphne had suffered in the past several years, a debilitating disease had not been numbered amongst their afflictions. Indeed, the making straight of their paths toward the future seemed trivial next to what she knew was Winifred's intractable confrontation with death.

"We have come to Bath that I might partake of the waters," she explained to Cressy's unspoken questions, her voice carried by the barest whiffs of a breath. "As you can see I am not in my best health, though I have improved a trifle since arriving here some months ago. Summers are always easier for me than winters."

Charlie looked up at his mother and stared at her solemnly. "Will she take care of me, Mama?" he asked, concerned. "She has a nice face. I like her."

"No, my darling," Winnie returned easily with a faint laugh, as she again caressed her child. To Cressida she added, "I have been in search of a—a nanny for Charlie, a place, a home for him with one or two children to play with."

Cressy regarded the child with an understanding of some of the difficulties before him. She knew what it was to lose a mother. On a cheerful note, she queried, "And where is your husband, Winnie? Is he in town with you? Do you live nearby? Does he accompany you to the Pump Room every day?"

Winifred appeared as though Cressida had struck her. "I don't know how to say this, Cressy, except to speak the words. It was several years ago when Charles died. He fell from his horse in a hunting accident. We had been married only a few months. Charlie had not even been born. I fear we've had a rough go of it since then."

"Oh, dear Winnie. I am sorry. No assistance from your family?"

Winifred shook her head. "An ancient and an unfortunate history, I fear. The squire had different plans for his son, and only my brother remains of my family, but he is unable to help us, I'm afraid."

Words failed Cressy after that.

Seeming to sense her discomfort, Winifred glanced at the fabric on the counter and exclaimed. "What a beautiful calico and such an exquisite tulle. Is this a gown you are having made up? A promenade dress, surely."

"It is for my aunt," she said. "I am earning my hire, as it were, by 'rigging her out in style.'" She then briefly explained about the death of her own parents, of the circumstances of her being in Bath, and how it happened she had come to reside with Mrs. Wanstrow. "You cannot imagine how grateful I am, for Daphne's sake, that we are permitted to live under her roof, and her societal wings! My sister's future is all but settled."

"I have heard! A marvelous connection—none better! And I'm sure that Lord Somersby—"

"Somersby?" Cressida interrupted immediately. "No, no! You are much mistaken. These are rumors only, though I do not hesitate to tell you that another good and quite worthy gentleman pursues her vigorously. I will not speak his name, but I have every expectation of an offer by summer's end."

Winifred shook her head, apparently mystified. "Are you sure it is not Somersby?" she asked, speaking slowly. "Why, the other day I saw her with him. At least, I am convinced it was Daphne I saw—for who could possibly mistake her angelic face—driving out with your aunt. She looked ever so happy."

Cressy laughed. "You must be mistaken. I'm sure it was another gentleman. Somersby is not permitted by his guardian to pay court to Daphne."

"I see," Winnie said, acquiescing, "then I must be mistaken. Well, I do wish her well, and you. But as for your circumstances, I wish to confess that I knew in part how you were fixed because I am acquainted with one of the ladies who you employ as a seamstress." She then bit her lip, an expression of consternation overtaking her features. "I never in my life expected to ask this of anyone, but I must." She paused, pressing her kerchief again to her lips briefly before continuing, "The fact is, I knew you were hiring ladies to sew for your aunt, and I have come here today hoping that I might see you and ask for employment of some kind. I am expert with the needle and any manner of thread or floss. I cannot, of course, do large work, but if you should perhaps have any smaller embroidery tasks or ruffling or ruching—" She broke off, taking a deep breath, and again began to cough.

When the spasm did not readily abate, Cressy led her to a chair and bade her sit down, the boy following with her, absolutely refusing to relinquish his hold on the skirts of her pelisse of a worn gray stuff.

Cressida looked down at the bent head and thin, bony neck. An old gray felt bonnet, trimmed with a red satin ribbon covered dusky curls, once gleaming with life in a girl's seminary, now dull. She remembered Winifred's high spirits, and infectious laughter from school days. She understood her well enough to know that charity was forbidden. She also knew what a long journey the words of help had taken to make, and so it was that she said, "How very fortunate that I should meet up with you today. My seamstresses have all they can do to stitch the many seams which my aunt's garments require. If I dare to mention an embroidered collar, or ruched ruff, or stand of gathered lace, I am fairly scowled at."

Winnie, whose fit of coughing had finally stopped, took Cressy's hand and squeezed it gently. "You were always kind, and we did have a great deal of fun, didn't we?"

"I should remind you of one or two episodes, but I fear you would be thrown into another coughing spell, so I shall refrain."

Winnie then searched in her reticule until she retrieved a card with her direction written on the back. Cressida was a little startled to see that her friend resided on Avon Street, a notorious habitat for the beggars of Bath.

"I know, I know," she responded with a faint smile of

despair. "It is ghastly, but if you would send a footman I'm sure all would be well, and I would be grateful. Ever so much, you've no idea." Upon ending her speech, Winnie rose, and taking her boy by the hand, thanked Cressy twice more before quitting the shop. Cressy offered to take her home, but Winnie stubbornly refused.

Cressida watched them go, her heart laden with sadness. It seemed in that moment that her life took one of its many shifts, her thoughts redirected from any complaints of her own situation to a sincere gratitude of all the good things which she possessed—her health, her sister, a proper house, excellent food, and the small competence which had enabled her to come to Bath in the first place and which, hopefully, would make it possible for her one day to open her own modiste.

Turning back to the fabric, she suddenly saw the garment she would make up for her aunt—a promenade confection with puffed sleeves, a fall of ruffled fabric about the bodice, a standing collar trimmed with lace, and between the bodice and the collar, a window of the sheer silk tulle, stitched with several miniscule pleats—enough work to keep Winnie occupied for a sennight or two.

Chapter Twenty-Two

A clerk followed Cressy from the shop onto the flagway, his arms laden with her purchases of the calico and tulle, and with a large parcel of muslin which Mrs. Wanstrow had ordered to underdrape all the windows fronting the town house. She was about to hire a waiting hackney when she noticed a familiar black curricle begin to slow before the linen-drapers, and with a start noticed that the equipage belonged to Mr. Rushton and was driven by him. Also to her surprise was the fact that he seemed to be guiding his carriage toward her.

She thought wryly that Miss Pritchard would be ecstatic to find she had erred in thinking Rushton would not be returning to Bath for a full fortnight. Only six days had passed, and here he was, come back and in apparent good health.

Once he had drawn his horses to a stop, he looked directly at her and asked politely, "May I escort you home, Miss Chalcot?"

Cressy wanted to refuse, nay, intended to refuse for she had rightly supposed he had meant to offer to take her up. But when she saw the expression of humble regret, albeit born proudly with a twinkle in his eye, Cressy found she could hardly refuse. "If you please, sir," she responded, afterward directing the clerk to pass the parcels to Mr. Rushton.

When this office had been performed, and the clerk had handed her up into the elegant equipage, Mr. Rushton gently laid a carriage rug over her lap and with a slap of the reins set his exquisite pair of grays in motion.

The sun was warm on Cressy's face as it peeked between streaks of clouds. A southwesterly breeze smelling of rain promised inclement weather in the near future, but for the present the sun was smiling, and Cressy smiled in return.

When the traffic surrounding the many shops on Milsom Street had been adequately navigated, Mr. Rushton said, "I happened to see you emerge from the linen-drapers just as I was returning to the White Hart. I could not resist coming to your aid, particularly when I saw the clerk laden with booty. I trust your expedition was prosperous?"

"Indeed, yes," she responded without amplification. He then made a polite remark on the excellent weather Bath inhabitants were enjoying of late, and inquired as to whether or not it had rained often since he had left for The Hall. She responded that it had rained only three times, but could not seem to formulate either a supportive comment upon the weather to satisfy the usual required verbal politeness or a counterquestion which might further conversation between them in general. Her thoughts were held in check by the image of Winnie caressing her son's head.

Generally, she was not given to dwelling upon misfortune, hers or anyone else's. But the realization that with the merest turn of Fate she could have just as easily been in similarly destitute circumstances as her friend, affected her deeply. She felt a compulsion to do more than just employ Winifred, but what else she could do, or even ought to do, she didn't know, not of the moment.

"And what air dreams are you spinning in that fervid brain of yours?"

Cressida glanced sharply at Rushton, who was looking

176

at her with an expression of bemused inquiry on his face. "Have I your attention at last?" he asked with almost an expression of hurt in his eyes. "Have I put myself beyond the pale? Is that why you are ignoring me and my apologies?"

"Your apologies?"

"There! I thought as much. I just made the most difficult speech of my entire existence, and you were spinning air dreams!"

Cressida blinked at him, still only half attending to what he was saying. "Oh, I am sorry," she returned indifferently.

"No, I don't think you are!" he exclaimed, pulling the horses hard to the left and bringing them to a halt in front of a row of offices.

"Whatever are you about, Rushton? Why have we stopped?"

"Because I will not continue this conversation, or rather, I will not continue to address you without looking into your eyes and determining for myself why you have been responding in monosyllables to my clever remarks and refusing to hear my humble speeches!"

Finally Cressida's mind cleared of all thoughts of Winnie, and she turned bodily toward him, determined to listen to what he had to say.

"Shall I begin again?" he queried.

"Yes, please do," she said. "I am sorry for not attending to you. My thoughts were engaged elsewhere. Pray, say what you will. I shall not let my thoughts drift again."

"About the other night, at the concert. I'm afraid I made a rather complete cake of myself and held your name up to the ridicule of any who might take delight in teasing you. I am very, very sorry for that wretched outburst, which I promise you shall never—"

She cut him off. "Really, Rushton, I wish you wouldn't. You see, I don't give a fig for any of it! Really, I don't. You are not the first person to be caught unawares by the untimely ending of a piece of music, and as for the rest, though I appreciate your apologies, they are meaningless to me. You were forgiven, if such forgiveness was even necessary, before you applied to me. And I assure you, no one teased me."

"No one dared," he said quietly, with a pensive frown between his brows.

She laughed lightly. "I think it is more that I am quite an insignificant entity in Bath. Besides, anyone knowing you as I do, would realize how absurd it would be for any of your friends to have supposed you had fallen in love with me. I am a penniless orphan, without a great deal of social aplomb to recommend me, and with a tongue not generally designed to please. So you see, you have nothing to concern you except perhaps your own conscience. I forgive you, but I think you are having a harder time forgiving yourself."

"There you are out!" he replied with spirit, at the same time slapping his reins across the backs of his horses, setting them in motion again. "I could easily forgive myself save that I have lost, or perhaps had never earned, your respect."

Cressida glanced at him in surprise. He was right of course, and so she remained silent.

The remainder of the journey was accomplished without a further exchange of words. Rushton seemed to have fallen into a brown study as he fixed his gaze upon the road before him.

When at last he drew his curricle into Landsdown Crescent, he said, "You seemed very much occupied by something or other when I first took you up. Do I impose by requesting to know what was distressing you? If I may say so, your expression was almost one of sadness."

Cressida, who felt that in the course of the journey she had wounded his pride, felt to some degree compelled to answer his query forthrightly. "I met a friend of mine from the school I attended several years ago. She has since been married and widowed, and she had a lovely child—a boy named Charlie—standing beside her. And, much to my dismay, I saw at once that she is very ill and that she is probably dying."

"I am sorry," he said quietly, instinctively laying his hand upon hers.

She was touched by his unexpected sympathy and felt her throat constrict. She lowered her gaze to look at the tan gloves covering his fingers. For some reason she was not in the least uncomfortable by his possession of her hand. She said, "I am not given to feeling overwhelmed by the unhappy circumstances of others, but in this case," she looked at Rushton and said, "I want to do something for her. I am going to employ her—that is, my aunt has hired several ladies to sew for her, and I'm sure she will be willing to give her some work, but it hardly seems enough of an effort on my, that is, on our part, considering how Winnie is situated. Oh, Rushton, it is really dreadful! You see, she is consumptive and is living on—on Avon Street!"

Unbidden tears now stung her eyes, and she quickly withdrew her hand from beneath his in order to search in her reticule for her handkerchief. Unable to find hers she was immensely relieved when he pressed his own kerchief into her hand. At the same time she was so struck by the neatness of the crisp, cambric square, which had been starched, ironed, and folded to perfection, that she was thoroughly diverted.

She looked at the handkerchief for a moment and then said with a wicked trembling of her lip, "I can't possibly sully your kerchief."

"Oh, the devil take it, you wretched vixen!" he tore the cloth from her fingers, shook it out of its tidy square with an angry flick of his wrist and bid her blow her nose.

Cressida did so with a vengeance. Afterward she turned to him and said, "Do come in for a little tea or sherry if you like. I know my aunt would be only to happy to receive you—" Here she looked at him with a challenging spark in her eye. It had escaped no one's attention that Mrs. Wanstrow was a toad eater of the first order.

"I should be delighted to—why you little minx! Do you know I begin to think you are in need of a sound thrashing, and I should be only too happy to oblige you if you don't take care."

"I'm trembling," she breathed, quite willing to tease him.

"I can see that you are! Now, if I take your hand, can you manage to clamber out of my curricle and fetch one of your aunt's footmen to see to my horses?"

With that, Cressida scooted forward to the edge of her seat, set aside her lap rug, took his right hand with her left, and eased her way backward out of the carriage. His horses were quite fresh, stamping their hooves in annoyance at having had their excursion cut short, and it was quite necessary for him to hold them in check until someone else could relieve him.

Once inside, sitting comfortably in a chair by the window near the fireplace, Rushton accepted a glass of sherry and responded politely to all of Mrs. Wanstrow's queries as to the state of his mother's health, as to his sister's progress on a piece of needlework which had kept her tambour frame employed for two years, as to whether or not he meant to attend the Lower Rooms Tuesday next.

Cressida watched him with interest as he gave his courteous answers to all her aunt's civil questions. She realized she had not been much in his company to know whether or not he was behaving as he usually did, or whether he was making a concerted effort to oblige her by addressing Mrs. Wanstrow with such politeness. She hoped something untoward would happen or be said, that she might catch him in some act of discourtesy and she did not have long to wait.

Much to her surprise, her aunt said, "We frequently have several of our intimate acquaintances join us on Sunday evenings—very informal. Sir Leighton-Jones, who has become one of my nieces' favorite squires, is often in attendance. If you should care to join us, I should be excessively pleased to have you—and perhaps Lord Somersby—grace my humble home."

Cressida felt a stir of impishness tickle her heart as she watched Rushton carefully, wondering how he would refuse her aunt. She knew he would not want to be included in such an invitation and for that reason could not keep from adding, "Yes, do come, Mr. Rushton! Your presence, and Somersby's, would be just the thing! Truly!"

He looked at her squarely, his eyes narrowed slightly. She saw the steely glint in his eye and wondered what he would say next.

He shifted his gaze back to Mrs. Wanstrow and much to Cressida's astonishment, responded, "I should consider it an honor. Though I can speak only for myself, I accept your invitation and will extend the same to Somersby."

"You're joking!" Cressida exclaimed, unthinking.

"Cressida!" her aunt cried. "You will make your apologies to Mr. Rushton at once. I have never seen such manners!"

Cressy bowed her head meekly and in a small voice which choked ever so slightly with laughter, said, "I beg your pardon, Mr. Rushton. I hope you can have no doubt of your being welcome here."

She then peeked at him from beneath her lashes and saw the appreciative gleam in his eye, which she had come to expect from him. At the same time, of all the peculiarities which comprised Rushton's character she wished more than anything he did not share her sense of humor, for when he got just that twinkle in his eye, then she felt truly in danger of losing her heart.

When, after visiting for a quarter hour, he drove away in his curricle, Mrs. Wanstrow strode to the window and watched him shout to his grays. "Would you look at that! Why I believe he could flick a fly off his leader's ear! He is quite a notable whip you know. He once won a race from London to Bristol!"

"Indeed," Cressy murmured. Out of deference to her vulnerable heart, she had chosen not to watch his performance, and instead was now settled into a corner of the sofa. Flipping through a copy of *La Belle Assemblee*, she said, "You must at least tell me this, dear Aunt, were you not surprised when Rushton accepted your invitation?"

She glanced up from her magazine to look at her aunt. What she found there surprised her, for Mrs. Wanstrow turned to regard her with a level eye and said, "Not at all, but you were, weren't you? Frankly, Cressida, I am not at all certain which is the greater simpleton, Daphne or yourself!"

And with that, she left Cressy to ponder the inscrutabilities of her aunt's character, which was daily proving more and more complex.

Chapter Twenty-Three

On Sunday evening, when Cressida entered the drawing room in preparation for Mrs. Wanstrow's informal evening, she was astonished to see that a fire had been lit in the grate. But when she realized that two branches of six candles each had been stationed and set ablaze just to each side of the mantel, thereby illuminating Aunt Liddy's portrait, the purpose of the fire became clear.

"An altar," she murmured to herself, as she stared up into the lovely visage of her aunt in her prime.

"What was that, my dear," Mrs. Wanstrow called to her from the doorway.

"Nothing to signify," Cressy responded, as she glanced at her aunt over her shoulder. She repressed a strong desire to place her cool hands upon cheeks which felt decidedly warm all of a sudden! She hoped Aunt Liddy had not heard her comment.

But Mrs. Wanstrow appeared oblivious to Cressida's reddened cheeks as she entered the chamber on a happy tread, humming a playful tune, and sporting a delighted smile. She was followed by a footman bearing two more heavy brass candelabras which she directed to be placed near the pianoforte opposite the windows. When she was satisfied with the arrangement, she turned to Cressida and said, "I trust you and Daphne are prepared to perform duets should any of our guests desire it?"

"Of course," Cressida responded. Daphne had a voice to match her lovely face, and whenever she performed, she never failed to please. Cressida, not being of a theatrical turn, was quite content to serve in the role of accompanist, both at the pianoforte as well as vocally as she sang in support of Daphne's musical, soprano voice.

Within half an hour the drawing room was comfortably full of guests. To Cressy's surprise, not only did Mr. Rushton make up one of the numbers, but his mother and sister attended as well. She learned from her aunt that upon consideration she felt it would be a slight not to extend the invitation to Mrs. Rushton and her pretty daughter, but Cressy could see by the satisfied gleam in her aunt's eye that civility was not the only force which prompted Mrs. Wanstrow to invite mother and daughter. There was no doubt in Cressy's mind that visions of an outraged, purple-faced Mrs. Pritchard had undoubtedly incited the supposed act of politeness.

For herself, Cressy was pleased with the combination of guests. Sir Leighton-Jones had brought with him an officer, a Major Heath, garrisoned, along with his regiment, in a nearby town. He was a tall, amiable gentleman, with curly brown hair, whose scarlet coat exactly matched the red silk-damask furnishings of the chamber.

Daphne had been busy over the past month in collecting a bevy of pretty young ladies about her, one of whom was Evangeline Rushton, and two others present were sisters, Mary and Elizabeth Hodges. These young women were both auburn-haired and hazel-eyed, though Elizabeth bore a spattering of freckles across her nose which were absent from lovely Mary's face. Their chief employment of the evening was giggling, which they did with a vengeance and effected the happy result of keeping Lord Somersby well entertained, as well as—to Cressida's relief—away from Daphne.

When she and Daphne were called upon to perform

their duets, Daphne delighted her audiences. Her voice was designed to please, being light and lyrical, and her simple, unaffected presentation did not fail to capture the attention of everyone present. When they began a third melody, Cressy played the familiar tune vigorously, but halfway through made the mistake of letting her mind wander a trifle from the music. Her gaze, too, slid from the notes in front of her and she was startled to find Rushton watching her with a curious expression on his face, not unlike the one he had sported at the concert, a full ten days earlier. She nearly lost her place in the music, and only by redoubling her concentration did she succeed in averting a dreadful lapse of timing.

She was rightly upset with herself. She had almost disturbed the flow of the music and merely because Rushton would look at her in just that way! Why was it she was so easily overset by the man?

At the conclusion of the song, Elizabeth Hodges leapt to her feet and begged Cressy to play a Scottish reel that she and Somersby—a companion from her childhood— might get up a dance. Mary seconded her sister's suggestion with a squeal, and in a truly charming manner begged Major Heath to partner her. This officer, dazzled by the red-haired beauties, acquiesced enthusiastically, and after the harp had been removed from the chamber and two of the larger chairs shifted against the walls, the dances began.

Cressida enjoyed being of service to her sister's friends and played vivaciously until her fingers ached. When a second dance had been brought to an end, Mary and Daphne began searching through her aunt's music in hopes of finding a waltz. They were unlucky in their attempt, but discovered one or two contredanses which the young ladies exclaimed would do just as well.

Rushton approached Cressida and asked politely whether or not she would prefer to dance instead of play. She responded with alacrity that she was well satisfied to continue to ply the keys, but Elizabeth took up Rushton's hint, and in a charming manner insisted she play the country dances with which she exclaimed she was quite familiar. Since it was well known she excelled in the art, Cressida relinquished her place at the pianoforte and immediately afterward discovered Rushton's true intention when he asked her to dance.

She was stunned, not least so because she had been sure when he recommended she cease playing it was due to his dislike of this form of amusement on a quiet, Sunday evening. Willing to tease him a little, she asked, "But does it not violate your sense of decorum to be dancing tonight? Here, without benefit of orchestra and polished ballroom floor?"

"Hush, vixen," he whispered with a devastating smile, then responded aloud for all to hear, "You know very little of me if you think I would reject partnering any of the young ladies present this evening. I've never met with a prettier assemblage of females in all my life!" Since a general, "Here! Here!" was raised by the rest of the male guests, the young women were inclined to be immensely pleased, Mary and Elizabeth in particular raising their giggles to the ceiling and beyond.

Cressida enjoyed herself hugely as she went down the country dance with Rushton. He was an excellent partner, which she had known from first dancing with him at the New Assembly Rooms some weeks ago. But he was also proving to be excellent company. She realized that when they were not brangling or pinching at one another, they shared many similar views and a decided appreciation for the ridiculous. And as the dance drew to a close and she accepted Major Heath's request for the next set, she knew an odd, fleeting sense of sadness as Rushton bowed her away.

After two country dances had been enjoyed, Mrs. Wanstrow announced that lemonade, ratafia, and Madeira, along with an assortment of desserts were being served in the dining room for any who wished for it. After the exertion of over an hour of dancing it was to no one's surprise that everyone repaired to partake of the refreshments.

Sipping a glass of iced lemonade, Cressida approached Mrs. Rushton and begged politely to know how she went on. Mrs. Rushton responded in kind, and after an innocuous exchange of pleasantries, the tall, elegant lady drew Cressy away from listening ears and said quietly, "I have been hoping to have a word with you this evening. In the general round of activities, day-to-day, one does not always have an opportunity for private discourse. I have been noticing for some time now two things—first, that your aunt has been parading before us in some of the most remarkable gowns imaginable, and secondly, that you do not go about in society as much as your sister is wont to do—in truth, you enjoy scarcely a fraction of the amusements which comprise Daphne's days."

Cressida felt decidedly uncomfortable and could think of nothing more to say in response than, "Very true."

Mrs. Rushton, whose congenial expression as well as the warmth of her blue eyes demanded confidence, dropped her voice even a little lower and said, "Gregory told me of having discovered you knee-deep in fabric and sketches. Am I presuming too much by asking whether or not your aunt keeps you employed as her private modiste?"

Cressy felt a blush of embarrassment cover her cheeks. "Madam, I pray you will not inquire further. I do not mean to give offense, but your incisive question places me in an intolerable position."

"I see," she responded with a knowing nod of her head. "Then I shall give you a little advice—just a hint, mind!—your aunt is as rich as Croesus! There! I can see by your expression you did not know, at least not to this extent. I thought as much. And to be quite candid, it goes sorely against the grain with me to see you ill-used in this manner." Her amiability gave way suddenly to a rather fierce, righteous indignation. "You should not have to earn your keep by sewing for Mrs. Wanstrow! It is quite beyond bearing. She ought to be taking you to her usual dressmaker instead of sending you to fetch and do for her!"

"Mrs. Rushton, I beg of you not to take a pelter!" Cressida responded in an urgent whisper. She firmly believed that regardless of the size of her aunt's fortune Mrs. Wanstrow had every right to dispose of her largess as she so desired. "I wish to assure you that I—that is, we—that Daphne and I have no claim upon my aunt! None whatsoever!"

"No claim!" Mrs. Rushton whispered angrily. "Only the bonds of familial connection! What do you mean, *no claim!* Of all the absurdities!"

Cressida pressed on. "An unfortunate breach occurred more years ago than can be numbered between my mother and her sister. Daphne and I came to Mrs. Wanstrow knowing we were not welcome. She could just as easily have sent us packing than have invited us to remain with her as she did."

"Not if she had even the smallest shred of conscience! You remain only in servitude, Cressida! Nothing more! Well, I can see that you are far more forgiving than I could ever be," she concluded, her nostrils flaring as Cressida had once seen Rushton's flare.

"But then," Cressy responded with a quivering lip, "you are far better situated to withhold pardon than I am."

Mrs. Rushton blinked with astonishment and gasped, her mouth falling slightly agape. "Upon my word!" she cried with a laugh. "Rushton told me you could be quite brazen, and the worst of it is I confess you are right. Only do remember what I have told you, and don't permit your aunt to complain of having to endure penury by having near-relations take up residence in her house!"

Since Mrs. Wanstrow had wandered near to Mrs. Rushton toward the end of her speech, it was not to be wondered at that she queried, "What is that you are saying to my niece, Mrs. Rushton?"

Cressida wondered what Mrs. Rushton would say to the formidable Mrs. Wanstrow. "Why nothing of great significance, only that you were to be commended for offering shelter to these poor, unfortunate, *orphaned* young women. And I do commend you, as I commend anyone who finally offers assistance where assistance has been long overdue."

Mrs. Wanstrow's blue eyes sharpened and narrowed. "Yes, well that is very kind of you, Margaret. I am sure, however, that anyone who knows how I am fixed must understand that heretofore I could do nothing for my darling nieces. Indeed, when I think of the laundering expenses alone—"

"Oh stubble it, Lydia. Do you take me for a flat? Good God, had I your fortune I could have purchased half of Bath and not spent a tithe of the whole! So you needn't pitch your gammon to me!" And with that, she smiled sweetly upon her hostess and moved to converse with Elizabeth Hodges who was batting her lashes at Major Heath and trying to keep from giggling as she sipped a glass of ratafia.

Mrs. Wanstrow took another bite of sweetmeat, afterward dabbing each side of her mouth with a small, linen table napkin. "I have never approved of that woman entirely. Ever since we were schoolgirls she has positively enjoyed making use of the most vulgar expressions! *Do you take me for a flat!* Cressida, I hope never to hear such a speech pass your lips!"

Cressy could not resist. "What?" she cried. "Do you take me for a flat? I would never employ such vulgarisms, 'pon my soul, I wouldn't!"

Cressida choked back the laughter she felt at the expression of astonishment on her aunt's visage and took the opportunity of expressing her desire to converse with Sir Leighton-Jones. Quitting Mrs. Wanstrow's side, she went in search of him, returning to the drawing room where he and Mary Hodges had their heads bent over a stack of musical pieces spread out upon the pianoforte.

When Mary lifted her head and caught sight of her, she exclaimed, "Cressida! Do look! We have found a waltz at last! But don't think I mean to ask you to play for us again. Mrs. Rushton has already insisted upon taking a turn."

"Mrs. Rushton?" Cressida queried, surprised.

"Indeed, yes! Have you had an opportunity to converse with her at length? She is such a complete hand! Oh, dear! I oughtn't to have said that. Mama would be horrified were she to know I had been speaking *cant* phrases!" She looked up at Sir Leighton-Jones, who stood over her by several inches, and dimpling, said, "You won't tell her, will you, sir?"

"Upon my honor, madam, I will not! I should think it a notorious lack of chivalry to betray a woman's confidence."

Mary, all smiles, dropped a quick curtsy. Lowering her eyes in a maidenly fashion, she batted her lashes and responded sweetly, "You are all kindness, I'm sure!"

Sir Leighton-Jones turned to glance at Cressida and smiled at her, rolling his eyes a trifle. Mary was quite possibly the most flirtatious female she had ever seen in her life.

When it was learned that a waltz was in the offing, the varied desserts were left behind at the prospect of seeing how cleverly the whirling steps to the dance could be managed by three or four couples within the confines of a relatively small drawing room. The mere challenge of the task at hand was enough to send spirits soaring and footsteps hurrying back to the narrow chamber.

Chapter Twenty-Four

Laughter ruled the elegant red-silk damask receiving room as the couples struggled to keep from plunging into one another with each dramatic turn of the dance. Cressida was held tightly in the arms of Sir Leighton-Jones, whose mastery of the waltz kept both of them from colliding more than once in five whirls with another couple. His weakened leg had regained its strength, and he was all she could desire in a partner. She laughed and laughed, unable to remember when she had enjoyed herself so much.

"I was wondering how you might look with your lovely face lit with amusement," her partner stated cheerfully. "And you are happy, aren't you?"

"Yes, of course, deliriously so, I think! I have not been so delightfully entertained since times out of mind!"

"I thought not," he responded quietly.

Something in the tone of his voice intrigued Cressida and she lifted her gaze, which had hitherto been directed toward the menacing elbows of the other dancers, and looked up at him. What she saw there led her to believe the good baronet had something of importance to say to her. Perhaps tonight she would learn the state of his heart where Daphne was concerned!

He began, "From the first it has struck me how much every particle of your being is spent upon seeing to your sister's future happiness. I cannot but admire you for such unflagging love and concern for your sibling. You are to be congratulated, and if I am not too hasty in saying as much, I believe all your hopes for your sister will soon be fulfilled."

Cressy felt her heart skip a beat. Was this his way of hinting at his own growing devotion to Daphne? Could it be true? Taking a deep breath in an effort to calm the excitement his words had engendered within her heart, she stated evenly, "I am sure most anyone in my situation would not have done less. I only wish I had brought Daphne to Bath sooner. I cannot begin to tell you how happy she is become since living under my aunt's roof, and—" here she paused before continuing with a careful smile, "and how very much your society pleases her. She speaks of you in the fondest of terms." She wished to say more by way of acknowledging his hints that Daphne's future with him would soon be settled, but did not want to appear overly eager.

"And what of you," he said in return, his voice low and confiding. "Do I please *you*, Cressida?"

"Oh, yes, very much," she answered without hesitation. "You are by far one of the kindest men I have ever known."

"Why, thank you," he responded, appearing satisfied. He then pulled her deftly to the right and cried, "Oh, dear! These spaces are cramped, aren't they? We almost collided with Rushton and Elizabeth. There, that's better." Smiling down at her, he continued, "I am very happy to hear you say that I in some manner please you. Daphne and I have become excellent friends, I think. She has, in fact, confided to me on more than one occasion. Has she mentioned as much to you? If so, I hope you don't think me an impertinent sort of fellow, since I have pursued her acquaintance with a purpose in mind."

Better and better, Cressy thought with an inward smile. "Now how could I possibly consider anything you might say or do an impertinence? I'm sure even Daphne would agree on that score."

"She is very charming, your sister, and quite beautiful, but—" here he paused and shook his head with mock sadness, "not precisely needle-witted, I fear."

Cressy smiled. "No, she is not." Then suddenly anxious that the baronet might be unhappy with her lack of intelligence, she queried, "You do not find her a trifle dull or a poor companion, do you?"

Sir Leighton-Jones, at his most affable, with each feature of his warm face blending into his friendliest of smiles, responded, "No, of course not! How could anyone, once having come to know the sweetness of her temperament as I have, possibly think her flawed for not possessing a keenness of wit. I would consider such a person above being pleased. Why, did you know for instance, that she has become acquainted with some children who frequent the Spring Gardens, and the moment they see her coming, they run to her arms? Is such a beauty of character to be despised for a mere lack of sense? No, a thousand times, no!"

"How good you are," Cressida said earnestly. "And it is so very much like Daphne to be beseiged by children. They have always flocked about her skirts, as far back as I can remember."

"I believe it is because she is still very innocent, just like a child—a most appealing quality, I assure you."

Cressida sighed deeply. Contentment and happiness combined to lift her spirits *aux anges*. Besides taking great pleasure in the simple amusements of the evening, she saw in the baronet's face and in the generous words he had just spoken, the fulfilling of her quest in bringing Daphne to Bath. A little more time, surely, and Daphne would bring the baronet up to scratch. She must encourage her sister, though, for to her eye she felt that Daphne had not been making a strong enough effort in attaching him to her side.

"Yes," Sir Leighton-Jones continued, warming to his theme. "And upon another occasion, the children were nigh to bowling her over, quite literally, with their enthusiastic play, but fortunately Lord Somersby was at hand to keep her from tumbling down a small hill."

Cressida was caught unawares by the introduction of the viscount into a subject in which, to her thinking, he had no place whatsoever. She responded uneasily, "Lord Somersby?"

"I think so," he said with a slight frown, attempting to recall the events of that particular day more firmly to mind. "Yes. I'm sure of it. He often attends your aunt to the Orange Grove and to the Gardens, as do any number of us."

Cressy realized he could not know how harshly his words were striking her. She stumbled in her steps, and the next moment, another couple collided with them— Daphne and Somersby!

"I—I am sorry, Daphne!" Cressida cried. "I tripped over my clumsy feet. Hello, Somersby!" The fact that the very persons who had caused her to miss her steps were not only upon her, but had been dancing together, nearly overset her completely. But that wouldn't do. She must compose herself quickly and discover, if she could, whether she had cause for concern.

Addressing the viscount, she said, "I haven't meant to ignore you this evening, Lord Somersby. I daresay I have not exchanged above a dozen words with you." She looked from one to the other, a feeling very much like panic rising within her.

He often attends your aunt to the Orange Grove and to the Gardens.

Were her sister and the viscount carrying on a secretive tryst? Surely not!

Lord Somersby bowed to Cressida and expressed his regrets as well, but said that he had been so much entertained by the Misses Hodges that he had scarcely spoken a word to anyone else, which was how he had come to dance with Daphne. "I thought at the very least I ought to stand up once with your sister, out of common civility. Miss Rushton has promised her hand to me as well."

Cressida could see nothing in his expression that might indicate his motives in dancing with Daphne were at all amorous. If the truth be known, he seemed completely disinterested. Glancing toward her sister, she wondered how Daphne would endure being slighted by a man who had once professed to love her, but there was nothing in Daphne's large blue eyes to indicate unhappiness. In fact, her expression was almost empty, as though she were devoid of any feeling for him whatsoever.

Could it be true?

If it was, Cressy thought she should have felt a little more comforted. Instead, Sir Leighton-Jones's words haunted her. Why had no one told her Somersby and Daphne had been together so frequently? Her aunt had never mentioned the matter to her. Nor had Olivia Pritchard, she thought wryly. But then Olivia would not have been included in the expeditions to the Gardens or to the promenade along the Orange Grove.

As the music drew to a close, Cressy again apologized both to her partner and to Daphne and Somersby. The latter pair jointly expressed the sentiment that she was being absurd for begging their pardon, and after speaking politely to one another for a minute or two, parted company—the viscount to seek out Miss Rushton, and Daphne to give her hand to Major Heath.

Seeing nothing in either Daphne's or Somersby's behavior to cause even the mildest concern, she shook off the oddly unsettled feeling which clung to her and was able to greet Rushton's request for the next waltz, if not with untrammeled enthusiasm, then with courtesy.

Just as he was about to take her hand, he seemed to experience a change of heart and asked her if she would care for a glass of ratafia instead. "For I am suddenly parched and could use a little Madeira myself."

Cressy was surprised and looked up at him with a question in her eyes. He narrowed his eyes expressively and offered her his arm. She took it, then permitted him to guide her back to the dining room, again feeling uneasy.

If she wondered what he was about, she did not have long to wait to discover his intentions, for he began, "I couldn't help but notice you are on uncommonly friendly terms with Sir Leighton-Jones."

Cressy felt the hackles upon the back of her neck immediately rise as they walked the length of the hall. She could not imagine what he meant to say to her with regard to a man she considered to be a complete gentleman, or why he had chosen to introduce the subject in the first place. Whatever his promptings, she had no intention of easing him through the conversation and responded, "If I am, I don't see what concern it is of yours."

When they reached the door of the dining room, he bade her remain in the hallway for a moment. He looked down at her, a frown between his thick arched brows. "I have debated bringing the subject forward," he began at last, "for reasons you infer. I have no right to concern myself with your affairs, none whatsoever. But after observing you with Sir Leighton-Jones, I feel compelled by what I believe to be the friendship which exists between you and myself to beg you to be mindful of—" he sought for words, and only continued after he had chosen the precise ones he wished to employ, "of his experience in society and your lack of it. I don't mean to be unkind, but I wish to make certain you understand that however much the gentleman he might appear, he has not remained a bachelor all these years without wounding a great many hearts."

Cressida did not know which she felt more strongly, relief or astonishment. Laughing slightly, she responded, "Mr. Rushton, are you telling me you are concerned that Sir Leighton-Jones will break my heart?"

"Yes, a little. And given the fact that you have not been much in society because of the trials of your existence heretofore, I wanted to advise you to be careful. You are not used to the advances and attentions of a great deal of men and perhaps therefore do not have the means with which to divine their motives."

Cressida turned away from him and pushed open the door to the dining room. There were no servants present, nor any of the other guests, so she felt perfectly safe in saying, "It is just like you, Rushton, to interfere where you are least wanted. I know I ought to be grateful for your attentions to the safety of my heart, but I believe I would rather you did not concern yourself. I have been governing my life, my emotions, my well-being for a number of years and feel perfectly capable of continuing to do so."

She walked up to the table, still laden resplendently with every manner of desserts.

"I meant no harm, Cressida, truly."

Cressy heard her Christian name, spoken as it was from behind her, and found herself a little startled by the gentle tone in his voice. "I'm sure you didn't," she responded quietly, her heart picking up its cadence. She turned around to face him and said, "And I didn't mean to speak brusquely. Sometimes with you I feel like a—a pugilist! Before you've so much as opened your mouth, I've lifted my fists, ready to have a go at you!"

"Now where did you learn of such things?" he queried, smiling.

"I beg you will tell no one, but years ago, my father dressed me up as a lad and took me to see a mill. I had begged him to do so for weeks, nay months. Finally, he consented. It was all so exciting until the bruising became rather marked! I'm 'fraid I became quite ill and forced my poor papa—who had wanted ever so much to see Molyeux box!—to take me home."

"You're a strange one, Cressida," Rushton said, looking down into her face, seeming to take in each of her features in turn.

She gazed back into piercing blue eyes and felt lost, all

197

over again, as she had several times before when he stood close to her and simply looked at her. Faintly from the drawing room she could hear the pianoforte marking the pulsing rhythm of the waltz. She and Rushton were alone, a thought which caused Cressy's knees to grow loose and unsteady. He oughtn't to be so handsome, she thought yet again. No wonder Miss Pritchard continued to be so entranced by him!

Taking a deep breath, she forced her gaze to shift to the window at the end of the table. She straightened her traitorous knees and summoning every ounce of her will, walked past him to stand by the window. In a breathy voice she said, "As it happens, I wish to assure you I am not in the least in danger of losing my heart to Sir Leighton-Jones. In fact, I wonder you even mention the matter since it is clear to me he is in pursuit of—of *Another*."

"*Another?*" Rushton queried.

Cressy bit her lip, as she stared down into the dark street, lit only by rushlights settled in the sconces of three or four of the town houses. Beyond the street, the green was dark and shadowless beneath a moonless sky. So still and peaceful was the vale that the hills on the opposite side of the valley appeared as though they had been tucked into a cosy bed and had fallen fast asleep.

Cressy didn't want Rushton to press her, but apparently he had found her allusion intriguing. "To whom do you refer, for I have observed no one tonight upon whom the baronet has turned his gaze so frequently as you."

Cressy thought he was speaking absurdities, but checked the impulse to say as much. Instead, she responded to his question, "To say more would be to expose someone else to mere conjecture on my part, so I will not."

Rushton joined her by the window, and stared down at her, his face lit with amusement. "You mean Daphne, don't you?" he cried. "Of all the hen-witted—Cressida,

198

you're a little fool!" He then laughed and strolled back toward the door. "It wouldn't do to set the tongues a-wagging so I will return post-haste to the drawing room. You have at least made my mind easy—I can see that you are not in a way to losing your heart to Sir Leighton-Jones. I have no more fears on that score."

"I'm so happy for you," she returned facetiously. So he thought her *a little fool,* curse the man! The worst of it was she might not be losing her heart to Sir Leighton-Jones, but she realized she was in a fair way to forming the most wretched *tendre* for a man who could make her as mad as fire with the mere lifting of his brow, and who was as unattainable as Zeus!

Chapter Twenty-Five

"So she is employed as her aunt's seamstress," Rushton said, glancing toward his mother. He could barely discern her features in the darkened coach, as Mrs. Rushton's barouche carried the family back to her town house in Queen's Square.

"Not her seamstress, precisely. I understand Cressida has hired several women to serve in that capacity, but there is no doubt she has taken the role of modiste to her aunt. She is quite a remarkable young woman."

Miss Rushton, who was a very youthful twenty, said, "She seemed to enjoy herself prodigiously this evening. She is not wont to do so, I am told. And though I suppose she possesses considerable abilities, I take more pleasure in her sister's company. Daphne is forever saying the funniest things. I realize she is not in the least clever, but her heart is warm, and her spirits are ever so lively. I hope she will take up a permanent residence in Bath, for then I shall have a new friend."

Rushton regarded his sister for a moment and thought two Seasons in London had done little to improve her mind. If it were possible, she seemed to have grown even more vain in her pursuits than before her first come-out ball. The fact that she would prefer Daphne to Cressida was a strong indication of the general tendency of her character and caused him to offer a small snort of disgust in response to her lively comments.

Evangeline Rushton, perfectly cognizant of her brother's contempt, stated, "I know what you will next say—that I would do a great deal better by pursuing an acquaintance with Cressida, but I'm not of a mind to. She seems forever occupied with something or other and does not attend to the conversations at hand. Why only this evening, I was in the midst of regaling Daphne and Elizabeth of a particular anecdote—involving Caroline Lamb and her latest escapade dressed up as a page, which they both found vastly amusing, I don't hesitate to tell you!—and what must Cressida do but stare at me with just that expression which I have seen you employ a hundred times—as though I were a wall she could see through!"

Mrs. Rushton, seeing that a well-rehearsed battle was about to ensue, addressed her daughter in a softened voice. "You must forgive such a one as Cressida Chalcot, who has attended almost exclusively to the care of her elder sister these five years and more. I, too, should like to see her a little less weighed down with the concerns of this life, but I had a letter from my good friend, Mrs. Cameley, about a fortnight ago, who gave me the most trying report of Daphne's wretched incompetence as a governess. Her daughters adored Daphne, of course, but it would seem even Cassie, who is but ten, could read better than your *new friend*. And tell me something, Evangeline, if you were suddenly cast upon the world, without a feather to fly with, how well would you fare should you have to earn your keep?"

Evangeline smiled brightly. "Why, it would be the easiest thing imaginable, I'm sure," she responded with a bouyancy found only in untried youth. "For I would become a famous actress like Sarah Siddons!"

Mrs. Rushton opened her mouth to try to reason with her daughter, but Rushton, who sat next to her, gave a single tug upon the sleeve of her redingote and said, "The task is hopeless, madam. I suggest you marry her off as soon as possible. It is the only solution!"

She glanced sharply at her son and queried, "To Sir Leighton-Jones?"

Rushton was surprised at his mother's perspicacity and nodded. "Just so."

"Sir Leighton-Jones!" Evangeline cried, horrified. "But he is ancient. Why he is nearly as old as you, Gregory. I should rather die first!"

Rushton would have argued that the baronet was quite five years his senior, but he knew the road was too short to give his horses their head, and so he merely crossed his arms over his chest.

Mrs. Rushton said, "Hush, Evangeline. Of course you shan't marry him." To her son she said, "Cressida's scheme would be a good one, if Sir Leighton-Jones hadn't evinced an interest in the wrong sister. Does she suspect the truth?"

"No, not at all. But what do you mean her scheme would be a good one? You can't approve of her machinations! Surely! I was only jesting when I said you ought to marry Evangeline off. Come, Mama! I have always believed you to be a woman of uncommonly good sense and forthrightness."

"Gregory, where have I failed in your education? How do you suppose any gently bred female must approach her future?"

He looked hard at her and after a pause of a full minute responded with, "I will say this much for Cressida, she does not seem to hold such a course for her own life. Her schemes, as you call them, have all been for Daphne."

"Rather like a mother, wouldn't you say?"

"I suppose so, but dash it all, I can't like it!"

"And why do you suppose Almack's is called the Marriage Mart? Our class aligns properties and fortunes and titles. I wish it weren't so, but really, you men can be so impractical at times. I for one hope for a chance to recommend Sir Leighton-Jones to Cressida! He would make an excellent husband for her. He is good and generous, though a little of a dandy. Did you see how much oil he wore in his hair this evening? At any rate, I mean to say as much to her when next we meet."

"I wish you wouldn't, Mama. Even if I agreed with you—which I don't!—marriage ought to be the result of a true and honest love between two people."

"Why, Gregory," Mrs. Rushton exclaimed. "I didn't know you were such a romantic fellow. Is that why you've never formed a lasting attachment? Have you never known love?"

"I suppose not," he murmured.

"I wonder if Cressida has."

Rushton had wondered the very same thing of late. He tried to imagine her exchanging vows with Sir Leighton-Jones, but somehow the image caused his jaw to clench painfully. He could not like the baronet, at least not in connection with Cressida.

But his mother was right. For a gently bred female, such as Cressida Chalcot, what better course than to marry a man of fortune and title, in order that she might bear her children in comfort?

He stamped his cane upon the floor of the coach. Damme, he couldn't like it!

Chapter Twenty-Six

Two days later, Cressy smoothed out the skirt of the promenade dress of calico cherries and silk tulle. It was everything she had hoped it would be, and even the seamstresses who had sewn every tiresome stitch had exclaimed over the final dazzling effect of the gown.

She called her aunt and Daphne to view the latest creation. Daphne covered her aunt's eyes with her hands and walked her awkwardly into the morning room, forcing her to keep her eyes shut. When she withdrew her hands, Mrs. Wanstrow took in the vision before her, blinked several times, and began exclaiming, "Oh, my dear! Oh, my goodness gracious! Exquisite! But are you sure it will not appear to disadvantage on my—my womanly girth! Oh, what do I care for that!" She approached the dress and touched the tulle which had been carefully stitched by Winifred. She drew in her breath. "Magnificent," she breathed and gasped and gasped again. "Oh, my dearest Cressida! you have been a godsend! My child, my child—" And so her raptures continued, until her maid was summoned to carry the walking dress carefully up the stairs where Mrs. Wanstrow intended to put it on, to decide which of her jewels would best set the cherries and gold stripes off to advantage, and to see whether or not she ought to purchase a new bonnet, or tear apart one of her old ones and have Cressida refashion it with a few red satin ribbons. "I have just remembered!" she added, with an upraised finger just before quitting the morning room. "I have some artificial cherries which are in excellent condition, that I wore some twenty years ago. How clever of me not to have thrown them out!"

The door closed behind Mrs. Wanstrow, and Daphne turned to smile upon her sister. "You have made her very happy, Cressy! I just can't believe that you are able to fashion all these gowns with so little effort. I mean, I know you take out your watercolors and make pretty pictures first, and you spend time at the linen-drapers, but really it seems to be so easy for you when I can't even arrange pattern cards without getting a headache!"

"And it seems so easy for you, Daphne, to collect a dozen friends about you. I am not so blessed. I was watching you on Sunday evening, sitting amongst your friends and laughing gaily. You are happy here, aren't you?"

"You can have no idea," Daphne said, tears suddenly shining in her large blue eyes.

Cressy went to her at once, hugged her, then begged her to sit in a chair beside the fireplace. "I'm so glad!" she cried, dropping beside her sister and taking Daphne's hands in her own. "I have been so worried all these years for you. Though I knew you enjoyed the children wherever you were employed, I knew equally as well that you were unhappy beyond words."

"I was," Daphne said. "But I didn't think you knew. I tried to be content, but it was so hard learning my letters."

"I know, I know. But that is all behind us now. And everything here, in Bath, seems to be progressing wonderfully well, wouldn't you agree?"

"Yes! Oh, yes," Daphne breathed.

Cressy looked into her sister's euphoric eyes and knew the time had come to press her about Sir Leighton-Jones.

She began, "I have only one concern at this time, Daphne."

Daphne nodded briskly several times, still smiling.

"Well, it is, of course, your future which I refer to." A little of Daphne's cheerfulness seemed to fade from her lovely face. Cressida continued. "I have reason to believe that a certain gentleman of your acquaintance has in part already lost his heart to you." Daphne's face fell further. "I am convinced with only the smallest effort—a hint that you would welcome his advances—his hand might be won."

"Who?" Daphne queried, her happy expression replaced by a worried frown. "I cannot imagine who you are referring to. Major Heath has quite lost his head to Mary, and Mr. Rushton certainly prefers your company to mine. Ev—that is, Lord Somersby—well I need not mention him I suppose. I can only think of Sir Leighton-Jones, and he is disposed to being in love with you as well."

Cressy shook her head. "No, my darling. There you are wrong. I am nearly certain he is fair and fast to tumbling head over ears in love with you. He needs but the smallest push and—what is it, my dear? Why do you hang your head?"

"I—" Daphne began in a whisper. She withdrew her hands from Cressy's grasp and pressed them to her cheeks, apparently unable to continue.

"Do you not hold Sir Leighton-Jones in affection? I had thought—I mean, the other day when we spoke of him, you fairly gushed with praise for him."

"I know. But that was because I thought—" She lifted her gaze, tears swimming in her large, blue eyes. "Cressy, aren't you in love him? When you asked me for my opinions of him, I supposed it was because you had fallen in love with Sir Leighton-Jones and meant to marry him and wanted to know if I liked the match."

"I?" Cressida cried, greatly shocked. "No, of course not. He is an amiable gentleman, but I have no intention

206

of marrying him or anyone else, for that matter. All my efforts have been on your behalf. Didn't you realize I was encouraging him that you might discover for yourself what an exemplary husband he would make for you?" She rose to her feet and moved to stand near the fireplace. On the mantel rested a watercolor sketch of a white satin gown which Cressy was hoping Daphne might wear for her nuptials.

Her thoughts began spinning dizzily about in her head at the sight of it. What if Daphne never married! Oh, it was not to be thought of, yet how had it come about that such a wretched piece of miscommunication had occurred! Hadn't Daphne spoken warmly of Sir Leighton Jones?

Convinced that the baronet's sentiments were indeed firmly attached to Daphne, Cressy moved to stand behind the winged chair in which her sister sat. Lightly laying her hands upon the soft velvet fabric, Cressida spoke in a quiet voice. "Daphne," she began slowly. "I can't conceive of how you came to think that Sir Leighton-Jones was in love with me or I with him. Nothing could be further from the truth, I assure you! Why, if you only knew how frequently he speaks of you—and always in the most ebullient manner—I am persuaded you would have no doubts as to his sentiments for you!

"Now that I have explained this to you, I wish to impress upon you how very much I believe him to be just the man to make you happy." She took a breath and waited for Daphne to respond. But a profound silence had settled over the yellow curls, still bent unhappily forward.

Feeling a knot form in the very pit of her stomach, Cressida stared down at the unresponsive, flaxen-haired beauty and knew both a sense of frustration as well as a wrenching of anxiety. She had not foreseen so unlikely a misunderstanding or her sister's extreme quietude.

When Daphne remained silent, Cressida decided it was necessary to explain the difficulties of their joint circumstances yet again to her shatterbrained sister. She took a deep breath and for a full quarter of an hour impressed upon Daphne the need for her to take into full measure the precariousness of her situation, the size of Sir Leighton-Jones's fortune, which would keep her in comfort all the years of her life, the kindness and affability which characterized him, and most importantly the fact that once the summer drew to a close, if Daphne had not got a husband, she and Cressida would again be cast upon the world to seek employment as governesses or companions. Was that what Daphne wanted?

"No," a small voice spoke from within the shelter of the velvet chair.

"So you see," Cressida finished at last, rounding the side of the chair and dropping to her knees in front of Daphne, "if you are to have a secure future, you must begin to accord Sir Leighton-Jones more and more of your attentions. I hope you will trust me in this Daphne—he will make you an excellent husband. Indeed, he will. And as I said before, he has already praised you to the skies and requires now only a little encouragement to see his heart won. You will try to oblige me by giving him a hint or two, won't you?"

The sober expression on Daphne's face caused Cressy to feel some hope, first that her sister had comprehended the whole of her speech, and secondly that she intended to make an effort.

Daphne opened to her mouth to speak, then closed it, an act which caused two perfect tears to roll in turn from each eye. "Of course," she responded at last.

Cressida frowned, wondering why her sister was crying. "Do you think marriage will end the gaieties which you have enjoyed this summer? Is that why you are so sad? My dear Daphne, do but think! If you were to marry Sir Leighton-Jones, he would bring you to Bath as often as you wished. His estates are not more than ten miles distant, and you would be near Miss Rushton and the Misses Hodges as well. Your society as a married woman is like to increase rather than decrease."

Daphne sniffed several times until Cressy procured a kerchief for her from her own reticule. Shortly after blowing her nose twice, Daphne quit the room and retired to her bedchamber. Cressida would have followed her and tried to offer her comfort, but upon consideration, she thought Daphne would do better to give some thought to all she had told her. After all, within the small scope of Daphne's brain, it had probably not occurred to her that Aunt Liddy was still planning to eject them from her town house when the leaves of the elms began to turn. Let her ponder the difficulties of her situation, Cressy adjured herself, then turned to the more enjoyable tasks of designing a gown for the alfresco luncheon her aunt had decided to hold on the following Saturday.

Once safely locked into her bedchamber, Daphne threw herself upon her bed and cried until she thought her heart would break. She had been so taken aback by her sister's insistence not only that Sir Leighton-Jones had fallen in love with her, but that it was essentially her duty to bring the baronet up to scratch—and that as quickly as possible!—that she had been able to do nothing more than listen, stunned, to Cressida's lecture.

She still could not believe it was true, nor that Cressy could be so blind to her own love for Somersby. Of course, Aunt Liddy had taught them both quite well how to carry on a tête-à-tête by schooling their features to indifference, and thereby keeping everyone in ignorance of the true state of their hearts. Still, she had not believed their charade to have been so effective as to have permitted Cressy to believe she would actually consider marrying Sir Leighton-Jones! He was well enough, she supposed, and might make some young lady an admirable husband, but she did not like the manner in which he addressed her as though she were five years old!

She thought back to the Sunday evening and the waltz she had shared with Evan. She blew her nose again and sniffed, then smiled into her pillow. Evan must have whispered his love to her a hundred times as they whirled and bumped their way through the enchanting set. With no one the wiser, she thought dreamily.

Several times she had scrutinized Somersby's face to see if he was keeping his features unenlivened, and he was! So much so, that had she not been well versed as to what he was doing, she would not have believed the words he spoke since he wore the expression of a dullard! As it was, every syllable had been a symphony in her ear!

Even Aunt Liddy had complimented her later that night upon the cleverness of their deception.

She laughed and blew her nose again. Oh, Evan, Evan, Evan! What are we to do? What am I to do?

Chapter Twenty-Seven

Bath society had been regulated for many years by the Master of Ceremonies, a position held in the prior century by Beau Nash, who laid down such laws as forced the gentry to meet in common places, such as assembly rooms, the theater, the concert room, and the card room. Private balls were, if not strictly forbidden, then heartily discouraged.

When Mrs. Wanstrow received permission, albeit reluctantly given by the Master of Ceremonies at the New Assembly Rooms, to hold a private alfresco luncheon on the banks of the Kennet-Avon Canal, she was as much astonished as Mrs. Pritchard was mad as fire, and she threw herself into the details of the event with great spirit. So much so, that by the time the day of the luncheon arrived, a week into the month of August, her exertions had cost her one of her chins, and two inches around the high waist of her gown.

Mrs. Wanstrow was ecstatic.

The welcome loss, however, dismayed Cressy since the promenade dress, so perfectly suited to a summary luncheon beside the canal, now hung upon her aunt like a dressing gown instead of the extremely well-fitted garment it was designed to be.

Calling the seamstresses together to marvel at the change in her aunt, she soon set them hurriedly plying new seams and "fishes" in the calico of cherries and stripes in order to better fit the gown to the renewed youth of her aunt's figure.

By half past four in the afternoon, four being the hour the luncheon was to take place, Cressida could see that her aunt's *fête* was destined to be a success. Two dozen guests had arrived to fill the air with trills of laughter and a constant chatter of bouyant conversation. Even Mrs. Wanstrow was prompted to announce that the party would surely take the wind out of Mrs. Pritchard's eye, once and for all!

The place chosen by Mrs. Wanstrow and Daphne for the *fête*, was on a sweeping green that led gently down to the edge of the canal where two brightly decorated water scows awaited to take members of the party on brief excursions up and down the narrow channel of water. The scows were pulled by horses hitched to the flat-bottomed boats by long ropes that extended to a well-worn path alongside the canal. The gentle plodding of the backs provided the precise, leisurely progress required for the younger ladies and gentlemen of the party to conduct lively flirtations away from the scrutiny of the older members, who were soon ensconced in chairs beneath a large, open canvas tent.

Laughter, therefore, echoed across the waters so long as the scows remained in motion—laughter, conversation, flattery, and every form of good-natured teasing, taunting, and humbug!

Cressida enjoyed the scows immensely, as much for the novelty of the experience as by the fact that Daphne kept Sir Leighton-Jones at her elbow on two successive trips. She breathed a sigh of relief as she saw Daphne smiling at the baronet, all the while holding her bonnet against the growing afternoon breeze. She had never looked prettier, and Sir Leighton-Jones had never worn so affectionate an expression on his face before. Daphne seemed to have taken her advice to heart, and the baronet was frequently seen gliding along in her wake.

"Now why is it," Rushton queried in a low voice, "do you appear as though you had just swallowed the mouse."

Cressida turned to look at the tall Leader of Fashion, and noted that he was, as always, dressed to perfection. His neckcloth was tied in a mode she recognized as à la Byron, and his coat of blue superfine appeared molded to his broad shoulders. He wore buff-colored pantaloons tucked into gleaming Hessians, the tassels of which swayed gently to the every shifting movement of the scow.

She felt a familiar tug of attraction as she smiled and returned easily, "My sister is very happy in Bath, and it brings me great pleasure to see her so. I hope you haven't any objection to that."

Rushton glanced toward the baronet, who was leaning on the tall side of the scow and listening to Daphne sing one of her favorite songs. "Does he still attend your aunt on Sunday evenings?" he queried.

Cressy nodded.

"And do you believe him caught by your sister's charms? Does he spend every moment waiting upon her next word?"

"I have observed that he pays her a great deal of attention, but whether or not he is *caught by my sister's charms,* is not for me to say. He seems content in her company."

"And is he as *content* in yours?"

Cressida looked beyond him to the sight of the descending sun reddening the horizon beyond the hills to the west. She knew what he inferred and so responded, "Sir Leighton-Jones's manners are such as make every lady feel *content* in his presence."

He chuckled softly. "Well said, Cressida. But tell me this, if it so, then why do you smile at Daphne's enjoyment of his company?"

"I wish you would stop," she whispered, feeling mildly irritated yet at the same time enjoying his teasing banter.

"If you were in my place, you would smile, too, and entertain every manner of hope—whether ill-founded or not!"

"In order to keep your spirits from plummeting?"

"Perhaps. Why do you press me, Rushton?"

"I suppose because I believe you are destined to be disappointed, severely so, and I don't wish to see it happen."

"That is very kind of you, but I don't think you need concern yourself. I have suffered more formidable disappointments and survived."

Rushton, gesturing to a bench provided for the guests, asked Cressy whether or not she wished to sit down. When she did, he took up a seat beside her and began to speak, much to her delight, upon any number of subjects—Byron's *Don Juan*, issues of reform, the canal he was having built upon his property at the priory.

Upon discussing the latter subject, Cressida was startled to learn that his earlier, hasty return to his estate—the very day following the concert at the New Assembly Rooms in which he had stated, for all to hear, that he had *not* fallen in love with her!—he had been called back because of the near-drowning of two of his workmen.

Cressida was reminded immediately of her earlier, ungenerous thoughts where he was concerned and made a clean breast of it, apologizing for having thought so little of him that she had actually believed he had quit Bath in order to avoid being teased by his friends and acquaintance.

He seemed astonished by her confession. "You needn't have told me as much, you know. I would never have had occasion to discover the nature of your ill opinion otherwise and therefore could never have snubbed you, which is what I long to do of the moment! How could you believe I would behave so cowardly?"

Cressida felt a familiar deviltry come over her. "How could I believe otherwise, is more to the point!" she cried, glancing down at her gloves of blue kid. She pretended to busy herself with smoothing out a small crease in the left one and struggled to keep a smile from overtaking her lips.

He leaned toward her and whispered, "Vixen!"

A smile vanquished her struggle to appear serious as she broke into a quiet trill of laughter. She liked it very much when he gracefully accepted her teasing and told him so.

Rushton looked into violet eyes which seemed to lighten to a delicate lavender beneath the warm, late-afternoon sun. It was very easy to be with Cressida, he realized. Not only easy but pleasurable, and it was with only the strongest hold on his impulses that he kept from caressing her. The moment she smiled he wanted nothing more than to take her hand in his, or to put his arm about her shoulder and pull her close, or to place his lips upon hers. Instead, he contented himself with watching her.

Cressida wondered what Rushton was thinking as he looked deeply into her eyes. There was just that expression on his face which she had seen so frequently before, that caused her heart to leap within her breast, robbed her of breath, and completely took away her desire for anything else save his company. She wanted to say something, but no words came to mind to break the spell of his unspoken thoughts.

After a time, when certain images began to assail her—in particular, of those moments when Rushton had taken her roughly in his arms and kissed her—she felt an overwhelming need to distance herself from him. Over the past fortnight since the Sunday evening when they had shared a cramped waltz in her aunt's drawing room, she had found herself frequently in Rushton's company. If she had previously felt disturbed by his presence, or in danger of her losing her heart to him, now she had begun an even worse occupation—that of looking for him wherever she happened to be, whether at the Pump Room, the milliner's, the Orange Grove, the linen-drapers, the shops on Milsom Street, the Spring Gardens, the theater, the New Assembly Rooms, or any other public place, even the streets where she might perchance see him driving his curricle on some errand or other.

Really, she'd become hopeless in her longing to see him and to exchange a word or two with him, so much so that as he looked upon her with what she believed was a blatant, wondrous desire to kiss her again, her throat constricted with tears.

To Rushton's credit, he had not overstepped the boundaries of social form. He had not tried to kiss her again, not since the tête-à-tête they had shared in her aunt's drawing room several weeks ago. He did not flirt outrageously with her, nor in any other fashion did he lead her to believe that his affections were engaged or that he desired any relationship with her beyond that of friendship.

For this reason, though she could sense that her heart was breaking before she had even admitted to herself the depth of her regard for Rushton, she tore her gaze away from his.

She swallowed hard, feeling tears sting her eyes, and was grateful that the waning sun, beginning its quick descent behind the Welsh mountains, obscured from everyone's view the obvious sign of her distress.

At the end of the flatboat, however, she chanced to witness an event which had the effect of causing her to gasp. It was a small thing, really. And if she had not witnessed it with her eyes, she would have sworn it could not have happened.

Yet it did. Or had the failing light played tricks on her eyes?

She thought she saw Lord Somersby stroll past Daphne, quite innocently, but slowly enough that his fingers entwined with hers. He then released them. They neither looked at one another, nor spoke. Somersby continued on toward the other side of the scow, and Daphne laughed at something or other Sir Leighton-

Jones said to her.

Had it really happened? What did it mean? Had their fingers truly touched? She did not know what to make of it.

She felt confused suddenly. Confused by the way Rushton would look at her, yet not reach for her, nor would he evince any other intention of pursuing her. And confused by Somersby and Daphne.

And why would Daphne, who also showed little interest in Somersby, not respond to having her fingers touched?

The remainder of the alfresco "luncheon," which really should have been termed a "dinner," progressed within a large circle of flaming rushlights as the sun slowly dropped behind the dark westerly mountains. Shawls and lap rugs were provided for any lady who felt chilled by the encroaching night air. A small orchestra of musicians, comprised of the stringed instruments exclusively, performed from a second tent during the course of dinner. A sumptuous feast was laid out on a long, makeshift, linen-covered table, the entrees provided by a scurrying bevy of servants, hired just for the occasion, and served from six enormous rush baskets.

Once the covers were removed, because of the dangers accorded to the mysterious night mists, the ladies and gentlemen immediately returned to their carriages to be conveyed home.

Mrs. Wanstrow, leaning her head against the plush, velvet squabs of her barouche, preened and glowed as she repeated every significant compliment upon the luncheon. Daphne sat serenely by, listening intently but saying nothing. Cressida watched her sister, fearful that what lay beneath Daphne's contentment was not love for the baronet, but a misguided hope that Somersby still loved her.

When they were each ensconced in their respective bedchambers, Cressida sought out her sister and asked Daphne if Somersby had indeed entwined his fingers with hers. Daphne, wide-eyed and innocent, replied that surely Cressida was mistaken, for she could remember nothing of the sort occurring. "I was quite engrossed in my conversation with Sir Leighton-Jones," she said, giving her blond curls a shake. "Oh, yes! I do remember now. He passed by me—or was it Major Heath—I can't recall, and his hand accidentally brushed against mine. But aren't you pleased with me Cressida, that I am earnestly pursuing the baronet?"

Cressy felt every tension of the day drain from her in this moment, as she looked into her sister's guileless blue eyes. "I am very pleased, my dear! Indeed, I am."

Once Cressy had quit her bedchamber Daphne composed yet another letter to her beloved. This one began on unhappy accents: "I am sick to death of so much deception, my darling Evan. Cressida saw you touch my fingers and I lied to her—I told such a whisker as you would not believe! How sorely it goes against the pluck with me to lie—and what is worse, I have become quite good at it. Please speak with Rushton and see if he will not agree to our marriage! I beseech you. I am not concerned that Sir Leighton-Jones might be falling in love with me. Indeed, our conversations are always about Cressida and how pretty he thinks she is, and how intelligent. But what of us, my darling? Again, I beg of you, pray speak with Rushton. Perhaps, when he comprehends the depths of your sentiments, he will agree to our marriage. Until tomorrow, my love, good night. Yours, affectionately, Daphne."

Chapter Twenty-Eight

Cressida stood in the black-and-white tiled entrance hall of her aunt's town house, carefully pulling on her gloves of yellow kid. She was dressed in a long-sleeved carriage gown of embroidered white muslin, made high to the neck, with a large ruff framing her chin. Over the gown, she wore a summer pelisse of twilled sarsenet in the shade of a delicate lavender.

When she had completed smoothing out her gloves, she tied a coal-scuttle bonnet over her light brown curls. The soft hat was quilted in a sarsenet to match her pelisse, dressed with large rosebuds of white tulle, and tied beneath her chin in a jaunty bow of white satin. She looked at herself in the mirror and with a laugh turned from side to side realizing that however fashionable the bonnet was, unless she looked straight on, at the object of her gaze, she could see only what was directly in front of her, views to either side obscured by the coal-scuttle design of the headgear.

Satisfied with her appearance, she considered the task before her—in particular, the part of town she meant to visit—and experienced a tightening of her chest.

For some reason she had not heard from Winifred in over nine days, nor had she received her most recent embroidery and ruffling assignments. She tried hard not to think of what she might find once she arrived at

Winnie's rooms, for with the delicate state of her health, the worst possibilities were also too close to reality to make Cressy in the least comfortable.

What had finally forced her to adopt so daring a scheme as to visit Avon Street was that Aunt Liddy had become nearly hysterical when she learned that her Venusian costume was not yet complete. Ever since Mrs. Wanstrow's alfresco picnic, Mrs. Pritchard had been seeking retribution in some form of societal entertainment—intended to completely eclipse decorated water scows on the Kennet-Avon Canal, and an orchestra in a tent! She had finally succeeded in her ambition when she persuaded the Master of Ceremonies to permit her to sponsor a masquerade ball at the New Assembly Rooms—a ball open to any who subscribed to the rooms. But she had not realized the depths of the anguish Aunt Liddy was suffering until this morning when her aunt had railed at her.

"You must go to your friend at once!" Mrs. Wanstrow had cried. "And bring back the pieces with you! If my costume is not far and away the most replendent among the assembly, I shall be undone by that—that platter-faced, butter-toothed stick insect who dares to call herself a hostess! Go fetch the embroidery, Cressida, or I shall turn you out of my home! Do you not realize what that woman means to do? I have learned from my Abigail that she intends to be carried into the assembly rooms, dressed as a water nymph and balanced upon the shoulders of two men, themselves dressed as lily pads! Of all the absurdities! Oh, that I had the powers of Venus, I should turn Mrs. Pritchard into an acorn and set the pigs on her!"

Cressy had stared at her aunt in astonishment. "Set the pigs on her?"

"Yes!" Mrs. Wanstrow barked. "I would do it! I would do it in an instant! And as for your *friend*, Cressida, I have no opinion of her, none whatsoever! You must go to her immediately and get the pieces before—before I fly off in a fit of apoplexy! You wouldn't want that on your conscience, would you? And as for your *friend*, I suggest once you have the embroidery in hand, you withhold payment! You mustn't permit these indigent women to take advantage of either you or me, Cressida. You are far too lenient. After all, look how greatly I have suffered, and all because one of your seamstresses has failed to get her work done!" She clutched her side. "I feel a spasm coming on!"

Cressida had recommended a glass of sherry to calm her aunt's nerves and perhaps the burning of a pastille or two. But Mrs. Wanstrow, who glanced at the clock and afterward at Daphne, stated firmly that her regular trip to the Pump Room, and her habitual three glasses of the mineral waters, would fix her up in a trice.

When her sister and aunt had quit the town house, Cressida had been left to consider what ought to be done next.

Her decision to go herself to Winnie's rooms had not been a difficult one to make. Now, with the clock striking half past nine, she adjusted the bow beneath her ear and was about to quit the town house when the knocker resounded loudly upon the door, startling her. Both Daphne and her aunt would not have returned yet, since they frequented the coffee house each day after the Pump Room. Who could it be, she wondered.

Stepping toward the staircase, away from the door, she nodded to the butler to respond to the summons of the knocker. A moment later he politely bowed a greatly agitated Mr. Rushton into the town house.

She had not seen him for over a sennight, having decided from the day of the alfresco luncheon that nothing good could possibly come of being in company with a man who caused her to feel the most persistent tremors in her heart. Even looking at him now, with his brow furrowed and anxious, she felt her knees quaver and her pulse quicken.

He wasted no time in revealing his purpose in coming

to her. "I was given to understand by Mrs. Wanstrow that you intend to visit your friend, whose name I cannot recall, in the Avon district."

Cressida glanced toward the butler and was not surprised to see a brief expression of astonishment curve his bushy gray brows into an arc above his eyes. "Yes, that is correct," she responded, returning her gaze to Rushton.

"Good God, my dear girl! Whatever are you thinking? Avon Street! Every footpad in England has undoubtedly made his way there at one time or another during the course of his career! You are ill-advised to go! And how came it about Mrs. Wanstrow would permit you to embark upon such a madcap excursion?"

Cressida gestured with a brief nod of her head for the butler to leave her alone with Mr. Rushton. When he had disappeared into the nether regions, Cressida responded quietly, "Mrs. Wanstrow did not *permit* me to go, precisely. She recommended it to me."

"What?" he cried. "Of all the shatterbrained females—I begin to think your aunt is one the most absurd creatures I have ever—"

"I beg your pardon?" Cressida cut him off with mock asperity. "Really, Rushton, you overstep yourself. She is my nearest relation, save Daphne, and I won't have you maligning her character to me. After all, she has offered us succor in time of gread need—"

"She's worked you to the bone! There isn't a soul in Bath who is ignorant of your industry on her behalf."

"What nonsense you speak!"

"Do you think I haven't noticed that you have turned her out in style all summer? It is nearly September. Do you intend to continue in this manner through the fall, although I must confess I look forward to seeing what you can concoct with velvets and bombazine."

"I would never make use of bombazine. It is a common fabric fit only for upper servants. Now if you were to speak of merino wool—"

"Cressida are you never at a loss? And how is it you retain your cheerfulness in a situation most of us would find intolerable. As for Mrs. Wanstrow, it is the outside of enough that you must be employed as her modiste instead of enjoying a holiday at her expense. How do you bear it? To be honest, I am as provoked by your indifference to her miserliness as I am by her willingness to make use of you. And this latest nonsense—recommending you repair to the Avon district yourself, really it is a great deal *too much!*"

"I pray you, Rushton, don't come the crab over me! I must go to Winnie, not only because I hired her to sew for my aunt, but because she is my friend. And if you must know, I am greatly distressed! I have not heard from her, or received any of the several embroidery pieces I contracted out to her. I told you she was ill, and I have the worst presentiment—" She stopped, her throat catching with tears. After the space of a scant few seconds she continued, "Good heavens! Why is it when one speaks the words, all these unbidden sentiments come flowing out—! For the past day or so I have kept the very same thoughts and fears held close within my mind without shedding a tear. But all I must do is hint at my distress with my lips, and what must I do but turn into a watering pot. She has a child, you see—" She could say nothing more.

She pressed her hand to her face and squeezed her eyes shut, trying to hold back her tears. She felt Rushton's arm about her shoulder as he said, "There, there! My dear girl!"

Rushton lifted her chin and looked into her dewy eyes. He thought that if her bonnet had not been such a damnable obstacle, he would have placed a comforting kiss on her lips. Instead, he smiled at her, wondering how it was he had ever thought the light brown of her hair had been an uninteresting shade since he could see the color precisely enhanced the violet of her eyes. "Do you know," he said, striving for a light tone, "looking at you,

223

with this cursed bonnet on your head, is like looking down a tunnel. Who the deuced conjured up such a creation in the first place!"

"It's all the crack you know," she responded, her lips quivering.

"Yes, I know it is. And it does set your beautiful face off to advantage, but I must confess, for a practiced flirt, it is one of the most inconvenient articles I have ever had the misfortune to encounter."

Cressy dropped her gaze to stare somewhat blindly at the top button of his coat. It was a pewter button, a hunting dog tooled into the soft metal. She tried to concentrate on the shape of the dog's head, or its feathered tail or its muzzle—anything to forget the sparkle in Rushton's eyes—but it seemed an impossible task. She wanted to move, but couldn't. Her brain might be rushing warning after warning to her feet, telling them to move away from a man who had the power to hurt her, but she couldn't even bring her toes to wriggle in response. Her senses became caught up in a whirlwind of impressions—the hunting dog on the button, the smell of Rushton's shaving soap, the knowledge his piercing eyes were staring down at her, the fuzzy sensation that his whole body was but inches from hers, the sound of his voice as he began beseeching her to terminate her scheme to visit Winnie.

Her mind strove to take the reins away from her senses. His words seemed to fall over each other until finally, from somewhere in her soul, where her will still held sway, she stepped toward the door, and pulling it wide, responded simply, "I must go."

She did not wait for him to respond, but set off quickly on foot down the hill leading to the town proper where she might hire a hackney to conduct her to Winnie's.

"Wait!" he called to her, but she refused to stop or to listen to his entreaties.

When she heard the sound of his curricle and pair, she presumed he meant to return to his hotel. She was greatly

224

startled, therefore, when he drew up beside her and extending his hand, said, "If you must be stubborn, then I shall accompany you. Come, Cressida, and pray don't argue with me."

Cressy was not certain whether or not to be grateful for his assistance. On the one hand, she was relieved at the knowledge that she would be protected on her journey. But on the other hand, she felt in serious danger of succumbing to certain improper promptings of her heart the longer she was in his company. "I won't argue," she said at last, accepting his hand with a smile. "I am by far too frightened by the prospect of venturing into that part of town to do more than acquiesce with extreme gratitude. Thank you, Rushton, you are a good friend."

"I accept your thanks, but what I wish to know is why Mrs. Wanstrow would not even send a footman along?"

Cressida felt a bubble of laughter swell in her chest as she turned to look at him, and she smiled broadly. "My aunt informed me she could not risk having one of her servants murdered because it takes such a long time to get the fellows properly trained to her household."

A variety of emotions seemed to overwhelm Rushton all at once. His face went from surprise to shock to anger, finally ending in amusement, as he responded, "Then it was just as well that I happened to speak with her this morning, since she can have no such worries where I am concerned. If I am set upon by footpads and summarily dispatched, the functioning of her household will not be disturbed in the least. As for you, though she might lose the advantage of your skill as a modiste, if she managed your burial correctly, I'm sure she could disclaim all connection, have you buried in a pauper's grave, and not have laid out a single groat for the effort."

"There is only one problem."

"What is that?" Rushton queried with a twitch of his lips.

"How would she explain Daphne?"

Rushton appeared to think for a moment, then

225

responded, "Gypsies. She could say that Daphne was her real niece, but that you had been left upon your parents' doorstep by Gypsies, and therefore she was under no obligation to accord you the ceremonies otherwise due upon your death."

"Gypsies," Cressy mused. "How very clever you are, Rushton, I have thought so times out of mind. And Daphne and I are sufficiently unalike to lend some credence to the theory. Really, should I survive this escapade, I shall recommend the notion to my aunt—in the event of some other untimely mishap."

Rushton leaned near to her, as he rounded the corner of Oxford Street heading south. "How is it the grimness of my humor has not caused you to experience a flurry of palpitations."

Cressy peeked at him from beneath her lashes, and down the long tunnel of her coal-scuttle bonnet, queried, "Were you being grim, Rushton? I hadn't noticed."

Chapter Twenty-Nine

The sound of the curricle as it made a slow progress down Avon Street, caused shadows and rag-covered lumps to come to life in the shape of the notorious beggars of Bath. Everywhere, creatures drew close to the carriage, running alongside the vehicle with hands outstretched, beseeching Cressy and Rushton with hopeless cries for mercy, for money. The paupers fought one another to gain the best advantage for calling out their practiced speeches of despairing words and tones which passed through rotten teeth and cracked lips.

Cressida was overwhelmed by the level of penury to be found in the Avon district, the squalor, the unkempt bodies, the emaciated, vicious dogs, the garbage disintegrating on the street, the vile odors which poured over her in relentless wave after wave. Had she been blindfolded she would have known where she was simply by the overpowering smells which emerged and faded only to emerge again with each spinning of the curricle's wheels. She thought she would be sick and hastily removed a perfumed kerchief from her reticule, holding it close to her nose and mouth.

"My God!" Rushton breathed in a hoarse whisper, his face twisted in disgust. "I should take you home. How could you have ever thought of coming here without protection? Damme, I *will* take you home, your friend be hanged!"

Cressy laid an imploring hand upon his sleeve. "Don't, I pray you. I must see Winifred! I must know if she is well. Her little boy—" She paused for a moment, then added, "Even if you should return me to my aunt's house, I will come again, make no mistake. Rushton, I must see her! Today!"

Her earnest manner seemed to settle the matter for Rushton. With a flick of his whip, he pressed his horses forward at a brisk trot, leaving the grasping crowds behind him.

Within a few minutes he located Winifred's house, one of a row of narrow stone houses in which several rooms were let to various persons and families. Speaking with the landlady, Cressida learned that Winnie's room was a small attic chamber, directly beneath the roof, a situation which promised unwelcome heat in the summer and freezing cold in the winter. If Winifred had been in Bath for over eight months, she was certain to have endured the worst of temperatures during the months of January and February. It was no wonder she was now weak with disease.

Cressida ascended the staircase alone to her friend's rooms. Rushton had had no choice but to remain in the street with his curricle. There might have been a dozen scruffy boys prepared to see to his horses, for a small fee, but not one appeared trustworthy enough in his opinion, or in Cressy's, to keep the entire equipage in tact.

When she reached the musty landing of the attic rooms, she knocked on the paint-scarred door, her heart thumping in her chest. Winifred's son opened the door to her. His face was drawn, his eyes dull with misery. "Hallo, Charlie," she began quietly. "May I come in and speak with your mother?"

Charlie pulled the door wide, backing up all the while, "If you please, ma'am," he said politely. "She's in bed and awful sick."

The quiet of the chamber was oppressive as she crossed the portals. The furnishings were bare in the front room, consisting of a wooden table, two chairs, and a straw mattress covered haphazardly by a threadbare blanket. The entire appearance of the little home was gray, save for a block of color in the purple calico tacked above the window. A doorway led to another chamber. Cressy knew a desire to flee, a peculiar sensation of unease swirling about her. Her mind seemed to grow weak and useless as she glanced from the boy to the bed to the flowered calico to the empty chairs and back again.

"Where is your mama?" she queried in a whisper, afraid to speak aloud lest she disturb things unseen.

He pointed toward the second chamber.

Cressida heard a whispered croak come from within the other room, followed by a fit of coughing punctuated with gasps.

The unease which had formerly afflicted her—accompanied now by a terrible sense of dread—kept her feet from moving until Charlie took her hand and began guiding her to the source of the coughing.

Cressy stood on the threshold aghast. She could see that Winifred was near to death. She lay on a beautiful bedstead of carved mahogany—undoubtedly the only surviving remnant of her once prosperous marriage. On her bed was a handsome embroidered counterpane of white linen and a length of sheer white muslin hung in a gentle drape across the window near the bed. Small dark spots on her pillow linen, and lighter red ones on her kerchief, bespoke the gravity of her illness.

The figure appeared shrouded by the counterpane, so thin had Winifred grown in such a short time. A pair of sunken eyes, open and blinking, were the only signs of life.

Cressy stood rooted to the doorway, staring at the hollow eyes, frozen by the specter of death awaiting to claim her friend. Not until Winnie finally closed her eyes and sighed did Cressy feel able to move.

Once in motion, Cressy was mobilized by the enormous need before her. She quickly set aside her reticule and pulled off her yellow kid gloves, laying both on a small table by the bed. "Winnie! Winnie!" she cried. "Why didn't you send for me? Surely you must have known I would have come on the instant!" She reached to pull back the counterpane slightly and petted Winifred's head in gentle strokes.

A frail hand reached from beneath the bedclothes and found Cressy's, giving her fingers a faint squeeze. Winnie smiled, but said nothing in response to Cressy's entreaty.

"What can I do for you?" she queried, feeling helpless. "Are you hungry? Are you cold? Only tell me what I can do!"

To these inquiries, Winnie shook her head. Cressy suspected that if her friend were to speak, she would begin another coughing seizure, which she knew must be painful for her in the extreme. Her suspicion was justified when Winnie finally summoned the energy to whisper, "Charlie hasn't eaten for days. He is afraid to go out alone. I have five pounds—from—from my earnings. I was ever so grateful for the employment. Indeed—" The fit of coughing that resulted from what was clearly for Winifred a lengthy speech, tore at the frail body which writhed beneath the bedclothes.

Cressy watched her friend, a cloud of despair descending on her own spirits as she waited for the terrible fit to end. When Winnie could again breathe, however raggedly, Cressida said, "I shall see to Charlie. Don't worry about him. I'll take care of him, I'll take care of everything."

Cressida watched tears fall from beneath Winnie's closed eyelids, dampening the pillow beneath her cheek.

Cressida left Winnie for a moment and crossed the room to open the window and call down to Rushton. He looked up at her, holding his hat to keep it from sliding off backward. She yelled down to him that she meant to

230

send Charlie to him and that he was to see that the boy had something to eat, at once! Rushton appeared confounded by her directive and appeared as though he wished to argue, but Cressida was not of a mind to begin brangling with him for all of Bath to hear.

She closed the window, and from a writing desk opposite the bed she pulled forward a sheet of paper and with quilled pen in hand, explained the dire nature of Winnie's circumstances to him, dwelling on the absolute necessity of seeing that the boy was properly fed.

She knew Rushton undoubtedly carried enough in his purse to see a hundred boys nourished, but on an impulse, she secreted a pound note into the folds of the letter. She believed he would not have hesitated in paying for Charlie's luncheon, but she did not want to be beholden to him—she had no right to trespass on his compassion.

She returned to the front room, where Charlie lay on his straw pallet. She realized now that the dullness in his eyes was nothing short of severe hunger. Taking him by the hand, she directed him to go to Rushton, to give him the letter, and wherever the fine gentleman wished to go, to go with him. "Mr. Rushton will take you to get something to eat. So be a very good boy, and perhaps he will let you handle the ribbons."

"Would he?" Charlie queried almost eagerly, his eyes beginning to shine. "And I am ever so hungry."

"Yes, my dear, I know. But Mr. Rushton will see to that. So go now, and mind!—do as he says!"

Charlie smiled and on an impulse gave her a hug which caused Cressy's eyes to fill with tears. He took the letter and with a sweet profession of thanks, hurried into the hall. His footsteps echoed loudly on the stairs as he thumped his way to the ground floor.

A sennight later Winifred died.

Chapter Thirty

Two days following Winifred's funeral Cressida stood in front of the empty shop on Union Street which had caught her eye the very first day of her arrival in Bath. The curved bowfront and its dozen panes would display her creations to perfection. She envisioned her gowns, as the seasons blended into one another, changing, as the leaves changed, in fabric and color. In addition, ever since Winifred's death she had been entertaining a certain notion where her shop was concerned.

Winnie's death had caused her several sleepless nights, in part because of Charlie. She had not revealed as much to either her aunt, or to Daphne, but she intended to adopt Charlie, if she discovered through corresponding with Winifred's only surviving relation, her brother, that Charlie had nowhere else to go. She remembered her conversation with Winifred some few weeks earlier to the effect that Charlie's father's family had cast off the connection entirely, and also that her brother was unable to offer assistance. Cressy did not expect help from any quarter and so had decided at last to keep him with her.

If Charles was indeed without concerned relatives, his fate as a parish orphan would be little more than a sentence to a life of the worst sort of drudgery, possibly including deformation or death, depending upon which industry he was apprenticed to. It was well known, for instance, that chimney sweeps utilized very small boys and girls to perform the worst chores and frequently forced their little charges to climb into chimneys which had caught fire, the diminuitive frame of the child being the only means by which the fire could be extinguished. Torture was a frequent abuse among sweeps, as well. It was not uncommon for the master to light a fire under the child, in order to force him or her up the chimney.

Out of respect and love for her friend, and a strong belief that because she was capable of helping this child she ought to do just that, Cressy intended to make Charlie her own.

If she could hire the shop and with her aunt's patronage quickly develop a vibrant enterprise, she would be well able to support herself and Charlie without fear of the poorhouse. But Charlie wasn't her only motivation to open her shop. The women she had hired to sew for her were not much better situated than Winifred had been. If she could provide them with excellent employment—believing she would be able to charge a fortune for her singular gowns—everyone would benefit.

With these thoughts filling her mind to bursting, it was with little wonder she did not at first hear a female voice addressing her. "I say again, Cressida, are you well? Do you hear me?"

Cressy turned to look into Mrs. Rushton's clear, concerned blue eyes. "Oh!" she cried. "I do beg your pardon. Yes, I hear you, and yes, I am well. My goodness! You must think I am crazed."

Mrs. Rushton glanced curiously at the shop. "What were you thinking, I wonder? Your expression was certainly rapt in appearance, almost mesmerized. What is it about this particular shop which fascinates you?"

"Oh, I don't know," she answered noncommitally. "The small-paned bow window, I suppose. I have been wondering how Mrs. Wanstrow's masquerade costume would appear framed inside the window."

Mrs. Rushton turned her gaze to the windows. The sun caught the glass, reflecting back slivers of light and causing the window to gleam. "Have you ambitions then, of a different sort?"

Cressy, who, from the first, had found an accepting spirit in Mrs. Rushton, returned quietly. "Yes, I do." She then explained her hopes of one day opening a shop of her own as a means of providing for her future, and even went so far as to confide her intention of caring for Charlie as well.

She was a little astonished when a rather wicked grin overtook the lovely matron's face, forcing Cressy to query, "My dear ma'am, whatever do you mean by teasing me with your smile?"

She did not expect Mrs. Rushton to respond and was surprised when she whispered conspiratorially, "I am considering the fact that my poor son has been hounded by Nemesis since you arrived in Bath—and rightly so."

"Whatever do you mean?"

"If I must explain my meaning to you, then you are as hopeless as Rushton, so I shan't discuss the matter further! But never mind, walk with me awhile, and tell me all about your schemes to set yourself up in business. I am intrigued by the notion, greatly so!"

Cressy was glad to have found a listening ear, and she accompanied Mrs. Rushton on the remainder of her shopping expedition.

When she returned to her aunt's town house at last, she was startled to find that nearly four hours had elapsed. Time had passed by quickly, and as she took her package of colored embroidery floss to the morning room, she realized she could not remember having enjoyed herself half so much before.

With a mild sinking of her heart, she also became aware, yet again, that when she opened her shop, she would lose her current enjoyment of society. The very nature of being employed in trade would place her far, far beneath the friends and acquaintance she had formed in

Bath since residing with her aunt. With a sigh she sat down in one of the winged chairs near the fireplace and began her embroidery work.

Mr. Brockley, who had been in Mrs. Wanstrow's service for twenty years, slipped cold fingers into the pocket of his waistcoat and fondled the sovereign residing there. Mrs. Wanstrow had always been a bird flying without all her feathers, and he had received her instructions to permit Mr. Rushton free rein in her house with only the mildest lifting of his brow. It would seem she was promoting a match which, to his own practiced eye, lacked a significant element, an insuperable one as it were—the younger Miss Chalcot had no dowry. And, unless a miracle were to transpire, it wasn't likely Mr. Rushton would have anything more in mind than a few exciting hugs conducted in secret.

The truth was, Brockley liked Mr. Rushton. For a moment he had almost returned the sovereign explaining t'weren't necessary. But then he thought of the jewjaws he could purchase with the additional largess—and bestow upon pretty Angelina, the new undermaid—and his former exemplary intentions sort of drifted away, quite suddenlike. He had left Mr. Rushton with a bow and hurried away to the nether regions, where he was now. Removing his hand from the pocket of his waistcoat, he pursed his lips. With a little luck he might catch Betty on the backstairs!

Cressy bent her head over a length of purple cotton upon which she was placing quick, sure embroidery stitches of silver-and-forest-green floss. Once the pattern of acanthus leaves had been completed, she would have one of her seamstresses quilt the fabric into a wide belt intending to represent Venus's famed cestus, which reputedly had powers to bring love to the wearer. The

235

cestus, or belt, had been a task assigned to Winifred, and it was one with which she now found herself somewhat burdened.

Her neck aching from the rigors of having to complete the project quickly, since the masquerade would take place in but two days, she reached up to rub her neck, letting her head roll about in a circle. Only then did she become aware that she was not alone in the chamber.

"Rushton!" she cried. "What a fright you have given me! And what are you doing standing there without saying a word! And how was it Brockley did not announce you?"

"I forbade him," he responded, advancing into the room purposefully.

She glanced down at her embroidery, set another stitch, and begged him to seat himself opposite her in one of the winged chairs by the empty grate. "I prefer it when my friends do not stand upon ceremony, but I still cannot believe you persuaded Brockley to let you come in here without his august presence to lend dignity and propriety to your visit."

"Perhaps it was the soveriegn I thrust into the palm of his hand," he suggested, taking up the proferred chair.

Cressy looked at him, uncertain whether to believe him or not. "You are a curious man," she stated at last. "Only tell me what business brings you to my aunt's home, for I cannot believe this is strictly a morning call." She continued to ply her needle, and when it ran out of thread she picked up the silver floss, rethreaded her needle, and began again.

"As it happens, I have come on a matter of some importance," he said quietly. "You see, I have learned from my mother that you intend to adopt Charlie."

Cressy nodded, resettling the purple fabric onto her lap and recommenced filling in the next leaf of the design. "Yes, it is true. Your mother asked me a great many questions about Charlie and what I hoped for his future. Of course you do know that I am trying to contact what little remains of his relations in hopes someone will want to love and raise him." She glanced at Rushton and watched as he nodded his head. "Yes, well, in the event he should be rejected by his kin, I cannot in good conscience cast him upon what is already an over-burdened parish. I believe I have the resources to care for him if not comfortably, then reasonably well—certainly far better than what he has known in the past several months, I'm sure. My only regret is that I didn't take the time to discern Winifred's difficulties sooner. Had I, I most certainly would have tried to help her beforehand in her misery. Poor, poor girl. My heart still aches for the utter sadness of her life."

"You are very good, Cressida," Rushton said softly, earnestly.

She looked up from her embroidery work and smiled. "You have not always thought so."

"There you are out. I always valued your goodness, it was your viper's tongue I frequently disliked and your infamous intention of seeing your sister wed to the first wealthy man she could attach to her side."

"If you were an impoverished female, I should have gladly listened to your complaints. As it was, there wasn't a single argument you could have employed, or now employ, to change my hopes of finding a husband for her."

He smiled faintly. "I have no wish to argue on that head," Rushton responded. "The truth is, I did not come to brangle with you about Daphne. Rather I wished to express my concern that caring for Charlie might prove to be more burdensome than you have as yet appre-hended. I am of the opinion—"

She cut him off, gently but firmly, "Though I value your opinion—"

"No you don't!" he responded brusquely, interrupting her just as quickly as she had brought his fine speech to an end. When she opened her eyes wide with surprise, he continued. "You don't value my opinion. If anything, you despise the ideas I put forth! Admit you do!"

Cressy's lips twitched. "Well, perhaps a little, but only what you deserve. And as I was saying, though I value your opinion—and in this matter I do, truly!—I cannot in good conscience do otherwise than offer Charlie my love and care. One thing I have learned from Winnie's sudden, yet not unexpected death, is that time is our most precious possession, and without the proper care, time is what Charlie will lose. Even you must agree with me in this."

"Perhaps you've misunderstood me then," he said, rising to his feet and moving to stand over her. "I wish to help you in some way. What I had meant to say, was that I cannot like the idea of your bearing the burden for Charlie alone. I was thinking perhaps I could pay for the boy's schooling. Eton first, then later perhaps the university, if he is so inclined."

Cressida was so surprised by his kindhearted offer, that she could do nothing more than simply stare up at him, her mouth unhandsomely agape. Her thoughts ranged from astonishment at his offer to the most overwhelming sensation of affection she had known in her entire existence. She felt a strong impulse to hug him, one which, before she knew what she was doing, she had followed. Casting her embroidery aside, she was in his arms, expressing her gratitude warmly, her words rushing and tumbling over one another.

"Eton!" she cried. "Oh, Rushton, you cannot know what this means. His schooling to be paid for! I would only have to think about food and shelter for us both— you cannot conceive of how much—! The relief. My dear sir!"

Cressy paused in her raptures to catch her breath. She saw in his expression an intensity which would have disturbed her greatly had it not been so familiar. He leaned toward her, his purpose clear and somehow— given Cressida's happiness—it did not seem so long a stretch in her sentiments to receive his lips quite willingly.

She threw her arms, with much abandon, about his neck, and held him close as he assaulted her mouth, tasting the nectar of her lips with his tongue, afterward placing a string of moist kisses over her cheek and the curved line of her chin. She gave herself to the wonderfully delectable feel of his body pressed closely to hers. The warmth of Rushton's masculine frame surrounded her with feelings of safety and love which served to increase a wholly feminine need she was experiencing, to belong completely to him.

His lips became a demand upon her mouth, as he tightened his arm about her waist, holding her even more firmly against him. When his tongue entered her mouth, she felt a terrible, enchanting sensation of weakness afflict her knees. She was certain that had she not been held in his arms, she would have dropped to the floor, so loose and ineffectual did her legs feel in this moment. She wanted his embrace, the feel of his tongue touching hers, to continue forever.

Rushton had not meant to take her in his arms and certainly would not have kissed her had she not thrown her arms about his shoulders, hugged him, and expressed her gratitude so fervently. Indeed, for several weeks he had been maintaining the strictest control of what had become a formidable desire to kiss Cressida again. He thought he had been succeeding quite admirably, especially since whenever he was in company with her, he had difficulty thinking of anything but the times he had kissed her previously—how she had felt in his arms, the depth of response she seemed to experience at the mere touch of his lips upon hers, the way her figure seemed molded to his.

Yet, with all his fine determination to keep his longings for her locked within the command of his will, here he was, assaulting her again, holding her as though each breath he took were dependent upon the closeness of her person, kissing her as though not to do so would cause him to forfeit his soul, touching his tongue to the secret depths of her mouth, as though she belonged to him, and to him alone.

He did not feel capable of drawing back from her. He felt consumed by desire for her. Yet, he did not comprehend why. He wasn't in love with her, surely not! And he could never marry her. When he wed, he intended to choose a female of equal if not exalted birth, someone with a large dowry, or perhaps even a property to bring to a union meant to enhance the name of Rushton.

It had always been his duty as heir to the Rushton estates—a duty impressed upon him again and again by his father whom he had loved and revered—and now as owner, to enlarge the family's wealth and prestige. He had always intended to do so by marriage. Miss Pritchard would have fulfilled this aspect of his ambitions, had she not unwittingly betrayed herself to him so many years ago. For he did not want a woman's substance alone, but her love as well. He wished for a moment he could blend Olivia and Cressida into one person, for then he would most assuredly have had all that he wanted in a wife.

These thoughts reminded him of the solemn promises he made to himself when he had first attained his majority to do nothing less than secure a wife who fulfilled all his needs. Upon this thought, with the knowledge that Cressida could never supply him with all he wanted in a spouse, the intensity of his feelings dimmed sufficiently to permit him to release her.

Cressy could scarcely breathe as she closed her eyes and savored the last exquisite sensations which seemed to have remained fixed within her body even after Rushton stepped away from her. To some extent she was surprised she could even stand. She sighed with immense satisfaction. She wondered what Rushton was thinking and feeling and longed to know whether he felt as she did—that the embrace they shared was magical. She opened her eyes and discovered that Rushton had moved toward the table upon which several lengths of cloth and at least a dozen of her sketches were scattered. She opened her mouth to speak, wanting to know if he was as consumed with passion as she was, when the door suddenly burst open. A young boy, dressed in nankeens and a fine velvet coat, ran into the room, with Daphne following close behind.

Chapter Thirty-One

Charlie skidded to a stop in front of Cressida and catapulted himself into her arms. She gave him a husky embrace and then directed his attention to Rushton.

Charlie, in the one or two easier moments of his life which he had enjoyed following Winnie's funeral, had talked of nothing else than the gentleman who had permitted him to handle the ribbons in style and to crack the whip over the horses' head.

"Mr. Rushton!" Charlie breathed, ecstatic, catching sight of him on the far side of the table. "Have you brought your prime 'uns today?"

"I have indeed," Rushton responded. "I don't suppose you would care to walk them up and down the street for a little while, would you?"

"Wouldn't I just!" Charlie cried. He turned beaming large, dove gray eyes upon Cressy and immediately began beseeching her in the most imploring of accents to allow him to go. She was more than inclined to do so, and bid him not to pester Mr. Rushton overly much.

"I won't, I won't, 'pon my honor, I won't!"

Cressy watched Rushton cross the chamber and take Charlie by the hand, the expression on his face kind and warm as he looked down at the little boy. She felt her heart swell with emotion at the sight of so much tenderness in his eyes. She was proud of Rushton in this moment and knew that this was the best part of him, the part of him she loved.

The part of him she loved.

The part of him she loved!

She could not credit that these words, these very specific, profound words had actually shaped themselves in her mind. An awareness of the precise nature of her sentiments toward Rushton clarified suddenly—and she knew at last that she loved him.

She loved him.

She was in love with Gregory Rushton. It was impossible, yet now that she had admitted the true state of her feelings, she realized she had been in love with him for some time, perhaps even from the first kiss, when he had so belligerently assaulted her while she was precariously seated in Mrs. Cameley's wretched cart.

How her heart quickened to the knowledge of her love for Rushton, so much so that she placed a hand against her bosom and gasped aloud, crying, "Good heavens! Whatever have I done?" Her next thought, following hard on the heels of so astonishing a revelation, caused her some anxiety. *Did Rushton love her in return?* If his embraces were to be believed, then of course he did, but men were so different from women, taking and enjoying a great deal of liberties and flirtations without a shred of conscience.

Did he love her?

"My goodness, my goodness," she again spoke to the air, shaking her head in wonderment and confusion. He was in so many respects, now that she examined the matter, precisely the sort of man she had once, in her most girlish of daydreams, envisioned marrying—a man with a generous, tender heart toward children, a man who could hold her in his arms and cause her to forget, even for a brief moment, all of life's difficulties, a man who, no matter how wrong he might be at times, stood firmly by his principles.

"Cressy, my dear," Daphne called to her. "You look as

white as a goose. Are you feeling ill? Shall I fetch your vinaigrette?" She had remained standing near the door, and now, as she blinked back at Cressy, wore a ruffle of frowns upon her brow.

"Indeed, please do not do anything of the kind. I assure you I am perfectly well." Since she followed up her assurances by dropping into a chair by the table in the center of the room, and pulling nervously upon the curls at the nape of her neck, Daphne was prompted to cross the room and place a gentle hand upon her shoulder.

"Did Rushton say unkind things to you as he is wont to do?"

"No, no!" Cressy breathed, a feeling very like rapture spreading over her heart. "He is the most considerate man I have ever known."

"Considerate?" Daphne queried. "Are you certain you mean Rushton? Wasn't it his fault we were cast out of Mrs. Cameley's home?"

"Well, as to that," Cressy began, preparing to defend him, until she suddenly recalled precisely why they had indeed been thrown from the manor. "Daphne!" she continued, incensed. "We quit Mrs. Cameley's employ because you were found kissing Somersby in the library, or have you forgotten?"

Daphne bit her lip and swallowed. With a guilty smile, she said, "I nearly did forget. How odd!"

"What a pea goose you are!" Cressy exclaimed. "How could you possibly forget such a—"

She would have continued, but at that moment Brockley appeared in the doorway and stated that if the Misses Chalcot were receiving visitors, Sir Leighton-Jones was wishful to pay a call.

Cressy glanced up at Daphne and wondered fleetingly if her sister had yet grown to love the baronet. Her cheeks showed a faint blush as she looked down at Cressy. "We ought to receive him, don't you think?" Daphne queried, her blush deepening to a rosy pink.

Her attention finally drawn away from thoughts of

Rushton, Cressy saw Daphne's conscious look and felt pleased. Could there be no greater sign of her sister's attachment to Sir Leighton-Jones than a fulsome blush enhancing her alabaster complexion? Pressing Daphne's hand, she directed her response to Brockley, "Pray show Sir Leighton-Jones to the drawing room. We shall be with him directly, and bring a little sherry round for him—I know he is fond of it."

When Brockley bowed, turned silently on his heel, and disappeared down the hall, Cressy rose to her feet. After smoothing out the skirts of her gown of a flowered, sprig muslin, she queried, "Where is Aunt Liddy? I had supposed she was with you and Charlie."

"She is abovestairs, reclining on her bed, I think. She complained earlier of having got a monstrous headache."

"I hope she is not succumbing to an illness."

"I don't think so. She said something about the useless chatter of children causing her head to feel as though it might explode. The funny thing was, when I begged Charlie to be quiet out of respect for poor Aunt Liddy, she said, 'I was not referring to Charlie!' Don't you think that was an odd thing for her to say? What do you suppose she meant by it?"

"I would tell you, Daphne, but of the moment my only concern is to keep Sir Leighton-Jones from kicking his heels any longer than necessary."

"Oh, yes, of course! We should go to him at once!"

By the enthusiasm in Daphne's voice Cressy was convinced her sister's future would soon be neatly settled. Taking her sister fondly by the hand she led the way toward the drawing room where they found Sir Leighton-Jones staring up into the youthful portrait of Mrs. Wanstrow, his mouth agape, his quizzing glass pressed to his right eye.

"Hallo, my good sir!" Cressy called to him warmly. "I hope you have not been waiting long."

"Not at all," he said, as he bowed to the young ladies. His brows were lifted in an expression of surprise as he gestured in confused circles with his quizzing glass in the general direction of the portrait. "Do you know your aunt's man, Brockley, told me this was a portrait of Mrs. Wanstrow when she was a few years younger? I didn't believe him, yet I cannot imagine what cause he would have to tell a whisker, so I take it, it's true!" When the ladies smiled and nodded, he continued, "I have been studying her portrait and only in fleeting moments can I make out the least resemblance. Quite remarkable. Pray don't speak a word of this to Mrs. Wanstrow, she would have my head if she knew of my astonishment. I do comprehend now, however, why she comports herself as she does. She has just that insolent air a beautiful, intelligent woman will affect when she prides herself on her appearance—your aunt still believes she is that woman!" He now leveled his quizzing glass at the portrait, and Cressy could not but think how right he was.

She did not, however, wish to speak ill of her aunt and responded politely, "She was quite beautiful, wasn't she? But how do you go on? Do sit down and make yourself comfortable. I have asked Brockley to bring some sherry."

The baronet sat on the sofa nearest the fireplace, crossed his legs, and thanked her for her attentions to his comfort. He then twirled his quizzing glass somewhat nervously about his fingers and in what Cressy thought was a rather fatherly fashion, smiled at Daphne. She was about to inquire after his health when he gave Daphne the queerest motion of his head, jerking it toward the door as though he wished her to leave.

Daphne responded instantly. She had just seated herself opposite the fireplace when she leapt lightly to her feet and after expressing her concern for her aunt's health, insisted upon seeing how Aunt Liddy fared.

The entire interchange smacked of duplicity!

Cressy felt her heart jump. She supposed that given Sir on-Jones's knowledge of the relationship the sisters shared—Cressida playing the role of parent—he intended to make a formal offer of marriage for Daphne's hand. Although, now that she thought on it, he should have sought Mrs. Wanstrow's permission rather than her own. Since she was overly delighted that all had progressed as she had hoped, she was certainly not of a mind to split hairs where propriety was concerned. Sir Leighton-Jones was welcome to request her permission to marry Daphne.

Cressida sat in a chair of smooth, red silk-damask situated near the fireplace directly across from the baronet. Her heart dancing in anticipation of receiving his request, she nervously began adjusting the skirts of her gown. By way of attempting to politely converse with the elegant gentleman, she directed his attention to the low position of the sun in the heavens and queried civilly as if he did not think the day had been one of the loveliest of the summer.

His response startled her. "How can I concern myself with such trivialities, my dearest Cressida, when my heart is near to bursting."

She was disconcerted by the earnest expression on his face and the use of an endearment connected so nearly as it was to her name and not to Daphne's. The boldness of his tone, and the reference to the state of his heart, employed words which should have been used when he next paid his addresses to her sister.

"Sir," she began quietly, her throat suddenly dry. "I cannot begin to wonder what you mean."

She smiled in encouragement and hoped he would explain himself, when he suddenly rose from the sofa, and before she knew what he was about, had fallen at her knees, taken her hands in his, and began pouring out word upon word of love.

She wasn't at first certain why he felt it necessary to humble himself upon her lap as he was, since surely he must have known she would gladly bestow Daphne upon him, as would her aunt. In quick stages, however, she

247

grew to an awareness of a profound error—Daphne was not his choice after all!

"I have been patient, my dearest, most treasured Cressida, but I can longer restrain the words which have begun burdening my heart and my lips past bearing. I determined to speak with you today, and so I beg you, Cressida Chalcot, will you not make me the happiest of men and accept of my hand in marriage?"

Cressy was infinitely grateful she was sitting in a chair for she was certain had she been standing, she would have collapsed into a mortifying faint at his feet. "You are not serious," she murmured, trying to extricate her hands from his painfully tight grasp.

He refused, however, to let her go. "I am most serious and I absolutely refuse to believe you have been oblivious to my sentiments all these weeks, surely not? And in like manner, I am persuaded, from the depths of my being, that you are not indifferent to me. Though I have not met with you so frequently in company as I have your lovely sister, yet each time you have greeted me in a manner only a simpleton could mistake as anything but replete with love. There has been such a warmth, such a welcoming expression in your eyes, indeed upon your lips as they would shape each bounteous word, that I have thought only shyness prevented you from encouraging me further—that is, in desiring me to speak my heart. Therefore, I have taken it upon myself to bring forward a subject which I believe to contain your fondest wish, as it does mine. Oh, my darling Cressida, say you will be mine!"

With that, the enamored baronet rose to his feet and, not having released hr hands, quickly drew her up next to him, caught her in a passionate embrace, and placed his eager lips upon hers.

Mr. Rushton had seen Sir Leighton-Jones enter the town house some few minutes earlier. Though he had fully intended to permit Charlie to walk his horses several times up and down the crescent, he found himself strangely anxious to return to Mrs. Wanstrow's home. He knew something odd was afoot by the fact that a man noted for his decorous conduct as Sir Leighton-Jones was, had actually been whistling when he jumped lightly down from his phaeton.

Whistling!

Rushton wondered if Cressy's scheme to see Daphne married to the good-natured baronet had actually succeeded, yet some other instinct warned him it was impossible. Rushton had for several weeks followed the progress of Cressy's schemes, and whenever Sir Leighton-Jones was in company with Daphne he watched the couple to see if Cupid had pulled back his bow and released an arrow or two. All that he had ever been able to divine, however, was that the baronet yawned frequently when in conversation with Daphne, save when Sir Leighton-Jones knew that Cressida was observing them.

Therefore, though Charlie had begged him to make one more circuit around Landsdown Crescent, he had sternly announced that the time had come to return to Mrs. Wanstrow's abode.

Oddly enough, a footman—as opposed to the butler—responded to his knock upon the door. When he and Charlie were led up the stairs to the drawing room located upon the first floor, he was not surprised to have caught up with Brockley—carrying a silver tray, a decanter of sherry, and a single glass—on the landing outside the drawing room.

Brockley waved the footman away, bid Charlie with a single lift of an imperious eyebrow to follow behind Rushton, and with a deft movement of his arm, threw the door wide.

When the butler did not immediately announce Rushton, a suspicion grew in Rushton's brain that all was not well within.

"Good grief!" Brockley murmured beneath his breath,

nearly upsetting his tray as he witnessed some unseen spectacle within the depths of the elegant chamber.

Rushton gently pushed past the butler and saw to his shock that Sir Leighton-Jones was not only holding Cressida in a rough embrace, but that to all appearances she was quite caught up in the pleasure of that man's kisses.

He felt Charlie grasp the tail of his coat, as the little boy gained admittance into the room and queried, "Why is that man biting Aunt Cressy?"

Chapter Thirty-Two

Cressida roamed her bedchamber like a wild horse plunging about an unfamiliar stable. She was overset in a way she had never known before—her head pounded with a fury that frightened her, and her stomach had drawn up into a knot which she strongly suspected would defy untying. Above all, she could not comprehend how it had come about that her world had just shattered into a dozen fragments and tumbled all about her feet. She would try to pick up one of the pieces—Sir Leighton-Jones's supposed love for Daphne—and the piece would leap from her hand. She would attempt to retrieve another—her need to have Daphne wed by summer's end—and the ragged bit of her life would turn and nip one of her fingers, afterward to fall hopelessly back to the scattered ruins on the carpet of her life.

She had thought all was settled! Good and settled!

Good Lord, what a ninnyhammer she had been about Sir Leighton-Jones! Why even Rushton had tried to warn her!

Rushton! her heart wailed.

When Sir Leighton-Jones had released her, she had stepped away from the terrors of his embrace only to turn and discover that the man she loved had seen her entangled in the baronet's arms. What must he think of her, when only a few minutes earlier she had permitted him, ever so eagerly, to importune her own lips.

She pressed her hands to her temples and walked in a furious cadence toward the windows, then whirled about to accomplish the distance to her wardrobe, only to turn abruptly and traverse the length of the chamber.

Never, as long as she lived, would she forget the wretched expression on Rushton's face—of complete bewilderment, pain, and disgust. He had said nothing. He had not advanced into the room to call Sir Leighton-Jones to book for his actions; he had only bid Charlie a fond farewell and as though he had been struck down mightily by the hand of God, left the room on a slow tread, his complexion ashen.

She needed to explain to Rushton what had really happened between herself and the baronet. Had she not been delayed by the absolute necessity of speaking with Sir Leighton-Jones immediately and setting to rest forever his hopes that she would ever become his wife, she would have pursued Rushton instantly.

As it was, the interchange with the baronet proved extremely painful since it had not taken her very long to realize how greatly at fault she had been in mistakenly giving every appearance of desiring his suit. He had repeatedly pointed out to her that when she beamed at him, and welcomed him so openly to her aunt's home, and positively glowed with affection whenever she laid her gaze upon his person, he had become convinced she was half in love with him.

Cressida sank into a chair near her bed and slipped anxious fingers through her light brown curls, squeezing her eyes shut in intense frustration. She saw it all now quite clearly. She had made a concerted effort to appear congenial and friendly with the baronet because of her desire to see Daphne wed to him.

Was it his fault he mistook her motives?

Hardly.

She was entirely to blame that such a good gentleman

would think he saw love where only self-serving attitudes prevailed. He could not know that her actions were full of guile. He could not know that she had purposely cultivated his affection in the hopes that he would fall in love with Daphne.

Shame caused her cheeks to burn hot beneath her fingers. She hadn't told him she had intended for him to fall in love with, and afterward wed, Daphne. She had merely begged forgiveness for having behaved in such a manner as to give him cause to believe she returned his affections.

He had left devastated, and she had climbed the stairs to her bedchamber feeling as though her slippered feet and stockinged ankles had become weighted with huge clots of mud.

One thought now pressed itself firmly into her mind: Rushton had been correct, completely so, in sternly warning her not to become involved in schemes and artifice. This was the result. Hot tears of self-reproach pricked her eyelids and drenched the fingers which still covered her face at the wretched thought that she had unwittingly brought pain to such a good, fine man as Sir Leighton-Jones.

At the same time, she realized that Daphne must have known something of the baronet's intentions. She recalled her sister's blushes when Sir Leighton-Jones was announced and how readily she had leapt to her feet on a signal from him, excusing herself from the drawing room on the pretext she wished to see how Aunt Liddy's headache fared. She struggled to understand her sister. She had believed Daphne to have been trying to win Sir Leighton-Jones's affections, just as she had told her to. It would seem now, however, that Daphne knew he had already become attached to the wrong sister. Why hadn't Daphne informed her of the truth?

Cressida sighed heavily as more unhappy tears stung her eyes. Perhaps Daphne was afraid to tell her. Cressy had pressured her time and again to pursue the baronet. It seemed reasonable then, that her sister would have remained silent. Had the situations been reversed, Cressida thought she would certainly have pretended that all was well, rather than disappoint Daphne.

In time she was certain that Sir Leighton-Jones would forgive her. But the erroneous object of his love brought a far more horrifying reality plunging in upon Cressida's awareness—Daphne was without a husband, and September was nearly upon them.

Later that evening Rushton sat in a wing chair in his chambers at the White Hart Inn staring at a pile of wood he had wrested earlier from the landlord and afterward stuffed into his fireplace.

He wasn't certain why it was so, but given the distress which held his brain captive he wanted to sit in front of a roaring wood fire, sip an entire decanter of brandy, and consider yet again the axiom "Frailty, thy name is woman!"

Using a candle, he set the crumpled paper, kindling, and logs ablaze. He poured himself out a generous snifter of brandy, enjoyed a deep pull, and immediately sensed a lessening of the tension which seemed to have stiffened every joint and limb of his body.

He sighed, the heat from the fire as it crackled, wheezed, and burst into life warming even the bottoms of his boots.

He sighed again.

Frailty, thy name is woman!

Not since he had been privy to Miss Pritchard's boastings of having lured and trapped the heart of *the elegant Mr. Gregory Rushton,* had he known such stomach-twisting agony as this. Somewhere in his heart he had believed Cressida above the reprehensible conduct she had exhibited in her aunt's drawing room.

In her aunt's drawing room! Had the woman no conscience whatsoever, to be kissing men in every room of her house! Well, at least in two of them—that he knew of!

Hell and damnation. He took another hearty swig of the rich, ancient brandy, coughed at the feel of the drink burning and swelling in his throat, and cursed again.

And to think only a scant few minutes earlier she had yet again permitted him to kiss her. What manner of female was she? Perhaps he had been mistaken in thinking of her as gently bred. Perhaps she would willingly become his mistress. Now there was an excellent notion, and the proper way to repay her for such an ignoble gesture as kissing Sir Leighton-Jones not ten minutes after having partaken of his own embraces!

Frailty, thy name is woman!

A knock on the door disturbed his happy thoughts.

"Come!" he bellowed sharply.

The door opened slowly, and the frightened features of his ward, Lord Somersby, appeared in the crack, his large brown eyes blinking with amazement. "Is that you, Rushton?" he queried. "Ah, so it is! I wasn't certain! Sounded for a moment like a crochety, old tutor I once had when I was seven. I'd stand in the doorway of the schoolroom, my knees shaking, and he'd bark 'Come,' the way you said it just then!"

Rushton, already feeling impatient with Somersby, responded curtly, "Well, do come in! You've created a draft and are pulling—Good God!" He looked back at the fireplace and noticed that a thick sheet of smoke was rolling out of the fireplace just beneath the mantel and creeping toward the ceiling.

He was on his feet at once, setting the brandy on a sideboard behind him, then checking to see if the flue was shut. When he found it open, he shook his head, "Lord, what next!"

"Wind is in the east," Somersby stated cryptically.

Rushton looked at him and scowled.

"No, it's true. The chimneys smoke when the wind is in the east. I'm sure of it. Always happens at my house in Oxfordshire."

"Well, there isn't a wind tonight, so you must think up another reason for all this—" he began coughing and backed away from the fireplace, "smoke."

Somersby snapped his fingers. "Of course! You've crammed the hearth full of wood. Who told me that's how you can get a fire to smoking? Perhaps it was Sir Leighton-Jones, but how the devil we came to speak of building fires, I can't imagine."

At the mere mention of the baronet's name, Rushton felt his head begin to pound with unwelcome and inexplicable emotion. "Yes, well, there's nothing for it then but to throw up the window and wait!"

Rushton crossed the room to the window. After opening it, he retrieved his brandy and begged to know if Somersby wished to join him.

"Indeed, I would!" Somersby responded with alacrity. "Man ought to be sustained a trifle when he's got something of importance—that is—" He began coughing but Rushton had the distinct impression the spasm had little to do with the smoke from his fire.

"Something of importance?" he queried. He poured out a brandy for Somersby and handed it to him. When he saw that the wall of smoke issuing from the fireplace had thinned perceptibly, he returned to his comfortable winged chair of green velvet, sat down, and took another sip.

"Something of importance," the viscount repeated almost absently. "Yes, very important." He drew forward a chair and placed himself near the fire, waving his hand about once or twice in an effort to clear the immediate surrounding area of some of the smoke. The effort was futile, but he seemed resigned to the discomfort and with a tic twitching his cheek, began. "I do have a request to make of you, Rushton, one which I hope you will agree to."

Rushton was feeling mightily the effects of swilling his brandy and saw his ward through a rosy haze. If a warning resounded at the earnest expression on Somersby's face, it did not seem to reach Rushton. Considering the matter, he supposed Evan's request was of a monetary nature—perhaps the viscount had been playing a trifle too deep at cards, or some such thing, and he found himself in need of an advance on next quarter's allowance. If so, Somersby had come to Rushton at precisely the right moment. He would gladly have given his ward a thousand pounds if for no other reason than to be rid of him.

"Whatever it is, Evan, you needn't worry. I'm of a mind to grant you anything tonight."

An expression of brightness flooded Somersby's face. Hope lit his features to a luminescent glow. "Anything?" he queried on a whisper.

"Anything within my power, old boy." Again he took a pull from the snifter and ran the brandy over his tongue several times before swallowing.

Lord Somersby took a kerchief from the pocket of his coat and began chewing on the corner of it. He didn't speak for a long moment, and when he did make his request, it was oddly run together and sounded like a repressed sneeze to Rushton's ears. "Dphn!" he cried.

Rushton leaned his head forward, stared hard at Somersby, and repeated with a confused shake of his head, "Dphn?"

"Yes," Somersby returned, nodding his head vigorously. "Daphne. I want to marry Daphne."

"Oh," Rushton said knowledgeably, the meaning of 'Dphn' preceding the more unwelcome implication. "Oh," he added slowly, in horrified accents the moment he realized what was being requested. "You want to marry her? Evan, for God's sake, I thought we had settled this business weeks, nay months ago. Of all the brain-baconed—that is—bacon-brained idiots! The answer is no, *no*, a thousand times no! When you have had several more seasons, perhaps a decade of them, doing the pretty amongst the ton, then you will discover what love is and what it is not! For the present, you must rely upon me to tell you that what love is not is marriage to a beautiful widgeon who will bore you within a fortnight and not have the least facility for managing your household! It would be unpardonable of me to grant your request. Absolutely unpardonable! Unthinkable and unpardonable!"

When Rushton observed that half the small square of cambric had now been sucked into Somersby's mouth, he exclaimed, "Hell and damnation, take that ridiculous thing out of your mouth!"

Somersby, who was staring at a burnished knot in one of the planks that made up the wood flooring of the chamber, jerked his gaze back to Rushton and immediately removed the offending kerchief. "So the answer is, *no?*" he queried, a deep frown furrowing his forehead.

"That's *eggzackly* right," Rushton said, his speech slurring as the brandy took hold of his tongue.

Somersby rose to his feet. "Very well," he said quietly, returning his untouched glass to the sideboard. "I'd best take my leave—I have a lot of planning to do."

Rushton felt an inclination to rise to his feet and escort his friend from the chamber, but when he tried to do so, he found his body would not obey him. He contented himself with waving to Somersby's back as his ward quit the chamber.

Rushton snorted as he returned to savoring his brandy. Marry Daphne Chalcot, he thought. Of all the absurdities! It suddenly occurred to him that it was a strange request to make since he could not recall a time during the past few weeks when Daphne seemed remotely interested in gaining Somersby's affections. She certainly did not try to flirt with him, nor did she seem in any manner *aux anges* in Somersby's presence. How odd, then, that Evan should beg permission to marry her!

Tomorrow, he had best pursue the subject with Somersby, just a trifle to make certain all was well, but for now, as his gaze became mesmerized by the leaping flames of the fire, he was content to be alone, happy to again be miserable with all his thoughts of Cressida's betrayal.

After leaving Rushton's chambers, Somersby stood in the hallway, remaining fixed in one spot rather like a lost cow, the kerchief dangling from the corner of his mouth as he chewed and ruminated upon his guardian's harsh refusal. Whatever was he to do now? He had followed his beloved's advice—though it had taken him nearly three weeks to summon the courage to do so—and asked Rushton to give his consent to a marriage between himself and Daphne, but the effort had failed.

He sighed heavily and rolled the mangled kerchief between his teeth. He must do something. He knew in his heart of hearts Daphne was the only female who could ever make him happy. She was, in truth, the only female he knew with whom he could claim the greater intelligence, and no matter what anyone else thought on the subject, he had never taken to the notion of wedding a woman of superior abilities—even if it was a sensible course to follow. After all, what man wanted to be despised by his wife?

Thinking of Daphne brought a warm glow to his heart. And she was so deuced pretty. He could spend hours just looking at her. Her complexion was enough to distract a man forever, all creamy white and suffused with the color of pink roses when he would touch her with no one the wiser. And children positively doted on her—only look how Charlie was wont to cling to her skirts and follow her everywhere. If nothing else had convinced him he had found the next Viscountess Somersby, the sight of that poor orphan tucked within the loving circle of Daphne's arms certainly had. Rushton be hanged!

His resolve strengthened by the happy stream of his thoughts, he walked briskly to the end of the hall and ran lightly down the stairs. Finding the landlord polishing glasses in the taproom, he begged of that good man directions to Scotland—more specifically, to Gretna Green.

Chapter Thirty-Three

Mrs. Pritchard did indeed arrive upon a palanquin, born upon the shoulders of two large, athletic men, dressed as lily pads, one of whom Cressida recognized as having carried her in a sedan chair up to Landsdown Crescent some few weeks earlier.

The entire body of guests milling excitedly about the ballroom of the New Assembly Rooms ceased all movement suddenly at Mrs. Pritchard's entrance, a hush descending over the elegant chamber. The only sound which could be heard was the occasional gasp erupting from the sight of Mrs. Pritchard, who had come to the Olympian masquerade not as the water nymph as she had promised, but as Medusa. Her headdress was comprised of nothing less than a score of snakelike appendages springing from her head in all directions. Her underdress was a sheer tulle embroidered in gold, over which was hung an exquisite scarlet velvet tunic. Gold sandals adorned bare feet which displayed several bejeweled rings upon the toes.

Cressida was duly impressed with the creativity and elegance of the unusual costume. She was herself begowned in only a simple gown of rose silk and a matching domino and regretted that she had not had sufficient time to sew a costume for herself. Mrs.

Pritchard had undoubtedly outshone the entire assemblage.

Mrs. Wanstrow had been one of the many who had literally gasped at the sight of Mrs. Pritchard's extraordinary costume. Cressy leaned toward Aunt Liddy and fairly exclaimed over the headdress which won from her aunt an unhappy harrumph. Cressy barely suppressed a smile. She could easily see that though Mrs. Wanstrow was gowned exquisitely as Venus in a creation of soft white cambric and silver embroidery, enhanced to perfection with the mock cestus of Venus, she was purple with jealousy over Mrs. Pritchard's success. She was not surprised therefore, when her aunt, having only one recourse with which to minimize the effects of her competitor's victory, decided it was to her best interest to fall into a loud, moaning faint beside her.

The ensuing uproar, which she could see her aunt observed from only partially closed eyes, was, if not all Mrs. Wanstrow hoped it would be, then at least sufficient to detract from Mrs. Pritchard's incredible entrance.

A flurry of ladies gathered round Mrs. Wanstrow, squealing and crying out and patting her hands and cheeks. After a moment she began to revive—or at least pretended to do so—and whispered weakly, "If I could be removed to a quieter place, perhaps on the palanquin . . ."

"Yes, of course!" her dear friend Mrs. Hodges cried. "Mrs. Pritchard! Mrs. Pritchard! You must come at once and permit Mrs. Wanstrow the use of your, er, slaves! She is become gravely ill and has been taken up in a swoon."

There was nothing for it. Mrs. Pritchard must give up her throne graciously.

To Cressida's surprise the hostess did not seem at all reluctant to do so, until, as Aunt Liddy was being removed from the ballroom, Cressy realized that Mrs. Pritchard not only had all the advantage of appearing magnanimous to the multitudes in being of service to her friend, but she had also been able to rid herself, for the moment, of her chief rival.

As the party surrounding Mrs. Wanstrow squeezed through the doorway into the octagonal court of the assembly rooms, Cressida heard Mrs. Pritchard open the ball by requesting the Master of Ceremonies to lead out the lady of noblest birth present, which happened this evening to be Sir Leighton-Jones's mother, Lady Leighton-Jones.

As Cressy caught one last glimpse of the assembly before passing through the doorway herself, she felt her cheeks burn at the sight of the Master of Ceremonies bowing before the baronet, who was dressed in a Roman toga and sported a wreath of silver leaves about his thick brown hair, and his mother. Two tedious days had passed since she had received Sir Leighton-Jones's passionate offer of marriage, but during the whole of that time Cressy had not ceased feeling immense regret for her ill-judged conduct. She had already spoken to the baronet on his arrival at the New Assembly Rooms and had apologized again for the dreadful misunderstanding which had prompted his declaration, but his recovery appeared satisfactorily underway when he begged her not to give the matter a moment's consideration. He had forgotten all about it himself and proved his desire for them to always remain friends by asking for her hand for the cotillion. Cressy had accepted, gratefully.

The ladies attended eagerly to Mrs. Wanstrow's affliction, the pungent smell of several proffered vinaigrettes effecting a general bout of coughing amongst them all.

Cressy, with Daphne beside her, backed away slightly, turned her head, and sneezed. "I fear she will suffocate with so much attention," she said.

Daphne nodded several times in agreement. "Or she might not be able to breathe with everyone crowded

263

about her so," she responded, wrinkling her nose. She was dressed as a country maid in a summery gown of flowing white muslin embroidered with lavender flowers and a half-mask of white silk stitched with the design of a strand of ivy wrapped about an oil lamp in gold floss. The lamp was a reference to the mortal, Psyche, who became the wife of Eros.

Cressy glanced at her sister and would have explained what *suffocated* meant when she realized for the first time that evening that Daphne was not in her best looks. Her complexion below her mask was perfectly white without even a touch of pink to soften the stark color of her skin. Even her lips seemed colorless.

Cressy leaned close to her sister and whispered, "Are you well, my dear? I can't remember seeing you so pale before."

At Cressy's words, Daphne responded like a startled fawn ready to flee. Her large blue eyes blinked rapidly, and she made several fitful movements with her hands and arms as though she would have liked to run somewhere and hide, but couldn't. "I—" she began nervously, then clamped her mouth shut and began uneasily adjusting the ribbons of her mask.

"What is it my dear? You are not well. Have you the headache? Daphne, why did you not say something to me? You should not be here. I am persuaded you are ill."

Daphne swallowed hard and took several deep breaths. She appeared sad beyond words, even with her mask covering part of her face. Were she and Cressida not in so public a place, Cressy would have gathered her up in her arms and comforted her. Instead, she gently took one of Daphne's hands and pressed it once. "Tell me what's troubling you."

Daphne drew in a breath on a quiet sob, and with tears blinding her eyes, she said, "I—I have so many friends here in Bath, Cressida, I don't wish to leave when summer is over. I want to stay here forever. I don't know what to do. I don't know what to do. I feel so blue-deviled about the summer—and—and about Sir Leighton-Jones—that he, that I—oh, I wish I could have loved him, and he, me! I'm sorry, Cressida, I'm ever so sorry."

Cressida felt her earlier chagrin pour over her in a molten stream of mortification. "You must never repine about Sir Leighton-Jones. I alone am at fault where he is concerned. And as for remaining in Bath, my dear sister, we must not give up hope that you will yet find someone who can love you and provide a home for you."

"But Cressy,' she whispered, squeezing her hand hard in return, "will you—I mean do you still love me, even though I do foolish and hateful things, and don't love where I ought?"

Cressida searched her sister's dew-laden eyes. "You still blame yourself for Sir Leighton-Jones? I wish you wouldn't. But if you desire an answer, yes, my darling, I will always love you. Always, no matter what foolish or hateful things you do. You are my dearest, best Daphne, and always shall be."

These last words seemed to give comfort, and Daphne's tears and unhappiness began to diminish as each minute passed.

When at last Mrs. Wanstrow was fully recovered, which required only several minutes into the first country dance to accomplish, all the ladies returned to the assembly room to watch the conclusion of Lady Leighton-Jones's dance with the Master of Ceremonies.

For the next two hours, quite beyond her ability to do otherwise, Cressy found herself caught up yet again in the reprehensible task of looking at all the eligible bachelors with a new eye. She tried not to think in terms of which of them would best make a suitable husband for Daphne—especially since her first effort had ended so miserably—but the knowledge of her sister's immense unhappiness seemed to force her to bring all her gentlemen acquaintance again under review.

265

That is, until she caught sight of Mr. Rushton scowling at her from across the chamber, behind his half-mask of black silk. Upon her arrival at the New Assembly Rooms, she had intended to approach Rushton and to explain to him how it had come about Sir Leighton-Jones had kissed her. Two full days had passed since that fateful moment when the baronet had offered for her, yet during that time Rushton had neither called upon her, nor, when they met in any of the several haunts frequented by the gentry, had he done more than bow civilly to her. She suspected he believed her at fault somehow, and her suspicions were confirmed by the current angry scowl upon his face.

Several times, over the course of what had become two very long days, she had recalled the last kiss they had shared, how it had resulted from his exceedingly kind offer to pay for Charlie's education. She had even admitted that she loved him. For that reason she had hoped beyond hope that he would beg to speak with her in private and that he would ask her forthrightly why she had been held tightly in Sir Leighton-Jones's arms. Once given an explanation, she then had pictured Rushton also dropping upon his knee, professing his love for her, and begging for her hand in marriage.

But these had been all the silliest daydreams. Rushton seemed determined to believe the worst of her.

As she held his gaze stubbornly, she felt an angry flush creep up her cheeks at the condemning expression on his face. And perhaps because of her embarrassment he decided to approach her. How very much she resented the proud set to his chin and the way he bore down upon her as though he intended to give her a severe dressing-down.

"You appear to be assessing the value of every gentleman in sight," he began on a brusque undertone. "Are you preparing to seduce your next victim? To what purpose, I wonder? Really, Miss Chalcot, did your

266

mother not teach you that you mustn't kiss every gentleman you meet?"

"How dare you!" Cressy whispered, stunned by the venom in his voice and the horrible aspersion of his words. She turned and walked away from him, unwilling to say more.

But he was not so easily gotten rid of, and followed after her. "Oh, did I offend you?" he began facetiously from behind her, whispering in her ear as she pressed toward the doors leading to the anteroom. "I meant no harm, only an indictment of your improper methods of going about in society."

"I do not *go about* in society, Mr. Rushton," she said over her shoulder. "Or have you not noticed? This is not my world, this is only a place in which I function, quite temporarily, in hopes, exclusively, of finding a husband for Daphne." Tears stung her eyes, and she quickly blinked them back, forging on through the crowds of costumes and masks, breaking through finally into the entrance to the New Assembly Rooms.

Mr. Rushton, his black domino floating over his evening dress, followed her into the foyer and begged her to stop for just a moment. He drew her aside and in a quieter, more compassionate voice, said, "I never faulted your motives where your sister was concerned, Cressida, but haven't you done enough harm already? If you do not take care, you will have Sir Leighton-Jones believing he is in love with you. After all, to be kissing every gentleman—"

"Every gentleman?" she cried. "Why do you keep saying that as though I accost every man with whom I converse!"

"Then tell me what I should think, what I should have thought when, the last we met, not a few moments after I had held you in my arms, *my arms,* and kissed you and felt you—" He paused briefly, as though he struggled to keep his emotions firmly in hand. "Only tell me why was it you kissed Sir Leighton-Jones. Oh, the devil take it, I don't want to know!''

He started to turn away, but Cressida prevented him by taking hold of his arm and squeezing hard. She strove to keep from being overwhelmed with anger, and after taking several deep breaths, whispered, "There is something, however, I want *you* to know. First, I have kissed but two men in the entire course of my life. One of them is a hopelessly selfish, arrogant man who dares to call himself a gentleman, and the other is Sir Leighton-Jones. And if you must know, he at least had the decency to beg for my hand in marriage before placing his lips upon mine, which is a great deal more than I can say for you! But then, you have never intended marriage, have you Rushton?''

The elegant Leader of Fashion blanched, started, and after closing his mouth, which had fallen unattractively agape, appeared as one who had been struck neatly over the head with a weighted object. "He asked for your hand in marriage?'' he asked, stunned.

"Indeed, he did. I can see you are dumbfounded, which is no happy reflection of your opinion of me.''

Rushton shook his head, as though attempting to clear it. "Did you accept his proposals?''

"No, of course I did not. Though I value him as one of the kindest gentlemen of my acquaintance, if the truth be known, I am not in love with him.''

"I don't understand,'' he responded, incredulous. "You would have done well to have married him. Your future would have been secured, your difficult path eased. You could have taken Daphne to London for the Little Season and disposed of her in a trice. I cannot credit you refused such an advantageous match.''

Cressy felt a terrible knot begin forming in her throat. These were not the words of a man who had been harboring thoughts of dropping to his knee and begging for her hand in marriage. "And I cannot believe you would countenance such a scheme, particularly after all your protestations where Daphne is concerned. But all this is quite beside the point. Now tell me if you can, have you ever intended marriage?"

He searched her eyes, his brow furrowed, his expression anxious. "As to my intentions where you are concerned," he began slowly, his voice hoarse and strained, "I can only say—oh, hang it all, I don't know what to say!" And with that he bowed politely and left her standing alone in the octagonal antechamber.

Chapter Thirty-Four

During the next several hours, Cressida felt as though she spoke, gestured, laughed, and danced through a deep fog. Her heart was as leaden as the night skies were heavy with rain and thunder and lightning. She knew a despair so intense that in order to keep from being consumed by heartache, she threw herself into the joys of dancing with an energy unusual for her.

The results were singular in that by eleven o'clock, when the Master of Ceremonies drew the masquerade to a close, she had not sat out for one set. Her feet ached abominably, and she believed one of her slippers was completely worn through.

Much she cared. What were sore limbs and blistered toes when her heart was doomed forever to belong to a man who could not return her love.

As the crowds began the slow process of quitting the assembly rooms, Cressida found her aunt deep in conversation with Mrs. Rushton to the side of the ballroom. Their choice of subjects—the merits of calico and muslin—ought to have pleased her, but of the moment she had interest in nothing more than her bed and a pillow upon which she could lay her weary, tormented head.

She took up her place beside Mrs. Wanstrow and

waited quietly, her gaze cast toward the floor. Vaguely, she wondered where Daphne was, but supposed in a few minutes, once the crowds thinned, her sister would be able to find them. When a quarter of an hour passed and still her sister did not appear, Cressida began scanning the assemblage of Olympian guests, growing concerned that she could not find among them the muslin country gown embroidered with violets and white mask which Daphne wore.

Aunt Liddy, becoming aware of Daphne's absence, turned quite abruptly to Cressy. "Where is your sister?" she asked, leaning her head near Cressida's. "I am become excessively fatigued and desire to return home."

Cressy shook her head. "I don't know, and now that I think on it, I cannot remember seeing her stand up for any of the last country dances. She is not a great one for cards, either, so I cannot imagine that she spent her hours in the card room, but where else might she have been all this time? When did you last see her?"

Mrs. Wanstrow shook her head. "Some time ago. I saw her speaking with a young gentleman wearing a rather strange pair of antlers. I didn't perceive who it was."

Mrs. Rushton, who had been attending their conversation, supplied the needed information. "You refer to Somersby."

"Was that Somersby, then, walking about and sticking the other guests with his headgear? But why on earth was he dressed as a deer?"

Mrs. Rushton responded, "His costume delineates a particular myth where a young man—whose name escapes me—was found watching the goddess Artemis bathing in a spring. When she found him so engaged, the goddess was furious and turned the young man, a skillful hunter, into a stag. He was thereafter hunted by his own bowsmen and slain."

"What a dreadful tale. But are you sure it was Somersby?"

"Yes. He and Daphne stood talking for several minutes. I remember it quite clearly because I had intended to call him over to me, but they left the ballroom shortly afterward. Daphne, if I recall, was quite agitated. I suppose he took her into the antechamber to restore her spirits."

Cressida experienced a strange sensation at the very pit of her stomach. Daphne's earlier unrest came to mind and her cryptic words, *do you still love me, even when I do foolish and hateful things, and don't love where I ought?* At the time Cressy had assumed she was referring to Sir Leighton-Jones, but now she questioned her initial supposition.

She turned to express her sudden concern that all was not well, when Miss Pritchard, upon the arm of Mr. Rushton, approached their small coterie. Miss Pritchard, begowned as a simple maid in a long robe of white cambric, her black hair pulled back à la Greque and tiered with several gold fillets, wore a smile Cressida could only conceive of as triumphant. Mr. Rushton's expression was inscrutable.

"And how did you enjoy Mama's masquerade, Miss Chalcot?" she queried with false warmth, unfurling her fan, her mask hanging by its ribbons from her wrist.

"Prodigiously," Cressy answered politely.

Miss Pritchard glanced up at Rushton and then back to Cressida. "You were certainly putting most of us to shame. I daresay your feet did not rest once in these last three hours or more."

"I daresay," Cressy responded flatly. She did not like the glint in Miss Pritchard's narrow green eyes.

"But your sister was not among the dancers this evening as she usually is, was she?"

"No, she was not. I expect she was fatigued."

"Undoubtedly. Was that why she left with Somersby, now what hour was it? Oh, yes, half past nine? Was he seeing her home? He was the gentleman sporting the large pair of antlers, was he not?"

Cressy stared at her, a fuzzy sensation of dread prickling her toes and fingers and causing the skin at the nape of her neck to run riot in gooseflesh.

Mrs. Rushton reprimanded her. "For heaven's sakes, Olivia! Such tales you bear. Somersby would not have done so without Mrs. Wanstrow's permission, and she has been waiting patiently here for Daphne to discover her."

Mrs. Wanstrow snorted. "Was it your mama who encouraged you to come to me in this brazen manner and tell such ridiculous whiskers? Of course Daphne is not gone off with Lord Somersby. She is by far too well-bred!"

Miss Pritchard smiled thinly, her green eyes narrowed with unkindness. "Oh, but I'm 'fraid in this you are mistaken. I followed them to the Alfred Street entrance, you see, and saw Daphne climb into a post-chaise with Somersby directly behind her. They had an unfortunate mishap when he stepped upon her muslin gown and tore part of it. I believe he saw me at that moment, for he became greatly distraught, fairly shoving poor Daphne into the coach. If I did not know better, I would suppose he had abducted your niece, particularly since he told the postillion to *spring-em!*" Here, she turned to Rushton, and wafting her painted fan over her satisfied features, begged of him. "Is that the correct expression, Gregory? *Spring 'em!* That is, when you have need of your horses to go very fast, do you cry out, *spring 'em?*"

Rushton's complexion had paled to a perfect shade of white. His blue eyes lost their sparkle in a cloud of confusion. "I don't understand," he murmured. "Why, why?"

"Perhaps he is in love with Daphne and intends to marry her out of hand," Olivia suggested helpfully.

The answering reproachful scowl caused her to flinch slightly and take a step away from him. She did not quaver in her attack, however, and pushed on gently, "I did not mean to offend you, Rushton. But honestly, the pair of them have smelled of April and May throughout the entire summer. I only wonder that you did not notice it. I'm certain, of course, that Mrs. Wanstrow did." Olivia turned to direct her infuriatingly smug expression toward Mrs. Wanstrow and continued. "I must have seen Somersby and Miss Chalcot in your company upon no fewer than two-score occasions. Should I ever wish to capture a man's fancy, I would wish for you to champion my cause."

Cressy turned suddenly and set her gaze squarely upon her aunt's calm visage. "Is this true, ma'am?" she asked, stunned. "Have you been encouraging an—an attachment, surreptitiously, between my sister and Lord Somersby?"

"As to that," Mrs. Wanstrow replied, "I'm sure I don't know what you mean. I merely permitted him, as I did any number of gentlemen and ladies, to attend us to the Spring Gardens and the like. Somersby is a truly amiable gentleman, whose company I approved of for my niece. As to his love for her, or Daphne's for him, as Miss Pritchard suggests—I saw nothing of it."

"Then were you conducting a flirtation with Somersby," Olivia queried, feigning astonishment. "For I vow, I saw any number of letters pass between you and his lordship. Observing for myself how many times Somersby and Daphne *chanced* to touch during the course of these outings, I had supposed you were serving as a messenger of love. Was I mistaken? Oh, how foolish I feel. But then, why do you suppose Somersby carried Daphne off, if not to marry her? Oh, I see Mama is waving to me. How odd she appears with snakes for hair. Well, I must beg my leave of you. Good night."

Rushton, to Cressy's surprise, followed after her. She could see that he was clearly overset by Olivia's revelations, and she supposed he meant to inquire further into precisely what had happened.

She remained standing very still beside her aunt, her mind in a whirlwind of bemusement. Olivia's speech seemed to indicate—if all that she said was true—that Aunt Liddy had somehow conspired with Daphne and Somersby.

Through the mist of her unsettled feelings she heard her aunt say, "I beg you will excuse us, Mrs. Rushton. It would seem Cressida and I must go in search of my niece. I don't for a moment believe, of course, that she is eloped—she is far too gently bred to adopt such a mode of conduct."

"Of course," Mrs. Rushton responded civilly, and with a polite bow moved toward the octagonal court.

"Aunt Liddy," Cressy began. "Pray do not tell me you have encouraged Daphne in her belief she has fallen in love with Somersby."

Mrs. Wanstrow, much to Cressy's surprise, set an imperious eye upon her. "Your sister has formed a lasting attachment to Lord Somersby, no matter what you might think. Even if she hadn't, our small circle of Bath intimates could provide no better husband for her than his lordship. And if I didn't know you better, I would suppose jealousy to be the reason for your dislike of the match. Since I have yet to detect even the slightest form of envy in your bones, I can only conclude some perversity of mind must have set you against such a propitious alliance."

"It is not a perversity of mind, as you phrase it, rather a wish to see my sister wed to a man of some intelligence."

"Whatever for?" was Mrs. Wanstrow's shocked response.

"I should think the nature of my explanation would be perfectly clear. Daphne requires a gentleman of some mental facility to counterbalance the deficiency of her own."

"Oh, I see," Aunt Liddy responded with some asperity. "You have decided upon what basis a perfect marriage ought to be arranged. I consider your reasonings, and therefore your actions toward Daphne, to hold the worst sort of arrogance and high-handedness I have ever had the occasion to witness. Who are you, Cressida Chalcot, to determine what manner of gentleman shall bring your sister her proper share of happiness? I have seen Somersby and Daphne together, and I know how extremely well-suited they are. When they are married— whether it be over the anvil, or at Bath Abbey—I will suppose them to have a score of children, to enjoy them completely, and to secure more happiness than most couples could hope to find together over the course of several lifetimes. If you choose to cast a rub in their way, I tell you now I shall oppose you with every power I possess."

By this time Cressida and Mrs. Wanstrow were the only guests remaining within the ballroom proper, though from the general rumbling of conversation issuing from the anteroom a great number of persons remained to board their respective carriages and return home.

Cressida felt as though her aunt had clubbed her neatly over the head with each word she had spoken. She dropped limply to a chair behind her and sighed. *Arrogant, high-handed!* These were terms with which she had frequently characterized Rushton. To hear them applied to her own person was unsettling in the extreme. Had she not considered Daphne's feelings? At the outset she had been so certain her sister was experiencing yet again a fleeting, transient *tendre* for the handsome peer. It had not occurred to her Daphne's sentiments might be engaged. Later, when she exhibited no appearance of love whatsoever—either when referring to Somersby in conversation or when dancing with him at the assembly rooms—she had supposed Daphne's feelings for the viscount to have simply run their course and disappeared.

Still, no matter what her aunt said, she could not like a marriage between Daphne and Somersby, not above half! The viscount had the intelligence no greater than a hunting dog, and Daphne! Well, she was a ninnyhammer born and bred! Aunt Liddy might speak all she wished to about *happiness*, but how much general contentment and productive living can two people spawn who possess the combined intelligence of a cabbage?

No, a marriage between them was unthinkable!

Chapter Thirty-Five

Rushton followed Miss Pritchard into the anteroom. The chamber was still crowded with costumed guests awaiting the arrival of their various carriages. A heavy rain had descended upon the town, making the departure of the masqueraders an even more difficult undertaking. Rushton, for his part, was not in a hurry to leave. He had a mission to accomplish first, and for that reason begged a word of Olivia, asking her to accompany him into the card room, which was already empty of guests.

"How very improper, to be sure, Gregory," Olivia said lightly, her head held perfectly straight. Once inside the chamber, she continued, "I hope you don't mean to be a bore and take me to task for imparting my knowledge of Daphne's horrid misconduct to Mrs. Wanstrow. Someone needed to tell her, and if you must know, I feel enormous pity for her—she cannot have enjoyed learning that her niece is engaged in an elopement, even if it was with Somersby."

"There you are out. I've little doubt her only concern was that a marriage take place—whether an elopement or not. She would surely triumph over your mother in either case, and having been in Mrs. Wanstrow's company several times over the course of the summer, I have come to understand that such a victory is her chief object. As for boring you by taking you to task for it, nothing could be further from my mind. I wished instead to address another subject entirely, one that relates more nearly to you than to Daphne or Somersby, mainly, my former love for you."

Olivia seemed a trifle startled, a crimson blush suffusing her cheeks. "Whatever do you mean?" she queried.

"I don't know if you are aware of this or not, but I had several years ago believed I had formed a lasting attachment for you. Your refinement, your self-assurance and poise, your elevated position in society all bespoke the precise manner of woman I wished to make my wife. I learned only moment's before I meant to offer for you that your heart carried a cruelness I had never experienced before. I'm sure you remember the day when you were boasting of having conquered my heart—and my lands—both to Mrs. Wanstrow and to other of your friends. Did you know I was standing nearby? I thought not."

The blush on her cheeks deepened ominously.

"Really, Rushton, what nonsense you speak," she denied, trying to hide her mortification behind a regal smile. "I cannot recall having said any such thing. You must be mistaken. And I am not cruel. You've simply not known me."

He shook his head. "I know you all too well, and your terrible unkindness in representing to Cressida your knowledge of her sister's scandalous conduct with the silky tongue of an adder is beneath your station. I am appalled by your conduct, and I suggest you save your compliments and best smiles for another gentleman. You are become a sour, manipulative, ape-leader, and I am grown to feel nothing but pity for you. Good-bye."

He turned around, took two steps then over his shoulder, and queried, "Do you know which way the post-chaise was headed?"

Olivia Pritchard finally admitted defeat. "You are in love with her, aren't you?" she asked, ignoring his question.

"You refer to Cressida?" When she nodded, he said, "As to that, I'm not of a mind to confess the condition of my heart to one who I am persuaded would use it against me in the very next moment. I ask again, which way were the horses pointed?"

Olivia sank down into a chair near a table covered in green baize. The former high color to her complexion had been replaced by a deathly pallor. She pressed her hand to her head and responded, "I have been such a fool. All these years I have thought of nothing but you, of winning your esteem, your affection—perhaps if I had had other interests, as Miss Chalcot seems to have—you might have found me more amusing."

"You are a very *amusing* woman, Olivia. It is your character which lacks, not your accomplishments. Only tell me which direction Somersby meant to go. I must stop the elopement if I am able."

Olivia sighed heavily. "There is more. I heard Somersby arguing earlier with Daphne. Of course I could not keep from listening to their discourse—"

"Of course you could not."

"That was unkind, Gregory. Whatever I may be, I am not a completely hopeless female. At least, even if I have been, I suppose it is time I thought of mending my ways." She rubbed her temple. "Somersby spoke of Gretna Green. Daphne implored him to reconsider, but he was insistent and finally persuaded her they must go since you were set against the match. That's all, I think."

Rushton regarded the unhappy form of Olivia Pritchard and knew a compassion hitherto unfamiliar to him. He went to her and placed a gentle hand on her shoulder. In a quiet voice he said, "I can be very unkind. You were right to say as much. Perhaps we have both been lacking in some of the finer qualities. I am sorry if I continued to give you hope these several years that my heart might yet be won. Perhaps, until recently, I never gave up hope that I might find in you the woman I once thought I loved."

Olivia looked up at him, her green eyes lusterless. "I trust we shall remain friends?"

"Yes, always."

With that, he quit the card room and nearly collided with Cressida.

Her expression was contorted with anxiety and distress. To his surprise he felt a profound desire to slip his arm about her shoulder and protect her from the miserable words he was about to speak. He did nothing more, however, than stand in front of her and in a low voice say, "I'm afraid it's Gretna." A clap of thunder followed his statement.

"Rushton, we must stop them!" she cried. "Can anything be more undesirable than their union?"

"You are opposed to the match?"

She lifted her brows in surprise. "Haven't I told you as much from the start? Mr. Rushton, do you never attend to me?"

Rain pummeled the roof of the post-chaise. The road was completely obscured by the onslaught of rain and wind. Somersby peered through the front glass of the carriage and in the distance saw a flickering light.

"There!" he cried. "We are arrived at last! I'm sure we are well into Shropshire, and in all this mud who could discover our trail?"

Daphne sniffled, as she had been for the three hours they had been journeying north. "I don't care if we are discovered or not! My whole side is bruised from being tossed about because of these dreadful roads. I knew we should not have come. I knew it!"

She burst into a hearty bout of tears, and Somersby, overcome with affection for his delicate love, gathered her up in his arms and said, "Sweetest nightingale, don't cry. You wound my heart when you get my neckcloth all wet with your tears."

Daphne attempted to control her sobs, pulling away

slightly in order to look up into his face. "You say the loveliest things to me, my dearest fox."

Somersby enjoyed hearing her call him such pet names and squeezed her tighter still. "My most precious little pansy, my dewy-eyed snowdrop, my snugly kitten."

"Oh, Evan," she whispered.

"Oh, Daphne," he responded, pressing his lips hard against hers. After a moment, as the coach began drawing up to the inn, he released her and said, "No regrets, my love? Pray tell me you have no regrets that we are to be wed in Scotland."

Daphne, who was still reeling from the intoxicating effects of his soft, affectionate words and sensual kiss, responded in a whisper, "Only a very little."

"That's my girl!" he returned with a smile. "You must be brave."

When they descended the carriage and ran into the taproom beneath a torrent of rain, they were met with the most disturbing news. It would seem that somewhere, about an hour into the journey, with the rain pouring down on both the postillion and the carriage in blinding sheets, a mistake had occurred. They were not in Shropshire at all, but had somehow made a great circuit and were some ten miles only to the west of Bath.

When Daphne learned of the error, she clutched her bosom and said, "It is the hand of God. We have been stopped in our hasty, ill-judged elopement and warned to return before it is too late!"

Somersby, who had also been greatly startled by the extraordinary nature of the error, did not at first respond. Instead, he saw his beloved settled in a chair by the fire, wrapped in a blanket, and plied with a little warm milk and brandy. After much cogitation, and a brief but intense discussion with the postillion on the dreadful condition of the roads leading to Bath after such a terrible rain, it was agreed that the best course was to remain fixed where they were.

Daphne, comforted and subdued by the strong potion

of brandy and milk, finally acquiesced to the scheme to be put to bed in one of the chambers abovestairs, but only after extracting a promise from her beloved that she be returned to her aunt on the morrow.

Lord Somersby, seeing that his darling bride—who might never become his wife—was not to be moved from her desire to be restored to her family, resigned himself to a life of utter loneliness. Once Rushton had him in his grasp, he would sweep him away from Bath, away from Daphne, before the cat could lick her ear!

Chapter Thirty-Six

The following morning, Cressida stood on the steps of Mrs. Wanstrow's town house with Charlie by her side, watching Mr. Rushton mount his curricle. The night's rain had prevented him from doing more than pace his chamber at the White Hart until a clearing sky and the dawn had caught him asleep in a chair by the window. He had arrived at the town house at half past eight and conveyed his regret to Cressida that the rain had prevented his leaving earlier.

"Even so," he had said with a slight frown furrowing his brow, "I expect to meet more muddy roads than I would wish to in the course of a year. At least Somersby and your sister cannot have gotten far."

Just as Rushton picked up the reins, preparing to give them a hearty slap, Cressy noticed a hackney turn into the crescent. "One moment, Rushton!" she cried.

Rushton turned to glance back at the carriage and let the reins fall slack. The horses, sensing something was amiss, began stamping their hooves and twitching their ears.

Cressy stepped away from the town house. She rightly divined that her sister and Somersby were within the post-chaise as Daphne's blond curls appeared out the window. She waved her hand and cried, "Cressy! Cressy! I've come home!"

Mrs. Wanstrow stared at the miscreants beneath a furious brow. She had begged Cressida and Mr. Rushton to spare her a few words alone with the wretched pair, and once they had quit the chamber, she did not mince words. "Why on earth did you return? For heaven's sakes! Everything was so neatly settled! And after all my scheming, is this what your ridiculous affair should come to—that Daphne must decide she will study to return to the employ of governess? I have never before exerted myself upon anyone's behalf, and now I recall why! There is so little gratitude among those whose cause you support! And don't keep telling me you're sorry you eloped, Daphne! You sound like a mewing kitten, what with all your whining and crying! Do you hear one word of reproach pass my lips? No, of course not! I wished you to go to Gretna Green. You know I did."

"But Cressida did not," Daphne said, wiping another tear from her cheek. "She is most particular in such matters, always instructing me about propriety and conduct. I know it was wrong of me to go, and now I mean to become a governess to make up for being such a wretched creature."

"Heaven deliver me from such an idiot," Mrs. Wanstrow cried, lifting her gaze imploringly toward the ceiling and wringing her hands. She then directed a question to Lord Somersby. "And what do you have to say, my lord? Do you mean to permit the woman you love to become a governess?"

He sucked on the kerchief ensconced within his mouth, and after a moment withdrew it. "I can't bear it when she cries. Rushton won't permit a marriage and means to hush up the elopement, so I don't see what I can do."

"Imbeciles," she murmured. She continued to pace the chamber, finally marching up to Somersby, who sat on the crimson silk-damask sofa by the fireplace, and stated, "You must learn to be very firm with men such as Rushton. He is just the sort determined to rule the roost wherever he might. I suggest you say to him, in the most adamant tone you can summon, *I intend to marry Daphne, if not this week, then next, or next year! But by God, I will marry her. I love her, she loves me, and—and the disparity in our stations be hanged!*"

"Aunt Liddy!" Daphne cried. "I have never heard you speak in such a manner."

"I was only trying to instruct your beau on just how he should go on."

Lord Somersby, who had returned the kerchief to his mouth, was mumbling words on top of the kerchief and sounded like he was speaking from behind a pillow.

"What is that you are saying?" Mrs. Wanstrow cried.

He popped the kerchief from his mouth and said, "I was practicing."

"Then keep practicing! I will fetch Mr. Rushton, and you may have your say, only *be firm!*"

Rushton stood by the window of the morning room, his hands clasped behind his back. Sunbeams poured through the windows in stark contrast to the rain of the night before, but for all the warmth of the day his heart remained steadfastly cold.

Cressida sat in her favorite wing chair by the fireplace, setting stitches in what she had informed him was the sleeve of a carriage dress. Charlie sat quietly on a footstool at her feet, his head resting on her knees. The little boy missed his mother a great deal, more it seemed as the days progressed, and every now and again Cressy would pause in her embroidery and pet his head.

Rushton stared down in the street, wanting to speak with Cressida, yet knowing there was nothing to be said.

In a few minutes, after Mrs. Wanstrow finished speaking with Somersby and Daphne, Rushton would remove Somersby from Mrs. Wanstrow's home and spirit him away to The Hall for the remainder of the summer. Even Cressy had agreed it would be best for all concerned if the young, impressionable viscount did not continue to reside in the same town as Daphne.

But the chill which had enveloped his heart had little to do with his ward. He glanced over his shoulder at the light brown curls bent over the embroidery work and watched Cressy give Charlie's ear a tug, a small, affectionate gesture which caused a faint smile to cross the boy's somber lips.

Another layer of frost seemed to settle upon Rushton's heart. He had come to an awareness throughout the long hours of the night that promised a measure of unhappiness he had never believed he would have to endure. Simply, he had fallen deeply and passionately in love with Cressida Chalcot, but could never—out of respect for his station in society, for the future of his estates, and for the esteem in which he held his deceased parent— wed her.

When he had discovered her held tightly within the arms of Sir Leighton-Jones, he had felt a fury which would have translated into a duel had he not quickly left the premises. Jealousy had so overpowered him in that moment that it was all he could do to keep from marching across the room, from tearing the baronet's arms from about Cressida, and from drawing his cork! But he had long been in the habit of placing the strictest control on his emotions and so had ignored the promptings of his jealous heart and had left Sir Leighton-Jones's nose properly in place.

After a day had passed and his temper had righted itself, he was then faced with trying to comprehend Cressida's outrageous conduct in having kissed two men within the space of a scant few minutes. Ironically, it had never occurred to him, until she baldly explained the episode to him, that Sir Leighton-Jones had actually offered for her hand in marriage. He was still reeling under the shock of the baronet, in his bachelorhood and station in life, having been so besotted with Cressida as to have offered for her! What's more, he was just as stunned that she had refused him.

The refusal, he decided, made the future all the harder to bear. For in her insistence not to marry where her affections were not engaged—a fact she had admitted to him not ten minutes earlier—he saw the woman he loved at her finest. Cressy's character, which he valued immensely, was as strong a pull upon his own affections as were her beauty and the sweet taste of her lips the few times he had importuned her.

His only thought now, as the sun beat upon his coat of blue superfine, was to be gone from Bath as quickly as possible that he might forget Cressida, forget her lovely lavender eyes, forget that he loved her more than he had ever believed possible.

When Rushton and Cressy returned to the drawing room—Charlie having been relegated to Angelina's care—Mrs. Wanstrow strode behind them and gesticulated with her fists the need for Somersby to pluck up and take charge of the situation.

To her infinite pleasure the viscount rose abruptly to his feet, took a stance very much like a man ready to employ his fisticuffs, and said, "I am being firm. *You* will marry Daphne at once. At once, I say!"

"What the devil—?" Rushton responded, startled.

When Somersby realized his error, he blinked several times and was in the process of lifting his kerchief to his mouth when he caught sight of Mrs. Wanstrow, who was still standing behind Rushton and Cressida, motioning to him to continue, her hands moving about wildly.

"I don't know what it is you are trying to say, Somersby," Rushton began, "But I think it the outside of enough that—"

"Hush!" Somersby commanded, causing his forbidding guardian to take a step backward. "I won't have it! I've asked for cursed little from you or anyone, and all I want is to make Daphne Chalcot my wife." He seemed to gain composure at the sight of Rushton's mouth agape and continued. "You will have to accept the fact, Gregory, that I love Daphne, and I mean to marry her. If not today, then tomorrow, or the next day, or the next month, or the next twelve-month, the next decade, or— let me see—the next quarter century, then half-century—"

"Evan," Daphne supplicated, rising to stand beside him and taking his hand in hers, "I shall be a very old woman by then, and I did so hope we could fill our nursery with a dozen children."

"What's that?" he said, then began laughing. "A half-century! I suppose I got a little carried away." He took her hand and pressed it tenderly to his lips. "We won't wait quite that long, my precious turnip top, I promise you."

Mrs. Wanstrow watched Cressida and Rushton exchange a long look of comprehension and knew that, for all his bumbling about, Somersby had won the day.

In late September Cressida watched her sister speak her vows in a voice that warbled beautifully throughout the majestic hall of Bath Abbey. The tears she shed were tears of perfect happiness, since the weeks that followed the aborted elopement proved to her beyond even the smallest doubt that Daphne had indeed found happiness in her beloved Somersby.

Rushton had tried to include in the marriage contract a settlement for her, but she would have none of it. There still remained enough of her initial inheritance, if not to permit her to lease a shop from the outset, then to hire lodgings for herself near Queen's Square. Here she could take in enough piece work from Mrs. Wanstrow's favorite modiste in order to begin saving for the day when she could set up an establishment of her own.

She told no one of her plans, but on the afternoon that Daphne and Somersby left for their honeymoon in Paris—a laden fourgon traveling behind Somersby's crested town coach—she simply announced her intention of removing to her lodgings.

Mrs. Wanstrow was astonished and began arguing strenuously that it would look very odd in her to be leaving the bosom of her nearest relation and residing with only little Charlie to keep her company in a part of town which was not even considered *genteel*. Cressy was impervious to her rebukes and the sound of her aunt's horrified and argumentative voice diminished only as she sent one of the footmen to fetch her a hackney.

"You cannot mean to do this to me, Cressida? What will my acquaintance say? I know you told me you only meant to remain through the summer—and I suppose I did seem to indicate that I would not permit you to stay longer—but all that has changed! Why, Daphne's brilliant marriage alone far outweighs the burden you both have been—"

Cressida cut her off abruptly with a fond smile, "Pray, Aunt Liddy, don't speak another word. Even if you were to beg me—us—Charlie and me to remain, we shouldn't! It has always been my intention to take my leave at summer's end, whether Daphne married or not. That she has, makes me happier than you can imagine, but I— we—don't need your assistance. Truly, we don't."

"Oh," Mrs. Wanstrow said, looking rather consternated. "But what do you mean to do, then? I trust you do not intend to pursue that most wretched of occupations and take up governessing as a means of earning your keep."

"Heavens, no," she responded. "I could hardly do so

with my little pet in tow, now could I?" She patted Charlie on the top of his head, and he looked up at her and smiled. She then extended her hand to her aunt, and said, "I hope you were well pleased with the gowns I created for you."

"Why, Cressy," she said, staring down at the unfriendly hand. She then startled her younger niece by throwing her arms about her and clasping her lovingly to her large, welcoming bosom. After a long moment, Mrs. Wanstrow pulled away from her and said, "I know I've never spoken of it, but I wanted you to know that I should never have kept the amethyst ring. I should have let Amelia have it. I think now of all the years I lost while my sister was alive, and the rest because of her unfortunate demise, and I realize how foolish I was."

"You quarreled over the ring, then?" Cressy asked.

Mrs. Wanstrow nodded, tears swimming in her blue eyes. "The ring and a thousand other insignificant things. It seems quite silly now, but at the time—" She shook her head. "We were both stubborn, your mother and I, like you are. Amelia and I shared the same failing, and it separated us forever. I trust that your stubbornness will not keep you from love."

Cressy did not know precisely what her aunt meant by offering such a strange piece of advice. Stubbornness, in her opinion, was not keeping her from love, rather her lack of fortune and consequence.

At the same time, in all the many weeks Cressida had been in her aunt's company, this was by far the most revealing speech her dear Aunt Liddy had ever delivered. She was not surprised, however, that in the very next moment Mrs. Wanstrow dried her tears and said, "Well, one cannot harbor regrets about the past, can one?" And the subject was dropped, undoubtedly forever as well.

Cressida felt strange tears of sudden loneliness bite her eyes as she moved to the entrance hall and tied her bonnet beneath her ear. She hadn't thought either that her aunt would embrace her so affectionately, or that she would feel a raging sense of despair at having to leave Landsdown Crescent. But so it was, and the distance between the entrance hall—with Charlie clutching her hand tightly—and the hackney awaiting them on the street was one of the longest she had ever had to traverse in all her life.

Chapter Thirty=Seven

Cressida had been settled in her rooms for not quite above a sennight when she received an unexpected visitor. She heard a knock on the door, and after separating herself from a current sketch she was contriving of a round gown—decorated daringly about the hem with no less than seven rows of elegant ruching—she was startled to find Mrs. Rushton standing on the threshold. Surprised by her visit, yet pleased, she welcomed Mrs. Rushton into her small, serviceable chambers, bidding Charlie to make his best bow.

Charlie did so with a smile, then returned to sit on the floor, where he resumed drawing a picture of a dog with very long ears.

For all the difficulties of Cressy's situation, she had no reason to be embarrassed by the charming effects she had created within the small confines of her rooms. Through long evenings of setting stitches into an elegant flowered chintz and a solid purple cotton stuff she had purchased from the linen-drapers, the window, sofa, two chairs, and bed all appeared fresh and lively against the dullness of the sight of chimneys and windows visible from across her second-floor chambers.

Mrs. Rushton, her hands tucked into a fur muff against the cool October morning, took in the room slowly and smiled. It seemed to Cressida that the fabrics and overall lively appearance of her home settled something in the elegant lady's mind. She permitted Cressida to take her muff and her pelisse and immediately began to speak on any number of unexceptionable subjects—how much she enjoyed Daphne's wedding, how Mrs. Pritchard had been in an uproar for obscure reasons and had taken Olivia to London, how the Master of Ceremonies had become ill suddenly with the gout, and how her son, Gregory, had removed to his home at The Hall.

"Which leads me in a completely circuitous route to the particular reason why I have called upon you, Miss Chalcot."

Cressy, having prepared tea, offered a cup to Mrs. Rushton, who took it gratefully, then continued. "I have been given to understand by your aunt—whose speech was quite difficult to follow since it was characterized by claims to the worst spasms and palpitations she has ever endured—but enough on that head!" She smiled conspiratorially, and Cressida could not keep from smiling in return. Mrs. Rushton continued. "Yes, as I was saying, I have been given to understand that you mean to take piecework from one of our local dressmakers. Is that true?"

Cressy nodded. "But only until, with a firm practice of economics, I can save enough largess to lease the shop on Union Street."

Mrs. Rushton nodded her head. "I suspected as much. Does Mrs. Wanstrow know of your plans?"

Cressy shook her head. "I feared she would go off in a fit of apoplexy were she to learn I meant to open my own establishment here in Bath, and thought I would spare her the pain until the moment actually occurred. Sewing in the privacy of my chambers must seem more genteel to her and therefore more acceptable than setting myself up in trade. As I perceive it, I shouldn't wonder that these months I must alone with my needles and threads will go a long way to preparing Aunt Liddy for the day I make my true ambitions known to the entire beau monde."

"Your plan is a good one, in general. But the fact is I have come here for no less a purpose than to overset them—in part."

Cressy was startled, unable to imagine what she intended to do. "Whatever do you mean, ma'am?"

"Only this. If you are willing to accept a loan from an anonymous investor—namely myself—you would have it within your power to open your shop immediately." From her reticule she withdrew a folded sheet of paper and handed it to Cressida with a very pleased expression sparkling from her sharp blue eyes. "The lease for that shop you admired so much—the one with the bow window and small panes. I know it is presumptuous, but if you wish for it, you may have it for the next twelve-month."

Cressy took the parchment with fingers that trembled. Her mind felt loose and strange as she tried to assimilate what Mrs. Rushton had done. 'You leased the shop—for me?"

"Yes. As I recall, you hoped one day to be able to hire several of your newly acquired—and quite indigent—friends to sew for you—the same ladies who constructed all of your aunt's quite intriguing costumes."

Cressy could only nod dumbly, confusion vying for a growing sense of excitement that the heavens had suddenly made her dreams a possibility. "But I don't understand! Not in the least! Why ever would you do this for me?"

Mrs. Rushton grew quite solemn for a moment, then replied, "My family, three generations ago, were silk merchants in Europe, who eventually emigrated to England and succeeded extraordinarily. My grandmama hence became a considerable heiress—*in Trade,* of course—and when she married into the gentry, her family was despised by her husband's relations. Now that is a prejudice I abhor, a peculiarity I inherited no doubt by her association!

"At any rate, something of my forebears' talents and interests has always caught my fancy. Why, I cannot pass by a linen-drapers without looking and touching and smelling the fabrics. I remember particularly when Gregory was quite young, I used to fashion my own garments. Like Charlie, Rushton would sit at my knee, hours on end. Your industry and skill has put me in mind of times past, in my grandmama's company and later when I would spread out my own fabrics and juggle my pattern cards. I'm afraid a most annoying rheumatic complaint has for many years made it impossible for me to indulge my own enjoyment of sewing—a great loss for me." Here she paused and rubbed her fingers in a faintly melancholy fashion. She sighed as though to set aside her disappointment, then continued. "But I would be telling only half the truth if I did not also hint that I have another reason for concerning myself with your affairs."

Cressida knew instinctively that she referred to Rushton. She longed to ask how he fared and whether or not he showed the least unhappiness in being separated from her. She had not been in company with him since Daphne and Somersby's wedding, and though she supposed she would see him upon occasion in the future, she held little hope that her love for him would ever be returned or fulfilled. For all her intense desire, however, to discover news of Rushton, she could not bring herself to ask after him.

Fortunately, Mrs. Rushton was not disinclined to assuage her silent curiosity. "I don't know what has happened to my poor boy," she began. "He is grown quite blue-deviled since Somersby's wedding. It is really quite alarming. Whenever I chance to speak with him I vow he does not hear half the questions I pose him, and if I inquire as to what unhappiness is afflicting him, he merely responds absently that the canal work on his estates is proceeding badly.

"I am not fooled for even a second, however. I am fully convinced something far weightier has gone awry, yet not even my most cleverly disguised questions have prompted more than the lift of an eyebrow in response—you know, that imperious stare of his which tells us mere mortals, we have overstepped our bounds. Quite provoking!"

Cressida remembered how many times she had seen just such an expression as Mrs. Rushton described, and smiling to herself, responded, "Indeed, exceedingly provoking."

Mrs. Rushton looked at her in a penetrating manner for a long moment, and said, "You'll do, Cressida. You'll do—as my grandmama used to say—to a cow's thumb!"

Within a fortnight, and three weeks into the month of October, Cressida opened her shop, startling all of her former acquaintance. If she felt a great deal of distress over the odd smiles and stares which met her a dozen times a day, she was amply compensated for it by a general rush of patronage from every quarter of the city—Mrs. Wanstrow's gowns had been their own advertisement, and the success of the shop was ensured instantly.

The ladies in her employ were each paid handsomely, their living arrangements improved beyond any former expectation, and Charlie had all the advantage, as he cavorted among the seamstresses, of being spoiled and petted by them all.

Each day for Cressida became an adventure as she waited upon one fashionable lady after another and weaved the magic of a gown, or a fur-trimmed fichu, or an embroidered muff, or a pelisse, or a velvet redingote, or any other manner of garment required to dress the woman of ton.

She received one letter from Daphne during the month that followed and did not expect to see her sister again until Christmas, when she and her contented husband would return from their honeymoon.

Mrs. Wanstrow visited the shop nearly every day. At first she had been horrified by Cressida's entry into the unfashionable world of trade and had paid her visits almost exclusively for the purpose of browbeating her into giving up her shop and returning to live with her at Landsdown Crescent.

Only after several weeks of unsuccessful hounding did Mrs. Wanstrow eventually turn her efforts from changing Cressida's mind, to begging her niece to design a Christmas balldress for her. It would seem Mrs. Pritchard was returning to Bath—with no less than an earl hanging upon Olivia's sleeve—and it simply wouldn't do for Mrs. Wanstrow to be seen in her outmoded costumes of the previous year! "An evening gown," she began, "and two or three new day dresses! And, oh, yes, a carriage dress such as one I saw in the *Repository!* And what do you think of a fur-lined cape of lavender silk?"

Grateful that her aunt had finally accepted the shift in Cressida's social status, she happily set about designing an entire winter wardrobe for her. When she absolutely refused payment for her services, save for the cost of the fabric and the seamstresses' labors, Mrs. Wanstrow was ecstatic. Thereafter, no further disparaging comments upon Cressida's unworthy occupation crossed her lips.

Charlie's cheeks began to grow fat with renewed health, and it was not long before Cressida moved into, if not fashionable, then more pleasing lodgings near the Royal Crescent.

She heard only the smallest scraps of news about Rushton, dropped unwittingly by the ladies who visited her shop weekly. He seemed to have adopted a pattern unfamiliar to him—as the ladies informed her— becoming almost reclusive as he tended to his business at The Hall.

Cressida could not hear his name mentioned without her heart beating erratically in her breast. She wondered if he thought of her. She missed him dreadfully, and yet each day she worked steadfastly at putting him out of her thoughts forever. The moment she felt certain she had succeeded, however, he crept stealthily into her dreams, driving recklessly through her nocturnal slumbers in his curricle, cracking his whip, and generally causing her to awaken with a feeling so much like despair dragging her heart down, that she often wondered, had she not had her work to keep her head and hands employed, and Charlie to keep her heart occupied, whether or not she would have fallen into a decline!

Thoughts of Rushton, whether fragments or fully conceived, made her terribly unhappy.

Chapter Thirty-Eight

"Has no one told you, then?" Mrs. Rushton queried, regarding her son with wide eyes from across the rim of her glass of sherry.

"I have not been much about, as you very well know, so it is only natural that I have not heard the latest gossip. What I don't understand is how it came about that Cressida opened a shop as a modiste! How could she? Has she not considered her sister or her brother-in-law's feelings in the matter?"

"I believe she was only concerned with seeing to her own livelihood that she would not need to rely on Somersby's beneficence. To own the truth, I quite admire her for it."

Rushton stood by the fireplace, his elbow propped on the mantel. He shook his head in consternation, trying to make sense of what had occurred. "I cannot credit what you have told me! Mother, are you certain you have the right of it?"

She held her arms wide and gestured to the gown she was wearing. "Cressy designed this for me, Rushton! She has a bevy of seamstresses fluttering about the shop, and really it is the most delightful establishment, all decorated in the most luscious colors, amaranth, a delicate shade of peach, the softest yellows—really, her sense of color and style is remarkable! Do you not admire my gown prodigiously?"

"You know I said as much the moment you strolled into the room," he responded with a sigh. The gown appeared to set off his mother's complexion and youthful figure to great advantage, and he was especially struck by the pretty ruffles about the hem. Mentally he calculated the number and was surprised to find seven rows. "Is this the latest mode, then, all these ruffles?"

"*Ruching*, my darling. But of course I wouldn't expect you to know as much. And if it is not the fashion, it very well might soon be! She is quite remarkable you know."

Rushton let his head tilt into his hand where he absently ran his fingers through his black hair. "Yes, I know," he responded quietly.

For the past several weeks, as he buried himself into the business of his estate, his thoughts had carried him back time and again to Cressida. He knew she was *remarkable*. He had never known a female quite like her in his entire existence. It was a great pity her origins and fortune were obscure. He had even been considering offering for her now that Somersby had lifted the family name of Chalcot from obscurity by marrying the sister.

Somehow, however, it did not serve to diminish his own dislike of either Somersby's match, or a possible one with Cressida herself. Love ought never to rule one's life. He believed that.

Rushton's heart felt as though it had been strapped with stones. He was making a valiant effort to live by such a precept, but the reality of each day came harshly to him. He missed Cressida's company so much that keeping from ordering his curricle brought round that he might fly to Bath just to see her had come to require a Herculean effort. He wanted to see her, to be with her, to be near her, to catch her hand to his lips, to see her violet eyes dance with amusement, to hear her scolding words, her laughter, her whispers! He longed to kiss her again.

She had even invaded his dreams. Once, in the midst of one particularly brilliant midnight reverie he had

actually touched her lips with his own, feeling all over
again the wondrous sensations of wholeness and
affection and passion which he had felt most especially
during the last kiss they had shared.

He had been jolted awake by the sensation only to find
himself covered in sweat and feeling as though he were
going mad. He wanted Cressida, desperately, yet each
time he thought of an alliance with her his heart would
constrict with a distress he could not fully comprehend,
save that his father would have been appalled at the
thought of his son marrying so improvidently.

When he realized his mother had risen from her chair,
he exclaimed, "What? Are you leaving? So soon?"

"I feel I ought to," she responded. "I can see that you
have a great many things on your mind. I can only trust
that all is well with your house?"

"Yes, of course it is," he answered, stunned by the
knowledge he had not heard a word she had said in the
past ten minutes, judging by the clock on the mantel.
"Even the canal prospers finally. We look to have it
completed by summer next."

"It shall be a burden off your shoulders then," Mrs.
Rushton responded kindly. "Now pray see me to my
carriage. I hope to see Cressida before I return to my
town house, and if I leave now, I shall most certainly pay
a call at her shop. She keeps a room abovestairs, you
know, to serve tea to her favorite patrons. A charming
little room with green shutters, and . . ."

His mother's voice faded to his own hearing, as he
pictured Cressida gowned as neat as a pin and her
exquisite eyes regarding her guests in the steadfast,
direct manner which most characterized her. An acute
sensation of longing so overwhelmed him that he could
not suppress the deepest sigh.

"I won't have it, Gregory!" his mother cried suddenly,
taking hold of his arm and giving it a gentle squeeze.

He glanced down at her as they walked through the
vaulted antechamber which connected the entrance hall

to the drawing room. "And what won't you have?" he queried, bemused. "Have I offended you somehow?"

"Yes, extremely so!" she said with a playful frown on her lips.

"How is this!" he exclaimed. Though he could see she was in some manner teasing him, he also knew her well enough to comprehend that he had caused her a measure of distress.

She appeared to need a moment to compose her thoughts as her gaze shifted inward. Her mouth fell slightly agape, and the expression on her face grew quite solemn. Finally, she began, "I don't know precisely how to say this, but I am become convinced that you have taken something your father has taught you a great deal too much to heart. I know that his family—your family—is an ancient one, whose line descends from 1066. And there is just reason for taking pride in such an ancient and honored lineage. But I would be greatly saddened if you let such a circumstance rule your judgment or your heart." She again gave his arm a squeeze, regarding him tenderly. "If you must know, it has not escaped my attention, Gregory, that you are exceedingly fond of Cressida and she, of you. I don't like to see your happiness jeopardized for antiquated reasons."

He was shocked. "She is *in Trade,* Mama. Does that mean nothing to you?"

"Not especially, since I hold the lease on her shop."

"You what?" he cried, unable to credit his ears.

She nodded and smiled. "Yes, my dear. I wished to help her. When she quit her aunt's house, I learned she had taken rooms in a rather shabby part of town." She explained the particulars of Cressida's situation and how only a little persuading had been necessary to convince Cressy to accept of her generous offer. "She had meant to spend the next several months saving every tuppence in order to open her shop. It seemed a small thing to pay for the lease myself—a loan, of course. Besides, every time I visit her establishment, I think of my grandmother, whose parents were silk mercers if you recall."

He ignored her reminiscence and said, "You should not have encouraged Cressida down this path."

With some asperity, she retorted, "Would you have prefered that she left Bath entirely and took up a position as a governess? Then I think you are very cruel. She is quite talented, if you must know, and has already made a success of her trade."

"Of course I would not have wished for her to become a governess, or any such thing. But surely Mrs. Wanstrow cannot have ejected her from her house. Surely!"

"No, that she did not. She begged Cressida, and Charlie, to stay with her. But Cressy would have none of it. She is quite an independent sort of female. If you do not take care, some worthy merchant will discover her, woo her, and make her his wife. She is far too pretty and too intelligent to remain unmarried for very long."

Rushton felt as though his mother were heaping coals upon his head. "I have a duty to this house—"

"You have a duty to yourself." When she saw that he was struggling mightily with his sentiments, she pressed him, "Do you not know why I have chosen to make my home in Bath, rather than London? There are so many amusing people here, of every manner of rank and occupation. And over half a century ago, Beau Nash leveled a number of the finer, more insidious grades between the classes. Did you know, for instance, that he would often request a peeress, even a duchess, to leave the assembly rooms if she gave just her fingers—instead of her whole hand—to a commoner in dance? There. I can see by your expression, that you are a little shocked. Good.

"Now. I have only one thing more to say to you, and then I shall go. I did not hold by your father's belief that you must add substantially to your estates through a proper marriage."

"But you've never said a word."

"I did not feel it was right to countermand anything your dear papa taught you about being a responsible proprietor of the Rushton lands—until now. Marry Cressida, Rushton. You will have my blessing and—and, besides! You would make Mrs. Wanstrow ever so happy!"

On this last remark, he started, a chuckle of laughter catching in his throat. "You nearly persuade me, Mama, by mentioning Cressida's aunt."

"I thought I might," she responded with sweet irony. "She will tell me an engagement between you and her niece will quite take the wind out of Mrs. Pritchard's eye. Oh, I almost forgot to tell you. Mrs. Pritchard has finally managed an alliance for Olivia. They return shortly to enjoy Christmas here in Bath."

Rushton saw, partly to his relief, that his mother had neatly drawn the subject of Cressida and matrimony to a close. "Indeed," he responded. "I am happy for her."

"I thought you would be. If I recall correctly you spoke to her privately the night of her mother's Olympian masquerade. You were right to end her hopes."

"Do your eyes never fail you?" he queried, astonished.

"Not often," she responded gaily, pulling on her gloves. "Now leave off playing the simpleton, and take yourself to Bath before it is too late! My solicitor was asking the most pointed questions about Cressida only the other day." She smiled mischievously upon him.

When at last he handed her up into her carriage, he clasped her fingers lightly and placed a kiss upon her hand. "Thank you, Mother," he whispered. "Thank you very much."

Chapter Thirty-Nine

"You are far too young to be losing your teeth, Charlie! Now tell me again, what happened?" Cressy dabbed at his bloody mouth with her kerchief then lifted the hysterical boy onto the counter in her shop, ignoring the three fashionable Misses Fulton waiting to be served.

Charlie, whose cheeks were streaked with tears and whose nose was bright red from crying, wiped his face with dirty hands and sobbed, "I was playing with my hoop and didn't look where I was going." A series of explosive hiccups followed these words. "And I r-ran straight on into the manure cart! Have I lost my teeth like Jimmy?" He had repeated this last query three times since returning to the shop following his accident. Jimmy was the milliner's son of seven, who could whistle through the empty spaces where he had lost two of his teeth, and for the present Charlie had no greater ambition than to lose at least two of his own.

"No, I'm afraid you haven't," she responded tenderly, checking his teeth one by one. She pronounced that they were all fully in tact, but that he had cut his lip. "But only a very little," she assured him. The lip had begun to turn purple and swell. He sobbed several more times, and Cressy gathered him up in her arms and cuddled him close.

"I wish I'd lost at least one of them," he cried.

"I know, dearest. I know. And I don't think you will have too much longer to wait, but you must be patient. After all, Jimmy is two years your senior."

She turned around with the lad still clinging to her and was about to ask her esteemed clients to pardon her for a few moments while she tended to Charlie when she was struck dumb by the sight of Rushton standing in the doorway. She was certain, by the lightness which invaded her mind, that had she not been so nearly grounded to the earth by the feel of the unhappy boy in her arms, she would have fainted.

"Rushton," she whispered.

The Misses Fulton, seated by the bow window in soft chairs upholstered in violet velvet, turned from staring at her to regarding Rushton in the utmost astonishment.

Rushton removed his tall beaver hat from his head and bowed politely to her. "I was hoping to have an opportunity to speak with you, Miss Chalcot, but I can see that the hour is inconvenient, perhaps I should return later?"

Cressy tried to move her mind quickly, but a rather dense fog seemed to have begun swirling about in her brain. She was completely incapacitated. She glanced at the ladies in a rather absent manner, wondering what she ought to do. They seemed to sense her stupefaction and with quick shakes of their sympathetic heads and a dozen giggles, motioned for her not to permit Rushton to leave. Their smiles of encouragement helped her to bring her mind and heart to order.

She did not hesitate to follow their advice. "I would prefer you remained, Rushton. Do come upstairs with Charlie and me. His nanny is upstairs, and my maid can prepare you a cup of tea, if you like."

Rushton turned toward the women and bowed politely. All three sighed in unison, and Cressy happened to glance back at Rushton the very moment he whispered his thanks to them for their kind assistance in aiding his cause.

Cressy, her heart full of too many emotions to make

307

her comfortable, mounted the stairs slowly with Charlie held tightly in her arms. His tears dwindled away with each step she took until she heard him greet Rushton from just above her shoulder. "Hallo, Mr. Rushton. I hurt my mouth."

"Hallo, scamp," he responded. "I can see you did."

"I have a very nice nanny named Sukey. Would you like to meet her?"

"Indeed, I would."

Once upstairs, Charlie refused to be led away by Sukey and instead took up residence upon Rushton's knee. He then begged to be told how the grays fared and soon engaged Rushton in an intense conversation upon the finer points of horseflesh. Cressida tried to interrupt the tête-à-tête, but Rushton suggested gently that she tend to her customers while he saw to Charlie's amusement.

Cressida was startled by the kindness in his voice as well as by his acceptance of her livelihood. She went downstairs and with her thoughts only partially engaged at the task at hand, waited on the Misses Fulton.

When they had quit the shop and her best seamstress had returned from an errand at the linen-drapers, Cressy left the operations in her assistant's capable hands. Remounting the stairs, she smoothed her hair and rearranged the skirts of her light blue woolen gown, trying without success to calm her rapidly beating heart.

Why had he come? She could not imagine. But how happy she was to see him! How sweet the air felt on her cheeks as she rapidly ascended the stairs, how soft the woolen cloth felt to her fingertips as she lifted her skirts, how joyous the days suddenly seemed as she reached the doorway of her tearoom, her gaze lighting upon the man she loved.

But why had he come? To what purpose?

She entered the small chamber, decorated with silk-damask in a gentle shade of orange and saw that Rushton was busily whispering in Charlie's ear. When Charlie caught sight of her, he said, "Here she is! Must I go? I want to hear what she says."

Rushton responded firmly, "Yes. Go to Sukey that I might have a few words *alone* with your Aunt Cressida."

"But are you going to ask her?"

"Yes, scamp. Now off with you!" He put Charlie off his knee and gave him a shove toward the nether regions.

Cressy felt her heart simply stop beating as she stared at Rushton. He was so dreadfully handsome, and his eyes were the same startling blue that she remembered so well. She longed to touch his face, to slip her arms about his neck, to feel his hair drift between her fingers. But that was impossible.

When Charlie had disappeared down the hall, Rushton rose to his feet, seeming to fill the small chamber with his fine broad shoulders and manly height. She smiled a trembling smile and said, "I'm glad you've come." And before the words were out, she added, "I've missed you terribly. I suppose I shouldn't have said as much, but I believe I quite got used to brangling with you."

"It is odd, isn't it?" he responded, a warm glint in his eye and an intensity to his expression which caused a shiver to travel all down her neck. "We do brangle don't we, and yet I, too, have missed you—more than life itself."

Cressy caught her breath. Everything around her seemed unreal suddenly. She wasn't even certain Rushton was truly standing before her. Was it possible she was trapped in a dream? Yet she knew it wasn't a dream.

She wondered if perhaps her hearing had failed her. Had he said he missed her *more than life itself?* Were these the words a gentleman spoke when paying a mere social call?

She swallowed, took two steps forward—neither of which she could feel upon the soles of her white slippers—and took up a chair at the linen-covered table where her maid had recently placed a silver pot of tea, a pitcher of thick cream, and a bowl of sugar.

"Very odd," she reiterated in a whisper.

She started to pour him a cup of tea, but before her hand could reach the teapot, he stopped her, sat down on the chair beside her and took possession of both her hands. "I have only one regret, Cressy, that I didn't come to you several weeks sooner and tell you what I wish to tell you now. I have been a perfect idiot, and I have only myself to blame for your having had to take up this shop in order to support yourself and Charlie."

"But, Rushton," she began, wanting to explain that he was not in any manner responsible for either herself or Charlie, but he wouldn't let her continue.

"No, don't speak," he said, bringing her hands to his warm lips and kissing each of them in turn. "Permit me, if you will, to finish my speeches, my darling Cressida."

Cressy felt her heart fairly disintegrate in her breast. She again felt dizzy as she had so many times when close to him. She was too overwhelmed by the feel of his hands holding hers, by the nearness of his beloved face, by the sincerity of his expression to do more than acquiesce.

He continued. "I have come to beg your hand in marriage, if you love me and if you are of a mind to become leg-shackled to one who is stubborn, at times unkind, but whose heart will always belong solely to you. I have loved you, I believe, from the first when you stood beside that ridiculous cart of Mrs. Cameley's and rang a peal over my head for driving too fast. You were so adorably impudent! How could I have done ought else but surrender my heart to you? But later, when at every turn you proved the goodness of your character to me, I was fully caught. Your unselfish, unflagging interest in your sister, your decision to care for Charlie yourself, your strength and determination in seeing this most extraordinary venture as a dressmaker to a happy conclusion—I am beyond praise for you! And each time I would importune you—Cressy, when I would hold you in my arms . . ." Here he again brought her hands up to his lips, drifting a string of slow kisses across the backs of

310

each hand as though to enact his meaning.

Cressy could not breathe. Her senses seemed to fail her as his lips assaulted the tender, white skin of her hands. She was completely overcome by his declaration. Tears smarted her eyes. She could not credit that only last night he had again visited her in her dreams, that she had again awakened to a terrible sense of despair, that she had yet again spent the entire morning driving him out of her thoughts. And now he was here, looking at her with a humility that was as pleasing as it was startling.

"But you can't wish to marry me," she responded, shaking her head. "I am set up in trade, as you have said. You would cause a scandal by embracing a woman of such an inferior station and fortune. It is unthinkable!"

"It is necessary," was his forthright response.

Cressida pulled her hands out of his grasp and rose from her seat to pace the small chamber. One of the windows was open slightly, and a cool November breeze gained enough entrance to buffet the white muslin curtains which hung in a billowy drape to the floor.

She tried to think. She wanted to say yes, she would marry him, but there was a part of her heart which caused her to believe that whatever Rushton might be feeling today, there would come a time when he would regret taking her to wife. She knew the depth of his sentiments all too well.

"What of your family, of your mother?" she queried, turning to look down at him.

"She wishes for the connection," he said, leaning back in his chair.

Cressida had suspected as much, yet she still could not help feeling some surprise. "I suppose she told you she hired this establishment for me."

"Yes, she did," Rushton responded. "Though I know she was to some degree motivated by her affection for you, I also have the strongest feeling she hoped it would teach me a lesson. In a conversation recently she gave me to understand she thought me a little too high in the

311

instep, a little too concerned with marrying advantage-ously."

Cressy took a deep breath. This was the heart of the matter. "As much as I wish to accept of your offer, Rushton—for I will confess that my heart is fully engaged, and that I am very much in love with you—I cannot marry you. I am persuaded you would come to despise me as unworthy of your family and your heritage. Particularly now that I own a shop."

"I don't give a fig for that," he replied, smiling tenderly upon her. "And perhaps you have forgotten that you are now exceedingly well-connected. Your sister, may I remind you, is the Countess of Somersby."

She felt frightened by the light bantering note in his voice, afraid that her conviction to refuse him might waver if he continued teasing her gently and looking at her with a mischievous light in his eye.

"Have you forgotten Charlie?" she pressed on. "I have promised to keep him by my side."

"I already told Charlie he would come and live with us should you decide to marry me."

"You told him that you were going to offer for me?"

"Yes. It seemed appropriate since you mean to adopt him. I thought I ought to have his approval since our marriage would mean he would have to change his residence yet again. But when I pointed out that he would be able to visit the grays every day in the stable, he hadn't the least objection."

Cressy was greatly moved by the fact that he had already committed himself to Charlie. Yet it changed nothing, nor was she unconvinced that in time Rushton would come to regret marrying beneath him.

Therefore she walked to the door leading to the stairs and said, "My answer must be no. I have already started down this path." Here she gestured belowstairs where the laughter of several customers floated up the stairwell. "And if you must know I am intending to remove to London and set up a new shop there, hopefully by

February or March. Since Daphne will be making her home in Oxfordshire, I know she will want to come frequently to Bath where my presence can only be a blight upon her social career. In London I shall remain a more obscure entity. And Rushton, you cannot want a dressmaker for a wife!"

"What nonsense you are speaking!" he cried, rising from his chair to approach her. "Or did you think I came here lightly, not having considered the very things which form your objections. I have been able to set aside the disparity in our stations. I am reconciled to it, completely, I most humbly beg you to believe me on that score. Of the moment I wouldn't care if you were a beggar on the streets. I would still wish you to become my wife!"

At that Cressy smiled. "Oh, I think you would hesitate to ask for the hand of a beggar," she responded teasingly.

He cocked his head, placing his hands upon her arms. "Perhaps that is coming it a bit too strong. But I love you, Cressida, I do. And I want you to be my wife."

"You would in time despise me. I know you all too well. You are deceiving yourself. Indeed, you are." She felt her throat constrict with unhappiness and in a whisper, said, "Pray, leave me in peace. I have made up my mind. I am going to London."

Rushton did the only sensible thing and pulled her into his arms, kissing her full upon the mouth.

Cressida felt the ache in her throat grow to unhappy proportions as tears began coursing down her cheeks. She slipped her arms gently about his shoulders and held him close, savoring this last moment in his arms, memorizing the sweetness of his lips upon hers, wishing that she could remain within the circle of his love forever.

Time disappeared as he drew her closer still, his body pressed against hers, the strength of his embrace enveloping her in a profound sensation of safety.

"I love you," he breathed, his lips moving gently over hers in a feathery sweep. "I love you."

"Rushton," she whispered. "If only it were possible."

"But it is, my darling. Only tell me you will have me."

He did not wait to hear her answer, but again assaulted her, his arms holding her so tightly against him that she felt she might disappear. She wanted to disappear and to believe that what he said was true, that he would never regret marrying her.

Knowing she could not accept his proposals, she finally drew back from him and said simply, "I will not marry you. I'm sorry. Please go."

She lowered her gaze that he might not see the tears which blinded her eyes.

"I see," he responded slowly. "And are you sure that your only objection is based solely upon the fact that you are in trade, and I am not?"

She nodded, wiping away her tears with the back of her hands.

"Then I will not distress you further," he said quietly. "Good-bye."

She felt her heart lurch within her breast. Was he really leaving? She did not want him to go, yet he must! He must!

She closed her eyes and listened to his footsteps as he quickly ran down the stairs. She thought she would remember the thudding, hollow sound as long as she lived.

Summoning her courage, strong in her belief that she had made the proper decision, she squeezed back the tears which threatened to conquer the resolution of her heart, straightened her shoulders, and after drying her eyes with a kerchief drawn hastily from the pocket of her gown, descended the stairs to greet her customers.

beneath his notice.

"Flowers for sale!" he cried, as one particularly irate whipster told him and his cart to go to the devil.

Cressy caught her hand to her mouth and smothered a laugh, tears, as they had earlier, again smarting her eyes. What a ridiculous figure he cut! Was he aware of it? Much he cared! Not Rushton!

From near the flagway, Cressy heard her aunt's voice call to her. "Cressida! Whatever is Rushton doing? Why he's pushing a flower cart! Of all the absurd starts!"

Cressy turned to glance toward her aunt, who was descending a hackney near the flagway, her eyes fairly popping from her head as she watched Rushton's progress.

Cressy responded, "I haven't the least notion why he is in possession of Mr. Batcombe's cart—oh, dear!" She realized suddenly that he was addressing the issue which lay between them in a most peculiar and persuasive way. She continued, "I believe he means to set himself up in trade."

"What?" Mrs. Wanstrow exclaimed, drawing close to Cressida, but staring at the sight of Rushton finally achieving the flagway. "Has he gone daft? Whyever would he want to do such a nonsensical thing as that?"

Cressy's heart had again begun leaping from one corner of her breast to the next. "Only for the most wonderful reason imaginable," she answered cryptically.

"I don't take your meaning, Cressida," Mrs. Wanstrow returned. "Whatever could he hope to gain by selling flowers when he has a fortune of no less than ten thousand a year! He must be making sport of you, Cressida! I would not speak to him, if I were you! He has put himself quite beyond the pale with his little joke. I see nothing *wonderful* at all in holding you up to the derision of others!"

By this time Rushton was nearly upon them, and he drew his cart just to the side of Cressida's front door. He removed his hat and bowed politely to both ladies, then begged them to forgive him, but he must now tend to business.

"Flowers for sale!" he again called out.

Mrs. Wanstrow took a deep breath and with a smoldering eye approached him. Her hands were clasped tightly together, her reticule dangling from her wrist. "We are not amused, Mr. Rushton!" she began, her cheeks flushed darkly. "My niece works very hard and has already established herself as the premiere modiste in our fair city. While, as for you, I can only suppose you mean to overset her and mock her! I find this mode of humor quite unforgivable. I suggest you remove yourself at once, or I shall be forced to summon the constable!"

Mr. Rushton removed several purple chrysanthemums from the cart and held them out for the passersby to inspect. At the same time he addressed Mrs. Wanstrow's complaint. "I assure you, ma'am, I am most sincere in my efforts. Though I had not intended upon setting myself up in trade, I will if it is the only way I can convince your niece that her current employment does not now, nor will it ever, have the smallest chance of diminishing my love for her. You see, I begged for her hand in marriage not an hour ago, and she refused me. She seems to think there is too great a discrepancy in our social rankings."

Mrs. Wanstrow, whose complexion now turned from an irritated red to a shocked white, rounded upon Cressida with the appearance of a fire-breathing dragon. "What?" she cried. "You refused Rushton's offer of marriage?"

"Yes, ma'am," Cressy responded with a sparkle of amusement quickening her heart. "I was fully persuaded that one day he would regret having been so nearly associated with one who *smelled of the shop*, as it were."

"How very vulgar!" she cried, repulsed by the cant phrase Cressida had used. "And how very absurd! If it does not matter to Mr. Rushton that you are a seamstress, then why should it matter to you? I insist you

318

apologize to Mr. Rushton for harboring such a ridiculous notion. You can see for yourself, especially since he was perfectly willing to sink to your level of absurdity, that your reasonings were unsound! For heaven's sake, child, take his hand, tell him you will meet him at the altar, and be done with it! I won't have a niece of mine playing the idiot." She thought for a moment and then amended, "Well, I will not have two nieces of mine playing the idiot. Daphne was enough to try the patience of the saintliest of women! Now do show a little sense, Cressida, and make Rushton the happiest of men!" she gestured toward him with a sweep of her hand. "Go to him, I say!"

Rushton, who stood with a pink rose in one hand, held his free hand out to her and said simply, "If you don't do as you are bid, I'm afraid I shall be here every day for the rest of your life, badgering your patrons into purchasing my flowers and generally making your life a misery."

His expression was so beseeching, and he was so wonderfully intent upon having her that Cressy saw nothing for it but to walk into his arms and accept both his proposals and his kisses.

After a long moment, when Mrs. Wanstrow's protests grew loud enough to pierce Cressida's hearing, she finally drew slightly away from Rushton. Still she held his hand tightly within her grasp, as though afraid she might awaken from one of her dreams. Looking up at him and with a worried frown on her brow, she said, "I cannot give up my shop. My seamstresses depend upon me for their livelihood."

Rushton smiled tenderly and drew her arm about his own. He patted her hand and said, "We'll manage something. Never fear! For now it is enough that I have won your hand."

"Rushton, I missed you so much."

"We need never be apart again."

He pulled her into his arms and would have started kissing her again, but Mrs. Wanstrow cleared her voice and told them to stop making a spectacle of themselves.

Only then did Cressida realize that a large assemblage had gathered about the flower cart and were listening intently to their entire exchange.

Cressy felt her cheeks grow hot with embarrassment, and she immediately withdrew, upon Rushton's arm, into the privacy of her establishment.

Later, as she served tea abovestairs to Rushton and her aunt, and a cup of chocolate to Charlie, she remembered back to the trying moment when she first decided to stake her small inheritance upon the prospect of finding a husband for Daphne in Bath. Her gambit, she realized, had succeeded beyond measure.

Her quiet reverie, as she handed Charlie a biscuit, was interrupted by her aunt. "Did I never tell you, Mr. Rushton, that it was *my* notion that the girls remove to Bath? I had been wishing for it, forever."

"*Aunt Liddy*," Rushton and Cressida cried in unison, their joint remonstration causing Mrs. Wanstrow to blush faintly.

"Well, if I hadn't been actually *wishing* for it forever, than I most certainly should have been. Daphne and Cressida have been a positive delight to me. I don't know how I used to get on without them! As you know, being a widow, and fixed as I am, it was no small thing to take on the additional expense of two such vivacious young ladies. Why the cost of candles alone, was quite prohibitive, not to mention the increases on the bills from the poulteress and the dairyman, which of course . . ."

Cressida did not attempt to interrupt her aunt's prattling. Nor was it at all necessary for the enjoyment of the moment, since Rushton had taken her hand in his and was even now bringing it to his lips.